THE MATADOR
OF THE FIVE TOWN

THE MATADOR
OF THE FIVE TOWNS

and Other Stories

by

ARNOLD BENNETT

1972
CHATTO & WINDUS
LONDON

Published by
Chatto & Windus Ltd
London

*

Clarke, Irwin & Co. Ltd
Toronto

ISBN 0 7011 1837 7

First published 1912
This edition first published 1972

© Mrs. Cheston Bennett 1912

Printed in Great Britain by
Redwood Press Ltd
Trowbridge, Wiltshire

CONTENTS

TRAGIC

FROLIC

THE MATADOR OF THE FIVE TOWNS

multitudinous books on every wall of the dining-room. The house was dadoed throughout with books.

" Rot! " said Brindley.

This was only my third visit to his home and to the Five Towns, but he and I had already become curiously intimate. My first two visits had been occasioned by official pilgrimages as a British Museum expert in ceramics. The third was for a purely friendly week-end, and had no pretext. The fact is, I was drawn to the astonishing district and its astonishing inhabitants. The Five Towns, to me, was like the East to those who have smelt the East: it " called."

" I'll tell you what we *could* do," said Mrs Brindley. " We could put him on to Dr Stirling."

" So we could! " Brindley agreed. " Wife, this is one of your bright, intelligent days. We'll put you on to the doctor, Loring. I'll impress on him that he must keep you constantly amused till I get back, which I fear it won't be early. This is what we call manners, you know—to invite a fellow-creature to travel a hundred and fifty miles to spend two days here, and then to turn him out before he's been in the house an hour. It's *us*, that is! But the truth of the matter is, the birthday business might be a bit serious. It might easily cost me fifty quid and no end of diplomacy. If you were a married man you'd know that the ten plagues of Egypt are simply nothing in comparison with your wife's re-lations. And she's over eighty, the old lady."

" *I'll* give you ten plagues of Egypt! " Mrs Brindley menaced her spouse, as she wafted the boys from the room. " Mr Loring, do take some more of that cheese if you fancy it." She vanished.

Within ten minutes Brindley was conducting me to the doctor's, whose house was on the way to the station. In its spacious porch he explained the circum-stances in six words, depositing me like a parcel. The doctor, who had once by mysterious medicaments saved

my frail organism from the consequences of one of
Brindley's Falstaffian "nights," hospitably protested
his readiness to sacrifice patients to my pleasure.

"It'll be a chance for MacIlroy," said he.

"Who's MacIlroy?" I asked.

"MacIlroy is another Scotchman," growled
Brindley. "Extraordinary how they stick together!
When he wanted an assistant, do you suppose he looked
about for some one in the district, some one who understood us and loved us and could take a hand at bridge?
Not he! Off he goes to Cupar, or somewhere, and comes
back with another stage Scotchman, named MacIlroy.
Now listen here, Doc! A charge to keep you have, and
mind you keep it, or I'll never pay your confounded
bill. We'll knock on the window to-night as we come
back. In the meantime you can show Loring your
etchings, and pray for me." And to me: "Here's a
latchkey." With no further ceremony he hurried away
to join his wife and children at Bleakridge Station. In
such singular manner was I transferred forcibly from
host to host.

II

THE doctor and I resembled each other in this: that
there was no offensive affability about either of us.
Though abounding in good-nature, we could not become
intimate by a sudden act of volition. Our conversation
was difficult, unnatural, and by gusts falsely familiar.
He displayed to me his bachelor house, his etchings, a
few specimens of modern *rouge flambé* ware made at
Knype, his whisky, his celebrated prize-winning fox-
terrier Titus, the largest collection of books in the Five
Towns, and photographs of Marischal College, Aber-
deen. Then we fell flat, socially prone. Sitting in his
study, with Titus between us on the hearthrug, we knew
no more what to say or do. I regretted that Brindley's

wife's grandmother should have been born on a fifteenth
of February. Brindley was a vivacious talker, he could be
trusted to talk.   I, too, am a good talker—with another
good talker.   With a bad talker I am just a little worse
than he is.   The doctor said abruptly after a nerve-
trying silence that he had forgotten a most important
call at Hanbridge, and would I care to go with him in
the car?   I was and still am convinced that he was
simply inventing.   He wanted to break the sinister
spell by getting out of the house, and he had not the face
to suggest a sortie into the streets of the Five Towns
as a promenade of pleasure.

So we went forth, splashing warily through the rich
mud and the dank mist of Trafalgar Road, past all those
strange little Indian-red houses, and ragged empty
spaces, and poster-hoardings, and rounded kilns, and
high, smoking chimneys, up hill, down hill, and up hill
again, encountering and overtaking many electric trams
that dipped and rose like ships at sea, into Crown
Square, the centre of Hanbridge, the metropolis of the
Five Towns.   And while the doctor paid his mysterious
call I stared around me at the large shops and the banks
and the gilded hotels.   Down the radiating street-vistas I
could make out the façades of halls, theatres, chapels.
Trams rumbled continually in and out of the square.
They seemed to enter casually, to hesitate a few
moments as if at a loss, and then to decide with a nonchalant clang of bells that they might as well go off somewhere else in search of something more interesting. They
were rather like human beings who are condemned to
live for ever in a place of which they are sick beyond
the expressiveness of words.

And indeed the influence of Crown Square, with its
large effects of terra cotta, plate glass, and gold letters,
all under a heavy skyscape of drab smoke, was depressing.   A few very seedy men (sharply contrasting with
the fine delicacy of costly things behind plate-glass)

stood doggedly here and there in the mud, immobilized
by the gloomy enchantment of the Square.   Two of
them turned to look at Stirling's motor-car and me.
They gazed fixedly for a long time, and then one said,
only his lips moving:

"Has Tommy stood thee that there quart o' beer
as he promised thee?"

No reply, no response of any sort, for a further long
period!   Then the other said, with grim resignation:

"Ay!"

The conversation ceased, having made a little oasis
in the dismal desert of their silent scrutiny of the car.
Except for an occasional stamp of the foot they never
moved.   They just doggedly and indifferently stood,
blown upon by all the nipping draughts of the square,
and as it might be sinking deeper and deeper into its
dejection.   As for me, instead of desolating, the harsh
disconsolateness of the scene seemed to uplift me;   I
savoured it with joy, as one savours the melancholy of
a tragic work of art.

"We might go down to the *Signal* offices and worry
Buchanan a bit," said the doctor, cheerfully, when he
came back to the car.   This was the second of his in-
spirations.

Buchanan, of whom I had heard, was another Scotchman and the editor of the sole daily organ of the Five
Towns, an evening newspaper cried all day in the streets
and read by the entire population.   Its green sheet appeared to be a permanent waving feature of the main
thoroughfares.   The offices lay round a corner close by,
and as we drew up in front of them a crowd of tattered
urchins interrupted their diversions in the sodden road
to celebrate our glorious arrival by unanimously yelling
at the top of their strident and hoarse voices:

"Hooray!   Hoo—bl—dy—ray!"

Abashed, I followed my doctor into the shelter of
the building, a new edifice, capacious and considerable

but horribly faced with terra cotta, and quite unimposing, lacking in the spectacular effect; like nearly everything in the Five Towns, carelessly and scornfully ugly! The mean, swinging double-doors returned to the assault when you pushed them, and hit you viciously. In a dark, countered room marked " Enquiries " there was nobody.

" Hi, there! " called the doctor.

A head appeared at a door.

" Mr Buchanan upstairs? "

" Yes," snapped the head, and disappeared.

Up a dark staircase we went, and at the summit were half flung back again by another self-acting door.

In the room to which we next came an old man and a youngish one were bent over a large, littered table, scribbling on and arranging pieces of grey tissue paper and telegrams. Behind the old man stood a boy. Neither of them looked up.

" Mr Buchanan in his — " the doctor began to question. " Oh! There you are! "

The editor was standing in hat and muffler at the window, gazing out. His age was about that of the doctor—forty or so; and like the doctor he was rather stout and clean-shaven. Their Scotch accents mingled in greeting, the doctor's being the more marked. Buchanan shook my hand with a certain courtliness, indicating that he was well accustomed to receive strangers. As an expert in small talk, however, he shone no brighter than his visitors, and the three of us stood there by the window awkwardly in the heaped disorder of the room, while the other two men scratched and fidgeted with bits of paper at the soiled table.

Suddenly and savagely the old man turned on the boy:

" What the hades are you waiting there for? "

" I thought there was something else, sir."

" Sling your hook."

Buchanan winked at Stirling and me as the boy

slouched off and the old man blandly resumed his writing.

" Perhaps you'd like to look over the place? " Buchanan suggested politely to me. " I'll come with you. It's all I'm fit for to-day. . . . 'Flu! " He glanced at Stirling, and yawned.

" Ye ought to be in bed," said Stirling.

" Yes. I know. I've known it for twelve years. I shall go to bed as soon as I get a bit of time to myself. Well, will you come? The half-time results are beginning to come in."

A telephone-bell rang impatiently.

" You might just see what that is, boss," said the old man without looking up.

Buchanan went to the telephone and replied into it: " Yes? What? Oh! Myatt? Yes, he's playing. . . . Of course I'm sure! Good-bye." He turned to the old man: " It's another of 'em wanting to know if Myatt is playing. Birmingham, this time."

" Ah! " exclaimed the old man, still writing.

" It's because of the betting," Buchanan glanced at me. " The odds are on Knype now—three to two."

" If Myatt is playing Knype have got me to thank for it," said the doctor, surprisingly.

" You? "

" Me! He fetched me to his wife this morning. She's nearing her confinement. False alarm. I guaranteed him at least another twelve hours."

" Oh! So that's it, is it? " Buchanan murmured. Both the sub-editors raised their heads.

" That's it," said the doctor.

" Some people were saying he'd quarrelled with the trainer again and was shamming," said Buchanan. " But I didn't believe that. There's no hanky-panky about Jos Myatt, anyhow."

I learnt in answer to my questions that a great and terrible football match was at that moment in progress at Knype, a couple of miles away, between the Knype Club and the Manchester Rovers. It was conveyed to me that the importance of this match was almost national, and that the entire district was practically holding its breath till the result should be known. The half-time result was one goal each.

" If Knype lose," said Buchanan, explanatorily, " they'll find themselves pushed out of the First League at the end of the season. That's a cert. . . . one of the oldest clubs in England! Semi-finalists for the English Cup in '78."

" '79," corrected the elder sub-editor.

I gathered that the crisis was grave.

" And Myatt's the captain, I suppose? " said I.

" No. But he's the finest full-back in the League."

I then had a vision of Myatt as a great man. By an effort of the imagination I perceived that the equivalent of the fate of nations depended upon him. I recollected, now, large yellow posters on the hoardings we had passed, with the names of Knype and of Manchester Rovers in letters a foot high and the legend " League match at Knype " over all. It seemed to me that the heroic name of Jos Myatt, if truly he were the finest full-back in the League, if truly his presence or absence affected the betting as far off as Birmingham, ought also to have been on the posters, together with possibly his portrait. I saw Jos Myatt as a matador, with a long ribbon of scarlet necktie down his breast, and embroidered trousers.

" Why," said Buchanan, " if Knype drop into the Second Division they'll never pay another dividend! It'll be all up with first-class football in the Five Towns! "

The interests involved seemed to grow more complicated. And here I had been in the district nearly four hours without having guessed that the district was quivering in the tense excitement of gigantic issues!

And here was this Scotch doctor, at whose word the great Myatt would have declined to play, never saying a syllable about the affair, until a chance remark from Buchanan loosened his tongue. But all doctors are strangely secretive. Secretiveness is one of their chief private pleasures.

"Come and see the pigeons, eh? " said Buchanan.

"Pigeons? " I repeated.

"We give the results of over a hundred matches in our Football Edition," said Buchanan, and added: "not counting Rugby."

As we left the room two boys dodged round us into it, bearing telegrams.

In a moment we were, in the most astonishing manner, on a leaden roof of the *Signal* offices. High factory chimneys rose over the horizon of slates on every side, blowing thick smoke into the general murk of the afternoon sky, and crossing the western crimson with long pennons of black. And out of the murk there came from afar a blue-and-white pigeon which circled largely several times over the offices of the *Signal*. At length it descended, and I could hear the whirr of its strong wings. The wings ceased to beat and the pigeon slanted downwards in a curve, its head lower than its wide tail. Then the little head gradually rose and the tail fell; the curve had changed, the pace slackened; the pigeon was calculating with all its brain; eyes, wings, tail and feet were being co-ordinated to the resolution of an intricate mechanical problem. The pinkish claws seemed to grope—and after an instant of hesitation the thing was done, the problem solved; the pigeon, with delicious gracefulness, had established equilibrium on the ridge of a pigeon-cote, and folded its wings, and was peering about with strange motions of its extremely movable head. Presently it flew down to the leads, waddled to and fro with the ungainly gestures of a fat woman of sixty, and disappeared into the cote. At the same moment the boy who had been dismissed from the sub-editor's room ran forward and entered the cote by a wire-screened door.

" Handy things, pigeons! " said the doctor as we approached to examine the cote.   Fifty or sixty pigeons were cooing and strutting in it.   There was a protest of wings as the boy seized the last arriving messenger.

" Give it here! " Buchanan ordered.

The boy handed over a thin tube of paper which he had unfastened from the bird's leg.   Buchanan unrolled it and showed it to me.   I read: " Midland Federation.   Axe United, Macclesfield Town.   Match abandoned after half-hour's play owing to fog.   Three forty-five."

" Three forty-five," said Buchanan, looking at his watch.   " He's done the ten miles in half an hour, roughly.   Not bad.   First time we tried pigeons from as far off as Axe.   Here, boy! "   And he restored the paper to the boy, who gave it to another boy, who departed with it.

" Man," said the doctor, eyeing Buchanan.   " Ye'd no business out here.   Ye're not precisely a pigeon."

Down we went, one after another, by the ladder, and now we fell into the composing-room, where Buchanan said he felt warmer.   An immense, dirty, white-washed apartment crowded with linotypes and other machines, in front of which sat men in white aprons, tapping, tapping—gazing at documents pinned at the level of their eyes—and tapping, tapping.   A kind of cavernous retreat in which monstrous iron growths rose out of the floor and were met half-way by electric flowers that had their roots in the ceiling!   In this jungle there was scarcely room for us to walk. Buchanan explained the linotypes to me.   I watched, as though romantically dreaming, the flashing descent of letter after letter, a rain of letters into the belly of the machine; then, going round to the back, I watched the same letters rising again in a close, slow procession, and sorting themselves by themselves at the top in readiness to answer again to the tapping, tapping of a man in a once-white apron. And while I was watching all that I could somehow, by a faculty which we have, at the same time see pigeons far overhead, arriving and arriving out of the murk from beyond the verge of chimneys.

"Ingenious, isn't it? " said Stirling.

But I imagine that he had not the faculty by which to see the pigeons.

A reverend, bearded, spectacled man, with his shirt-sleeves rolled up and an apron stretched over his hemispherical paunch, strolled slowly along an alley, glancing at a galley-proof with an ingenuous air just as if he had never seen a galley-proof before.

"It's a stick more than a column already," said he confidentially, offering the long paper, and then gravely looking at Buchanan, with head bent forward, not through his spectacles but over them.

The editor negligently accepted the proof, and I read a series of titles: " Knype *v.* Manchester Rovers. Record Gate. Fifteen thousand spectators. Two goals in twelve minutes. Myatt in form. Special Report."

Buchanan gave the slip back without a word.

"There you are! " said he to me, as another compositor near us attached a piece of tissue paper to his machine. It was the very paper that I had seen come out of the sky, but its contents had been enlarged and amended by the sub-editorial pen. The man began tapping, tapping, and the letters began to flash downwards on their way to tell a quarter of a million people that Axe *v.* Macclesfield had been stopped by fog.

"I suppose that Knype match is over by now? " I said.

"Oh no! " said Buchanan. " The second half has scarcely begun."

"Like to go? " Stirling asked.

" Well," I said, feeling adventurous, " it's a notion, isn't it? "

" You can run Mr Loring down there in five or six minutes," said Buchanan. " And he's probably never seen anything like it before. You might call here as you come home and see the paper on the machines."

III

WE went on the Grand Stand, which was packed with men whose eyes were fixed, with an unconscious but intense effort, on a common object. Among the men were a few women in furs and wraps, equally absorbed. Nobody took any notice of us as we insinuated our way up a rickety flight of wooden stairs, but when by misadventure we grazed a human being the elbow of that being shoved itself automatically and fiercely outwards, to repel. I had an impression of hats, caps, and woolly overcoats stretched in long parallel lines, and of grimy raw planks everywhere presenting possibly dangerous splinters, save where use had worn them into smooth shininess. Then gradually I became aware of the vast field, which was more brown than green. Around the field was a wide border of infinitesimal hats and pale faces, rising in tiers, and beyond this border fences, hoardings, chimneys, furnaces, gasometers, telegraph-poles, houses, and dead trees. And here and there, perched in strange perilous places, even high up towards the sombre sky, were more human beings clinging. On the field itself, at one end of it, were a scattered handful of doll-like figures, motionless; some had white bodies, others red; and three were in black; all were so small and so far off that they seemed to be mere unimportant casual incidents in whatever recondite affair it was that was proceeding. Then a whistle shrieked, and all these figures began simultaneously to move, and then I saw a ball in the air.   An obscure, uneasy murmuring rose from the immense multitude like an invisible but audible vapour. The next instant the vapour had condensed into a sudden shout.   Now I saw the ball rolling solitary in the middle of the field, and a single red doll racing towards it; at one end was a confused group of red and white, and at the other two white dolls, rather lonely in the expanse.   The single red doll overtook the ball and scudded along with it at his twinkling toes.   A great voice behind me bellowed with an incredible volume of sound:

" Now, Jos! "

And another voice, further away, bellowed:

" Now, Jos! "

And still more distantly the grim warning shot forth from the crowd:

" Now, Jos!   Now, Jos! "

The nearer of the white dolls, as the red one approached, sprang forward.   I could see a leg.   And the ball was flying back in a magnificent curve into the skies; it passed out of my sight, and then I heard a bump on the slates of the roof of the grand stand, and it fell among the crowd in the stand-enclosure.   But almost before the flight of the ball had commenced, a terrific roar of relief had rolled formidably round the field, and out of that roar, like rockets out of thick smoke, burst acutely ecstatic cries of adoration:

" Bravo, Jos! "

" Good old Jos! "

The leg had evidently been Jos's leg.   The nearer of these two white dolls must be Jos, darling of fifteen thousand frenzied people.

Stirling punched a neighbour in the side to attract his attention.

" What's the score? " he demanded of the neighbour, who scowled and then grinned.

" Two—one — agen uz! " The other growled.
" It'll take our b——s all their time to draw. They're
playing a man short."

" Accident? "

" No! Referee ordered him off for rough play."

Several spectators began to explain, passionately,
furiously, that the referee's action was utterly bereft of
common sense and justice; and I gathered that a less
gentlemanly crowd would undoubtedly have lynched
the referee. The explanations died down, and everybody except me resumed his fierce watch on the field.

I was recalled from the exercise of a vague curiosity
upon the set, anxious faces around me by a crashing,
whooping cheer which in volume and sincerity of joy surpassed all noises in my experience. This massive cheer
reverberated round the field like the echoes of a battle-
ship's broadside in a fiord. But it was human, and
therefore more terrible than guns. I instinctively
thought: " If such are the symptoms of pleasure, what
must be the symptoms of pain or disappointment? "
Simultaneously with the expulsion of the unique noise
the expression of the faces changed. Eyes sparkled;
teeth became prominent in enormous, uncontrolled
smiles. Ferocious satisfaction had to find vent in ferocious gestures, wreaked either upon dead wood or upon
the living tissues of fellow-creatures. The gentle,
mannerly sound of hand-clapping was a kind of light
froth on the surface of the billowy sea of heartfelt applause. The host of the fifteen thousand might have just
had their lives saved, or their children snatched from
destruction and their wives from dishonour; they might
have been preserved from bankruptcy, starvation,
prison, torture; they might have been rewarding with
their impassioned worship a band of national heroes.
But it was not so. All that had happened was that the
ball had rolled into the net of the Manchester Rovers'
goal. Knype had drawn level. The reputation of the

Five Towns before the jury of expert opinion that could
distinguish between first-class football and second-class
was maintained intact.   I could hear specialists around
me proving that though Knype had yet five League
matches to play, its situation was safe.   They pointed
excitedly to a huge hoarding at one end of the ground on
which appeared names of other clubs with changing
figures.   These clubs included the clubs which Knype
would have to meet before the end of the season, and the
figures indicated their fortunes on various grounds
similar to this ground all over the country.   If a goal
was scored in Newcastle, or in Southampton, the very
Peru of first-class football, it was registered on that
board and its possible effect on the destinies of Knype
was instantly assessed.   The calculations made were
dizzying.

Then a little flock of pigeons flew up and separated,
under the illusion that they were free agents and masters
of the air, but really wafted away to fixed destinations
on the stupendous atmospheric waves of still-continued
cheering.

After a minute or two the ball was restarted, and
the greater noise had diminished to the sensitive uneasy
murmur which responded like a delicate instrument to
the fluctuations of the game.   Each feat and manœuvre
of Knype drew generous applause in proportion to its
intention or its success, and each sleight of the Manchester Rovers, successful or not, provoked a holy
disgust.   The attitude of the host had passed beyond
morality into religion.

Then, again, while my attention had lapsed from the
field, a devilish, a barbaric, and a deafening yell broke
from those fifteen thousand passionate hearts.   It
thrilled me; it genuinely frightened me.   I involuntarily made the motion of swallowing.   After the
thunderous crash of anger from the host came the thin
sound of a whistle.   The game stopped.   I heard the

same word repeated again and again, in divers tones
of exasperated fury:

" Foul! "

I felt that I was hemmed in by potential homicides,
whose arms were lifted in the desire of murder and whose
features were changed from the likeness of man into the
corporeal form of some pure and terrible instinct.

And I saw a long doll rise from the ground and
approach a lesser doll with threatening hands.

" Foul! Foul! "

" Go it, Jos! Knock his neck out! Jos! He
tripped thee up! "

There was a prolonged gesticulatory altercation between the three black dolls in leather leggings and several
of the white and the red dolls. At last one of the man-
nikins in leggings shrugged his shoulders, made a definite
gesture to the other two, and walked away towards the
edge of the field nearest the stand. It was the unprin-
cipled referee; he had disallowed the foul. In the pro-
tracted duel between the offending Manchester forward
and the great, honest Jos Myatt he had given another
point to the enemy. As soon as the host realized the
infamy it yelled once more in heightened fury. It
seemed to surge in masses against the thick iron railings
that alone stood between the referee and death. The
discreet referee was approaching the grand stand as the
least unsafe place. In a second a handful of execu-
tioners had somehow got on to the grass. And in
the next second several policemen were in front of
them, not striking nor striving to intimidate, but heavily
pushing them into bounds.

" Get back there! " cried a few abrupt, commanding
voices from the stand.

The referee stood with his hands in his pockets and
his whistle in his mouth. I think that in that moment
of acutest suspense the whole of his earthly career must
have flashed before him in a phantasmagoria. And

then the crisis was past. The inherent gentlemanliness of the outraged host had triumphed and the referee was spared.

"Served him right if they'd man-handled him!" said a spectator.

"Ay!" said another, gloomily, "ay! And th' Football Association 'ud ha' fined us maybe a hundred quid and disqualified th' ground for the rest o' th' season!"

"D——n th' Football Association!"

"Ay! But you canna'!"

"Now, lads! Play up, Knype! Now, lads! Give 'em hot hell!" Different voices heartily encouraged the home team as the ball was thrown into play.

The fouling Manchester forward immediately resumed possession of the ball. Experience could not teach him. He parted with the ball and got it again, twice. The devil was in him and in the ball. The devil was driving him towards Myatt. They met. And then came a sound quite new: a cracking sound, somewhat like the snapping of a bough, but sharper, more decisive.

"By Jove!" exclaimed Stirling. "That's his bone!"

And instantly he was off down the staircase and I after him. But he was not the first doctor on the field. Nothing had been unforeseen in the wonderful organization of this enterprise. A pigeon sped away and an official doctor and an official stretcher appeared, miraculously, simultaneously. It was tremendous. It inspired awe in me.

"He asked for it!" I heard a man say as I hesitated on the shore of the ocean of mud.

Then I knew that it was Manchester and not Knype that had suffered. The confusion and hubbub were in a high degree disturbing and puzzling. But one emotion emerged clear: pleasure. I felt it myself. I was aware of joy in that the two sides were now levelled to ten men apiece. I was mystically identified with the Five Towns, absorbed into their life. I could discern on every face the conviction that a divine providence was in this affair, that God could not be mocked.   I toc had this conviction.   I could discern also on every face the fear lest the referee might give a foul against the hero Myatt, or even order him off the field, though of course the fracture was a simple accident.   I too had this fear.   It was soon dispelled by the news which swept across the entire enclosure like a sweet smell, that the referee had adopted the theory of a simple accident. I saw vaguely policemen, a stretcher, streaming crowds, and my ears heard a monstrous universal babbling.   And then the figure of Stirling detached itself from the moving disorder and came to me.

"Well, Myatt's calf was harder than the other chap's, that's all," he said.

"Which *is* Myatt?" I asked, for the red and the white dolls had all vanished at close quarters, and were replaced by unrecognizably gigantic human animals, still clad, however, in dolls' vests and dolls' knickerbockers.

Stirling warningly jerked his head to indicate a man not ten feet away from me.   This was Myatt, the hero of the host and the darling of populations.   I gazed up at him.   His mouth and his left knee were red with blood, and he was piebald with thick patches of mud from his tousled crown to his enormous boot.   His blue eyes had a heavy, stupid, honest glance; and of the three qualities stupidity predominated.   He seemed to be all feet, knees, hands and elbows.   His head was very small— the sole remainder of the doll in him.

A little man approached him, conscious—somewhat too obviously conscious — of his right to approach. Myatt nodded.

"Ye'n settled *him*, seemingly, Jos!" said the little man.

"Well," said Myatt, with slow bitterness.   "Hadn't he been blooming well begging and praying for it, aw afternoon?   Hadn't he now?"

The little man nodded. Then he said in a lower tone:
" How's missis, like? "

" Her's altogether yet," said Myatt.   " Or I'd none
ha' played! "

" I've bet Watty half-a-dollar as it inna' a lad! "
said the little man.

Myatt seemed angry.

" Wilt bet me half a *quid* as it inna' a lad? " he
demanded, bending down and scowling and sticking out
his muddy chin.

" Ay! " said the little man, not blenching.

" Evens? "

" Evens."

" I'll take thee, Charlie," said Myatt, resuming his
calm.

The whistle sounded. And several orders were given
to clear the field. Eight minutes had been lost over a
broken leg, but Stirling said that the referee would
surely deduct them from the official time, so that after
all the game would not be shortened.

" I'll be up yon, to-morra morning," said the little
man.

Myatt nodded and departed. Charlie, the little man,
turned on his heel and proudly rejoined the crowd. He
had been seen of all in converse with supreme greatness.

Stirling and I also retired; and though Jos Myatt
had not even done his doctor the honour of seeing him,
neither of us, I think, was quite without a consciousness
of glory: I cannot imagine why. The rest of the game
was flat and tame. Nothing occurred. The match
ended in a draw.

IV

WE were swept from the football ground on a furious
flood of humanity—carried forth and flung down a slope

into a large waste space that separated the ground from
the nearest streets of little reddish houses.   At the
bottom of the slope, on my suggestion, we halted for a
few moments aside, while the current rushed forward
and, spreading out, inundated the whole space in one
marvellous minute.   The impression of the multitude
streaming from that gap in the wooden wall was like
nothing more than the impression of a burst main which
only the emptying of the reservoir will assuage.   Anybody who wanted to commit suicide might have stood
in front of that gap and had his wish.   He would not
have been noticed.   The interminable and implacable
infantry charge would have passed unheedingly over
him.   A silent, preoccupied host, bent on something
else now, and perhaps teased by the inconvenient
thought that after all a draw is not as good as a win!
It hurried blindly, instinctively outwards, knees and
chins protruding, hands deep in pockets, chilled feet
stamping.   Occasionally someone stopped or slackened
to light a pipe, and on being curtly bunted onward by
a blind force from behind, accepted the hint as an atom
accepts the law of gravity.   The fever and ecstasy were
over.   What fascinated the Southern in me was the grim
taciturnity, the steady stare (vacant or dreaming), and
the heavy, muffled, multitudinous tramp shaking the
cindery earth.   The flood continued to rage through the
gap.

Our automobile had been left at the Haycock
Hotel; we went to get it, braving the inundation.
Nearly opposite the stableyard the electric trams started
for Hanbridge, Bursley and Turnhill, and for Longshaw.
Here the crowd was less dangerous, but still very formidable—to my eyes.   Each tram as it came up was
savagely assaulted, seized, crammed and possessed, with
astounding rapidity.   Its steps were the western bank of
a Beresina.   At a given moment the inured conductor,
brandishing his leather-shielded arm with a pitiless

gesture, thrust aspirants down into the mud and the tram rolled powerfully away.   All this in silence.

After a few minutes a bicyclist swished along through the mud, taking the far side of the road, which was comparatively free.   He wore grey trousers, heavy boots, and a dark cut-away coat, up the back of which a line of caked mud had deposited itself.   On his head was a bowler hat.

" How do, Jos? " cried a couple of boys, cheekily. And then there were a few adult greetings of respect.

It was the hero, in haste.

" Out of it, there! " he warned impeders, between his teeth, and plugged on with bent head.

" He keeps the Foaming Quart up at Toft End," said the doctor.   " It's the highest pub in the Five Towns. He used to be what they call a pot-hunter, a racing bicyclist, you know.   But he's got past that and he'll soon be past football.   He's thirty-four if he's a day. That's one reason why he's so independent—that and because he's almost the only genuine native in the team."

" Why? " I asked.   " Where do they come from, then? "

" Oh! " said Stirling as he gently started the car. " The club buys 'em, up and down the country.   Four of 'em are Scots.   A few years ago an Oldham club offered Knype £500 for Myatt, a big price—more than he's worth now!   But he wouldn't go, though they guaranteed to put him into a first-class pub—a free house.   He's never cost Knype anything except his wages and the goodwill of the Foaming Quart."

" What are his wages? "

" Don't know exactly.   Not much.   The Football Association fix a maximum.   I daresay about four pounds a week   *Hi there !   Are you deaf ?* "

" Thee mind what tha'rt about! " responded a stout loiterer in our path.   "Or I'll take thy ears home for my tea, mester."

Stirling laughed.

In a few minutes we had arrived at Hanbridge, splashing all the way between two processions that crowded either footpath. And in the middle of the road was a third procession of trams,—tram following tram, each gorged with passengers, frothing at the step with passengers; not the lackadaisical trams that I had seen earlier in the afternoon in Crown Square; a different race of trams, eager and impetuous velocities. We reached the *Signal* offices. No crowd of urchins to salute us this time!

Under the earth was the machine-room of the *Signal*. It reminded me of the bowels of a ship, so full was it of machinery. One huge machine clattered slowly, and a folded green thing dropped strangely on to a little iron table in front of us. Buchanan opened it, and I saw that the broken leg was in it at length, together with a statement that in the *Signal's* opinion the sympathy of every true sportsman would be with the disabled player. I began to say something to Buchanan, when suddenly I could not hear my own voice. The great machine, with another behind us, was working at a fabulous speed and with a fabulous clatter. All that my startled senses could clearly disentangle was that the blue arc-lights above us blinked occasionally, and that folded green papers were snowing down upon the iron table far faster than the eye could follow them. Tall lads in aprons elbowed me away and carried off the green papers in bundles, but not more quickly than the machine shed them. Buchanan put his lips to my ear. But I could hear nothing. I shook my head. He smiled, and led us out from the tumult.

"Come and see the boys take them," he said at the foot of the stairs.

In a sort of hall on the ground floor was a long counter, and beyond the counter a system of steel railings in parallel lines, so arranged that a person entering at the public door could only reach the counter by passing up or down each alley in succession. These steel lanes, which absolutely ensured the triumph of right over might, were packed with boys—the ragged urchins whom we had seen playing in the street. But not urchins now; rather young tigers! Perhaps half a dozen had reached the counter; the rest were massed behind, shouting and quarrelling. Through a hole in the wall, at the level of the counter, bundles of papers shot continuously, and were snatched up by servers, who distributed them in smaller bundles to the hungry boys; who flung down metal discs in exchange and fled, fled madly as though fiends were after them, through a third door, out of the pandemonium into the darkling street. And unceasingly the green papers appeared at the hole in the wall and unceasingly they were plucked away and borne off by those maddened children, whose destination was apparently Aix or Ghent, and whose wings were their tatters.

" What are those discs? " I inquired.

" The lads have to come and buy them earlier in the day," said Buchanan. " We haven't time to sell this edition for cash, you see."

" Well," I said as we left, " I'm very much obliged."

" What on earth for? " Buchanan asked.

" Everything," I said.

We returned through the squares of Hanbridge and by Trafalgar Road to Stirling's house at Bleakridge. And everywhere in the deepening twilight I could see the urchins, often hatless and sometimes scarcely shod, scudding over the lamp-reflecting mire with sheets of wavy green, and above the noises of traffic I could hear the shrill outcry: " *Signal*. Football Edition. Football Edition. *Signal*." The world was being informed of the might of Jos Myatt, and of the averting of disaster from Knype, and of the results of over a hundred other matches—not counting Rugby.

V

DURING the course of the evening, when Stirling had
thoroughly accustomed himself to the state of being in
sole charge of an expert from the British Museum,
London, and the high walls round his more private soul
had yielded to my timid but constant attacks, we grew
fairly intimate.   And in particular the doctor proved
to me that his reputation for persuasive raciness with
patients was well founded.   Yet up to the time of dessert
I might have been justified in supposing that that much-
praised " manner " in a sick-room was nothing but a
provincial legend.   Such may be the influence of a quite
inoffensive and shy Londoner in the country.   At half-
past ten, Titus being already asleep for the night in an
arm-chair, we sat at ease over the fire in the study telling each other stories.   We had dealt with the arts, and
with medicine; now we were dealing with life, in those
aspects of it which cause men to laugh and women uneasily to wonder.   Once or twice we had mentioned the
Brindleys.   The hour for their arrival was come.   But
being deeply comfortable and content where I was, I felt
no impatience.   Then there was a tap on the window.

" That's Bobbie! " said Stirling, rising slowly from
his chair.   " *He* won't refuse whisky, even if you do.
I'd better get another bottle."

The tap was repeated peevishly.

" I'm coming, laddie! " Stirling protested.

He slippered out through the hall and through the
surgery to the side door, I following, and Titus sneezing
and snuffing in the rear.

" I say, mester," said a heavy voice as the doctor
opened the door.   It was not Brindley, but Jos Myatt.
Unable to locate the bell-push in the dark, he had characteristically attacked the sole illuminated window.
He demanded, or he commanded, very curtly, that the

doctor should go up instantly to the Foaming Quart at Toft End.

Stirling hesitated a moment.

" All right, my man," said he, calmly.

" Now? " the heavy, suspicious voice on the door-step insisted.

" I'll be there before ye if ye don't sprint, man. I'll run up in the car." Stirling shut the door. I heard footsteps on the gravel path outside.

" Ye heard? " said he to me. " And what am I to do with ye? "

" I'll go with you, of course," I answered.

" I may be kept up there a while."

" I don't care," I said roisterously. " It's a pub and I'm a traveller."

Stirling's household was in bed and his assistant gone home. While he and Titus got out the car I wrote a line for the Brindleys: " Gone with doctor to see patient at Toft End. Don't wait up.—A. L." This we pushed under Brindley's front door on our way forth. Very soon we were vibrating up a steep street on the first speed of the car, and the yellow reflections of dis-tant furnaces began to shine over house roofs below us. It was exhilaratingly cold, a clear and frosty night, tonic, bracing after the enclosed warmth of the study. I was joyous, but silently. We had quitted the kingdom of the god Pan; we were in Lucina's realm, its consequence, where there is no laughter. We were on a mission.

" I didn't expect this," said Stirling.

" No? " I said. " But seeing that he fetched you this morning—"

" Oh! That was only in order to be sure, for himself. His sister was there, in charge. Seemed very capable. Knew all about everything. Until ye get to the high social status of a clerk or a draper's assistant people seem to manage to have their children without professional assistance."

" Then do you think there's anything wrong? " 1 asked.

" I'd not be surprised."

He changed to the second speed as the car topped the first bluff. We said no more. The night and the mission solemnized us. And gradually, as we rose towards the purple skies, the Five Towns wrote themselves out in fire on the irregular plain below.

" That's Hanbridge Town Hall," said Stirling, pointing to the right. " And that's Bursley Town Hall," he said, pointing to the left. And there were many other beacons, dominating the jewelled street-lines that faded on the horizon into golden-tinted smoke.

The road was never quite free of houses. After occurring but sparsely for half a mile, they thickened into a village—the suburb of Bursley called Toft End. I saw a moving red light in front of us. It was the reverse of Myatt's bicycle lantern. The car stopped near the dark façade of the inn, of which two yellow windows gleamed. Stirling, under Myatt's shouted guidance, backed into an obscure yard under cover. The engine ceased to throb.

" Friend of mine," he introduced me to Myatt. " By the way, Loring, pass me my bag, will you? Mustn't forget that." Then he extinguished the acetylene lamps, and there was no light in the yard except the ray of the bicycle lantern which Myatt held in his hand. We groped towards the house. Strange, every step that I take in the Five Towns seems to have the genuine quality of an adventure!

VI

IN five minutes I was of no account in the scheme of things at Toft End, and I began to wonder why I had come. Stirling, my sole protector, had vanished up the dark stairs of the house, following a stout, youngish woman in a white apron, who bore a candle. Jos Myatt, behind, said to me: " Happen you'd better go in there, mester," pointing to a half-open door at the foot of the stairs. I went into a little room at the rear of the bar-parlour. A good fire burned in a small old-fashioned grate, but there was no other light. The inn was closed to customers, it being past eleven o'clock. On a bare table I perceived a candle, and ventured to put a match to it. I then saw almost exactly such a room as one would expect to find at the rear of the bar-parlour of an inn on the outskirts of an industrial town. It appeared to serve the double purpose of a living-room and of a retreat for favoured customers. The table was evidently one at which men drank. On a shelf was a row of bottles, more or less empty, bearing names famous in newspaper advertisements and in the House of Lords. The dozen chairs suggested an acute bodily discomfort such as would only be tolerated by a sitter all of whose sensory faculties were centred in his palate. On a broken chair in a corner was an insecure pile of books. A smaller table was covered with a chequered cloth on which were a few plates. Along one wall, under the window, ran a pitch-pine sofa upholstered with a stuff slightly dissimilar from that on the table. The mattress of the sofa was uneven and its surface wrinkled, and old newspapers and pieces of brown paper had been stowed away between it and the framework. The chief article of furniture was an effective walnut bookcase, the glass doors of which were curtained with red cloth. The window, wider than it was high, was also curtained with red cloth. The walls, papered in a saffron tint, bore framed advertisements and a few photographs of self-conscious persons. The ceiling was as obscure as heaven; the floor tiled, with a list rug in front of the steel fender.

I put my overcoat on the sofa, picked up the candle and glanced at the books in the corner: Lavater's indestructible work, a paper-covered *Whitaker*, the *Licensed Victuallers' Almanac*, *Johnny Ludlow*, the illustrated catalogue of the Exhibition of 1856, *Cruden's Concordance*, and seven or eight volumes of *Knight's Penny Encyclopædia*. While I was poring on these titles I heard movements overhead—previously there had been no sound whatever—and with guilty haste I restored the candle to the table and placed myself negligently in front of the fire.

"Now don't let me see ye up here any more till I fetch ye!" said a woman's distant voice—not crossly, but firmly. And then, crossly: "Be off with ye now!"

Reluctant boots on the stairs! Jos Myatt entered to me. He did not speak at first; nor did I. He avoided my glance. He was still wearing the cut-away coat with the line of mud up the back. I took out my watch, not for the sake of information, but from mere nervousness, and the sight of the watch reminded me that it would be prudent to wind it up.

"Better not forget that," I said, winding it.

"Ay!" said he, gloomily. "It's a tip." And he wound up his watch; a large, thick, golden one.

This watch-winding established a basis of intercourse between us.

"I hope everything is going on all right," I murmured.

"What dun ye say?" he asked.

"I say I hope everything is going on all right," I repeated louder, and jerked my head in the direction of the stairs, to indicate the place from which he had come.

"Oh!" he exclaimed, as if surprised. "Now what'll ye have, mester?" He stood waiting. "It's my call to-night."

I explained to him that I never took alcohol. It was not quite true, but it was as true as most general propositions are.

" Neither me! " he said shortly, after a pause.

" You're a teetotaller too? " I showed a little involuntary astonishment.

He put forward his chin.

" What do *you* think? " he said confidentially and scornfully. It was precisely as if he had said: " Do you think that anybody but a born ass would *not* be a teetotaller, in my position? "

I sat down on a chair.

" Take th' squab, mester," he said, pointing to the sofa. I took it.

He picked up the candle; then dropped it, and lighted a lamp which was on the mantelpiece between his vases of blue glass. His movements were very slow, hesitating and clumsy. Blowing out the candle, which smoked for a long time, he went with the lamp to the bookcase. As the key of the bookcase was in his right pocket and the lamp in his right hand he had to change the lamp, cautiously, from hand to hand. When he opened the cupboard I saw a rich gleam of silver from every shelf of it except the lowest, and I could distinguish the forms of ceremonial cups with pedestals and immense handles.

" I suppose these are your pots? " I said.

" Ay! "

He displayed to me the fruits of his manifold victories. I could see him straining along endless cinder-paths and highroads under hot suns, his great knees going up and down like treadles amid the plaudits and howls of vast populations. And all that now remained of that glory was these debased and vicious shapes, magnificently useless, grossly ugly, with their inscriptions lost in a mess of flourishes.

" Ay! " he said again, when I had fingered the last of them.

" A very fine show indeed! " I said, resuming the sofa.

He took a penny bottle of ink and a pen out of the bookcase, and also, from the lowest shelf, a bag of money and a long narrow account book. Then he sat down at the table and commenced accountancy. It was clear that he regarded his task as formidable and complex. To see him reckoning the coins, manipulating the pen, splashing the ink, scratching the page; to hear him whispering consecutive numbers aloud, and muttering mysterious anathemas against the untamable naughtiness of figures—all this was painful, and with the painfulness of a simple exercise rendered difficult by inaptitude and incompetence. I wanted to jump up and cry to him: " Get out of the way, man, and let me do it for you! I can do it while you are wiping hairs from your pen on your sleeve." I was sorry for him because he was ridiculous—and even more grotesque than ridiculous. I felt, quite acutely, that it was a shame that he could not be for ever the central figure of a field of mud, kicking a ball into long and grandiose parabolas higher than gasometers, or breaking an occasional leg, surrounded by the violent affection of hearts whose melting-point was the exclamation, " Good old Jos! " I felt that if he must repose his existence ought to have been so contrived that he could repose in impassive and senseless dignity, like a mountain watching the flight of time. The conception of him tracing symbols in a ledger, counting shillings and sixpences, descending to arithmetic, and suffering those humiliations which are the invariable preliminaries to legitimate fatherhood, was shocking to a nice taste for harmonious fitness. . . . What, this precious and terrific organism, this slave with a specialty — whom distant towns had once been anxious to buy at the prodigious figure of five hundred pounds—obliged to sit in a mean chamber and wait silently while the woman of his choice encountered the supreme peril! And he would " soon be past football! " He was " thirty-four if a day!" It was the verge of senility! He was no longer worth five hundred pounds. Perhaps even now this jointed merchandise was only worth two hundred pounds! And "they"—the shadowy directors, who could not kick a ball fifty feet and who would probably turn sick if they broke a leg—"they" paid him four pounds a week for being the hero of a quarter of a million of people! He was the chief magnet to draw fifteen thousand sixpences and shillings of a Saturday afternoon into a company's cash box, and here he sat splitting his head over fewer sixpences and shillings than would fill a half-pint pot! Jos, you ought in justice to have been José, with a thin red necktie down your breast (instead of a line of mud up your back), and embroidered breeches on those miraculous legs, and an income of a quarter of a million pesetas, and the languishing acquiescence of innumerable mantillas. Every moment you were getting older and stiffer; every moment was bringing nearer the moment when young men would reply curtly to their doddering elders: " Jos Myatt—who was *'e ?*"

The putting away of the ledger, the ink, the pen and the money was as exasperating as their taking out had been. Then Jos, always too large for the room, crossed the tiled floor and mended the fire. A poker was more suited to his capacity than a pen. He glanced about him, uncertain and anxious, and then crept to the door near the foot of the stairs and listened. There was no sound; and that was curious. The woman who was bringing into the world the hero's child made no cry that reached us below. Once or twice I had heard muffled movements not quite overhead—somewhere above—but naught else. The doctor and Jos's sister seemed to have retired into a sinister and dangerous mystery. I could not dispel from my mind pictures of what they were watching and what they were doing. The vast, cruel, fumbling clumsiness of Nature, her lack of majesty in crises that ought to be majestic, her incurable indignity, disgusted me, aroused my disdain. I wanted, as a philosopher of all the cultures, to feel that the present was indeed a majestic crisis, to be so esteemed by a superior man. I could not. Though the crisis possibly intimidated me somewhat, yet, on behalf of Jos Myatt, I was ashamed of it. This may be reprehensible, but it is true.

He sat down by the fire and looked at the fire. I could not attempt to carry on a conversation with him, and to avoid the necessity for any talk at all, I extended myself on the sofa and averted my face, wondering once again why I had accompanied the doctor to Toft End. The doctor was now in another, an inaccessible world. I dozed, and from my doze I was roused by Jos Myatt going to the door on the stairs.

" Jos," said a voice. " It's a girl."

Then a silence.

I admit there was a flutter in my heart. Another soul, another formed and unchangeable temperament, tumbled into the world! Whence? Whither? . . . As for the quality of majesty—yes, if silver trumpets had announced the advent, instead of a stout, aproned woman, the moment could not have been more majestic in its sadness. I say " sadness," which is the inevitable and sole effect of these eternal and banal questions, " Whence? Whither? "

" Is her bad? " Jos whispered.

" Her's pretty bad," said the voice, but cheerily. " Bring me up another scuttle o' coal."

When he returned to the parlour, after being again dismissed, I said to him:

" Well, I congratulate you."

" I thank ye! " he said, and sat down. Presently I could hear him muttering to himself, mildly: " Hell! Hell! Hell! "

I thought: " Stirling will not be very long now, and

we can depart home." I looked at my watch. It was a quarter to two. But Stirling did not appear, nor was there any message from him or sign. I had to submit to the predicament. As a faint chilliness from the window affected my back I drew my overcoat up to my shoulders as a counterpane. Through a gap between the red curtains of the window I could see a star blazing. It passed behind the curtain with disconcerting rapidity. The universe was swinging and whirling as usual.

VII

SOUNDS of knocking disturbed me. In the few seconds that elapsed before I could realize just where I was and why I was there, the summoning knocks were repeated. The early sun was shining through the red blind. I sat up and straightened my hair, involuntarily composing my attitude so that nobody who might enter the room should imagine that I had been other than patiently wide-awake all night. The second door of the parlour—that leading to the bar-room of the. Foaming Quart—was open, and I could see the bar itself, with shelves rising behind it and the upright handles of a beer-engine at one end. Someone whom I could not see was evidently unbolting and unlocking the principal entrance to the inn. Then I heard the scraping of a creaky portal on the floor.

" Well, Jos lad! "

It was the voice of the little man, Charlie, who had spoken with Myatt on the football field.

" Come in quick, Charlie. It's cowd [cold]," said the voice of Jos Myatt, gloomily.

" Ay! Cowd it is, lad! It's above three mile as I've walked, and thou knows it, Jos. Give us a quartern o' gin."

The door grated again and a bolt was drawn.

The two men passed together behind the bar, and so within my vision.   Charlie had a grey muffler round his neck; his hands were far in his pockets and seemed to be at strain, as though trying to prevent his upper and his lower garments from flying apart.   Jos Myatt was extremely dishevelled.   In the little man's demeanour towards the big one there was now none of the self-conscious pride in the mere fact of acquaintance that I had noticed on the field.   Clearly the two were intimate friends, perhaps relatives.   While Jos was dispensing the gin, Charlie said, in a low tone:

" Well, what luck, Jos? "

This was the first reference, by either of them, to the crisis.

Jos deliberately finished pouring out the gin. Then he said:

" There's two on 'em, Charlie."

" Two on 'em? What mean'st tha', lad? "

" I mean as it's twins."

Charlie and I were equally startled.

" Thou never says! " he murmured, incredulous.

" Ay! One o' both sorts," said Jos.

" Thou never says! " Charlie repeated, holding his glass of gin steady in his hand.

" One come at summat after one o'clock, and th' other between five and six.   I had for fetch old woman Eardley to help.   It were more than a handful for Susannah and th' doctor."

Astonishing, that I should have slept through these events!

"How is her?" asked Charlie, quietly, as it were casually.   I think this appearance of casualness was caused by the stoic suppression of the symptoms of anxiety.

" Her's bad," said Jos, briefly.

" And I am na' surprised," said Charlie.   And he lifted the glass.   " Well—here's luck."   He sipped the gin, savouring it on his tongue like a connoisseur, and gradually making up his mind about its quality. Then he took another sip.

" Hast seen her? "

" I seed her for a minute, but our Susannah wouldna' let me stop i' th' room.   Her was raving like."

" Missis? "

" Ay! "

" And th' babbies—hast seen *them* ? "

" Ay!   But I can make nowt out of 'em.   Mrs Eardley says as her's never seen no finer."

" Doctor gone? "

"That he has na'!   He's bin up there all the blessed night, in his shirt-sleeves.   I give him a stiff glass o' whisky at five o'clock and that's all as he's had."

Charlie finished his gin.   The pair stood silent.

" Well," said Charlie, striking his leg.   " Swelp me bob!   It fair beats me!   Twins!   Who'd ha' thought it?   Jos, lad, thou mayst be thankful as it isna' triplets. Never did I think, as I was footing it up here this morning, as it was twins I was coming to! "

" Hast got that half quid in thy pocket? "

" What half quid? " said Charlie, defensively.

" Now then.   Chuck us it over! " said Jos, suddenly harsh and overbearing.

" I laid thee half quid as it 'ud be a wench," said Charlie, doggedly.

" Thou'rt a liar, Charlie! " said Jos.   " Thou laidst half a quid as it wasna' a boy."

" Nay, nay! "   Charlie shook his head.

" And a boy it is! " Jos persisted.

" It being a lad *and* a wench," said Charlie, with a judicial air, " and me 'aving laid as it 'ud be a wench, I wins."   In his accents and his gestures I could discern the mean soul, who on principle never paid until he was absolutely forced to pay.   I could see also that Jos Myatt knew his man.

"Thou laidst me as it wasna' a lad," Jos almost shouted. "And a lad it is, I tell thee."

"*And* a wench!" said Charlie; then shook his head.

The wrangle proceeded monotonously, each party repeating over and over again the phrases of his own argument. I was very glad that Jos did not know me to be a witness of the making of the bet; otherwise I should assuredly have been summoned to give judgment.

"Let's call it off, then," Charlie suggested at length. "That'll settle it. And it being twins—"

"Nay, thou old devil, I'll none call it off. Thou owes me half a quid, and I'll have it out of thee."

"Look ye here," Charlie said more softly. "I'll tell thee what'll settle it. Which on 'em come first, th' lad or th' wench?"

"Th' wench come first," Jos Myatt admitted, with resentful reluctance, dully aware that defeat was awaiting him.

"Well, then! Th' wench is thy eldest child. That's law, that is. And what was us betting about, Jos lad? Us was betting about thy eldest and no other. I'll admit as I laid it wasna' a lad, as thou sayst. And it *wasna'* a lad. First come is eldest, and us was betting about eldest."

Charlie stared at the father in triumph.

Jos Myatt pushed roughly past him in the narrow space behind the bar, and came into the parlour. Nodding to me curtly, he unlocked the bookcase and took two crown pieces from a leathern purse which lay next to the bag. Then he returned to the bar and banged the coins on the counter with fury.

"Take thy brass!" he shouted angrily. "Take thy brass! But thou'rt a damned shark, Charlie, and if anybody 'ud give me a plug o' bacca for doing it, I'd bash thy face in."

The other sniggered contentedly as he picked up his money.

" A bet's a bet," said Charlie.

He was clearly accustomed to an occasional violence of demeanour from Jos Myatt, and felt no fear. But he was wrong in feeling no fear. He had not allowed, in his estimate of the situation, for the exasperated condition of Jos Myatt's nerves under the unique experiences of the night.

Jos's face twisted into a hundred wrinkles and his hand seized Charlie by the arm whose hand held the coins.

" Drop 'em! " he cried loudly, repeating his naïve honesty. " Drop 'em! Or I'll—"

The stout woman, her apron all soiled, now came swiftly and scarce heard into the parlour, and stood at the door leading to the bar-room.

" What's up, Susannah? " Jos demanded in a new voice.

" Well may ye ask what's up! " said the woman. " Shouting and brangling there, ye sots! "

" What's up? " Jos demanded again, loosing Charlie's arm.

" Her's gone! " the woman feebly whimpered. " Like that! " with a vague movement of the hand indicating suddenness. Then she burst into wild sobs and rushed madly back whence she had come, and the sound of her sobs diminished as she ascended the stairs, and expired altogether in the distant shutting of a door.

The men looked at each other.

Charlie restored the crown-pieces to the counter and pushed them towards Jos.

" Here! " he murmured faintly.

Jos flung them savagely to the ground. Another pause followed.

" As God is my witness," he exclaimed solemnly, his voice saturated with feeling, " as God is my witness," he repeated, " I'll ne'er touch a footba' again! "

Little Charlie gazed up at him sadly, plaintively, for what seemed a long while.

" It's good-bye to th' First League, then, for Knype! " he tragically muttered, at length.

VIII

DR STIRLING drove the car very slowly back to Bursley. We glided gently down into the populous valleys. All the stunted trees were coated with rime, which made the sharpest contrast with their black branches and the black mud under us. The high chimneys sent forth their black smoke calmly and tirelessly into the fresh blue sky. Sunday had descended on the vast landscape like a physical influence. We saw a snake of children winding out of a dark brown Sunday school into a dark brown chapel. And up from the valleys came all the bells of all the temples of all the different gods of the Five Towns, chiming, clanging, ringing, each insisting that it alone invited to the altar of the one God. And priests and acolytes of the various cults hurried occasionally along, in silk hats and bright neckties, and smooth coats with folded handkerchiefs sticking out of the pockets, busy, happy and self-important, the convinced heralds of eternal salvation: no doubt nor hesitation as to any fundamental truth had ever entered their minds. We passed through a long, straight street of new red houses with blue slate roofs, all gated and gardened. Here and there a girl with her hair in pins and a rough brown apron over a gaudy frock was stoning a front step. And half-way down the street a man in a scarlet jersey, supported by two women in blue bonnets, was beating a drum and crying aloud: " My friends, you may die to-night. Where, I ask you, where—? " But he had no friends; not even a boy heeded him. The drum continued to bang in our rear.

I enjoyed all this. All this seemed to me to be fine, seemed to throw off the true, fine, romantic savour of life. I would have altered nothing in it. Mean, harsh, ugly, squalid, crude, barbaric—yes, but what an intoxicating sense in it of the organized vitality of a vast community unconscious of itself! I would have altered nothing even in the events of the night. I thought of the rooms at the top of the staircase of the Foaming Quart—mysterious rooms which I had not seen and never should see, recondite rooms from which a soul had slipped away and into which two had come, scenes of anguish and of frustrated effort! Historical rooms, surely! And yet not a house in the hundreds of houses past which we slid but possessed rooms ennobled and made august by happenings exactly as impressive in their tremendous inexplicableness.

The natural humanity of Jos Myatt and Charlie, their fashion of comporting themselves in a sudden stress, pleased me. How else should they have behaved? I could understand Charlie's prophetic dirge over the ruin of the Knype Football Club. It was not that he did not feel the tragedy in the house. He had felt it, and because he had felt it he had uttered at random, foolishly, the first clear thought that ran into his head.

Stirling was quiet. He appeared to be absorbed in steering, and looked straight in front, yawning now and again. He was much more fatigued than I was. Indeed, I had slept pretty well. He said, as we swerved into Trafalgar Road and overtook the aristocracy on its way to chapel and church:

" Well, ye let yeself in for a night, young man! No mistake! "

He smiled, and I smiled.

" What's going to occur up there? " I asked, indicating Toft End.

" What do you mean? "

" A man like that—left with two babies! "

"Oh!" he said. "They'll manage that all right. His sister's a widow. She'll go and live with him. She's as fond of those infants already as if they were her own."

We drew up at his double gates.

" Be sure ye explain to Brindley," he said, as I left him, " that it isn't my fault ye've had a night out of bed. It was your own doing. I'm going to get a bit of sleep now. See you this evening. Bob's asked me to supper."

A servant was sweeping Bob Brindley's porch and the front door was open. I went in. The sound of the piano guided me to the drawing-room. Brindley, the morning cigarette between his lips, was playing Maurice Ravel's " L'heure espagnole." He held his head back so as to keep the smoke out of his eyes. His children in their blue jerseys were building bricks on the carpet.

Without ceasing to play he addressed me calmly:

" You're a nice chap! Where the devil have you been? "

And one of the little boys, glancing up, said, with roguish, imitative innocence, n his high, shrill voice:

" Where the del you been? "

MIMI

I

ON a Saturday afternoon in late October Edward Coe, a satisfactory average successful man of thirty-five, was walking slowly along the King's Road, Brighton. A native and inhabitant of the Five Towns in the Midlands, he had the brusque and energetic mien of the Midlands. It could be seen that he was a stranger to the south; and, in fact, he was now viewing for the first time the vast and glittering spectacle of the southern pleasure city in the unique glory of her autumn season. A spectacle to enliven any man by its mere splendour! And yet Edward Coe was gloomy. One reason for his gloom was that he had just left a bicycle, with a deflated back tyre, to be repaired at a shop in Preston Street. Not perhaps an adequate reason for gloom! . . . Well, that depends. He had been informed by the blue-clad repairer, after due inspection, that the trouble was not a common puncture, but a malady of the valve mysterious.

And the deflation was not the sole cause of his gloom. There was another. He was on his honeymoon. Understand me—not a honeymoon of romance, but a real honeymoon. Who that has ever been on a real honeymoon can look back upon the adventure and faithfully say that it was an unmixed ecstasy of joy? A honeymoon is in its nature and consequences so solemn, so dangerous, and so pitted with startling surprises, that the most irresponsible bridegroom, the most light-hearted, the least in love, must have moments of grave anxiety.

And Edward Coe was far from irresponsible. Nor was
he only a little in love. Moreover, the circumstances
of his marriage were peculiar, and he had married a
dark, brooding, passionate girl.

Mrs Coe was the younger of two sisters named Olive
Wardle, well known in the most desirable circles in the
Five Towns. I mean those circles where intellectual
and artistic tastes are united with sound incomes and
excellent food delicately served. It will certainly be
asked why two sisters should be named Olive. The
answer is that though Olive One and Olive Two were
treated as sisters, and even treated themselves as sisters,
they were not sisters. They were not even half-sisters.
They had first met at the age of nine. The father of
Olive One, a widower, had married the mother of Olive
Two, a widow. Olive One was the elder by a few
months. Olive Two gradually allowed herself to be
called Wardle because it saved trouble. They got on
with one another very well indeed, especially after the
death of both parents, when they became joint mis-
tresses, each with a separate income, of a nice house
at Sneyd, the fashionable residential village on the rim
of the Five Towns. Like all persons who live long
together, they grew in many respects alike. Both were
dark, brooding and passionate, and to this deep similarity a superficial similarity of habits and demeanour
was added. Only, whereas Olive One was rather
more inclined to be the woman of the world, Olive Two
was rather more inclined to study and was particularly
interested in the theory of music.

They were sought after, naturally. And yet they
had reached the age of twenty-five before the world perceived that either of them was not sought after in vain.
The fact, obvious enough, that Pierre Émile Vaillac had
become an object of profound human interest to Olive
One—this fact excited the world, and the world would
have been still more excited had it been aware of an-

other fact that was not at all obvious: namely, that
Pierre Emile Vaillac was the cause of a secret and terrible
breach between the two sisters.   Vaillac, a widower with
two young children, Mimi and Jean, was a Frenchman,
and a great authority on the decoration of egg-shell
china, who had settled in the Five Towns as expert
partner in one of the classic china firms at Longshaw.
He was undoubtedly a very attractive man.

Olive One, when the relations between herself and
Vaillac were developing into something unmistakable,
had suddenly, and without warning, accused Olive Two
of poaching.   It was a frightful accusation, and a frightful scene followed it, one of those scenes that are seldom
forgiven and never forgotten.   It altered their lives; but
as they were women of considerable common sense and
of good breeding, each did her best to behave afterwards
as though nothing had happened.

Olive Two did not convince Olive One of her innocence, because she did not bring forward the supreme
proof of it.   She was too proud—in her brooding and her
mystery—to do so.   The supreme proof was that at this
time she herself was secretly engaged to be married to
Edward Coe, who had conquered her heart with un-
imaginable swiftness a few weeks before she was about
to sit for a musical examination at Manchester.   " Let
us say nothing till after my exam.," she had suggested
to her betrothed.   " There will be an enormous fuss,
and it will put me off, and I shall fail, and I don't want
to fail, and you don't want me to fail."   He agreed
rapturously.   Of course she did fail, nevertheless.   But
being obstinate she said she would go in again, and they
continued to make a secret of the engagement.   They
found the secret delicious.   Then followed the devastat-
ing episode of Vaillac.   Shortly afterwards Olive One
and Vaillac were married, and then Olive Two was alone
in the nice house.   The examination was forgotten, and
she hated the house.   She wanted to be married; Coe

also. But nothing had been said. Difficult to announce
her engagement just then! The world would say that
she had married out of imitation, and her sister would
think that she had married out of pique. Besides, there
would be the fuss, which Olive Two hated. Already the
fuss of her sister's marriage, and the effort at the wedding of pretending that nothing had happened between
them, had fatigued the nerves of Olive Two.

Then Edward Coe had had the brilliant and seductive
idea of marrying in secret. To slip away, and then to
return, saying, "We are married. That's all!" . . .
Why not? No fuss! No ceremonial! The accomplished fact, which simplifies everything!

It was, therefore, a secret honeymoon that Edward
Coe was on; delightful—but surreptitious, furtive! His
mental condition may be best described by stating that,
though he was conscious of rectitude, he somehow could
not look a policeman in the face. After all, plain people
do not usually run off on secret honeymoons. Had he
acted wisely? Perhaps this question, presenting itself
now and then, was the chief cause of his improper gloom.

II

However, the spectacle of Brighton on a fine Saturday afternoon in October had its effect on Edward Coe
—the effect which it has on everybody. Little by little
it inspired him with the joy of life, and straightened his
back, and put a sparkle into his eyes. And he was filled
with the consciousness of the fact that it is a fine thing
to be well-dressed and to have loose gold in your pocket,
and to eat, drink, and smoke well; and to be among
crowds of people who are well-dressed and have loose
gold in their pockets, and eat and drink and smoke well ;
and to know that a magnificent woman will be waiting
for you at a certain place at a certain hour, and that

upon catching sight of you her dark orbs will take on an enchanting expression reserved for you alone, and that she is utterly yours. In a word, he looked on the bright side of things again. It could not ultimately matter a bilberry whether his marriage was public or private.

He lit a cigarette gaily. He could not guess that untoward destiny was waiting for him close by the newspaper kiosque.

A little girl was leaning against the palisade there, and gazing somewhat restlessly about her. A quite little girl, aged, perhaps, eleven, dressed in blue serge, with a short frock and long legs, and a sailor hat (H.M.S. *Formidable*), and long hair down her back, and a mild, twinkling, trustful glance. Somewhat untidy, but nevertheless the image of grace.

She saw him first. Otherwise he might have fled. But he was right upon her before he saw her. Indeed, he heard her before he saw her.

" Good afternoon, Mr Coe."

" Mimi! "

The Vaillacs were in Brighton! He had chosen practically the other end of the world for his honeymoon, and lo! by some awful clumsiness of fate the Vaillacs were at the same end! The very people from whom he wished to conceal his honeymoon until it was over would know all about it at the very start! Relations between the two Olives would be still more strained and difficult! In brief, from optimism he swung violently back to darkest pessimism. What could be worse than to be caught red-handed in a surreptitious honeymoon?

She noticed his confusion, and he knew that she noticed it. She was a little girl. But she was also a little woman, a little Frenchwoman, who spoke English perfectly—and yet with a difference! They had flirted together, she and Mr Coe. She had a new mother now, but for years she had been without a mother, and she

would receive callers at her father's house (if he happened
to be out) with a delicious imitation of a practised hostess.

He raised his hat and shook hands and tried to play
the game.

" What are you doing here, Mimi? " he asked.

" What are *you* doing here? " she parried, laughing.
And then, perceiving his increased trouble, and that
she was failing in tact, she went on rapidly, with a
screwing up of the childish shoulders and something
between a laugh and a grin: " It's my back. It seems
it's not strong. And so we've taken an ever so jolly
little house for the autumn, because of the air, you
know. Didn't you know? "

No, he did not know. That was the worst of strained
relations. You were not informed of events in advance.

" Where? " he asked.

" Oh! " she said, pointing. " That way. On the
road to Rottingdean. Near the big girls' school. We
came in on that lovely electric railway — along the
beach. Have you been on it, Mr Coe? "

Terrible! Rottingdean was precisely the scene of his
honeymoon. The hazard of fate was truly appalling.
He and his wife might have walked one day straight
into the arms of her sister! He went hot and cold.

" And where are the others? " he asked nervously.

" Mamma "—she coloured as she used this word, so
strange on her lips—" mamma's at home. Father may
come to-night. And Ada has brought us here so that
Jean can have his hair cut. He didn't want to come
without me."

" Ada? "

" Ada's a new servant. She's just gone in there
again to see how long the barber will be." Mimi indicated a barber's shop opposite. " And I'm waiting
here," she added.

" Mimi," he said, in a confidential tone, " can you
keep a secret? "

She grew solemn. "Yes." She smiled seriously.
"What?"

"About meeting me. Don't tell anybody you've
met me to-day. See?"

"Not Jean?"

"No, not Jean. But later on you can tell—when I
give you the tip. I don't want anybody to know just
now."

It was a shame. He knew it was a shame. He
deliberately flattered her by appealing to her as to a
grown woman. He deliberately put a cajoling tone into
his voice. He would not have done it if Mimi had not
been Mimi—if she had been an ordinary sort of English
girl. But she was Mimi. And the temptation was
very strong. She promised, gravely. He knew that
he could rely on her.

Hurrying away lest Jean and the servant might
emerge from the barber's, he remembered with com-
punction that he had omitted to show any curiosity
about Mimi's back.

III

THE magnificent woman was to be waiting for him in
the lounge of the Royal York Hotel at a quarter to
four. She was coming in to Brighton by the Rottingdean omnibus, which function, unless the driver changes
his mind, occurs once in every two or three hours. He,
being under the necessity of telephoning to London on
urgent business, had hired a bicycle and ridden in.
Despite the accident to this prehistoric machine, he
arrived at the Royal York half a minute before the
Rottingdean omnibus passed through the Old Steine
and set down the magnificent woman his wife. The
sight of her stepping off the omnibus really did thrill
him. They entered the hotel together, and, accustomed
though the Royal York is to the reception of magnificent

women, Olive made a sensation therein. As for him,
he could not help feeling just as though he had eloped
with her. He could not help fancying that all the
brilliant company in the lounge was murmuring under
the strains of the band: "That johnny there has
certainly eloped with that splendid creature!"

"Ed," she asked, fixing her dark eyes upon him,
"is anything the matter?"

They were having tea at a little Moorish table in the
huge bay window of the lounge.

"No," he said. This was the first lie of his career
as a husband. But truly he could not bring himself to
give her the awful shock of telling her that the Vaillacs
were close at hand, that their secret was discovered,
and that their peace and security depended entirely
upon the discretion of little Mimi and upon their not
meeting other Vaillacs.

"Then it's having that puncture that has upset
you," his wife insisted. You see her feelings towards
him were so passionate that she could not leave him
alone. She was utterly preoccupied by him.

"No," he said guiltily.

"I'm afraid you don't very much care for this
place," she went on, because she knew now that he
was not telling her the truth, and that something, indeed, was the matter.

"On the contrary," he replied, "I was informed
that the finest tea and the most perfect toast in
Brighton were to be had in this lounge, and upon my
soul I feel as if I could keep on having tea here for ever
and ever amen!'"

He was trying to be gay, but not very successfully.

"I don't mean just here," she said. "I mean all
this south coast."

"Well—" he began judicially.

"Oh! Ed!" she implored him. "*Do* say you
don't like it!"

"Why!" he exclaimed. "Don't *you*?"

She shook her head. "I much prefer the north," she remarked.

"Well," he said, "let's go. Say Scarborough."

"You're joking," she murmured. "You adore this south coast."

"Never!" he asserted positively.

"Well, darling," she said, "if you hadn't said first that you didn't care for it, of course I shouldn't have breathed a word——"

"Let's go to-morrow," he suggested.

"Yes." Her eyes shone.

"First train! We should have to leave Rottingdean at six o'clock a.m."

"How lovely!" she exclaimed. She was enchanted by this idea of a capricious change of programme. It gave such a sense of freedom, of irresponsibility, of romance!

"More toast, please," he said to the waiter, joyously.

It cost him no effort to be gay now. He could not have been sad. The world was suddenly transformed into the best of all possible worlds. He was saved! They were saved! Yes, he could trust Mimi. By no chance would they be caught. They would stick in their rooms all the evening, and on the morrow they would be away long before the Vaillacs were up. Papa and "mamma" Vaillac were terrible for late rising. And when he had got his magnificent Olive safe in Scarborough, or wherever their noses might lead them, then he would tell her of the risk they had run.

They both laughed from mere irrational glee, and Edward Coe nearly forgot to pay the bill. However, he did pay it. They departed from the Royal York. He put his Olive into the returning Rottingdean omnibus, and then hurried to get his repaired bicycle. He had momentarily quaked lest Mimi and company might be in the omnibus. But they were not. They must have left earlier, fortunately, or walked.

IV

WHEN he was still about a mile away from Rottingdean, and the hour was dusk, and he was walking up a hill, he caught sight of a girl leaning on a gate that led by a long path to a house near the cliffs. It was Mimi. She gave a cry of recognition. He did not care now —he was at ease now—but really, with that house so close to the road and so close to Rottingdean, he and his Olive had practically begun their honeymoon on the summit of a volcano!

Mimi was pensive. He felt remorse at having bound her to secrecy. She was so pensive, and so wistful, and her eyes were so loyal, that he felt he owed her a more complete confidence.

" I'm on my honeymoon, Mimi," he said. It gave him pleasure to tell her.

" Yes," she said simply, " I saw Auntie Olive go by in the omnibus."

That was all she said. He was thunderstruck, as much by her calm simplicity as by anything else. Children were astounding creatures.

" Did Jean see her, or anyone? " he asked.

Mimi shook her head.

Then he told her they were leaving the next morning at six.

" Shall you be in a carriage? " she inquired.

" Yes."

" Oh! Do let me come out and see you go past," she pleaded. " Nobody else in our house will be up till hours afterwards! . . . Do! "

He was about to say " No," for it would mean re-

vealing the whole affair to his wife at once. But after
an instant he said " Yes." He would not refuse that
exquisite, appealing gesture. Besides, why keep anything whatever from Olive, even for a day?

At dinner he told his wife, and was glad to learn
that she also thought highly of Mimi and had confidence in her.

V

MIMI lay in bed in the nursery of the hired house on
the way to Rottingdean, which, considering that it
was not "home," was a fairly comfortable sort of
abode. The nursery was immense, though an attic.
The white blinds of the two windows were drawn, and
a fire burned in the grate, lighting it pleasantly and
behaving in a very friendly manner. At the other
end of the room, in the deep shadow, was Jean's bed.

The door opened quietly and someone came into
the room and pushed the door to without quite
shutting it.

" Is that you, mamma? " Jean demanded in his
shrill voice, from the distance of the bed in the corner.
His age was exactly eight.

" Yes, dear," said the new stepmother.

The menial Ada had arranged the children for the
night, and now the stepmother had come up to kiss
them and be kind. She was a conscientious young
woman, full of a desire to do right, and she had determined not to be like the traditional stepmother.

She kissed Jean, who had taken quite a fancy to
her, and tickled him agreeably, and tucked him up
anew, and then moved silently across the room to
Mimi. Mimi could see her face in the twilight of the
fire. A handsome, good-natured face; yet very determined, and perhaps a little too full of common sense.
It had a responsible, somewhat grave look. After all,

these two young children were a responsibility, especially Mimi with her back; and, moreover, Pierre Emile Vaillac had disappointed both her and her step-children by telegraphing that he could not arrive that night. Olive One, the bride of three months, had put on fine raiment for nothing.

" Well, Mimi," she said in her low, vibrating voice, as she stood over the bed, " I do hope you didn't overtire yourself this afternoon." Then she kissed Mimi.

" Oh no, mamma! " The little girl smiled.

" It seems you waited outside the barber's while Jeannot was having his hair cut."

" Yes, mamma. I didn't like to go in."

" Ada didn't stay with you all the time? "

" No, mamma. First of all she took Jeannot in, and then she came out to me, and then she went in again to see how long he would be."

" I'm sorry she left you alone in the street. She ought not to have done so, and I've told her. . . . The King's Road, with all kinds of people about! "

Mimi said nothing. The new Madame Vaillac moved a little towards the fire.

" Of course," the latter went on, " I know you're a regular little woman, and perhaps I needn't tell you but you must never speak to anyone in the street."

" No, mamma."

" Particularly in Brighton. . . . You never do, do you? "

" No, mamma."

" Good-night."

The stepmother left the room. Mimi could feel her heart beating. Then Jean called out:

" Mimi."

She made no reply. The fact was she was too disturbed to be able to reply.

Jean called again and then got out of bed and thudded across the room to her bedside.

" I say, Mimi," he screeched in his insistent treble,
who *was* it you were talking to? "

Mimi's heart did not beat, it jumped.

" When? Where? "

" This afternoon, when I was having my hair cut."

" How do you know I was talking to anybody? "

" Ada saw you through the window of the barber's."

" When did she tell you? "

" She didn't. I heard her telling mamma."

There was a silence. Then Mimi hid her face, and
Jean could hear sobbing.

" You might tell me! " Jean insisted. He was too
absorbed by his own curiosity, and too upset by the full
realization of the fact that she had kept something from
him, to be touched by her tears.

" It's a secret," she muttered into the pillow.

" You might tell me! "

" Go away, Jeannot! " she burst out hysterically.

He gave an angry lunge against the bed.

" I tell you everything; and it's not fair. *C'est pas
juste !* " he said savagely, but there were tears in his
voice too. He was a creature at once sensitive and
violent, passionately attached to Mimi.

He thudded back to his bed. But even before he
had reached his bed Mimi could hear him weeping.

She gradually stilled her own sobs, and after a
time Jean's ceased. And then she guessed that Jean
had gone to sleep. But Mimi did not go to sleep. She
knew that chance, and Mr Coe, and that odious new
servant, Ada, had combined to ruin her life. She saw
the whole affair clearly. Ada was officious and fussy,
also secretive and given to plotting. Ada's leading idea
was that children had to be circumvented. Imagine
the detestable woman spying on her from the window,
and then saying nothing to her, but sneaking off to tell
tales to her mamma! Imagine it! Mimi's strict sense
of justice could not blame her mamma. She was sure

that the new stepmother meant well by her. Her mamma had given her every opportunity to confess, to admit of her own accord that she had been talking to somebody in the street, and she had not confessed. On the contrary, she had lied. Her mamma would probably say nothing more on the matter, for she had a considerable sense of honour with children, and would not take an unfair advantage. Having tried to obtain a confession from Mimi by pretending that she knew nothing, and having failed, she was not the woman to turn round and say, "Now I know all about it. So just confess at once!" Her mamma would accept the situation, would try to behave as if nothing had happened, and would probably even say nothing to her father.

But Mimi knew that she was ruined for ever in her stepmother's esteem.

And she had quarrelled with Jean, which was exceedingly hateful and exceedingly rare. And there was also the private worry of her mysterious back. And there was another thing. The mere fact that her friend, Mr Coe, had gone and married somebody. For long she had had a weakness for Mr Coe. They had been intimate at times. Once, last year, in the stern of a large sailing-boat at Morecambe, while her friends were laughing and shouting at the prow, she and Mr Coe had had a most beautiful quiet conversation about her thoughts on the world in general; she had stroked his hand. . . . No! She had no dream whatever of growing up into a woman and then marrying Mr Coe! Certainly not. But still, that he should have gone and married, like that . . . it was . . .

The fire died out into blackness, thus ceasing to be a friend. Still she did not sleep. Was it likely that she should sleep, with the tragedy and woe of the entire universe crushing her?

VI

Mr Edward Coe and Olive Two arose from their bed the next morning in great spirits. Mr Coe had told both his wife and Mimi that the hour of departure from Rottingdean would be six o'clock. But this was an exaggeration. So far as his wife was concerned he had already found it well to exaggerate on such matters. A little judicious exaggeration lessened the risk of missing trains and other phenomena which cannot be missed without confusion and disappointment.

As a fact it was already six o'clock when Edward Coe looked forth from the bedroom window. He was completely dressed. His wife also was completely dressed. He therefore felt quite safe about the train. The window, which was fairly high up in the world, gave on the south-east, so that he had a view, not only of the vast naked downs billowing away towards Newhaven, but also of the Channel, which was calm, and upon which little parcels of fog rested. The sky was clear overhead, of a greenish sapphire colour, and the autumnal air bit and gnawed on the skin like some friendly domestic animal, and invigorated like an expensive tonic. On the dying foliage of a tree near the window millions of precious stones hung. Cocks were boasting. Cows were expressing a justifiable anxiety. And in the distance a small steamer was making a great deal of smoke about nothing, as it puffed out of Newhaven harbour.

" Olive," he said.

" What is it? "

She was putting hats into the top of her trunk. She had a special hat-box, but the hats were too large for it, and she packed minor trifles in the hat-box, such as skirts. This was one of the details which first indicated to an astounded Edward Coe that a woman is never less like a man than when travelling.

" Come here," he commanded her.

She obeyed.

" Look at that," he commanded her, pointing to the scene of which the window was the frame.

She obeyed. She also looked at him with her dark, passionate, and yet half-mocking eyes.

" Yes," she said, " and who's going to make that trunk lock? "

She snapped her fingers at the sweet morning influences of Nature, to which he was peculiarly sensitive. And yet he was delighted. He found it entirely delicious that she should say, when called upon to admire Nature: " Who's going to make that trunk lock? "

He stroked her hair.

" It's no use trying to keep your hair decent at the seaside," she remarked, pouting exquisitely.

He explained that his hand was offering no criticism of her hair. And then there was a knock at the bedroom door, and Olive Two jumped a little away from her husband.

"Come in," he cried, pretending to be as bold as a lion.

However, he had forgotten that the door was locked, and he had to go and open it.

A tray with coffee and milk and sugar and slices of bread-and-butter was in the doorway, and behind the tray the little parlour-maid of the little hotel. He greeted the girl and instructed her to carry the tray to the table by the window.

" You are prompt," said Olive Two, kindly. She had got up so miraculously early herself that she was startled to see any other woman up quite as early. And also she was a little surprised that the parlour-maid showed no surprise at these very unusual hours.

" Yes'm," replied the parlour-maid, wondering why

Olive Two was so excited. The parlour-maid arose at five-thirty every morning of her life, except on special occasions, when she arose at four-thirty to assist in pastoral affairs.

"All right, this coffee, eh?" murmured Edward Coe as he put down the steaming cup after his first sip. They were alone again, seated opposite each other at the small table by the window.

Olive Two nodded.

It must not be supposed that this was the one unique dreamed-of hotel in England where the coffee is good of its own accord. No! In the matter of coffee this hotel was just like all other hotels. Only Olive Two had taken special precautions about that coffee. She had been into the hotel kitchen on the previous evening about that coffee.

" By the way," she asked, " where's the sun? "

" The sun doesn't happen to be up yet," said Edward. He looked at his diary and then at his watch. " Unless something goes wrong, you'll be seeing it inside of three minutes."

" Do you mean to say we shall see the sun rise? " she exclaimed.

He nodded.

" Well! " cried she, absurdly gleeful, " I never heard of such a thing! "

She watched the sunrise like a child who sees for the first time the inside of a watch. And when the sun had risen she glanced anxiously round the disordered room.

" For heaven's sake," she muttered, " don't let's forget these tooth-brushes! "

" You are so ridiculous," said he, " that I must kiss you."

The truth is that they were no better than two children out on an adventure.

It was the same when down in the hotel-yard they got into the small and decrepit victoria which was destined to take them and their luggage to Brighton. It was the same, but more so. They were both so pleased with themselves that their joy was bubbling continually out in manifestations that could only be described as infantile. The mere drive through the village, with the pony whisking his tail round corners, and the driver steadying the perilous hat-box with his left hand, was so funny that somehow they could not help laughing.

Then they had left the village and were climbing the exposed highroad, with the wavy blue-green downs on the right, and the immense glittering flat floor of the Channel on the left. And the mere sensation of being alive almost overwhelmed them.

And further on they passed a house that stood by itself away from the road towards the cliffs. It had a sloping garden and a small greenhouse. The gate leading to the road was ajar, but the blinds of all the windows were drawn, and there was no sign of life anywhere.

" That's the house," said Edward Coe, briefly.

" I might have known it," Olive Two replied. " Olive One is certainly the worst getter-up that I ever had anything to do with, and I believe Pierre Emile isn't much better."

" Well," said Edward, " it's no absolute proof of sluggardliness not to be up and about at six forty-five of a morning, you know."

" I was forgetting how early it was! " said Olive Two, and yawned. The yawn escaped her before she was aware of it. She pulled herself together and kissed her hands mockingly, quizzically, to the house. " Goodbye, house! Good-bye, house! "

They were saved now. They could not be caught now on their surreptitious honeymoon. And their spirits went even higher.

" I thought you said Mimi would be waiting for us? " Olive Two remarked.

Edward Coe shrugged his shoulders. " Probably

overslept herself! Or she may have got tired of waiting. I told her six o'clock."

On the whole Olive Two was relieved that Mimi
was invisible.

"It wouldn't really matter if she *did* split on us,
would it? " said the bride.

"Not a bit," the bridegroom agreed. Now that
they had safely left the house behind them, they were
both very valiant. It was as if they were both saying:
"Who cares?" The bridegroom's mood was entirely
different from his sombre apprehensiveness of the
previous evening. And the early sunshine on the dew-
drops was magnificent.

But a couple of hundred yards further on, at a
bend of the road, they saw a little girl shading her
eyes with her hand and gazing towards the sun. She
wore a short blue serge frock, and she had long restless
legs, and the word *Formidable* was on her forehead, and
her eyes were all screwed up in the strong sunshine.
And in her hand were flowers.

"There she is, after all! " said Edward, quickly.

Olive Two nodded. Olive Two also blushed, for
Mimi was the first person acquainted with her to see
her after her marriage. She blushed because she was
now a married woman.

Mimi, who with much prudence had managed so
that the meeting should not occur exactly in front of
the house, came towards the carriage. The pony was
walking up a slope. She bounded forward with her
childish grace and with the awkwardness of her long
legs, and her hair loose in the breeze, and she laughed
nervously.

"Good morning, good morning," she cried.
"Shall I jump on the step? Then the horse won't
have to stop."

And she jumped lightly on to the step and giggled,
still nervously, looking first at the bridegroom and then

at the bride.   The bridegroom held her securely by the shoulder.

"Well, Mimi," said Olive Two, whose shyness vanished in an instant before the shyness of the child. "This *is* nice of you."

The two women kissed.   But Mimi did not offer her cheek to the bridegroom.   He and she simply shook hands as well as they could with a due regard for Mimi's firmness on the step.

"And who woke you up, eh? " Edward Coe demanded.

"Nobody," said Mimi; " I got up by myself, and," turning to Olive Two, " I've made this bouquet for you, auntie.   There aren't any flowers in the fields.   But I got the chrysanthemum out of the greenhouse, and put some bits of ferns and things round it.   You must excuse it being tied up with darning wool."

She offered the bouquet diffidently, and Olive Two accepted it with a warm smile.

"Well," said Mimi, " I don't think I'd better go any further, had I? "

There was another kiss and hand-shaking, and the next moment Mimi was standing in the road and waving a little crumpled handkerchief to the receding victoria, and the bride and bridegroom were cricking their necks to respond.   She waved until the carriage was out of sight, and then she stood moveless, a blue and white spot on the green landscape, with the morning sun and the sea behind her.

"Exactly like a little woman, isn't she? " said Edward Coe, enchanted by the vision.

"Exactly! " Olive Two agreed.   " Nice little thing! But how tired and unwell she looks!   They did well to bring her away."

"Oh! " said Edward Coe, " she probably didn't sleep well because she was afraid of oversleeping herself.   She looked perfectly all right yesterday."

THE SUPREME ILLUSION

I

PERHAPS it was because I was in a state of excited annoyance that I did not recognize him until he came right across the large hall of the hotel and put his hand on my shoulder.

I had arrived in Paris that afternoon, and driven to that nice, reasonable little hotel which we all know, and whose name we all give in confidence to all our friends; and there was no room in that hotel. Nor in seven other haughtily-managed hotels that I visited! A kind of archduke, who guarded the last of the seven against possible customers, deigned to inform me that the season was at its fullest, half London being as usual in Paris, and that the only central hotels where I had a chance of reception were those monstrosities the Grand and the Hôtel Terminus at the Gare St Lazare. I chose the latter, and was accorded room 973 in the roof.

I thought my exasperations were over. But no! A magnificent porter within the gate had just consented to get my luggage off the cab, and was in the act of beginning to do so, when a savagely-dressed, ugly and ageing woman, followed by a maid, rushed neurotically down the steps and called him away to hold a parcel. He obeyed! At the same instant the barbaric and repulsive creature's automobile, about as large as a railway carriage, drove up and forced my frail cab down the street. I had to wait, humiliated and helpless, the taximeter of my cab industriously adding penny to

penny, while that offensive hag installed herself, with
the help of the maid, the porter and two page-boys,
in her enormous vehicle. I should not have minded
had she been young and pretty. If she had been young
and pretty she would have had the right to be rude and
domineering. But she was neither young nor pretty.
Conceivably she had once been young; pretty she could
never have been. And her eyes were hard—hard.

Hence my state of excited annoyance.

" Hullo! How goes it? " The perfect colloquial
English was gently murmured at me with a French
accent as the gentle hand patted my shoulder.

" Why," I said, cast violently out of a disagreeable
excitement into an agreeable one, " I do believe you
are Boissy Minor! "

I had not seen him for nearly twenty years, but I
recognized in that soft and melancholy Jewish face,
with the soft moustache and the soft beard, the wistful
features of the boy of fifteen who had been my companion at an " international " school (a clever invention
for inflicting exile upon patriots) with branches at
Hastings, Dresden and Versailles.

Soon I was telling him, not without satisfaction,
that, being a dramatic critic, and attached to a London
daily paper which had decided to flatter its readers by
giving special criticisms of the more important new
French plays, I had come to Paris for the production
of *Notre Dame de la Lune* at the Vaudeville.

And as I told him the idea occurred to me for
positively the first time:

" By the way, I suppose you aren't any relation of
Octave Boissy? "

I rather hoped he was; for after all, say what you
like, there is a certain pleasure in feeling that you have
been to school with even a relative of so tremendous
a European celebrity as Octave Boissy—the man who
made a million and a half francs with his second play,

which was nevertheless quite a good play. All the
walls of Paris were shouting his name.

"I'm the johnny himself," he replied with timi-
dity, naïvely proud of his Saxon slang.

I did not give an astounded *No !* An astounded
No ! would have been rude. Still, my fear is that I
failed to conceal entirely my amazement. I had to
fight desperately against the natural human tendency
to assume that no boy with whom one has been to
school can have developed into a great man.

"Really!" I remarked, as calmly as I could, and
added a shocking lie: "Well, I'm not surprised!"
And at the same time I could hear myself saying a
few days later at the office of my paper: "I met
Octave Boissy in Paris. Went to school with him,
you know."

"You'd forgotten my Christian name, probably,"
he said.

"No, I hadn't," I answered. "Your Christian name
was Minor. You never had any other!" He smiled
kindly. "But what on earth are you doing here?"

Octave Boissy was a very wealthy man. He even
looked a very wealthy man. He was one of the darlings
of success and of an absurdly luxurious civilization.
And he seemed singularly out of place in the vast,
banal foyer of the Hôtel Terminus, among the shifting,
bustling crowd of utterly ordinary, bourgeois, moder-
ately well-off tourists and travellers and needy touts.
He ought at least to have been in a very select private
room at the Meurice or the Bristol, if in any hotel at all!

"The fact is, I'm neurasthenic," he said simply,
just as if he had been saying, "The fact is, I've got a
wooden leg."

"Oh!" I laughed, determined to treat him as
Boissy Minor, and not as Octave Boissy.

"I have a morbid horror of walking in the open
air. And yet I cannot bear being in a small enclosed

space, especially when it's moving.   This is extremely
inconvenient. *Mais que veux-tu? . . . Suis comme
ça !* "

  " *Je te plains,*" I put in, so as to return his familiar
and flattering " thou " immediately.

  " I was strongly advised to go and stay in the
country," he went on, with the same serious, wistful
simplicity, " and so I ordered a special saloon carriage
on the railway, so as to have as much breathing room
as possible; and I ventured from my house to this
station in an auto.   I thought I could surely manage
that.   But I couldn't!   I had a terrible crisis on
arriving at the station, and I had to sit on a luggage-
truck for four hours.   I couldn't have persuaded myself to get into the saloon carriage for a fortune!   I
couldn't go back home in the auto!   I couldn't walk!
So I stepped into the hotel.   I've been here ever since."

  " But when was this? "

  " Three months ago.   My doctors say that in
another six weeks I shall be sufficiently recovered
to leave.   It is a most distressing malady.   *Mais que
veux-tu ?*   I have a suite in the hotel and my own
servants.   I walk out here into the hall because it's so
large.   The hotel people do the best they can, but of
course—"   He threw up his hands.   His resigned,
gentle smile was at once comic and tragic to me.

  " But do you mean to say you couldn't walk out
of that door and go home? " I questioned.

  " Daren't! " he said, with finality.   " Come to my
rooms, will you, and have some tea."

II

A LITTLE later his own valet served us with tea in
a large private drawing-room on the sixth or seventh
floor, to reach which we had climbed a thousand and

5

one stairs; it was impossible for Octave Boissy to use
the lift, as he was convinced that he would die in it if
he took such a liberty with himself. The room was
hung with modern pictures, such as had certainly never
been seen in any hotel before. Many knick-knacks and
embroideries were also obviously foreign to the hotel.

" But how have you managed to attend the rehearsals of the new play? " I demanded.

" Oh! " said he, languidly, " I never attend any
rehearsals of my plays. Mademoiselle Lemonnier sees
to all that."

" She takes the leading part in this play, doesn't
she, according to the posters? "

" She takes the leading part in all my plays,"
said he.

" A first-class artiste, no doubt? I've never seen
her act."

" Neither have I! " said Octave Boissy. And as
I now yielded frankly to my astonishment, he added:
" You see, I am not interested in the theatre. Not
only have I never attended a rehearsal, but I have
never seen a performance of any of my plays. Don't you
remember that it was engineering, above all else, that
attracted me? I have a truly wonderful engineering
shop in the basement of my house in the Avenue du
Bois. I should very much have liked you to see it;
but you comprehend, don't you, that I'm just as much
cut off from the Avenue du Bois as I am from Timbuctoo.
My malady is the most exasperating of all maladies."

" Well, Boissy Minor," I observed, " I suppose it has
occurred to you that your case is calculated to excite
wonder in the simple breast of a brutal Englishman."

He laughed, and I was glad that I had had the
courage to reduce him definitely to the rank of Boissy
Minor.

" And not only in the breast of an Englishman! "
he said. " *Mais que veux-tu?* One must live."

" But I should have thought you could have made a comfortable living out of engineering. In England consulting engineers are princes."

" Oh yes! "

" And engineering might have cured your neuras-thenia, if you had taken it in sufficiently large quantities."

" It would," he agreed quietly.

" Then why the theatre, seeing that the theatre doesn't interest you? "

" In order to live," he replied. " And when I say ' live,' I mean *live*. It is not a question of money, it is a question of *living*."

" But as you never go near the theatre—"

" I write solely for Blanche Lemonnier," he said. I was at a loss. Perceiving this, he continued inti-mately: " Surely you know of my admiration for Blanche Lemonnier? "

I shook my head.

" I have never even heard of Blanche Lemonnier, save in connection with your plays," I said.

" She is only known in connection with my plays," he answered. " When I met her, a dozen years ago, she was touring the provinces, playing small parts in third-rate companies. I asked her what was her greatest ambition, and she said that it was to be applauded as a star on the Paris stage. I told her that I would satisfy her ambition, and that when I had done so I hoped she would satisfy mine. That was how I began to write plays. That was my sole reason. It is the sole reason why I keep on writing them. If she had desired to be a figure in Society I should have gone into politics."

" I am getting very anxious to see this lady," I said. " I feel as if I can scarcely wait till to-night."

" She will probably be here in a few minutes," said he.

" But how did you do it? " I asked. " What was your plan of campaign? "

" After the success of my first play I wrote the second specially for her, and I imposed her on the management. I made her a condition. The management kicked, but I was in a position to insist. I insisted."

" It sounds simple." I laughed uneasily.

" If you are a dramatic critic," he said, " you will guess that it was not at first quite so simple as it sounds. Of course it is simple enough now. Blanche Lemonnier is now completely identified with my plays. She is as well known as nearly any actress in Paris. She has the glory she desired." He smiled curiously. " Her ambition is satisfied—so is mine." He stopped.

" Well," I said, " I've never been so interested in any play before. And I shall expect Mademoiselle Lemonnier to be magnificent."

" Don't expect too much," he returned calmly. " Blanche's acting is not admired by everybody. And I cannot answer for her powers, as I've never seen her at work."

" It's that that's so extraordinary! "

"Not a bit! I could not bear to see her on the stage. I hate the idea of her acting in public. But it is her wish. And after all, it is not the actress that concerns me. It is the woman. It is the woman alone who makes my life worth living. So long as she exists and is kind to me my neurasthenia is a matter of indifference, and I do not even trouble about engineering."

He tried to laugh away the seriousness of his tone, but he did not quite succeed. Hitherto I had been amused at his singular plight and his fatalistic acceptance of it. But now I was touched.

" I'm talking very freely to you," he said.

" My dear fellow," I burst out, " do let me see her portrait."

He shook his head.

" Unfortunately her portrait is all over Paris. She likes it so. But I prefer to have no portrait myself. My feeling is—"

At that moment the valet opened the door and we heard vivacious voices in the corridor.

" She is here," said Octave Boissy, in a whisper suddenly dramatic. He stood up; I also. His expression had profoundly changed. He controlled his gestures and his attitude, but he could not control his eye. And when I saw that glance I understood what he meant by "living." I understood that, for him, neither fame nor artistic achievement nor wealth had any value in his life. His life consisted in one thing only.

" *Eh bien, Blanche !* " he murmured amorously.

Blanche Lemonnier invaded the room with arrogance. She was the odious creature whose departure in her automobile had so upset my arrival.

THE LETTER AND THE LIE

I

A S he hurried from his brougham through the sombre hall to his study, leaving his secretary far in the rear, he had already composed the first sentence of his address to the United Chambers of Commerce of the Five Towns; his mind was full of it; he sat down at once to his vast desk, impatient to begin dictating. Then it was that he perceived the letter, lodged prominently against the gold and onyx inkstand given to him on his marriage by the Prince and Princess of Wales. The envelope was imperfectly fastened, or not fastened at all, and the flap came apart as he fingered it nervously.

"Dear Cloud,—This is to say good-bye, finally—"

He stopped. Fear took him at the heart, as though he had been suddenly told by a physician that he must submit to an operation endangering his life. And he skipped feverishly over the four pages to the signature, "Yours sincerely, Gertrude."

The secretary entered.

"I must write one or two private letters first," he said to the secretary. "Leave me. I'll ring."

"Yes, sir. Shall I take your overcoat?"

"No, no."

A discreet closing of the door.

"—finally. I can't stand it any longer. Cloud, I'm gone to Italy. I shall use the villa at Florence, and trust you to leave me alone. You must tell our friends. You can start with the Bargraves to-night. I'm sure they'll agree with me it's for the best—"

It seemed to him that this letter was very like the sort of letter that gets read in the Divorce Court and printed in the papers afterwards; and he felt sick.

"—for the best. Everybody will know in a day or two, and then in another day or two the affair will be forgotten. It's difficult to write naturally under the circumstances, so all I'll say is that we aren't suited to each other, Cloud. Ten years of marriage has amply proved that, though I knew it six—seven—years ago. You haven't guessed that you've been killing me all these years; but it is so—"

Killing her! He flushed with anger, with indignation, with innocence, with guilt—with Heaven knew what!

"—it is so. *You've* been living *your* life. But what about me? In five more years I shall be old, and I haven't begun to live. I can't *stand* it any longer. I can't stand this awful Five Towns district—"

Had he not urged her many a time to run up to South Audley Street for a change, and leave him to continue his work? Nobody wanted her to be always in Staffordshire!

"—and I can't stand *you*. That's the brutal truth. You've got on my nerves, my poor boy, with your hurry, and your philanthropy, and your commerce, and your seriousness. My poor nerves! And you've been too busy to notice it. You fancied I should be content if you made love to me absent-mindedly, *en passant*, between a political dinner and a bishop's breakfast."

He flinched. She had stung him.

" I sting you—"

No! And he straightened himself, biting his lips!

"—I sting you! I'm rude! I'm inexcusable! People don't say these things, not even hysterical wives to impeccable husbands, eh? I admit it. But I was bound to tell you. You're a serious person, Cloud, and

I'm not. Still, we were both born as we are, and I've
just as much right to be unserious as you have to be
serious. That's what you've never realized. You
aren't better than me; you're only different from me.
It is unfortunate that there are some aspects of the
truth that you are incapable of grasping. However,
after this morning's scene—"

Scene? What scene? He remembered no scene,
except that he had asked her not to interrupt him while
he was reading his letters, had asked her quite politely,
and she had left the breakfast-table. He thought she
had left because she had finished. He hadn't a notion
—what nonsense!

"—this morning's scene, I decided not to 'interrupt'
you any more—"

Yes. There was the word he had used—how
childish she was!

"—any more in the contemplation of those aspects
of the truth which you *are* capable of grasping. Good-
bye! You're an honest man, and a straight man, and
very conscientious, and very clever, and I expect you're
doing a lot of good in the world. But your responsi-
bilities are too much for you. I relieve you of one,
quite a minor one—your wife. You don't want a wife.
What you want is a doll that you can wind up once a
fortnight to say 'Good-morning, dear,' and 'Good-
night, dear.' I think I can manage without a husband
for a very long time. I'm not so bitter as you might
guess from this letter, Cloud. But I want you
thoroughly to comprehend that it's finished between us.
You can do what you like. People can say what they
like. I've had enough. I'll pay any price for freedom.
Good luck. Best wishes. I would write this letter
afresh if I thought I could do a better one.—Yours
sincerely, Gertrude."

He dropped the letter, picked it up and read it again
and then folded it in his accustomed tidy manner and

replaced it in the envelope. He sat down and propped
the letter against the inkstand and stared at the address in her careless hand: " The Right Honourable
Sir Cloud Malpas, Baronet." She had written the
address in full like that as a last stroke of sarcasm.
And she had not even put " Private."

He was dizzy, nearly stunned; his head rang.

Then he rose and went to the window. The high hill
on which stood Malpas Manor—the famous Rat Edge—
fell away gradually to the south, and in the distance
below him, miles off, the black smoke of the Five Towns
loomed above the yellow fires of blast-furnaces. He
was the demi-god of the district, a greater landowner
than even the Earl of Chell, a model landlord, a model
employer of four thousand men, a model proprietor of
seven pits and two iron foundries, a philanthropist, a
religionist, the ornamental mayor of Knype, chairman
of a Board of Guardians, governor of hospitals, president of Football Association—in short, Sir Cloud, son
of Sir Cloud and grandson of Sir Cloud.

He stared dreamily at his dominion. Scandal,
then, was to touch him with her smirching finger, him
the spotless! Gertrude had fled. He had ruined
Gertrude's life! Had he? With his heavy and severe
conscientiousness he asked himself whether he was to
blame in her regard. Yes, he thought he was to blame.
It stood to reason that he was to blame. Women,
especially such as Gertrude, proud, passionate, reserved,
don't do these things for nothing.

With a sigh he passed into his dressing-room and
dropped on to a sofa.

She would be inflexible—he knew her. His mind
dwelt on the beautiful first days of their marriage, the
tenderness and the dream! And now—!

He heard footsteps in the study; the door was
opened! It was Gertrude! He could see her in the dusk.
She had returned! Why? She tripped to the desk,

leaned forward and snatched at the letter. Evidently
she did not know that he was in the house and had
read it.

The tension was too painful. A sigh broke from
him, as it were of physical torture.

" Who's there? " she cried, in a startled voice. " Is
that you, Cloud? "

" Yes," he breathed.

" But you're home very early! " Her voice shook.

" I'm not well, Gertrude," he replied. " I'm tired.
I came in here to lie down. Can't you do something for
my head? I must have a holiday."

He heard her crunch up the letter, and then she
hastened to him in the dressing-room.

" My poor Cloud! " she said, bending over him in
the mature elegance of her thirty years. He noticed
her travelling costume. " Some eau de Cologne? "

He nodded weakly.

" We'll go away for a holiday," he said, later, as she
bathed his forehead.

The touch of her hands on his temples reminded
him of forgotten caresses. And he did really feel as
though, within a quarter of an hour, he had been
through a long and dreadful illness and was now convalescent.

II

" THEN you think that after starting she thought
better of it? " said Lord Bargrave after dinner that
night. " And came back? "

Lord Bargrave was Gertrude's cousin, and he and
his wife sometimes came over from Shropshire for a
week-end. He sat with Sir Cloud in the smoking-
room; a man with greying hair and a youngish, equable
face.

" Yes, Harry, that was it. You see, I'd just

happened to put the letter exactly where I found it.
She's no notion that I've seen it."

" She's a thundering good actress! " observed Lord
Bargrave, sipping some whisky. " I knew something
was up at dinner, but I didn't know it from *her* : I
knew it from you."

Sir Cloud smiled sadly.

" Well, you see, I'm supposed to be ill—at least, to
be not well."

" You'd best take her away at once," said Lord
Bargrave. " And don't do it clumsily. Say you'll go
away for a few days, and then gradually lengthen it out.
She mentioned Italy, you say. Well, let it be Italy.
Clear out for six months."

" But my work here? "

" D—n your work here! " said Lord Bargrave.
" Do you suppose you're indispensable here? Do you
suppose the Five Towns can't manage without you?
Our caste is decayed, my boy, and silly fools like you
try to lengthen out the miserable last days of its importance by giving yourselves airs in industrial dis-
tricts! Your conscience tells you that what the dema-
gogues say is true—we *are* rotters on the face of the
earth, we *are* mediæval; and you try to drown your conscience in the noise of philanthropic speeches. There
isn't a sensible working-man in the Five Towns who
doesn't, at the bottom of his heart, assess you at your
true value—as nothing but a man with a hobby, and
plenty of time and money to ride it."

" I do not agree with you," Sir Cloud said
stiffly.

" Yes, you do," said Lord Bargrave. " At the same
time I admire you, Cloud. I'm not built the same way
myself, but I admire you—except in the matter of
Gertrude. There you've been wrong—of course from
the highest motives: which makes it all the worse. A
man oughtn't to put hobbies above the wife of his

bosom. And, besides, she's one of *us*. So take her away and stay away and make love to her."

"Suppose I do? Suppose I try? I must tell her!"

"Tell her what?"

"That I read the letter. I acted a lie to her this afternoon. I can't let that lie stand between us. It would not be right."

Lord Bargrave sprang up.

"Cloud," he cried. "For heaven's sake, don't be an infernal ass. Here you've escaped a domestic catastrophe of the first magnitude by a miracle. You've made a sort of peace with Gertrude. She's come to her senses. And now you want to mess up the whole show by the act of an idiot! What if you did act a lie to her this afternoon? A very good thing! The most sensible thing you've done for years! Let the lie stand between you. Look at it carefully every morning when you awake. It will help you to avoid repeating in the future the high-minded errors of the past. See?"

III

AND in Lady Bargrave's dressing-room that night Gertrude was confiding in Lady Bargrave.

"Yes," she said, "Cloud must have come in within five minutes of my leaving—two hours earlier than he was expected. Fortunately he went straight to his dressing-room. Or was it unfortunately? I was half-way to the station when it occurred to me that I hadn't fastened the envelope! You see, I was naturally in an awfully nervous state, Minnie. So I told Collins to turn back. Fuge, our new butler, is of an extremely curious disposition, and I couldn't bear the idea of him prying about and perhaps reading that letter before Cloud got it. And just as I was picking up the letter to fasten it I heard Cloud in the next room. Oh! I never felt so queer in all my life! The poor boy was quite unwell. I screwed up the letter and went to him. What else could I do? And really he was so tired and white—well, it moved me! It moved me. And when he spoke about going away I suddenly thought: ' Why not try to make a new start with him?' After all . . ."

There was a pause.

" What did you say in the letter? " Lady Bargrave demanded. " How did you put it? "

" I'll read it to you," said Gertrude, and she took the letter from her corsage and began to read it. She got as far as " I can't stand this awful Five Towns district," and then she stopped.

" Well, go on," Lady Bargrave encouraged her.

" No," said Gertrude, and she put the letter in the fire. " The fact is," she said, going to Lady Bargrave's chair, " it was too cruel. I hadn't realized. . . . I must have been very worked-up. . . . One does work oneself up. . . . Things seem a little different now. . . ." She glanced at her companion.

" Why, Gertrude, you're crying, dearest! "

" What a chance it was! " murmured Gertrude, in her tears. " What a chance! Because, you know, if he *had* once read it I would never have gone back on it. I'm that sort of woman. But as it is, there's a sort of hope of a sort of happiness, isn't there? "

" Gertrude! " It was Sir Cloud's voice, gentle and tender, outside the door.

" Mercy on us! " exclaimed Lady Bargrave. " It's half-past one. Bargrave will have been asleep long since."

Gertrude kissed her in silence, opened the door, and left her.

THE GLIMPSE *

I

WHEN I was dying I had no fear. I was simply indifferent, partly, no doubt, through exhaustion caused by my long illness. It was a warm evening in August. We ought to have been at Blackpool, of course, but we were in my house in Trafalgar Road, and the tramcars between Hanley and Bursley were shaking the house just as usual. Perhaps not quite as usual; for during my illness I had noticed that a sort of tiredness, a soft, nice feeling, seems to come over everything at sunset of a hot summer's day. This universal change affected even the tramcars, so that they rolled up and down the hill more gently. Or it may have been merely my imagination. Through the open windows I could see, dimly, the smoke of the Cauldon Bar Iron Works slowly crossing the sky in front of the sunset. Margaret sat in my grandfather's oak chair by the gas-stove. There was only Margaret, besides the servant, in the house; the nurse had been obliged to go back to Pirehill Infirmary for the night. I don't know why. Moreover, it didn't matter.

I began running my extraordinarily white fingers

* Some years ago the editor of *Black and White* commissioned me to write a story for his Christmas Number. I wrote this story. He expressed a deep personal admiration for it, but said positively that he would not dare to offer it to his readers. I withdrew the story, and gave him instead a frolic tale about a dentist. (See page 136.) Afterwards, I was glad that I had withdrawn the story, for I perceived that its theme could only be treated adequately in a novel. I accordingly wrote the novel, which was duly published under the same title.—A. B.

along the edge of the sheet. I was doing this quite mechanically when I noticed a look of alarm in Margaret's face, and I vaguely remembered that playing with the edge of the sheet was supposed to be a trick of the dying. So I stopped, more for Margaret's sake than for anything else. I could not move my head much, in fact scarcely at all; hence it was difficult for me to keep my eyes on objects that were not in my line of vision as I lay straight on my pillows. Thus my eyes soon left Margaret's. I forgot her. I thought about nothing. Then she came over to the bed, and looked at me, and I smiled at her, very feebly. She smiled in return. She appeared to me to be exceedingly strong and healthy. Six weeks before I had been the strong and healthy one—I was in my prime, forty, and had a tremendous appetite for business—and I had always regarded her as fragile and delicate; and now she could have crushed me without effort! I had an unreasonable, instinctive feeling of shame at being so weak compared to her. I knew that I was leaving her badly off; we were both good spenders, and all my spare profits had gone into the manufactory; but I did not trouble about that. I was almost quite callous about that. I thought to myself, in a confused way: " Anyhow, I shan't be here to see it, and she'll worry through somehow! " Nor did I object to dying. It may be imagined that I resented death at so early an age, and being cut off in my career, and prevented from getting the full benefit of the new china-firing oven that I had patented. Not at all! It may be imagined that I was preoccupied with a future life, and thinking that possibly we had given up going to chapel without sufficient reason. No! I just lay there, submitting like a person without will or desires to the nursing of my wife, which was all of it accurately timed by the clock.

I just lay there and watched the gradual changing of the sky, and, faintly, heard clocks striking and the quiet swish of my wife's dress. Once my ear would have caught the ticking of our black marble clock on the mantelpiece; but not now—it was lost to me. I watched the gradual changing of the sky, until the blue of the sky had darkened so that the blackness of the smoke was merged in it. But to the left there appeared a faint reddish glare, which showed where the furnaces were; this glare had been invisible in daylight. I watched all that, and I waited patiently for the last trace of silver to vanish from a high part of the sky above where the sunset had been—and it would not. I would shut my eyes for an age, and then open them again, and the silver was always in the sky. The cars kept rumbling up the hill and bumping down the hill. And there was still that soft, languid feeling over everything. And all the heat of the day remained. Sometimes a waft of hot air moved the white curtains. Margaret ate something off a plate. The servant stole in. Margaret gave a gesture as though to indicate that I was asleep. But I was not asleep. The servant went off. Twice I restrained my thin, moist hands from playing with the edge of the sheet. Then I closed my eyes with a kind of definite closing, as if finally admitting that I was too exhausted to keep them open.

II

DIFFICULT to describe my next conscious sensations, when I found I was not in the bed! I have never described them before. You will understand why I've never described them to my wife. I meant never to describe them to anyone. But as you came all the way from London, Mr Myers, and seem to understand all this sort of thing, I've made up my mind to tell you for what it's worth. Yes, what you say about the difficulty of sticking to the exact truth is quite correct.

I feel it. Still, I don't think I over-flatter myself in saying that I am a more than ordinarily truthful man.

Well, I was looking at the bed. I was not in the bed. I can't be precisely sure where I was standing, but I think it was between the two windows, half behind the crimson curtains. Anyhow, I must have been near the windows, or I couldn't have seen the foot of the bed and the couch that is there. I could most distinctly hear Cauldon Church clock, more than two miles away, strike two. I was cold. Margaret was leaning over the bed, and staring at a face that lay on the pillows. At first it did not occur to me that this face on the pillows was my face. I had to reason out that fact. When I had reasoned it out I tried to speak to Margaret and tell her that she was making a mistake, gazing at that thing there on the pillows, and that the real one was standing in the cold by the windows. I could not speak. Then I tried to attract her attention in other ways; but I could do nothing. Once she turned sharply, as if startled, and looked straight at me. I strove more frantically than ever to make signs to her; but no, I could not. Seemingly she did not see.

Then I thought: "I'm dead! This is being dead! I've died!"

Margaret ran to the dressing-table and picked up her hand-mirror. She rubbed it carefully on the counterpane, and then held it to the mouth and nostrils of that face on the pillows, and then examined it under the gas. She was very agitated; the whole of her demeanour had changed; I scarcely recognized her. I could not help thinking that she was mad. She put down the mirror, glanced at the clock, even glanced out of the window (she was much closer to me than I am now to you), and then flew back to the bed. She seized the scissors that were hanging from her girdle, and cut a hole in the top pillow, and drew from it a flock of down, which she carefully placed on the lips of that face. The down did not even tremble. Then she bared the breast of the body on the bed, and laid her ear upon the region of the heart; I could see her eyes blinking as she listened intensely. After she had listened some time she raised her head, with a little sob, and frantically pulled the bell-rope. I could hear the bell; we could both hear it. There was no response; nothing but a fearful silence. Margaret, catching her breath, rushed out of the room. I was sick with the most awful disgust that I could not force her to see where I was. I had been helpless before, when I lay in the bed, but I was far more completely helpless now. Talk about the babe unborn!

She came back with the servant, and the two women stood on either side of the bed, gazing at that body. The servant whispered:

" They do say that if you put a full glass of water on the chest you can tell for sure."

Margaret hesitated. However, the servant began to fill a glass of water on the washstand, and they poised it on the chest of that body. Not the slightest vibration troubled its surface. I was—not angry; no, tremendously disgusted is the only term I can use—at all this flummery with that body on the bed. It was shocking to me that they should confuse that body with me. I thought them silly, wilfully silly. I thought their behaviour monstrously blind. There was I, the master of the house, standing chilled between the windows, and neither Margaret nor the servant would take the least notice of me!

The servant said:

" I'd better run for the doctor, ma'am." And she lifted off the glass.

"What use can the doctor be? " Margaret asked. " Only spoil the poor man's night for nothing. And he's had a lot of bad nights lately. He told me to be— prepared."

The servant said:

" Yes, mum. But I'd better run for him. That's what doctors is for."

As soon as the front-door banged on the excited servant, my wife fell on that body with a loud cry, and stroked it passionately, and I could see her tears dropping on it. She wept without any restraint. She loved me very much; I knew that. But the fact that she loved me only increased my horror that she should be caressing that body, which was not me at all, which had nothing whatever to do with me, which was loathsome, vile, and as insensible as a log to the expressions of her love. She was not weeping over me. She was weeping over an abomination. She was all wrong, all tragically wrong, and I could not set her right. Her woe desolated me. We had been happy together for sixteen years. Her error desolated me, as a painful farce. But a slow, horrible change in my own consciousness made me forget her grief in my own increasing misery.

III

I DO not suppose that the feeling which came over me is capable of being described in human language. It can only be hinted at, not truly conveyed. If I say that I was utterly overcome by the sensation of being *cut off from everything*, I shall perhaps not impress you very much with a notion of my terror. But I do not see how I can better express myself. No one who has not been through what I have been through—it is a pretty awful thought that all who die do probably go through it—can possibly understand the feeling of acute and frightful loneliness that possessed me as I stood near the windows, that wrapped me up and enveloped me, as it were, in an icy sheet. A few people in England are possibly in my case—they have *been*, and they have returned, like me. They will understand, and only they. I was solitary in the universe. I was invisible, and I was forgotten. There was my poor wife lavishing her immense sorrow on that body on the bed, which had ceased to have any connection with me, which was emphatically not me, and to which I felt the strongest repugnance. I was even jealous of that lifeless, unresponsive, decaying mass. You cannot guess how I tried to yell to my wife to come to me and warm me with her companionship and her sympathy— and I could accomplish nothing, not the faintest whisper.

I had no home, no shelter, no place in the world, no share in life. I was cast out. The changeless purposes of nature had ejected me from humanity. It was as though humanity had been a fortified city and the gates had been shut on me, and I was wandering round and round the unscalable smooth walls, and beating against their stone with my hands. That is a good simile, except that I could not move. Of course if I could have moved I should have gone to my wife. But I could not move. To be quite exact, I could move very slightly, perhaps about an inch or two inches, and in any direction, up or down, to left or right, backwards or forwards; this by a great straining, fatiguing effort. I was stuck there on the surface of the world, desolate and undone. It was the most cruel situation that you can imagine; far worse, I think, than any conceivable physical torture. I am perfectly sure that I would have exchanged my state, then, for the state of no matter what human being, the most agonized martyr, the foulest criminal. I would have given anything, made any sacrifice, to be once more within the human pale, to feel once more that human life was not going on without me.

There was a knocking below. My wife left that

body on the bed, and came to the window and put her head out into the nocturnal, gaslit silence of Trafalgar Road. She was within a foot of me—and I could do nothing.

She whispered : " Is that you, Mary ? "

The voice of the servant came : " Yes, mum. The doctor's been called away to a case. He's not likely to be back before five o'clock."

My wife said, with sad indifference : " It doesn't matter now. I'll let you in."

She went from the room. I heard the opening and shutting of the door. Then both women returned into the room, and talked in low voices.

My wife said : " As soon as it's light you must . . ." She stopped and corrected herself. " No, the nurse will be back at seven o'clock. She said she would. She will attend to all that. Mary, go and get a little rest, if you can."

" Aren't you going to put the pennies on his eyes, mum ? " the servant asked.

" Ought I ? " said my wife. " I don't know much about these things."

" Oh yes, mum. And tie his jaw up," the servant said.

His eyes ! *His* jaw ! I was terribly angry in my desolation. But it was a futile anger, though it raged through me like a storm. Could they not understand, would they never understand, that they were gro-tesquely deceived ? How much longer would they continue to fuss over that body on the bed while I, *I*, the person whom they were supposed to be sorry for, suffered and trembled in dire need just behind them ?

A ridiculous bother over pennies. There was only one penny in the house, they decided, after searching. I knew the exact whereabouts of two shillings' worth of copper, rolled in paper in my desk in the dining-room. It had been there for many weeks ; I had

brought it home one day from the works. But they
did not know. I wanted to tell them, so as to end the
awful exacerbation of my nerves. But of course I
could not. In spite of Mary's superstitious protest, my
wife put a penny on one eye and half-a-crown on the
other. Mary seemed to regard this as a desecration,
or at best as unlucky. Then they bound up the jaw
of that body with one of my handkerchiefs. I thought
I had never seen anything more wantonly absurd.
Their trouble in straightening the arms—the legs were
quite straight—infuriated me. I wanted to weep in
my tragic vexation. It seemed as though tears would
ease me. But I could not weep.

The servant said: " You'd better come away now,
mum, and rest on the sofa in the drawing-room."

Margaret, with red-bordered, glittering eyes,
answered, staring all the while at that body: " No,
Mary. It's no use. I can't leave him. I won't leave
him! "

But she wasn't thinking about me at all. There I
was, neglected and shivering, near the windows; and
she would not look at me!

After an interminable palaver Margaret induced the
servant to leave the room. And she sat down on the
chair nearest the bed, and began to cry again, not
troubling to wipe her eyes. She sobbed, more and
more loudly, and kept touching that body. She seized
my gold watch, which hung over the bed, and which
she wound up every night, and kissed it and put it
back. Her sobs continued to increase. Then the door
opened quietly, and the servant, half-undressed, crept
in, and without saying a word gently led Margaret out
of the room. Margaret's last glance was at that body.
In a moment the servant returned and extinguished the
gas, and departed again, very carefully closing the
door. I was now utterly abandoned.

IV

ALL that had happened to me up to now was strange; but what followed was still more strange and still less capable of being described in human language.

I became aware that I was gradually losing the sensation of being cut off from intercourse, at any-rate that the sensation was losing its painfulness. I didn't seem to care, now, whether I was neglected or not. And to be cast out from humanity grew into a matter of indifference to me. I became aware, too, of the approach of a mysterious freedom. I was not free, I could still move only an inch or so in any direction; but I felt that a process of dissolving of bonds had begun. What manner of bonds? I don't know. I felt—that was all. My indifference slowly passed into a sad and deep pity for the world. The world seemed to me so pathetic, so awry, so obstinate in its honest illusions, so silly in its dishonest pretences. " Have I been content with *that* ? " I thought, staggered. And I was sorry for what I had been. I perceived that the ideals of my life were tawdry, that even the best were poor little things. And I perceived that it was the same with everyone, and that even the greatest men, those men that I had so profoundly admired as of another clay than mine, were as like the worst as one sheep was like another sheep. Weep—because nature had ejected me from that petty little world, with its ridiculous and conceited wrongness? What an idea! Why, I said to myself, that world spends nearly the whole of its time in moving physical things from one place to another. Change the position of matter—that is all it does, all it thinks of. I remembered a states-man who had referred to the London and North-Western Railway as being one of the glories of Eng-land! Parcels! Parcels! Parcels, human, brute,

insensate! Nothing but parcel-moving! I smiled.
And then I perceived that I could understand and solve
problems which had defied thousands of years of human
philosophy, problems which we on earth called fundamental. And lo! They were not in the least fundamental, but were trifles, as simple as Euclid. It was
surprising that the solution of them had not presented
itself to me before! I thought: With one word, one
single word, I could enlighten the human race beyond
all that it has ever learned. Feeble-bodied, feeble-
minded humanity!

And then I had a glimpse. . . . I was in the bedroom, near the windows, all the time, but nevertheless
I was nowhere, nowhere in space. I could feel the roll
of the earth as it turned lumberingly on its axis—a faint
shaking which did not affect me. Still, I was in the
bedroom, near the windows. And I had a glimpse. . . .
The heralds of a new vitality swept trumpeting through
me, and a calm, intense, ineffable joy followed in their
train. I had a glimpse. . . . And my eyes were not
dazzled. I yearned and strained towards what I saw,
towards the exceeding brightness of undreamt com-
panionships, hopes, perceptions, activities, and sorrows.
Yes, sorrows! But what noble sorrows they were
that I felt awaited me there! I strained at my mysterious bonds. It seemed that they were about to
break and that I should be winged away into other
dimensions. . . .

And then, I knew that they were tightening again,
and the brightness very slowly faded, and I lost faith
in the gift of vision which momentarily had enabled me
to see the illusions and the littleness of the world. And
I was slowly, slowly drawn away from the window. . . .
And then I felt heavy weights on my eyes, and I could
not move my jaw. I shuddered convulsively, and a
coin struck the floor and ran till it fell flat. And the
door swiftly opened. . . .

V

YES, my whole character is changed, within; though externally it may seem the same. Externally I may seem to have resumed the affections and the interests which occupied me before my illness and my remarkable recovery. Yet I am different. Certainly I have lost again the strange transcendental knowledge which was mine for a few instants. Certainly I have descended again to the earthly level. All those magic things have slipped away, except hope. In a sure hope, in a positive faith, I am waiting. I am waiting for all that magic to happen to me again. I know that the pain of loneliness, when again I shall see my own body from the outside, will be exquisite, but—the reward! The reward! That is what is always at the back of my mind, the source of the calm joy in which I wait. Externally I am the successful earthenware manufacturer, happily married, getting rich on a china-firing oven, employing a couple of hundred workmen, etcetera, who was once given up for dead. But I am more than that. I have seen God.

JOCK-AT-A-VENTURE

I

A LL this happened at a Martinmas Fair in Bursley, long ago in the fifties, when everybody throughout the Five Towns pronounced Bursley " Bosley " as a matter of course; in the tedious and tragic old times, before it had been discovered that hell was a myth, and before the invention of pleasure or even of half-holidays. Martinmas was in those days a very important moment in the annual life of the town, for it was at Martinmas that potters' wages were fixed for twelve months ahead, and potters hired themselves out for that term at the best rate they could get. Even to the present day the housewives reckon chronology by Martinmas. They say, " It'll be seven years come Martinmas that Sal's babby died o' convulsions." Or, " It was that year as it rained and hailed all Martinmas." And many of them have no idea why it is Martinmas, and not Midsummer or Whitsun, that is always on the tips of their tongues.

The Fair was one of the two great drunken sprees of the year, the other being the Wakes. And it was meet that it should be so, for intoxication was a powerful aid to the signing of contracts. A sot would put his name to anything, gloriously; and when he had signed he had signed. Thus the beaver-hatted employers smiled at Martinmas drunkenness, and smacked it familiarly on the back; and little boys swilled themselves into the gutter with their elders, and felt intensely proud of the feat. These heroic old times have gone by, never to return.

It was on the Friday before Martinmas, at dusk. In the centre of the town, on the waste ground to the

north of the "Shambles" (as the stone-built meat
market was called), and in the space between the
Shambles and the as yet unfinished new Town Hall, the
showmen and the showgirls and the showboys were
titivating their booths, and cooking their teas, and
watering their horses, and polishing the brass rails of
their vans, and brushing their fancy costumes, and
hammering fresh tent-pegs into the hard ground, and
lighting the first flares of the evening, and yarning, and
quarrelling, and washing—all under the sombre purple
sky, for the diversion of a small crowd of loafers, big
and little, who stood obstinately with their hands in
their pockets or in their sleeves, missing naught of the
promising spectacle.

Now, in the midst of what in less than twenty-four
hours would be the Fair, was to be seen a strange and
piquant sight—namely, a group of three white-tied,
broad-brimmed dissenting ministers in earnest converse with fat Mr Snaggs, the proprietor of Snaggs's—
Snaggs's being the town theatre, a wooden erection,
generally called by patrons the "Blood Tub," on
account of its sanguinary programmes. On this occasion Mr Snaggs and the dissenting ministers were for
once in a way agreed. They all objected to a certain
feature of the Fair. It was not the roundabouts, so
crude that even an infant of to-day would despise them.
It was not the shooting-galleries, nor the cocoanut shies.
It was not the arrangements of the beersellers, which
were formidably Bacchic. It was not the boxing-
booths, where adventurous youths could have teeth
knocked out and eyes smashed in free of charge. It
was not the monstrosity-booths, where misshapen and
maimed creatures of both sexes were displayed all alive
and nearly nude to anybody with a penny to spare.
What Mr Snaggs and the ministers of religion objected
to was the theatre-booths, in which the mirror, more or
less cracked and tarnished, was held up to nature.

Mr Snaggs's objection was professional. He considered that he alone was authorized to purvey drama to the town; he considered that among all purveyors of drama he alone was respectable, the rest being upstarts, poachers, and lewd fellows. And as the dissenting ministers gazed at Mr Snaggs's superb moleskin waistcoat, and listened to his positive brazen voice, they were almost convinced that the hated institution of the theatre could be made respectable and that Mr Snaggs had so made it. At any rate, by comparison with these flashy and flimsy booths, the Blood Tub, rooted in the antiquity of thirty years, had a dignified, even a reputable air—and did not Mr Snaggs give frequent performances of Cruickshanks' *The Bottle*, a sermon against intemperance more impressive than any sermon delivered from a pulpit in a chapel? The dissenting ministers listened with deference as Mr Snaggs explained to them exactly what they ought to have done, and what they had failed to do, in order to ensure the success of their campaign against play-acting in the Fair; a campaign which now for several years past had been abortive—largely (it was rumoured) owing to the secret jealousy of the Church of England.

" If ony on ye had had any gumption," Mr Snaggs was saying fearlessly to the parsons, " ye'd ha' gone straight to th' Chief Bailiff and ye'd ha'—Houch! " He made the peculiar exclamatory noise roughly indicated by the last word, and spat in disgust; and without the slightest ceremony of adieu walked ponderously away up the slope, leaving his sentence unfinished.

" It is remarkable how Mr Snaggs flees from before my face," said a neat, alert, pleasant voice from behind the three parsons. " And yet save that in my unregenerate day I once knocked him off a stool in front of his own theayter, I never did him harm nor wished him anything but good. . . . Gentlemen! "

A rather small, slight man of about forty, with tiny

feet and hands, and " very quick on his pins," saluted
the three parsons gravely.

" Mr Smith! " one parson stiffly inclined.

" Mr Smith! " from the second.

" Brother Smith! " from the third, who was Jock
Smith's own parson, being in charge of the Bethesda in
Trafalgar Road where Jock Smith worshipped and where
he had recently begun to preach as a local preacher.

Jock Smith, herbalist, shook hands with vivacity
but also with self-consciousness. He was self-conscious
because he knew himself to be one of the chief characters
and attractions of the town, because he was well aware
that wherever he went people stared at him and pointed
him out to each other. And he was half proud and half
ashamed of his notoriety.

Even now a little band of ragged children had
wandered after him, and, undeterred by the presence
of the parsons, were repeating among themselves, in a
low audacious monotone:

" Jock-at-a-Venture! Jock-at-a-Venture! "

II

HE was the youngest of fourteen children, and when
he was a month old his mother took him to church to
be christened. The rector was the celebrated Rappey,
sportsman, who (it is said) once pawned the church
Bible in order to get up a bear-baiting. Rappey asked
the name of the child, and was told by the mother that
she had come to the end of her knowledge of names,
and would be obliged for a suggestion. Whereupon
Rappey began to cite all the most ludicrous names in
the Bible, such as Aholibamah, Kenaz, Iram, Baal-
hanan, Abiasaph, Amram, Mushi, Libni, Nepheg,
Abihu. And the mother laughed, shaking her head.
And Rappey went on: Shimi, Carmi, Jochebed. And

at Jochebed the mother became hysterical with laughter. " Jock-at-a-Venture," she had sniggered, and Rappey, mischievously taking her at her word, christened the infant Jock-at-a-Venture before she could protest; and the infant was stamped for ever as peculiar.

He lived up to his name. He ran away twice, and after having been both a sailor and a soldier, he returned home with the accomplishment of flourishing a razor, and settled in Bursley as a barber. Immediately he became the most notorious barber in the Five Towns, on account of his gab and his fisticuffs. It was he who shaved the left side of the face of an insulting lieutenant of dragoons (after the great riots of '45, which two thousand military had not quelled), and then pitched him out of the shop, soapsuds and all, and fought him to a finish in the Cock Yard and flung him through the archway into the market-place with just half a magnificent beard and moustache. It was he who introduced hair-dyeing into Bursley. Hair-dyeing might have grown popular in the town if one night, owing to some confusion with red ink, the Chairman of the Bursley Burial Board had not emerged from Jock-at-a-Venture's with a vermilion top-knot and been greeted on the pavement by his waiting wife with the bitter words: " Thou foo! "

A little later Jock-at-a-Venture abandoned barbering and took up music, for which he had always shown a mighty gift. He was really musical and performed on both the piano and the cornet, not merely with his hands and mouth, but with the whole of his agile expressive body. He made a good living out of public-houses and tea-meetings, for none could play the piano like Jock, were it hymns or were it jigs. His cornet was employed in a band at Moorthorne, the mining village to the east of Bursley, and on his nocturnal journeys to and from Moorthorne with the beloved instrument he had had many a set-to with the maraud-

ing colliers who made the road dangerous for cowards.
One result of this connection with Moorthorne was that
a boxing club had been formed in Bursley, with Jock
as chief, for the upholding of Bursley's honour against
visiting Moorthorne colliers in Bursley's market-place.

Then came Jock's conversion to religion, a blazing
affair, and his abandonment of public-houses. As tea-
meetings alone would not keep him, he had started
again in life, for the fifth or sixth time—as a herbalist
now. It was a vocation which suited his delicate
hands and his enthusiasm for humanity. At last, and
quite lately, he had risen to be a local preacher. His
first two sermons had impassioned the congregations,
though there were critics to accuse him of theatricality.
Accidents happened to him sometimes. On this very
afternoon of the Friday before Martinmas an accident
had happened to him. He had been playing the piano
at the rehearsal of the Grand Annual Evening Concert
of the Bursley Male Glee-Singers. The Bursley Male
Glee-Singers, determined to beat records, had got a
soprano with a foreign name down from Manchester.
On seeing the shabby perky little man who was to
accompany her songs the soprano had had a moment
of terrible misgiving. But as soon as Jock, with a
careful-careless glance at the music, which he had never
seen before, had played the first chords (with a " How's
that for time, missis? "), she was reassured. At the end
of the song her enthusiasm for the musical gifts of the
local artist was such that she had sprung from the platform and simply but cordially kissed him. She was a
stout, feverish lady. He liked a lady to be stout; and
the kiss was pleasant and the compliment enormous.
But what a calamity for a local preacher with a naughty
past to be kissed in full rehearsal by a soprano from
Manchester! He knew that he had to live that kiss
down, and to live down also the charge of theatricality.

Here was a reason, and a very good one, why he

deliberately sought the company of parsons in the middle of the Fair-ground. He had to protect himself against tongues.

III

" I DON'T know," said Jock-at-a-Venture to the parsons, gesturing with his hands and twisting his small, elegant feet, " I don't know as I'm in favour of stopping these play-acting folk from making a living; stopping 'em by force, that is."

He knew that he had said something shocking, something that when he joined the group he had not in the least meant to say. He knew that instead of protecting himself he was exposing himself to danger. But he did not care. When, as now, he was carried away by an idea, he cared for naught. And, moreover, he had the consciousness of being cleverer, acuter, than any of these ministers of religion, than anybody in the town! His sheer skill and resourcefulness in life had always borne him safely through every difficulty—from a prize-fight to a soprano's embrace.

" A strange doctrine, Brother Smith! " said Jock's own pastor.

The other two hummed and hawed, and brought the tips of their fingers together.

" Nay! " said Jock, persuasively smiling. " 'Stead o' bringing 'em to starvation, bring 'em to the House o' God! Preach the gospel to 'em, and then when ye've preached the gospel to 'em, happen they'll change their ways o' their own accord. Or happen they'll put their play-acting to the service o' God. If there's plays agen drink, why shouldna' there be plays agen the devil, and *for* Jesus Christ, our Blessed Redeemer? "

" Good day to you, brethren," said one of the parsons, and departed. Thus only could he express his horror of Jock's sentiments.

In those days churches and chapels were not so empty that parsons had to go forth beating up congregations. A pew was a privilege. And those who did not frequent the means of grace had at any rate the grace to be ashamed of not doing so. And, further, strolling players, in spite of John Wesley's exhortations, were not considered salvable. The notion of trying to rescue them from merited perdition was too fantastic to be seriously entertained by serious Christians. Finally, the suggested connection between Jesus Christ and a stage-play was really too appalling! None but Jock-at-a-Venture would have been capable of such an idea.

" I think, my friend—" began the second remaining minister.

" Look at that good woman there! " cried Jock-at-a-Venture, interrupting him with a dramatic outstretching of the right arm, as he pointed to a very stout but comely dame, who, seated on a three-legged stool, was calmly peeling potatoes in front of one of the more resplendent booths. " Look at that face! Is there no virtue in it? Is there no hope for salvation in it? "

" None," Jock's pastor replied mournfully. " That woman—her name is Clowes—is notorious. She has eight children, and she has brought them all up to her trade. I have made inquiries. The elder daughters are actresses and married to play-actors, and even the youngest child is taught to strut on the boards. Her troupe is the largest in the Midlands."

Jock-at-a-Venture was certainly dashed by this information.

" The more reason," said he, obstinately, " for saving her! . . . And all hers! "

The two ministers did not want her to be saved. They liked to think of the theatre as being beyond the pale. They remembered the time, before they were

ordained, and after, when they had hotly desired to see
the inside of a theatre and to rub shoulders w:th wickedness.   And they took pleasure in the knowledge that
the theatre was always there, and the wickedness thereof, and the lost souls therein.   But Jock-at-a-Venture
genuinely longed, in that ecstasy of his, for the total
abolition of all forms of sin.

"And what would you do to save her, brother? "
Jock's pastor inquired coldly.

"What would I do?   I'd go and axe her to come to
chapel Sunday, her and hers.   I'd axe her kindly, and
I'd crack a joke with her.   And I'd get round her for
the Lord's sake."

Both ministers sighed.   The same thought was in
their hearts, namely, that brands plucked from the
burning (such as Jock) had a disagreeable tendency to
carry piety, as they had carried sin, to the most ridiculous and inconvenient lengths.

IV

" THOSE are bonny potatoes, missis! "

" Ay! "   The stout woman, the upper part of whose
shabby dress seemed to be subjected to considerable
strains, looked at Jock carelessly, and then, attracted
perhaps by his eager face, smiled with a certain facile
amiability.

" But by th' time they're cooked your supper'll be
late, I'm reckoning."

" Them potatoes have naught to do with our supper,"
said Mrs Clowes.   " They're for to-morrow's dinner.
There'll be no time for peeling potatoes to-morrow.
Kezia! "   She shrilled the name.

A slim little girl showed herself between the heavy
curtains of the main tent of Mrs Clowes's caravanserai.

" Bring Sapphira, too! "

" Those yours? " asked Jock.

" They're mine," said Mrs Clowes. " And I've six more, not counting grandchildren and sons-in-law like."

" No wonder you want a pailful of potatoes! " said Jock.

Kezia and Sapphira appeared in the gloom. They might have counted sixteen years together. They were dirty, tousled, graceful and lovely.

" Twins," Jock suggested.

Mrs Clowes nodded. " Off with this pail, now! And mind you don't spill the water. Here, Kezia! Take the knife. And bring me the other pail."

The children bore away the heavy pail, staggering, eagerly obedient. Mrs Clowes lifted her mighty form from the stool, shook peelings from the secret places of her endless apron, and calmly sat down again.

" Ye rule 'em with a rod of iron, missis," said Jock.

She smiled good-humouredly and shrugged her vast shoulders—no mean physical feat.

" I keep 'em lively," she said. " There's twelve of 'em in my lot, without th' two babbies. Someone's got to be after 'em all the time."

" And you not thirty-five, I swear! "

" Nay! Ye're wrong."

Sapphira brought the other pail, swinging it. She put it down with a clatter of the falling handle and scurried off.

" Am I now? " Jock murmured, interested; and, as it were out of sheer absent-mindedness, he turned the pail wrong side up, and seated himself on it with a calm that equalled the calm of Mrs Clowes.

It was now nearly dark. The flares of the showmen were answering each other across the Fair-ground; and presently a young man came and hung one out above the railed platform of Mrs Clowes's booth; and Mrs Clowes blinked. From behind the booth floated the sounds of the confused chatter of men, girls and youngsters,

together with the complaint of an infant. A few yards
away from Mrs Clowes was a truss of hay; a pony sidled
from somewhere with false innocence up to this truss,
nosed it cautiously, and then began to bite wisps from
it. Occasionally a loud but mysterious cry swept
across the ground. The sky was full of mystery.
Against the sky to the west stood black and clear the
silhouette of the new Town Hall spire, a wondrous erection; and sticking out from it at one side was the form
of a gigantic angel. It was the gold angel which, from
the summit of the spire, has now watched over Bursley
for half a century, but which on that particular Friday
had been lifted only two-thirds of the way to its final
home.

Jock-at-a-Venture felt deeply all the influences of
the scene and of the woman. He was one of your
romantic creatures; and for him the woman was magnificent. Her magnificence thrilled.

"And what are you going to say?" she quizzed him.
"Sitting on my pail!"

Now to quiz Jock was to challenge him.

"Sitting on your pail, missis," he replied, "I'm
going for to say that you're much too handsome a
woman to go down to hell in eternal damnation."

She was taken aback, but her profession had taught
her the art of quick recovery.

"You belong to that Methody lot," she mildly
sneered. "I thought I seed you talking to them white-
chokers."

"I do," said Jock.

"And I make no doubt you think yourself very
clever."

"Well," he vouchsafed, "I can splice a rope, shave
a head, cure a wart or a boil, and tell a fine woman with
any man in this town. Not to mention boxing, as I've
given up on account of my religion."

"I *was* handsome once," said Mrs Clowes, with

apparent, but not real, inconsequence. " But I'm all
run to fat, like. I've played Portia in my time. But
now it's as much as I can do to get through with Maria
Martin or Belladonna."

" Fat! " Jock protested. " Fat! I wouldn't have
an ounce taken off ye for fifty guineas."

He was so enthusiastic that Mrs Clowes blushed.

" What's this about hell-fire? " she questioned.
" I often think of it— I'm a lonely woman, and I often
think of it."

" You lonely! " Jock protested again. " With all
them childer? "

" Ay! "

There was a silence.

" See thee here, missis! " he exploded, jumping up
from the pail. " Ye must come to th' Bethesda down
yon, on Sunday morning, and hear the word o' God.
It'll be the making on ye."

Mrs Clowes shook her head.

" Nay! "

" And bring yer children," he persisted.

" If it was you as was going to preach like! " she
said, looking away.

" It is me as is going to preach," he answered loudly
and proudly. " And I'll preach agen any man in this
town for a dollar! "

Jock was forgetting himself: an accident which
often happened to him.

V

THE Bethesda was crowded on Sunday morning; partly
because it was Martinmas Sunday, and partly because
the preacher was Jock-at-a-Venture. That Jock
should have been appointed on the " plan " [rota of
preachers] to discourse in the principal local chapel

of the Connexion at such an important feast showed
what extraordinary progress he had already made in
the appreciation of that small public of experts which
aided the parson in drawing up the quarterly plan.
At the hands of the larger public his reception was sure.
Some sixteen hundred of the larger public had crammed
themselves into the chapel, and there was not an empty
place either on the ground floor or in the galleries.
Even the " orchestra " (as the " singing-seat " was then
called) had visitors in addition to the choir and the
double-bass players. And not a window was open.
At that date it had not occurred to people that fresh air
was not a menace to existence. The whole congregation was sweltering, and rather enjoying it; for in some
strangely subtle manner perspiration seemed to be a
help to religious emotion. Scores of women were
fanning themselves; and among these was a very stout
peony-faced woman of about forty in a gorgeous yellow
dress and a red-and-black bonnet, with a large boy and
a small girl under one arm, and a large boy and a small
girl under the other arm. The splendour of the group
appeared somewhat at odds with the penury of the
" Free Seats," whither it had been conducted by a
steward.

In the pulpit, dominating all, was Jock-at-a-Venture,
who sweated like the rest. He presented a rather noble
aspect in his broadcloth, so different from his careless,
shabby week-day attire. His eye was lighted; his
arm raised in a compelling gesture. Pausing effectively,
he lifted a glass with his left hand and sipped. It was
the signal that he had arrived at his peroration. His
perorations were famous. And this morning everybody felt, and he himself knew, that all previous perorations were to be surpassed. His subject was the wrath
to come, and the transient quality of human life on
earth. " Yea," he announced, in gradually-increasing
thunder, " all shall go. And loike the baseless fabric o'

a vision, the cloud-capped towers, the gorgeous palaces, the solemn temples, the great globe itself— Yea, I say, all which it inherit shall dissolve, and, like this insubstantial payjent faded, leave not a rack behind."

His voice had fallen for the last words. After a dramatic silence, he finished, in a whisper almost, and with eyebrows raised and staring gaze directed straight at the vast woman in yellow: " We are such stuff as drames are made on; and our little life is rounded with a sleep. May God have mercy on us. Hymn 442."

The effect was terrific. Men sighed and women wept, in relief that the strain was past. Jock was an orator; he wielded the orator's dominion. Well he knew, and well they all knew, that not a professional preacher in the Five Towns could play on a congregation as he did. For when Jock was roused you could nigh see the waves of emotion sweeping across the upturned faces of his hearers like waves across a wheatfield on a windy day.

And this morning he had been roused.

VI

But in the vestry after the service he met enemies, in the shape and flesh of the chapel-steward and the circuit-steward, Mr Brett and Mr Hanks respectively. Both these important officials were local preachers, but, unfortunately, their godliness did not protect them against the ravages of jealousy. Neither of them could stir a congregation, nor even fill a country chapel.

" Brother Smith," said Jabez Hanks, shutting the door of the vestry. He was a tall man with a long, greyish beard and no moustache. " Brother Smith, it is borne in upon me and my brother here to ask ye a question."

" Ask! " said Jock.

"Were them yer own words—about cloud-capped towers and baseless fabrics and the like? I ask ye civilly."

"And I answer ye civilly, they were," replied Jock.

"Because I have here," said Jabez Hanks, maliciously, "Dod's *Beauties o' Shakspere*, where I find them very same words, taken from a stage-play called *The Tempest*."

Jock went a little pale as Jabez Hanks opened the book.

"They may be Shakspere's words too," said Jock, lightly.

"A fortnight ago, at Moorthorne Chapel, I suspected it," said Jabez.

"Suspected what?"

"Suspected ye o' quoting Shakspere in our pulpits."

"And cannot a man quote in a sermon? Why, Jabez Hanks, I've heard ye quote Matthew Henry by the fathom."

"Ye've never heard me quote a stage-play in a pulpit, Brother Smith," said Jabez Hanks, majestically. "And as long as I'm chapel-steward it wunna' be tolerated in this chapel."

"Wunna it?" Jock put in defiantly.

"It's a defiling of the Lord's temple; that's what it is!" Jabez Hanks continued. "Ye make out as ye're against stage-plays at the Fair, and yet ye come here and mouth 'em in a Christian pulpit. *You* agen stage-plays! Weren't ye seen talking by the hour to one o' them trulls, Friday night—? And weren't ye seen peeping through th' canvas last night? And now—"

"Now what?" Jock inquired, approaching Jabez on his springy toes, and looking up at Jabez's great height.

Jabez took breath. "Now ye bring yer fancy women into the House o' God! You—a servant o' Christ, you—"

Jock-at-a-Venture interrupted the sentence with his
daring fist, which seemed to lift Jabez from the ground
by his chin, and then to let him fall in a heap, as though
his clothes had been a sack containing loose bones.

" A good-day to ye, Brother Brett," said Jock,
reaching for his hat, and departing with a slam of the
vestry door.

He emerged at the back of the chapel and got by
" back-entries " into Aboukir Street, up which he
strolled with a fine show of tranquillity, as far as the
corner of Trafalgar Road, where stood and stands the
great Dragon Hotel. The congregations of several
chapels were dispersing slowly round about this famous
corner, and Jock had to salute several of his own audi-
ence. Then suddenly he saw Mrs Clowes and her four
children enter the tap-room door of the Dragon.

He hesitated one second and followed the variegated
flotilla and its convoy.

The tap-room was fairly full of both sexes. But
among them Jock and Mrs Clowes and her children
were the only persons who had been to church or chapel.

" Here's preacher, mother! " Kezia whispered,
blushing, to Mrs Clowes.

" Eh," said Mrs Clowes, turning very amiably.
" It's never you, mester! It was that hot in that chapel
we're all on us dying of thirst. . . . Four gills and a
pint, please! " (This to the tapster.)

" And give me a pint," said Jock, desperately.

They all sat down familiarly. That a mother should
take her children into a public-house and give them
beer, and on a Sunday of all days, and immediately
after a sermon! That a local preacher should go direct
from the vestry to the gin-palace and there drink ale
with a strolling player! These phenomena were simply
and totally inconceivable! And yet Jock was in presence of them, assisting at them, positively acting in
them! And in spite of her enormities, Mrs Clowes still

struck him as a most agreeable, decent, kindly, motherly woman—quite apart from her handsomeness. And her offspring, each hidden to the eyes behind a mug, were a very well-behaved lot of children.

"It does me good," said Mrs Clowes, quaffing. "And ye need summat to keep ye up in these days! We did *Belphegor* and *The Witch* and a harlequinade last night. And not one of these children got to bed before half after midnight. But I was determined to have 'em at chapel this morning. And not sorry I am I went! Eh, mester, what a Virginius you'd ha' made! I never heard preaching like it—not as I've heard much!"

"And you'll never hear anything like it again, missis," said Jock, "for I've preached my last sermon."

"Nay, nay!" Mrs Clowes deprecated.

"I've preached my last sermon," said Jock again. "And if I've saved a soul wi' it, missis . . . !" He looked at her steadily and then drank.

"I won't say as ye haven't," said Mrs Clowes, lowering her eyes.

VII

RATHER less than a week later, on a darkening night, a van left the town of Bursley by the Moorthorne Road on its way to Axe-in-the-Moors, which is the metropolis of the wild wastes that cut off northern Staffordshire from Derbyshire. This van was the last of Mrs Clowes's caravanserai, and almost the last to leave the Fair. Owing to popular interest in the events of Jock-at-a-Venture's public career, in whose meshes Mrs Clowes had somehow got caught, the booth of Mrs Clowes had succeeded beyond any other booth, and had kept open longer and burned more naphtha and taken far more money. The other vans of the stout lady's enterprise (there were three in all) had gone forward in advance, with all her elder children and her children-in-law and her grandchildren, and the heavy wood and canvas of the booth. Mrs Clowes, transacting her own business herself, from habit, invariably brought up the rear of her procession out of a town; and sometimes her leisurely manner of settling with the town authorities for water, ground-space and other necessary commodities, left her several miles behind her tribe.

The mistress's van, though it would not compare with the glorious vehicles that showmen put upon the road in these days, was a roomy and dignified specimen, and about as good as money could then buy. The front portion consisted of a parlour and kitchen combined, and at the back was a dormitory. In the dormitory Kezia, Sapphira and the youngest of their brothers were sleeping hard. In the parlour and kitchen sat Mrs Clowes, warmly enveloped, holding the reins with her right hand and a shabby, paper-covered book in her left hand. The book was the celebrated play, *The Gamester*, and Mrs Clowes was studying therein the rôle of Dulcibel. Not a rôle for which Mrs Clowes was physically fitted; but her prolific daughter, Hephzibah, to whom it appertained by prescription, could not possibly play it any longer, and would, indeed, be incapacitated from any rôle whatever for at least a month. And the season was not yet over; for folk were hardier in those days.

The reins stretched out from the careless hand of Mrs Clowes and vanished through a slit between the double doors, which had been fixed slightly open. Mrs Clowes's gaze, penetrating now and then the slit, could see the gleam of her lamp's ray on a horse's flank. The only sounds were the hoof-falls of the horse, the crunching of the wheels on the wet road, the occasional rattle of a vessel in the racks when the van happened to descend violently into a rut, and the steady murmur of

Mrs Clowes's voice rehearsing the grandiloquence of the part of Dulcibel.

And then there was another sound, which Mrs Clowes did not notice until it had been repeated several times; the cry of a human voice out on the road:

" Missis! "

She opened wide the doors of the van and looked prudently forth. Naturally, inevitably, Jock-at-a-Venture was trudging alongside, level with the horse's tail! He stepped nimbly—he was a fine walker—but none the less his breath came short and quick, for he had been making haste up a steepish hill in order to overtake the van. And he carried a bundle and a stick in his hands, and on his head a superb but heavy beaver hat.

" I'm going your way, missis," said Jock.

" Seemingly," agreed Mrs Clowes, with due caution.

" Canst gi' us a lift? " he asked.

" And welcome," she said, her face changing like a flash to suit the words.

" Nay, ye needna' stop! " shouted Jock.

In an instant he had leapt easily up into the van, and was seated by her side therein on the children's stool.

" That's a hat—to travel in! " observed Mrs Clowes.

Jock removed the hat, examined it lovingly and replaced it.

" I couldn't ha' left it behind," said he, with a sigh, and continued rapidly in another voice: " Missis, we'n seen a pretty good lot o' each other this wik, and yet ye slips off o'this'n, without saying good-bye, nor a word about yer soul! "

Mrs Clowes heaved her enormous breast and shook the reins.

" I've had my share of trouble," she remarked mysteriously.

" Tell me about it, missis! "

And lo! in a moment, lured on by his smile, she was

telling him quite familiarly about the ailments of her younger children, the escapades of her unmarried daughter aged fifteen, the surliness of one of her sons-in-law, the budding dishonesty of the other, the perils of infant life, and the need of repainting the big van and getting new pictures for the front of the booth. Indeed, all the worries of a queen of the road!

" And I'm so fat! " she said, " and yet I'm not forty, and shan't be for two year—and me a grand-mother! "

" I knowed it! " Jock exclaimed.

" If I wasn't such a heap o' flesh—"

" Ye're the grandest heap o' flesh as I ever set eyes on, and I'm telling ye! " Jock interrupted her.

VIII

THEN there were disconcerting sounds out in the world beyond the van. The horse stopped. The double doors were forced open from without, and a black figure, with white eyes in a black face, filled the doorway. The van had passed through the mining village of Moorthorne, and this was one of the marauding colliers on the outskirts thereof. When the colliers had highroad business in the night they did not trouble to wash their faces after work. The coal-dust was a positive aid to them, for it gave them a most useful resemblance to the devil.

Jock-at-a-Venture sprang up as though launched from a catapult.

" Is it thou, Jock? " cried the collier, astounded.

" Ay, lad! " said Jock, briefly.

And caught the collier a blow under the chin that sent him flying into the obscurity of the night. Other voices sounded in the road. Jock rushed to the doorway, taking a pistol from his pocket. And Mrs Clowes, all dithering like a jelly, heard shots. The horse started into a gallop. The reins escaped from the hands of the mistress, but Jock secured them, and lashed the horse to greater speed with the loose ends of them.

"I've saved thee, missis!" he said later. "I give him a regular lifter under the gob, same as I give Jabez, Sunday. But where's the sense of a lone woman wandering about dark roads of a night wi' a pack of childer? . . . Them childer 'ud ha' slept through th' battle o' Trafalgar," he added.

Mrs Clowes wept.

"Well may you say it!" she murmured. "And it's not the first time as I've been set on!"

"Thou'rt nowt but a girl, for all thy flesh and thy grandchilder!" said Jock. "Dry thy eyes, or I'll dry 'em for thee!"

She smiled in her weeping. It was an invitation to him to carry out his threat.

And while he was drying her eyes for her, she asked: "How far are ye going? Axe?"

"Ay! And beyond! Can I act, I ask ye? Can I fight, I ask ye? Can ye do without me, I ask ye, you a lone woman? And yer soul, as is mine to save?"

"But that business o' yours at Bursley?"

"Here's my bundle," he said, "and here's my best hat. And I've money and a pistol in my pocket. The only thing I've clean forgot is my cornet; but I'll send for it and I'll play it at my wedding. I'm Jock-at-a-Venture."

And while the van was rumbling in the dark night across the waste and savage moorland, and while the children were sleeping hard at the back of the van, and while the crockery was restlessly clinking in the racks and the lamp swaying, and while he held the reins, the thin, lithe, greying man contrived to take into his arms the vast and amiable creature whom he desired. And the van became a vehicle of high romance.

THE HEROISM OF
THOMAS CHADWICK

I

" HAVE you heard about Tommy Chadwick? "
one gossip asked another in Bursley.
" No."
" He's a tram-conductor now."
This information occasioned surprise, as it was
meant to do, the expression on the faces of both gossips
indicating a pleasant curiosity as to what Tommy Chadwick would be doing next.

Thomas Chadwick was a " character " in the Five
Towns, and of a somewhat unusual sort.   " Characters "
in the Five Towns are generally either very grim or
very jolly, either exceptionally shrewd or exceptionally
simple; and they nearly always, in their outward aspect, depart from the conventional.   Chadwick was not
thus.   Aged fifty or so, he was a portly and ceremonious
man with an official gait.   He had been a policeman in
his youth, and he never afterwards ceased to look like
a policeman in plain clothes.   The authoritative mien
of the policeman refused to quit his face.   Yet, beneath
that mien, few men (of his size) were less capable of
exerting authority than Chadwick.   He was, at
bottom, a weak fellow.   He knew it himself, and
everybody knew it.   He had left the police force because he considered that the strain was beyond his
strength.   He had the constitution of a she-ass, and
the calm, terrific appetite of an elephant; but he maintained that night duty in January was too much for

him. He was then twenty-seven, with a wife and two small girls. He abandoned the uniform with dignity. He did everything with dignity. He looked for a situation with dignity, saw his wife and children go hungry with dignity, and even went short himself with dignity. He continually got fatter, waxing on misfortune. And — another curious thing — he could always bring out, when advisable, a shining suit of dark blue broadcloth, a clean collar and a fancy necktie. He was not a consistent dandy, but he could be a dandy when he liked.

Of course, he had no trade. The manual skill of a policeman is useless outside the police force. One cannot sell it in other markets. People said that Chadwick was a fool to leave the police force. He was; but he was a sublime and dignified fool in his idle folly. What he wanted was a position of trust, a position where nothing would be required from him but a display of portliness, majesty and incorruptibility. Such positions are not easy to discover. Employers had no particular objection to portliness, majesty and incorruptibility, but as a rule they demanded something else into the bargain. Chadwick's first situation after his defection from the police was that of night watchman in an earthenware manufactory down by the canal at Shawport. He accepted it regretfully, and he firmly declined to see the irony of fate in forcing such a post on a man who conscientiously objected to night duty. He did not maintain this post long, and his reasons for giving it up were kept a dark secret. Some said that Chadwick's natural tendency to sleep at night had been taken amiss by his master.

Thenceforward he went through transformation after transformation, outvying the legendary chameleon. He was a tobacconist, a park-keeper, a rent collector, a commission agent, a clerk, another clerk, still another clerk, a sweetstuff seller, a fried fish merchant, a coal agent, a book agent, a pawnbroker's assistant, a dog-breeder, a door-keeper, a board-school keeper, a chapel-keeper, a turnstile man at football matches, a coachman, a carter, a warehouseman, and a chucker-out at the Empire Music Hall at Hanbridge. But he was nothing long. The explanations of his changes were invariably vague, unseizable. And his dignity remained unimpaired, together with his broadcloth. He not only had dignity for himself, but enough left over to decorate the calling which he happened for the moment to be practising. He was dignified in the sale of rock-balls, and especially so in encounters with his creditors; and his grandeur when out of a place was a model to all unemployed.

Further, he was ever a pillar and aid of the powers. He worshipped order, particularly the old order, and wealth and correctness. He was ever with the strong against the weak, unless the weak happened to be an ancient institution, in which case he would support it with all the valour of his convictions. Needless to say, he was a very active politician. Perhaps the activity of his politics had something to do with the frequency of his transformations—for he would always be his somewhat spectacular self; he would always call his soul his own, and he would quietly accept a snub from no man.

And now he was a tram-conductor. Things had come to that.

In the old days of the steam trams, where there were only about a score of tram-conductors and eight miles of line in all the Five Towns, the profession of tram-conductor had still some individuality in it, and a conductor was something more than a number. But since the British Electric Traction Company had invaded the Five Towns, and formed a subsidiary local company, and constructed dozens of miles of new line, and electrified everything, and raised prices, and abolished season tickets, and quickened services, and built hundreds of cars and engaged hundreds of conductors—since then a tram-conductor had been naught but an unhuman automaton in a vast machine-like organization. And passengers no longer had their favourite conductors.

Gossips did not precisely see Thomas Chadwick as an unhuman automaton for the punching of tickets and the ringing of bells and the ejaculation of street names. He was never meant by nature to be part of a system. Gossips hoped for the best. That Chadwick, at his age and with his girth, had been able, in his extremity, to obtain a conductorship was proof that he could bring influences to bear in high quarters. Moreover, he was made conductor of one of two cars that ran on a little branch line between Bursley and Moorthorne, so that to the village of Moorthorne he was still somebody, and the chances were just one to two that persons who travelled by car from or to Moorthorne did so under the majestic wing of Thomas Chadwick. His manner of starting a car was unique and stupendous. He might have been signalling " full speed ahead " from the bridge of an Atlantic liner.

II

CHADWICK's hours aboard his Atlantic liner were so long as to interfere seriously, not only with his leisure, but with his political activities. And this irked him the more for the reason that at that period local politics in the Five Towns were extremely agitated and interesting. People became politicians who had never been politicians before. The question was, whether the Five Towns, being already one town in practice, should not become one town in theory—indeed, the twelfth largest town in the United Kingdom! And the district was divided into Federationists and anti-Federationists. Chadwick was a convinced anti-Federationist. Chadwick, with many others, pointed to the history of Bursley, " the mother of the Five Towns," a history which spread over a thousand years and more; and he asked whether " old Bursley " was to lose her identity merely because Hanbridge had insolently outgrown her. A poll was soon to be taken on the subject, and feelings were growing hotter every day, and rosettes of different colours flowered thicker and thicker in the streets, until nothing but a strong sense of politeness prevented members of the opposing parties from breaking each other's noses in St Luke's Square.

Now on a certain Tuesday afternoon in spring Tommy Chadwick's car stood waiting, opposite the Conservative Club, to depart to Moorthorne. And Tommy Chadwick stood in all his portliness on the platform. The driver, a mere nobody, was of course at the front of the car. The driver held the power, but he could not use it until Tommy Chadwick gave him permission; and somehow Tommy's imperial attitude seemed to indicate this important fact.

There was not a soul in the car.

Then Mrs Clayton Vernon came hurrying up the slope of Duck Bank and signalled to Chadwick to wait for her. He gave her a wave of the arm, kindly and yet deferential, as if to say, " Be at ease, noble dame! You are in the hands of a man of the world, who knows what is due to your position. This car shall stay here till you reach it, even if Thomas Chadwick loses his situation for failing to keep time."

And Mrs Clayton Vernon puffed into the car. And Thomas Chadwick gave her a helping hand, and raised his official cap to her with a dignified sweep; and his glance seemed to be saying to the world, " There, you see what happens when *I* deign to conduct a car! Even Mrs Clayton Vernon travels by car then." And the whole social level of the electric tramway system was apparently uplifted, and conductors became fine, portly court-chamberlains.

For Mrs Clayton Vernon really was a personage in the town—perhaps, socially, the leading personage. A widow, portly as Tommy himself, wealthy, with a family tradition behind her, and the true grand manner in every gesture! Her entertainments at her house at Hillport were unsurpassed, and those who had been invited to them seldom forgot to mention the fact. Thomas, a person not easily staggered, was nevertheless staggered to see her travelling by car to Moorthorne— even in his car, which to him in some subtle way was not like common cars—for she was seldom seen abroad apart from her carriage. She kept two horses. Assuredly both horses must be laid up together, or her coachman ill. Anyhow, there she was, in Thomas's car, splendidly dressed in a new spring gown of flowered silk.

" Thank you," she said very sweetly to Chadwick, in acknowledgment of his assistance.

Then three men of no particular quality mounted the car.

" How do, Tommy? " one of them carelessly greeted the august conductor. This impertinent youth was Paul Ford, a solicitor's clerk, who often went to Moorthorne because his employer had a branch office there, open twice a week.

Tommy did not respond, but rather showed his displeasure. He hated to be called Tommy, except by a few intimate coevals.

" Now then, hurry up, please! " he said coldly.

" Right oh! your majesty," said another of the men, and they all three laughed.

What was still worse, they all three wore the Federationist rosette, which was red to the bull in Thomas Chadwick. It was part of Tommy's political creed that Federationists were the " rag, tag, and bob-tail " of the town. But as he was a tram-conductor, though not an ordinary tram-conductor, his mouth was sealed, and he could not tell his passengers what he thought of them.

Just as he was about to pull the starting bell, Mrs Clayton Vernon sprang up with a little " Oh, I was quite forgetting! " and almost darted out of the car. It was not quite a dart, for she was of full habit, but the alacrity of her movement was astonishing. She must have forgotten something very important.

An idea in the nature of a political argument suddenly popped into Tommy's head, and it was too much for him. He was obliged to let it out. To the winds with that impartiality which a tram company expects from its conductors!

" Ah! " he remarked, jerking his elbow in the direction of Mrs Clayton Vernon and pointedly addressing his three Federationist passengers, " she's a lady, she is! *She* won't travel with anybody, she won't! *She chooses her company—and quite right too, I say !* "

And then he started the car. He felt himself richly avenged by this sally for the " Tommy " and the " your majesty " and the sneering laughter.

Paul Ford winked very visibly at his companions, but made no answering remark. And Thomas Chadwick entered the interior of the car to collect fares. In his hands this operation became a rite. His gestures seemed to say, " No one ever appreciated the importance of the vocation of tram-conductor until I came. We will do this business solemnly and meticulously. Mind what money you give me, count your change, and don't lose, destroy, or deface this indispensable ticket that I hand to you. Do you hear the ting of my bell? It is a sign of my high office. I am fully authorized."

When he had taken his toll he stood at the door of the car, which was now jolting and climbing past the loop-line railway station, and continued his address to the company about the aristocratic and exclusive ex-

cellences of his friend Mrs Clayton Vernon. He proceeded to explain the demerits and wickedness of federation, and to descant on the absurdity of those who
publicly wore the rosettes of the Federation party, thus
branding themselves as imbeciles and knaves; in fact,
his tongue was loosed. Although he stooped to accept
the wages of a tram-conductor, he was not going to
sacrifice the great political right of absolutely free speech.

"If I wasn't the most good-natured man on earth,
Tommy Chadwick," said Paul Ford, "I should write
to the tram company to-night, and you'd get the boot
to-morrow."

"All I say is," persisted the singular conductor—
"all I say is—she's a lady, she is—a regular real lady!
She chooses her company—and quite right too! That
I do say, and nobody's going to stop my mouth." His
manner was the least in the world heated.

"What's that?" asked Paul Ford, with a sudden
start, not inquiring what Thomas Chadwick's mouth
was, but pointing to an object which was lying on the
seat in the corner which Mrs Clayton Vernon had too
briefly occupied.

He rose and picked up the object, which had the
glitter of gold.

"Give it here," said Thomas Chadwick, command-
ingly. "It's none of your business to touch findings in
my car;" and he snatched the object from Paul Ford's
hands.

It was so brilliant and so obviously costly, however,
that he was somehow obliged to share the wonder of it
with his passengers. The find levelled all distinctions
between them. A purse of gold chain-work, it indis-
creetly revealed that it was gorged with riches. When
you shook it the rustle of banknotes was heard, and the
chink of sovereigns, and through the meshes of the purse
could be seen the white of valuable paper and the tawny
orange discs for which mankind is so ready to commit

all sorts of sin. Thomas Chadwick could not forbear to open the contrivance, and having opened it he could not forbear to count its contents. There were, in that purse, seven five-pound notes, fifteen sovereigns, and half a sovereign, and the purse itself was probably worth twelve or fifteen pounds as mere gold.

"There's some that would leave their heads behind 'em if they could!" observed Paul Ford.

Thomas Chadwick glowered at him, as if to warn him that in the presence of Thomas Chadwick noble dames could not be insulted with impunity.

"Didn't I say she was a lady?" said Chadwick, holding up the purse as proof. "It's lucky it's *me* as has laid hands on it!" he added, plainly implying that the other occupants of the car were thieves whenever they had the chance.

"Well," said Paul Ford, "no doubt you'll get your reward all right!"

"It's not—" Chadwick began; but at that moment the driver stopped the car with a jerk, in obedience to a waving umbrella. The conductor, who had not yet got what would have been his sea-legs if he had been captain of an Atlantic liner, lurched forward, and then went out on to the platform to greet a new fare, and his sentence was never finished.

III

THAT day happened to be the day of Thomas Chadwick's afternoon off; at least, of what the tram company called an afternoon off. That is to say, instead of ceasing work at eleven-thirty p.m. he finished at six-thirty p.m. In the ordinary way the company housed its last Moorthorne car at eleven-thirty (Moorthorne not being a very nocturnal village), and gave the conductors the rest of the evening to spend exactly as they liked;

but once a week, in turn, it generously allowed them a complete afternoon beginning at six-thirty.

Now on this afternoon, instead of going home for tea, Thomas Chadwick, having delivered over his insignia and takings to the inspector in Bursley market-place, rushed away towards a car bound for Hillport. A policeman called out to him:

" Hi! Chadwick! "

" What's up? " asked Chadwick, unwillingly stopping.

" Mrs Clayton Vernon's been to the station an hour ago or hardly, about a purse as she says she thinks she must have left in your car.   I was just coming across to tell your inspector."

" Tell him, then, my lad," said Chadwick, curtly, and hurried on towards the Hillport car.   His manner to policemen always mingled the veteran with the comrade, and most of them indeed regarded him as an initiate of the craft.   Still, his behaviour on this occasion did somewhat surprise the young policeman who had accosted him.   And undoubtedly Thomas Chadwick was scarcely acting according to the letter of the law. His proper duty was to hand over all articles found in his car instantly to the police—certainly not to keep them concealed on his person with a view to restoring them with his own hands to their owners.   But Thomas Chadwick felt that, having once been a policeman, he was at liberty to interpret the law to suit his own convenience.   He caught the Hillport car, and nodded the professional nod to its conductor, asking him a technical question, and generally showing to the other passengers on the platform that he was not as they, and that he had important official privileges.   Of course, he travelled free; and of course he stopped the car when, its conductor being inside, two ladies signalled to it at the bottom of Oldcastle Street.   He had meant to say nothing whatever about his treasure and his errand to the other conductor; but somehow, when fares had been duly collected, and these two stood chatting on the platform, the gold purse got itself into the conversation, and presently the other conductor knew the entire history, and had even had a glimpse of the purse itself.

Opposite the entrance to Mrs Clayton Vernon's grounds at Hillport Thomas Chadwick slipped neatly, for all his vast bulk, off the swiftly-gliding car. (A conductor on a car but not on duty would sooner perish by a heavy fall than have a car stopped in order that he might descend from it.) And Thomas Chadwick heavily crunched the gravel of the drive leading up to Mrs Clayton Vernon's house, and imperiously rang the bell.

" Mrs Clayton Vernon in? " he officially asked the responding servant.

" She's *in*," said the servant. Had Thomas Chadwick been wearing his broadcloth she would probably have added " sir."

" Well, will you please tell her that Mr Chadwick—Thomas Chadwick—wants to speak to her? "

" Is it about the purse? " the servant questioned, suddenly brightening into eager curiosity.

" Never you mind what it's about, miss," said Thomas Chadwick, sternly.

At the same moment Mrs Clayton Vernon's grey-curled head appeared behind the white cap of the servant. Probably she had happened to catch some echo of Thomas Chadwick's great rolling voice. The servant retired.

" Good-evening, m'm," said Thomas Chadwick, raising his hat airily. " Good-evening." He beamed.

" So you did find it? " said Mrs Vernon, calmly smiling. " I felt sure it would be all right."

" Oh, yes, m'm." He tried to persuade himself that this sublime confidence was characteristic of great ladies, and a laudable symptom of aristocracy. But he would have preferred her to be a little less confident. After all, in the hands of a conductor less honourable than himself, of a common conductor, the purse might not have been so " all right " as all that! He would have preferred to witness the change on Mrs Vernon's features from desperate anxiety to glad relief. After all, £50, 10s. was money, however rich you were!

" Have you got it with you? " asked Mrs Vernon.

" Yes'm," said he. " I thought I'd just step up with it myself, so as to be sure."

" It's very good of you! "

" Not at all," said he; and he produced the purse. " I think you'll find it as it should be."

Mrs Vernon gave him a courtly smile as she thanked him.

" I'd like ye to count it, ma'am," said Chadwick, as she showed no intention of even opening the purse.

" If you wish it," said she, and counted her wealth and restored it to the purse. " *Quite* right—*quite* right! Fifty pounds and ten shillings," she said pleasantly. " I'm very much obliged to you, Chadwick."

" Not at all, m'm! " He was still standing in the sheltered porch.

An idea seemed to strike Mrs Clayton Vernon.

" Would you like something to drink? " she asked.

" Well, thank ye, m'm," said Thomas.

" Maria," said Mrs Vernon, calling to someone within the house, " bring this man a glass of beer." And she turned again to Chadwick, smitten with another idea. " Let me see. Your eldest daughter has two little boys, hasn't she? "

" Yes'm," said Thomas—" twins."

" I thought so. Her husband is my cook's cousin. Well, here's two threepenny bits—one for each of them." With some trouble she extracted the coins from a

rather shabby leather purse—evidently her household
purse. She bestowed them upon the honest conductor
with another grateful and condescending smile. "I
hope you don't *mind* taking them for the chicks," she
said. "I *do* like giving things to children. It's so
much *nicer*, isn't it?"

"Certainly, m'm."

Then the servant brought the glass of beer, and Mrs
Vernon, with yet another winning smile, and yet more
thanks, left him to toss it off on the mat, while the
servant waited for the empty glass.

IV

On the following Friday afternoon young Paul Ford was
again on the Moorthorne car, and subject to the official
ministrations of Thomas Chadwick. Paul Ford was a
man who never bore malice when the bearing of malice
might interfere with the gratification of his sense of
humour. Many men—perhaps most men—after being
so grossly insulted by a tram-conductor as Paul Ford
had been insulted by Chadwick, would at the next
meeting have either knocked the insulter down or coldly
ignored him. But Paul Ford did neither. (In any case,
Thomas Chadwick would have wanted a deal of knocking down.) For some reason, everything that Thomas
Chadwick said gave immense amusement to Paul Ford.
So the young man commenced the conversation in the
usual way:

"How do, Tommy?"

The car on this occasion was coming down from
Moorthorne into Bursley, with its usual bump and rattle
of windows. As Thomas Chadwick made no reply,
Paul Ford continued:

"How much did she give you—the perfect lady, I
mean?"

Paul Ford was sitting near the open door. Thomas Chadwick gazed absently at the Town Park, with its terra-cotta fountains and terraces, and beyond the Park, at the smoke rising from the distant furnaces of Red Cow. He might have been lost in deep meditation upon the meanings of life; he might have been prevented from hearing Paul Ford's question by the tremendous noise of the car. He made no sign. Then all of a sudden he turned almost fiercely on Paul Ford and glared at him.

" Ye want to know how much she gave me, do ye? " he demanded hotly.

" Yes," said Paul Ford.

" How much she gave me for taking her that there purse? " Tommy Chadwick temporized.

He was obliged to temporize, because he could not quite resolve to seize the situation and deal with it once for all in a manner favourable to his dignity and to the ideals which he cherished.

" Yes," said Paul Ford.

" Well, I'll tell ye," said Thomas Chadwick— " though I don't know as it's any business of yours. But, as you're so curious! . . . She didn't give me anything. She asked me to have a little refreshment, like the lady she is. But she knew better than to offer Thomas Chadwick any pecooniary reward for giving her back something as she'd happened to drop. She's a lady, she is! "

" Oh! " said Paul Ford. " It don't cost much, being a lady! "

" But I'll tell ye what she *did* do," Thomas Chadwick went on, anxious, now that he had begun so well, to bring the matter to an artistic conclusion—" I'll tell ye what she did do. She give me a sovereign apiece for my grandsons—my eldest daughter's twins." Then, after an effective pause: " Ye can put that in your pipe and smoke it! . . . A sovereign apiece! "

" And have you handed it over? " Paul Ford inquired mildly, after a period of soft whistling.

" I've started two post-office savings bank accounts for 'em," said Thomas Chadwick, with ferocity.

The talk stopped, and nothing whatever occurred until the car halted at the railway station to take up passengers. The heart of Thomas Chadwick gave a curious little jump when he saw Mrs Clayton Vernon coming out of the station and towards his car. (Her horses must have been still lame or her coachman still laid aside.) She boarded the car, smiling with a quite particular effulgence upon Thomas Chadwick, and he greeted her with what he imagined to be the true antique chivalry. And she sat down in the corner opposite to Paul Ford, beaming.

When Thomas Chadwick came, with great respect, to demand her fare, she said:

" By the way, Chadwick, it's such a short distance from the station to the town, I think I should have walked and saved a penny. But I wanted to speak to you. I wasn't aware, last Tuesday, that your other daughter got married last year and now has a dear little baby. I gave you threepenny bits each for those dear little twins. Here's another one for the other baby. I think I ought to treat all your grandchildren alike—otherwise your daughters might be jealous of each other "—she smiled archly, to indicate that this passage was humorous—" and there's no knowing what might happen! "

Mrs Clayton Vernon always enunciated her remarks in a loud and clear voice, so that Paul Ford could not have failed to hear every word. A faint but beatific smile concealed itself roguishly about Paul Ford's mouth, and he looked with a rapt expression on an advertisement above Mrs Clayton Vernon's head, which assured him that, with a certain soap, washing-day became a pleasure.

Thomas Chadwick might have flung the threepenny bit into the road. He might have gone off into language unseemly in a tram-conductor and a grandfather. He might have snatched Mrs Clayton Vernon's bonnet off and stamped on it. He might have killed Paul Ford (for it was certainly Paul Ford with whom he was the most angry). But he did none of these things. He said, in his best unctuous voice:

" Thank you, m'm, I'm sure! "

And, at the journey's end, when the passengers descended, he stared a harsh stare, without winking, full in the face of Paul Ford, and he courteously came to the aid of Mrs Clayton Vernon. He had proclaimed Mrs Clayton Vernon to be his ideal of a true lady, and he was heroically loyal to his ideal, a martyr to the cause he had espoused. Such a man was not fitted to be a tram-conductor, and the Five Towns Electric Traction Company soon discovered his unfitness—so that he was again thrown upon the world.

UNDER THE CLOCK

I

I T was one of those swift and violent marriages which
occur when the interested parties are so severely
wounded by the arrow of love that only immediate and
constant mutual nursing will save them from a fatal issue.
(So they think.)   Hence when Annie came from Sneyd
to inhabit the house in Birches Street, Hanbridge, which
William Henry Brachett had furnished for her, she
really knew very little of William Henry save that he was
intensely lovable, and that she was intensely in love with
him.   Their acquaintance extended over three months.
And she knew equally little of the manners and customs
of the Five Towns.   For although Sneyd lies but a few
miles from the immense seat of pottery manufacture, it is
not as the Five Towns are.   It is not feverish, grimy,
rude, strenuous, Bacchic, and wicked.   It is a model
village, presided over by the Countess of Chell.   The
people of the Five Towns go there on Thursday after-
noons (eightpence, third class return), as if they were
going to Paradise.   Thus, indeed, it was that William
Henry had met Annie, daughter of a house over whose
door were writ the inviting words, " Tea and Hot Water
Provided.'

There were a hundred and forty-two residences in
Birches Street, Hanbridge, all alike, differing only in the
degree of cleanliness of their window-curtains.   Two
front doors together, and then two bow-windows, and
then two front doors again, and so on all up the street
and all down the street.   Life was monotonous, but on

127

the whole respectable.   Annie came of an economical
family, and, previous to the wedding, she had been
afraid that William Henry's ideal of economy might fall
short of her own.   In this she was mistaken.   In fact,
she was startlingly mistaken.   It was some slight shock
to her to be informed by William Henry that owing to
slackness of work the honeymoon ought to be reduced
to two days.   Still, she agreed to the proposal with joy.
(For her life was going to be one long honeymoon.)
When they returned from the brief honeymoon, William
Henry took eight shillings from her, out of the money
he had given her, and hurried off to pay it into the Going
Away Club, and there was scarcity for a few days.   This
happened in March.   She had then only a vague idea of
what the Going Away Club was.   But from William
Henry's air, and his fear lest he might be late, she
gathered that the Going Away Club must be a very important institution.   Brachett, for a living, painted blue
Japanese roses on vases at Gimson & Nephews' works.
He was nearly thirty years of age, and he had never
done anything else but paint blue Japanese roses on
vases.   When the demand for blue Japanese roses on
vases was keen, he could earn what is called "good
money"—that is to say, quite fifty shillings a week.
But the demand for blue Japanese roses on vases was
subject to the caprices of markets—especially Colonial
markets—and then William Henry had undesired days
of leisure, and brought home less than fifty shillings,
sometimes considerably less.   Still, the household over
which Annie presided was a superiorly respectable household and William Henry's income was, week in, week out,
one of the princeliest in the street; and certainly Annie's
window-curtains, and her gilt-edged Bible and artificial
flowers displayed on a small table between the window-
curtains was not to be surpassed.   Further, William was
"steady," and not quite raving mad about football
matches; nor did he bet on horses, dogs or pigeons.

Nevertheless Annie—although, mind you, extraordinarily happy—found that her new existence, besides being monotonous, was somewhat hard, narrow and lacking in spectacular delights. Whenever there was any suggestion of spending more money than usual, William Henry's fierce chin would stick out in a formidable way, and his voice would become harsh, and in the result more money than usual was not spent. His notion of an excursion, of a wild and costly escapade, was a walk in Hanbridge Municipal Park and two shandy-gaffs at the Corporation Refreshment House therein. Now, although the Hanbridge Park is a wonderful triumph of grass-seed and terra-cotta over cinder-heaps and shard-rucks, although it is a famous exemplar to other boroughs, it is not precisely the Vale of Llangollen, nor the Lake District. It is the least bit in the world tedious, and by the sarcastic has been likened to a cemetery. And it seemed to symbolize Annie's life for her, in its cramped and pruned and smoky regularity. She began to look upon the Five Towns as a sort of prison from which she could never, never escape.

I say she was extraordinarily happy; and yet she was unhappy too. In a word, she resembled all the rest of us—she had "somehow expected something different" from what life actually gave her. She was astonished that her William Henry seemed to be so content with things as they were. Far, now, from any apprehension of his extravagance, she wished secretly that he would be a little more dashing. He did not seem to feel the truth that, though prudence is all very well, you can only live your life once, and that when you are dead you are dead. He did not seem to understand the value of pleasure. Few people in the Five Towns did seem to understand the value of pleasure. He had no distractions except his pipe. Existence was a harsh and industrious struggle, a series of undisturbed daily habits. No change, no gaiety, no freak! Grim, changeless monotony!

And once, in July, William Henry abandoned even his pipe for ten days. Work, and therefore pay, had been irregular, but that was not in itself a reason sufficient for cutting off a luxury that cost only a shilling a week. It was the Going Away Club that swallowed up the tobacco money. Nothing would induce William Henry to get into arrears with his payments to that mysterious Club. He would have sacrificed not merely his pipe, but his dinner—nay, he would have sacrificed his wife's dinner—to the greedy maw of that Club. Annie hated the Club nearly as passionately as she loved William Henry.

Then on the first of August (a Tuesday) William Henry came into the house and put down twenty sovereigns in a row on the kitchen table. He did not say much, being (to Annie's mild regret) of a secretive disposition.

Annie had never seen so much money in a row before. " What's that? " she said weakly.

" That? " said William Henry. " That's th' going away money."

II

A FLAT barrow at the door, a tin trunk and two bags on the barrow, and a somewhat ragged boy between the handles of the barrow! The curtains removed from the windows, and the blinds drawn! A double turn of the key in the portal! And away they went, the ragged boy having previously spit on his hands in order to get a grip of the barrow. Thus they arrived at Hanbridge Railway Station, which was a tempest of traffic that Saturday before Bank Holiday. The whole of the Five Towns appeared to be going away. The first thing that startled Annie was that William Henry gave the ragged boy a shilling, quite as much as the youth could have earned in

a couple of days in a regular occupation. William Henry
was also lavish with a porter. When they arrived,
after a journey of ten minutes, at Knype, where they
had to change for Liverpool, he was again lavish with a
porter. And the same thing happened at Crewe, where
they had to change once more for Liverpool. They had
time at Crewe for an expensive coloured drink. On the
long seething platform William Henry gave Annie all
his money to keep.

"" Here, lass! " he said. " This'll be safer with you
than with me."

She was flattered.

When it came in, the Liverpool train was crammed
to the doors. And two hundred people pumped themselves into it, as air is forced into a pneumatic tyre.
The entire world seemed to be going to Liverpool. It
was uncomfortable, but it was magnificent. It was joy,
it was life. The chimneys and kilns of the Five Towns
were far away. And Annie, though in a cold perspiration lest she might never see her tin trunk again, was
feverishly happy. At Liverpool William Henry demanded silver coins from her. She had a glimpse of her
trunk. Then they rattled and jolted and whizzed in an
omnibus to Prince's Landing Stage. And William
Henry demanded more coins from her. A great ship
awaited them. Need it be said that Douglas was their
destination? The deck of the great ship was like a
market-place. Annie had never seen such a thing.
They climbed up into the market-place among the shouting, gesticulating crowd. There was a real shop, at
which William Henry commanded her to buy a hat-
guard. The hat-guard cost sixpence. At home sixpence was sixpence, and would buy seven pounds of fine
mealy potatoes; but here sixpence was nothing—certainly it was not more than a halfpenny. They wandered and found other shops. Annie could not believe
that all those solid shops and the whole market-place

could move. And she was not surprised, a little later, to see Prince's Landing Stage sliding away from the ship, instead of the ship sliding away from Prince's Landing Stage. Then they went underground, beneath the market-place, and Annie found marble halls, colossal staircases, bookshops, trinket shops, highly-decorated restaurants, glittering bars, and cushioned drawing-rooms. They had the most exciting meal in the restaurant that Annie had ever had; also the most expensive; the price of it indeed staggered her; still, William Henry did not appear to mind that one meal should exceed the cost of two days living in Birches Street. Then they went up into the market-place again, and lo! the market-place had somehow of itself got into the middle of the sea!

Before the end of the voyage they had tea at three-pence a cup. Annie reflected that the best " Home and Colonial " tea cost eighteenpence a pound, and that a pound would make two hundred and twenty cups. Similarly with the bread and butter which they ate, and the jam! But it was glorious. Not the jam (which Annie could have bettered), but life! Particularly as the sea was smooth! Presently she descried a piece of chalk sticking up against the horizon, and it was Douglas lighthouse.

III

THERE followed six days of delirium, six days of the largest conceivable existence. The holiday-makers stopped in a superb boarding-house on the promenade, one of about a thousand superb boarding-houses. The day's proceedings began at nine o'clock with a regal breakfast, partaken of at a very long table which ran into a bow window. At nine o'clock, in all the thousand boarding-houses, a crowd of hungry and excited men and women sat down thus to a very long table, and consumed the same dishes, that is to say, Manx herrings, and bacon and eggs, and jams. Everybody ate as much as he could. William Henry was never content with less than two herrings, two eggs, about four ounces of bacon, and as much jam as would render a whole Board school sticky. And in four hours after that he was ready for an enormous dinner, and so was she; and in five hours after that they neither of them had the slightest disinclination for a truly high and complex tea. Of course, the cost was fabulous. Thirty-five shillings per week each. Annie would calculate that, with thirty boarders and extras, the boarding-house was taking in money at the rate of over forty pounds a week. She would also calculate that about a hundred thousand herrings and ten million little bones were swallowed in Douglas each day.

But the cost of the boarding-house was as naught. It was the flowing out of coins between meals that deprived Annie of breath. They were always doing something. Sailing in a boat! Rowing in a boat! Bathing! The Pier! Sand minstrels! Excursions by brake, tram and train to Laxey, Ramsey, Sulby Glen, Port Erin, Snaefell! Morning shows! Afternoon shows! Evening shows! Circuses, music-halls, theatres, concerts! And then the public balls, with those delicious tables in corners, lighted by Chinese lanterns, where you sat down and drew strange liquids up straws. And it all meant money. There were even places in Douglas where you couldn't occupy a common chair for half a minute without paying for it. Each night Annie went to bed exhausted with joy. On the second night she counted the money in her bag, and said to William Henry:

"How much money do you think we've spent already? Just—"

"Don't tell me, lass!" he interrupted her curtly. 'When I want to know, I'll ask ye."

And on the fifth evening of this heaven he asked her:

" What'n ye got left? "

She informed him that she had five pounds and two-pence left, of which the boarding-house and tips would absorb four pounds.

" H'm! " he replied.   " It's going to be a bit close."

On the seventh day they set sail.   The dream was not quite over, but it was nearly over.   On the ship, when the porter had been discharged, she had two and twopence, and William Henry had the return tickets. Still, this poverty did not prevent William Henry from sitting down and ordering a fine lunch for two (the sea being again smooth).   Having ordered it, he calmly told his wife that he had a sovereign in his waistcoat pocket.   A sovereign was endless riches.   But it came to an end during a long wait for the Five Towns train at Crewe.   William Henry had apparently decided to finish the holiday as he had begun it.   And the two and twopence also came to an end, as William Henry, sud-denly remembering the children of his brother, was deter-mined to buy gifts for them on Crewe platform.   At Hanbridge man and wife had sixpence between them. And the boy with the barrow, who had been summoned by a postcard, was not visible.   However, a cab was visible.   William Henry took that cab.

" But, Will—"

" Shut up, lass! " he stopped her.

They plunged into the smoke and squalor of the Five Towns, and reached Birches Street with pomp, while Annie wondered how William Henry would contrive to get credit from a cabman.   The entire street would certainly gather round if there should be a scene.

" Just help us in with this trunk, wilt? " said William Henry to the cabman.   This, with sixpence in his pocket!

Then turning to his wife, he whispered:

" Lass, look under th' clock on th' mantelpiece in th' parlour. Ye'll find six bob."

He explained to her later that prudent members of Going Away Clubs always left money concealed behind them, as this was the sole way of providing against a calamitous return. The pair existed on the remainder of the six shillings and on credit for a week. William Henry became his hard self again. The prison life was resumed. But Annie did not mind, for she had lived for a week at the rate of a thousand a year. And in a fortnight William Henry began grimly to pay his subscriptions to the next year's Going Away Club.

THREE EPISODES IN THE LIFE OF MR COWLISHAW DENTIST

I

THEY all happened on the same day. And that day was a Saturday, the red Saturday on which, in the unforgettable football match between Tottenham Hotspur and the Hanbridge F.C. (formed regardless of expense in the matter of professionals to take the place of the bankrupt Knype F.C.), the referee would certainly have been murdered had not a Five Towns crowd observed its usual miraculous self-restraint.

Mr Cowlishaw — aged twenty-four, a fair-haired bachelor with a weak moustache—had bought the practice of the retired Mr Rapper, a dentist of the very old school. He was not a native of the Five Towns. He came from St Albans, and had done the deal through an advertisement in the *Dentists' Guardian*, a weekly journal full of exciting interest to dentists. Save such knowledge as he had gained during two preliminary visits to the centre of the world's earthenware manufacture, he knew nothing of the Five Towns; practically, he had everything to learn. And one may say that the Five Towns is not a subject that can be " got up " in a day.

His place of business—or whatever high-class dentists choose to call it—in Crown Square was quite ready for him when he arrived on the Friday night: specimen " uppers " and " lowers " and odd teeth shining in their glass case, the new black-and-gold door-plate on the

door, and the electric filing apparatus which he had purchased, in the operating-room. Nothing lacked there.
But his private lodgings were not ready; at least, they
were not what he, with his finicking Albanian notions,
called ready, and, after a brief altercation with his landlady, he went off with a bag to spend the night at the
Turk's Head Hotel. The Turk's Head is the best hotel
in Hanbridge, not excepting the new Hotel Metropole
(Limited, and German-Swiss waiters). The proof of its
excellence is that the proprietor, Mr Simeon Clowes,
was then the Mayor of Hanbridge, and Mrs Clowes one
of the acknowledged leaders of Hanbridge society.

Mr Cowlishaw went to bed. He was a good sleeper;
at least, he was what is deemed a good sleeper in St
Albans. He retired about eleven o'clock, and re-
quested one of the barmaids to instruct the boots to
arouse him at 7 a.m. She faithfully promised to do so.

He had not been in bed five minutes before he heard
and felt an earthquake. This earthquake seemed to
have been born towards the north-east, in the direction
of Crown Square, and the shock seemed to pass southwards in the direction of Knype. The bed shook; the
basin and ewer rattled together like imperfect false
teeth in the mouth of an arrant coward; the walls of the
hotel shook. Then silence! No cries of alarm, no cries
for help, no lamentations of ruin! Doubtless, though
earthquakes are rare in England, the whole town had
been overthrown and engulfed, and only Mr Cowlishaw's
bed left standing. Conquering his terror, Mr Cowlishaw
put his head under the clothes and waited.

He had not been in bed ten minutes before he heard
and felt another earthquake. This earthquake seemed
to have been born towards the north-east, in the direction of Crown Square, and to be travelling southwards;
and Mr Cowlishaw noticed that it was accompanied by a
strange sound of heavy bumping. He sprang courageously out of bed and rushed to the window. And it

so happened that he caught the earthquake in the very act of flight. It was one of the new cars of the Five Towns Electric Traction Company, Limited, guaranteed to carry fifty-two passengers. The bumping was due to the fact that the driver, by a too violent application of the brake, had changed the form of two of its wheels from circular to oval. Such accidents do happen, even to the newest cars, and the inhabitants of the Five Towns laugh when they hear a bumpy car as they laugh at *Charley's Aunt*. The car shot past, flashing sparks from its overhead wire and flaming red and green lights of warning, and vanished down the main thoroughfare. And gradually the ewer and basin ceased their colloquy. The night being the night of the 29th December, and exceedingly cold, Mr Cowlishaw went back to bed.

"Well," he muttered, "this is a bit thick, this is!" (They use such language in cathedral towns.) "However, let's hope it's the last."

It was not the last. Exactly, it was the last but twenty-three. Regularly at intervals of five minutes the Five Towns Electric Traction Company, Limited, sent one of their dreadful engines down the street, apparently with the object of disintegrating all the real property in the neighbourhood into its original bricks. At the seventeenth time Mr Cowlishaw trembled to hear a renewal of the bump-bump-bump. It was the oval-wheeled car, which had been to Longshaw and back. He recognized it as an old friend. He wondered whether he must expect it to pass a third time. However, it did not pass a third time. After several clocks in and out of the hotel had more or less agreed on the fact that it was one o'clock, there was a surcease of earthquakes. Mr Cowlishaw dared not hope that earthquakes were over. He waited in strained attention during quite half an hour, expectant of the next earthquake. But it did not come. Earthquakes were, indeed, done with till the morrow.

It was about two o'clock when his nerves were suffi-

ciently tranquillized to enable him to envisage the possibility of going to sleep. And he was just slipping,
gliding, floating off when he was brought back to realities
by a terrific explosion of laughter at the head of the
stairs outside his bedroom door. The building rang like
the inside of a piano when you strike a wire directly.
The explosion was followed by low rumblings of laughter
and then by a series of jolly, hearty "Good-nights." He
recognized the voices as being those of a group of commercial travellers and two actors (of the Hanbridge
Theatre Royal's specially selected London Panto-
mime Company), who had been pointed out to him with
awe and joy by the aforesaid barmaid. They were telling each other stories in the private bar, and apparently
they had been telling each other stories ever since. And
the truth is that the atmosphere of the Turk's Head,
where commercial travellers and actors forgather every
night except perhaps Sundays, contains more good
stories to the cubic inch than any other resort in the
county of Staffordshire. A few seconds after the explosion there was a dropping fusillade—the commercial
travellers and the actors shutting their doors. And
about five minutes later there was another and more
complicated dropping fusillade — the commercial
travellers and actors opening their doors, depositing
their boots (two to each soul), and shutting their doors.

Then silence.

And then out of the silence the terrified Mr Cowlishaw
heard arising and arising a vast and fearful breathing,
as of some immense prehistoric monster in pain. At
first he thought he was asleep and dreaming. But he
was not. This gigantic sighing continued regularly,
and Mr Cowlishaw had never heard anything like it
before. It banished sleep.

After about two hours of its awful uncanniness, Mr
Cowlishaw caught the sound of creeping footsteps in the
corridor and fumbling noises. He got up again. He

was determined, though he should have to interrogate burglars and assassins, to discover the meaning of that horrible sighing. He courageously pulled his door open, and saw an aproned man with a candle marking boots with chalk, and putting them into a box.

"I say!" said Mr Cowlishaw.

"Beg yer pardon, sir," the man whispered. "I'm getting forward with my work so as I can go to th' fut-baw match this afternoon. I hope I didn't wake ye, sir."

"Look here!" said Mr Cowlishaw. "What's that appalling noise that's going on all the time?"

"Noise, sir?" whispered the man, astonished.

"Yes," Mr Cowlishaw insisted. "Like something breathing. Can't you hear it?"

The man cocked his ears attentively. The noise veritably boomed in Mr Cowlishaw's ears.

"Oh! *That!*" said the man at length. "That's th' blast furnaces at Cauldon Bar Ironworks. Never heard that afore, sir? Why, it's like that every night. Now you mention it, I *do* hear it! It's a good couple o' miles off, though, that is!"

Mr Cowlishaw closed his door.

At five o'clock, when he had nearly, but not quite, forgotten the sighing, his lifelong friend, the oval-wheeled electric car, bumped and quaked through the street, and the ewer and basin chattered together busily, and the seismic phenomena definitely recommenced. The night was still black, but the industrial day had dawned in the Five Towns. Long series of carts with-out springs began to jolt past under the window of Mr Cowlishaw, and then there was a regular multitudinous clacking of clogs and boots on the pavement. A little later the air was rent by first one steam-whistle, and then another, and then another, in divers tones an-nouncing that it was six o'clock, or five minutes past, or half-past, or anything. The periodicity of earth-quakes had by this time quickened to five minutes, as at midnight. A motor-car emerged under the archway of the hotel, and remained stationary outside with its engine racing. And amid the earthquakes, the motor-car, the carts, the clogs and boots, and the steam muezzins calling the faithful to work, Mr Cowlishaw could still distinguish the tireless, monstrous sighing of the Cauldon Bar blast furnaces. And, finally, he heard another sound. It came from the room next to his, and, when he heard it, exhausted though he was, exasperated though he was, he burst into laughter, so comically did it strike him.

It was an alarm-clock going off in the next room.

And, further, when he arrived downstairs, the barmaid, sweet, conscientious little thing, came up to him and said, "I'm so sorry, sir. I quite forgot to tell the boots to call you!"

II

THAT afternoon he sat in his beautiful new surgery and waited for dental sufferers to come to him from all quarters of the Five Towns. It needs not to be said that nobody came. The mere fact that a new dentist has " set up " in a district is enough to cure all the toothache for miles around. The one martyr who might, perhaps, have paid him a visit and a fee did not show herself. This martyr was Mrs Simeon Clowes, the mayoress. By a curious chance, he had observed, during his short sojourn at the Turk's Head, that the landlady thereof was obviously in pain from her teeth, or from a particular tooth. She must certainly have informed herself as to his name and condition, and Mr Cowlishaw thought that it would have been a graceful act on her part to patronize him, as he had patronized the Turk's Head. But no! Mayoresses, even the most tactful, do not always do the right thing at the right moment.

Besides, she had doubtless gone, despite toothache,

to the football match with the Mayor, the new club
being under the immediate patronage of his Worship.
All the potting world had gone to the football match.
Mr Cowlishaw would have liked to go, but it would have
been madness to quit the surgery on his opening day.
So he sat and yawned, and peeped at the crowd crowding to the match at two o'clock, and crowding back in
the gloom at four o'clock; and at a quarter past five he
was reading a full description of the carnage and the
heroism in the football edition of the *Signal*. Though
Hanbridge had been defeated, it appeared from the
Signal that Hanbridge was the better team, and that
Rannoch, the new Scotch centre-forward, had fought
nobly for the town which had bought him so dear.

Mr Cowlishaw was just dozing over the *Signal* when
there happened a ring at his door. He did not precipi-
tate himself upon the door. With beating heart he retained his presence of mind, and said to himself that of
course it could not possibly be a client. Even dentists
who bought a practice ready-made never had a client on
their first day. He heard the attendant answer the ring,
and then he heard the attendant saying, " I'll see, sir."

It was, in fact, a patient. The servant, having
asked Mr Cowlishaw if Mr Cowlishaw was at liberty,
introduced the patient to the Presence, and the Presence trembled.

The patient was a tall, stiff, fair man of about thirty,
with a tousled head and inelegant but durable clothing.
He had a drooping moustache, which prevented Mr
Cowlishaw from adding his teeth up instantly.

" Good afternoon, mister," said the patient,
abruptly.

" Good afternoon," said Mr Cowlishaw. " Have
you . . . Can I . . ."

Strange; in the dental hospital and school there had
been no course of study in the art of pattering to
patients!

"It's like this," said the patient, putting his hand in his waistcoat pocket.

"Will you kindly sit down," said Mr Cowlishaw, turning up the gas, and pointing to the chair of chairs.

"It's like this," repeated the patient, doggedly. "You see these three teeth?"

He displayed three very real teeth in a piece of reddened paper. As a spectacle, they were decidedly not appetizing, but Mr Cowlishaw was hardened.

"Really!" said Mr Cowlishaw, impartially, gazing on them.

"They're my teeth," said the patient. And thereupon he opened his mouth wide, and displayed, not without vanity, a widowed gum. "'Ont 'eeth," he exclaimed, keeping his mouth open and omitting preliminary consonants.

"Yes," said Mr Cowlishaw, with a dry inflection. "I saw that they were upper incisors. How did this come about? An accident, I suppose?"

"Well," said the man, "you may call it an accident; I don't. My name's Rannoch; centre-forward. Ye see? Were ye at the match?"

Mr Cowlishaw understood. He had no need of further explanation; he had read it all in the *Signal*. And so the chief victim of Tottenham Hotspur had come to him, just him! This was luck! For Rannoch was, of course, the most celebrated man in the Five Towns, and the idol of the populace. He might have been M.P. had he chosen.

"Dear me!" Mr Cowlishaw sympathized, and he said again, pointing more firmly to the chair of chairs, "Will you sit down?"

"I had 'em all picked up," Mr Rannoch proceeded, ignoring the suggestion. "Because a bit of a scheme came into my head. And that's why I've come to you, as you're just commencing dentist. Supposing you put these teeth on a bit of green velvet in the case in

your window, with a big card to say as they're guaranteed to be my genuine teeth, knocked out by that
blighter of a Tottenham half-back, you'll have such a
crowd as was never seen around your door. All the
Five Towns 'll come to see 'em. It'll be the biggest
advertisement that either you or any other dentist ever
had. And you might put a little notice in the *Signal*
saying that my teeth are on view at your premises; it
would only cost ye a shilling. . . . I should expect ye
to furnish me with new teeth for nothing, ye see."

In his travels throughout England Mr Rannoch
had lost most of his Scotch accent, but he had not lost
his Scotch skill in the art and craft of trying to pay less
than other folks for whatever he might happen to want.

Assuredly the idea was an idea of genius. As an
advertisement it would be indeed colossal and unique.
Tens of thousands would gaze spellbound for hours at
those relics of their idol, and every gazer would inevitably be familiarized with the name and address of Mr
Cowlishaw, and with the fact that Mr Cowlishaw was
dentist-in-chief to the heroical Rannoch. Unfortunately, in dentistry there is etiquette. And the etiquette
of dentistry is as terrible, as unbending, as the etiquette
of the Court of Austria.

Mr Cowlishaw knew that he could not do this thing
without sinning against etiquette.

" I'm sorry I can't fall in with your scheme," said
he, " but I can't."

" But, *man !* " protested the Scotchman, " it's the
greatest scheme that ever was."

" Yes," said Mr Cowlishaw, " but it would be un-
professional."

Mr Rannoch was himself a professional. " Oh,
well," he said sarcastically, " if you're one of those
amateurs—"

" I'll put you the job in as low as possible," said Mr
Cowlishaw, persuasively.

But Scotchmen are not to be persuaded like that. Mr Rannoch wrapped up his teeth and left.

What finally happened to those teeth Mr Cowlishaw never knew. But he satisfied himself that they were not advertised in the *Signal*.

III

Now, just as Mr Cowlishaw was personally conducting to the door the greatest goal-getter that the Five Towns had ever seen there happened another ring, and thus it fell out that Mr Cowlishaw found himself in the double difficulty of speeding his first visitor and welcoming his second all in the same breath. It is true that the second might imagine that the first was a client, but then the aspect of Mr Rannoch's mouth, had it caught the eye of the second, was not reassuring. However, Mr Rannoch's mouth happily did not catch the eye of the second.

The second was a visitor beyond Mr Cowlishaw's hopes, no other than Mrs Simeon Clowes, landlady of the Turk's Head and Mayoress of Hanbridge; a tall and well-built, handsome, downright woman, of something more than fifty and something less than sixty; the mother of five married daughters, the aunt of fourteen nephews and nieces, the grandam of seven, or it might be eight, assorted babies; in short, a lady of vast influence. After all, then, she had come to him! If only he could please her, he regarded his succession to his predecessor as definitely established and his fortune made. No person in Hanbridge with any yearnings for style would dream, he trusted, of going to any other dentist than the dentist patronized by Mrs Clowes.

She eyed him interrogatively and firmly. She probed into his character, and he felt himself pierced.

" You *are* Mr Cowlishaw? " she began.

" Good afternoon, Mrs Clowes," he replied. " Yes, I am. Can I be of service to you? "

" That depends," she said.

He asked her to step in, and in she stepped.

" Have you had any experience in taking teeth out? " she asked in the surgery. Her hand stroked her left cheek.

" Oh yes," he said eagerly. " But, of course, we try to avoid extraction as much as possible."

" If you're going to talk like that," she said coldly, and even bitterly, " I'd better go."

He wondered what she was driving at.

" Naturally," he said, summoning all his latent powers of diplomacy, " there are cases in which extraction is unfortunately necessary."

" How many teeth have you extracted? " she inquired.

" I really couldn't say," he lied. " Very many."

" Because," she said, " you don't look as if you could say ' Bo! ' to a goose."

He observed a gleam in her eye.

" I think I can say ' Bo! ' to a goose," he said.

She laughed.

" Don't fancy, Mr Cowlishaw, that if I laugh I'm not in the most horrible pain. I am. When I tell you I couldn't go with Mr Clowes to the match—"

" Will you take this seat? " he said, indicating the chair of chairs; " then I can examine."

She obeyed. " I do hate the horrid, velvety feeling of these chairs," she said; " it's most creepy."

" I shall have to trouble you to take your bonnet off."

So she removed her bonnet, and he took it as he might have taken his firstborn, and laid it gently to rest on his cabinet. Then he pushed the gas-bracket so that the light came through the large crystal sphere, and made the Mayoress blink.

"Now," he said soothingly, "kindly open your mouth—wide."

Like all women of strong and generous character, Mrs Simeon Clowes had a large mouth. She obediently extended it to dimensions which must be described as august, at the same time pointing with her gloved and chubby finger to a particular part of it.

"Yes, yes," murmured Mr Cowlishaw, assuming a tranquillity which he did not feel. This was the first time that he had ever looked into the mouth of a Mayoress, and the prospect troubled him.

He put his little ivory-handled mirror into that mouth and studied its secrets.

"I see," he said, withdrawing the mirror. "Exposed nerve. Quite simple. Merely wants stopping. When I've done with it the tooth will be as sound as ever it was. All your other teeth are excellent."

Mrs Clowes arose violently out of the chair.

"Now just listen to me, please," she said. "I don't want any stopping; I won't have any stopping; I want that tooth out. I've already quarrelled with one dentist this afternoon because he refused to take it out. I came to you because you're young, and I thought you'd be more reasonable. Surely a body can decide whether she'll have a tooth out or not! It's my tooth. What's a dentist for? In my young days dentists never did anything else but take teeth out. All I wish to know is, will you take it out or will you not?"

"It's really a pity—"

"That's my affair, isn't it?" she stopped him, and moved towards her bonnet.

"If you insist," he said quickly, "I will extract."

"Well," she said, "if you don't call this insisting, what do you call insisting? Let me tell you I didn't have a wink of sleep last night!"

"Neither did I, in your confounded hotel!" he nearly retorted; but thought better of it.

The Mayoress resumed her seat, taking her gloves off.

" It's decided then? " she questioned.

" Certainly," said he. " Is your heart good? "

" Is my heart good? " she repeated. " Young man, what business is that of yours? It's my tooth I want you to deal with, not my heart."

" I must give you gas," said Mr Cowlishaw, faintly.

" Gas! " she exclaimed. " You'll give me no gas, young man. No! My heart is not good. I should die under gas. I couldn't bear the idea of gas. You must take it out without gas, and you mustn't hurt me. I'm a perfect baby, and you mustn't on any account hurt me."

The moment was crucial. Supposing that he refused—a promising career might be nipped in the bud; would, undoubtedly, be nipped in the bud. Whereas, if he accepted the task, the patronage of the aristocracy of Hanbridge was within his grasp. But the tooth was colossal, monumental. He estimated the length of its triple root at not less than ·75 inch.

" Very well, madam," he said, for he was a brave youngster.

But he was in a panic. He felt as though he were about to lead the charge of the Light Brigade. He wanted a stiff drink. (But dentists may not drink.) If he failed to wrench the monument out at the first pull the result would be absolute disaster; in an instant he would have ruined the practice which had cost him so dear. And could he hope not to fail with the first pull? At best he would hurt her indescribably. However, having consented, he was obliged to go through with the affair.

He took every possible precaution. He chose his most vicious instrument. He applied to the vicinity of the tooth the very latest substitute for cocaine; he prepared cotton wool and warm water in a glass. And at length, when he could delay the fatal essay no longer, he said:

"Now, I think we are ready."

"You won't hurt me?" she asked anxiously.

"Not a bit," he replied, with an admirable simulation of gaiety.

"Because if you do—"

He laughed. But it was a hysterical laugh. All his nerves were on end. And he was very conscious of having had no sleep during the previous night. He had a sick feeling. The room swam. He collected himself with a terrific effort.

"When I count one," he said, "I shall take hold; when I count two you must hold very tight to the chair; and when I count three, out it will come."

Then he encircled her head with his left arm—brutally, as dentists always are brutal in the thrilling crisis. "Wider!" he shouted.

And he took possession of that tooth with his fiendish contrivance of steel.

"One—two—"

He didn't know what he was doing.

There was no three. There was a slight shriek and a thud on the floor. Mrs Simeon Clowes jumped up and briskly rang a bell. The attendant rushed in. The attendant saw Mrs Clowes gurgling into a handkerchief, which she pressed to her mouth with one hand, while with the other, in which she held her bonnet, she was fanning the face of Mr Cowlishaw. Mr Cowlishaw had fainted from nervous excitement under fatigue. But his unconscious hand held the forceps; and the forceps, victorious, held the monumental tooth.

"O-o-pen the window," spluttered Mrs Clowes to the attendant. "He's gone off; he'll come to in a minute."

She was flattered. Mr Cowlishaw was for ever endeared to Mrs Clowes by this singular proof of her impressiveness. And a woman like that can make the fortune of half a dozen dentists.

CATCHING THE TRAIN

I

ARTHUR COTTERILL awoke. It was not exactly with a start that he awoke, but rather with
a swift premonition of woe and disaster. The strong,
bright glare from the patent incandescent street lamp
outside, which the lavish Corporation of Bursley kept
burning at the full till long after dawn in winter, illuminated the room (through the green blind) almost
as well as it illuminated Trafalgar Road. He clearly
distinguished every line of the form of his brother
Simeon, fast and double-locked in sleep in the next bed.
He saw also the open trunk by the dressing-table in
front of the window. Then he looked at the clock on
the mantelpiece, the silent witness of the hours. And a
pair of pincers seemed to clutch his heart, and an anvil
to drop on his stomach and rest heavily there, producing
an awful nausea. Why had he not looked at the clock
before? Was it possible that he had been awake even
five seconds without looking at the clock—the clock
upon which it seemed that his very life, more than his
life, depended? The clock showed ten minutes to
seven, and the train went at ten minutes past. And it
was quite ten minutes' walk to the station, and he had
to dress, and button those new boots, and finish packing—and the porter from the station was late in coming
for the trunk! But perhaps the porter had already
been; perhaps he had rung and rung, and gone away in
despair of making himself heard (for Mrs Hopkins slept
at the back of the house).

Something had to be done. Yet what could he do with those hard pincers pinching his soft, yielding heart, and that terrible anvil pressing on his stomach? He might even now, by omitting all but the stern necessities of his toilet, and by abandoning the trunk and his brother, just catch the train, the indispensable train. But somehow he could not move. Yet he was indubitably awake.

"Simeon!" he cried at length, and sat up.

The younger Cotterill did not stir.

"Sim!" he cried again, and, leaning over, shook the bed.

"What's up?" Simeon demanded, broad awake in a second, and, as usual, calm, imperturbable.

"We've missed the train! It's ten—eight—minutes to seven," said Arthur, in a voice which combined reproach and terror. And he sprang out of bed and began with hysteric fury to sort out his garments.

Simeon turned slowly on his side and drew a watch from under his pillow. Putting it close to his face, Simeon could just read the dial.

"It's all right," he said. "Still, you'd better get up. It's eight minutes to six. We've got an hour and eighteen minutes."

"What do you mean? That clock was right last night."

"Yes. But I altered it."

"When?"

"After you got into bed."

"I never saw you."

"No. But I altered it."

"Why?"

"To be on the safe side."

"Why didn't you tell me?"

"If I'd told you, I might just as well have not altered it. The man who puts a clock on and then goes gabbling all over the house about what he has done is an ass; in fact, to call him an ass is to flatter him."

Arthur tried to be angry.

" That's all very well—" he began to grumble.

But he could not be angry. The pincers and the anvil had suddenly ceased their torment. He was free. He was not a disgraced man. He would catch the train easily. All would be well. All would be as the practical Simeon had arranged that it should be. And in advancing the clock Simeon had acted for the best. Of course, it *was* safer to be on the safe side! In an affair such as that in which he was engaged, he felt, and he honestly admitted to himself, that he would have been nowhere without Simeon.

" Light the stove first, man," Simeon enjoined him. " There's been a change in the weather, I bet. It's as cold as the very deuce."

Yes, it was very cold. Arthur now noticed the cold. Strange—or rather not strange—that he had not noticed it before! He lit the gas stove, which exploded with its usual disconcerting *plop*, and a marvellously agreeable warmth began to charm his senses. He continued his dressing as near as possible to the source of this exquisite warmth. Then Simeon, in his leisurely manner, arose out of bed without a word, put his feet into slippers and lit the gas.

" I never thought of that," said Arthur, laughing nervously.

" Shows what a state you're in," said Simeon.

Simeon went to the window and peeped out into the silence of Trafalgar Road.

" Slight mist," he observed.

Arthur felt a faint return of the pincers and anvil.

" But it will clear off," Simeon added.

Then Simeon put on a dressing-gown and padded out of the room, and Arthur heard him knock at another door and call:

" Mrs Hopkins, Mrs Hopkins! " And then the sound of a door opening.

" She was dressed and just going downstairs," said Simeon when he returned to their bedroom. " Breakfast ready in ten minutes. She set the table last night. I told her to."

" Good! " Arthur murmured.

At sixteen minutes past six they were both dressed, and Simeon was showing Arthur that Simeon alone knew how to pack a trunk. At twenty minutes past six the trunk was packed, locked and strapped.

" What about getting the confounded thing downstairs? " Arthur asked.

"When the porter comes," said Simeon, " he and I will do that. It's too heavy for you to handle."

At six twenty-one they were having breakfast in the little dining-room, by the heat of another gas-stove. And Arthur felt that all was well, and that in postponing their departure till that morning in order not to upset the immemorial Christmas dinner of their Aunt Sarah, they had done rightly. At half-past six they had, between them, drunk five cups of tea and eaten four eggs, four slices of bacon, and about a pound and a half of bread. Simeon, with what was surely an exaggeration of imperturbability, charged his pipe, and began to smoke. They had forty minutes in which to catch the Loop-Line train, even if it was prompt. There would then be forty minutes to wait at Knype for the London express, which arrived at Euston considerably before noon. After which there would be a clear ninety minutes before the business itself—and less than a quarter of a mile to walk! Yes, there was a rich and generous margin for all conceivable delays and accidents.

" The porter ought to be coming," said Simeon. It was twenty minutes to seven, and he was brushing his hat.

Now such a remark from that personification of

calm, that living denial of worry, Simeon, was decidedly
unsettling to Arthur. By chance, Mrs Hopkins came
into the room just then to assure herself that the young
men whose house she kept desired nothing.

"Mrs Hopkins," Simeon asked, "you didn't forget
to call at the station last night?"

"Oh no, Mr Simeon," said she; "I saw the
second porter, Merrith. He knows me. At least, I
know his mother—known her forty year—and he
promised me he wouldn't forget. Besides, he never
has forgot, has he? I told him particular to bring his
barrow."

It was true the porter never had forgotten! And
many times had he transported Simeon's luggage to
Bleakridge Station. Simeon did a good deal of commercial travelling for the firm of A. & S. Cotterill, teapot makers, Bursley. In many commercial hotels he
was familiarly known as Teapot Cotterill.

The brothers were reassured by Mrs Hopkins.
There was half an hour to the time of the train—and
the station only ten minutes off. Then the chiming
clock in the hall struck the third quarter.

"That clock right?" Arthur nervously inquired,
assuming his overcoat.

"It's a minute late," said Simeon, assuming *his*
overcoat.

And at that word "late," the pincers and the anvil
revisited Arthur. Even the confidence of Mrs Hopkins
in the porter was shaken. Arthur looked at Simeon,
depending on him. It was imperative that they should
catch the train, and it was imperative that the trunk
should catch the train. Everything depended on a
porter. Arthur felt that all his future career, his happiness, his honour, his life depended on a porter. And,
after all, even porters at a pound a week are human.
Therefore, Arthur looked at Simeon.

Simeon walked through the kitchen into the backyard. In a shed there an old barrow was lying. He drew out the barrow, and ticklishly wheeled it into the house, as far as the foot of the stairs.

"Mrs Hopkins," he called. "And you too!" he glanced at Arthur.

"What are you going to do?" Arthur demanded.

"Wheel the trunk to the station myself, of course," Simeon replied. "If we meet the porter on the way, so much the better for us . . . and so much the worse for him!" he added.

II

It was just as dark as though it had been midnight—dark and excessively cold; not a ray of hope in the sky; not a sign of life in the street. All Bursley, and, indeed, all the Five Towns, were sleeping off the various consequences of Christmas on the human frame. Trafalgar Road, with its double row of lamps, each exactly like that one in front of the house of the Cotterills, stretched downwards into the dead heart of Bursley, and upwards over the brow of the hill into space. And although Arthur Cotterill knew Trafalgar Road as well as Mrs Hopkins knew the hundred and twenty-first Psalm, the effect of the scene on him was most uncanny. He watched Simeon persuade the loaded barrow down the step into the tiny front garden, not daring to help him, because Simeon did not like to be helped by clumsy people in delicate operations. Mrs Hopkins was rapidly pouring all the goodness of her soul into his ear, when Simeon and the barrow reached the pavement, and Simeon staggered and recovered himself.

"Look out, Arthur," Simeon cried. "The road's like glass. It's rained in the night, and now it's freezing. Come along."

Arthur bade adieu to Mrs Hopkins.

" Eh, Mr Arthur," said she. " Things'll be different when ye come back, this time a month."

He said nothing. The pincers and the anvil were at him again. He thought of falls, torn garments, broken legs.

Simeon lifted the arms of the barrow, and then dropped them.

" Have you got it? " he demanded of Arthur.

" Got what? "

" *It.*"

" Yes," said Arthur, comprehending.

" Are you sure? Show it me. Better give it me. It will be safer with me."

Arthur unbuttoned his overcoat, took off his left glove, and drew from one of his pockets a small, bright object, which shone under the street lamp. Simeon took it silently. Then he definitely seized the arms of the barrow, and the procession started up the street.

No time had been lost, for Simeon had an extraordinary gift of celerity. It was eleven minutes to seven. Nevertheless, Arthur felt the pincers, and the feel of the pincers made him look at his watch.

" See here," said Simeon, briefly. " You needn't worry. *We shall catch that train.* We've got twenty minutes, and we shall get to the station in nine." The exertion of wheeling the barrow over what was practically a sheet of rough ice made him speak in short gasps.

Impossible for the pincers and the anvil to remain in face of that assured, almost god-like tone!

" Good! " murmured Arthur. " By Jove, but it's cold though! "

" I've never been hotter in my life," said Simeon, puffing. " Except in my hands."

" Can't I take it for a bit? "

" No, you can't," said Simeon. At the robust finality of the refusal Arthur laughed. Then Simeon laughed. The party became gay. The pincers and the anvil were gone for ever.   Simeon turned gingerly into Pollard Street—half-way to the station.   They had but to descend Pollard Street and climb the path across the cinder-heaps beyond, and they would be, as it were, in harbour.   In Pollard Street Simeon had the happy idea of taking to the roadway.   It was rougher, and, therefore, less dangerous, than the pavement.   At intervals he shoved the wheel of the barrow by main force over a stone.

"Put my hat straight, will you? " he asked of Arthur, and Arthur obeyed.   It was becoming a task under the winter stars.

Then Arthur happened to notice the wheel of the barrow—its sole wheel.

" I say," he said, " what's up with that wheel? "

" It's rocky, that's what that wheel is," replied Simeon.   " I hope it will hold out."

Instead of pushing the barrow he was now holding it back, down the slant of Pollard Street.   The mist had cleared.   And Arthur could see the red gleam of a signal in the neighbourhood of the station.   But now the pincers and the anvil were at him again, for Simeon's tone was alarming.   It indicated that the wobbling wheel of the barrow might not hold out.

The catastrophe happened when they were climbing the cinder-slope and within two hundred yards of the little station.   Simeon was propelling with all his might, and he propelled the wheel against half a brick.   The wheel collapsed.   There was a splintering even of the main timbers of the vehicle as the immense weight of the trunk crashed to the solid earth.

Simeon fell, and rose with difficulty, standing on one leg, and terribly grimacing.

He said nothing, but consulted his watch by the aid of a fusee.

" We must carry it," Arthur suggested wildly.

" We can't carry it up here.   It's much too heavy."

Arthur remembered the tremendous weight of even his share of it as they had slid it down the stairs.

No. It could not be carried.

" Besides," said Simeon, " I've sprained my ankle, I fear." And he sat down on the trunk.

" What are we to do? " Arthur asked tragically.

" Do? Why, it's perfectly simple! You must go without me. Anyhow, run to the station, and try to get the porter down here with another barrow."

Man of infinite calm, of infinite resource. Though the pincers and the anvil were horribly torturing him at that moment, Arthur could not but admire his younger brother's astounding *sangfroid*.

And he set off.

" Here! " Simeon called him peremptorily. " Take this—in case you don't come back."

And he handed him the small bright object.

" But I must come back. I can't possibly go without the trunk. All my things are in it."

" I know that, man. *But perhaps you'll have to go without it.* Hurry! "

Arthur ran. He encountered the senior porter at the gate of the station.

" Where's Merrith? " he began. " He was to have—"

" Merrith's mother is dead—died at five o'clock," said the senior porter. " And I'm here all alone."

Arthur stopped as if shot.

" Well," he recovered himself. " Lend me a barrow."

" I shall lend ye no barrow. It's against the rules. Since they transferred our stationmaster to Clegg there's been an inspector down here welly [well nigh] every day."

" But I must *have* a barrow."

" I shall lend ye no barrow," said the senior porter, a brute.

A signal close to the signal-box clattered down from red to green.

" Her's signalled," said the senior porter. " Are ye travelling by her? "

Arthur had to decide in a moment. Must he or must he not abandon Simeon and the trunk? The train, a procession of lights, could be seen in the distance under the black sky. He gave one glance in the direction of Simeon and the trunk, and then entered the station.

Simeon had been right. He did catch the train.

It was fortunate that there was a wide margin between the advertised time of arrival of the Loop-Line train at Knype and the departure therefrom of the London express. For, beyond Hanbridge, the Loop-Line train came to a standstill, and obstinately remained at a standstill for near upon forty minutes. Dawn began and completed itself while that train reposed there. Things got to such a point that, despite the intense cold, the few passengers stuck their heads out of the windows and kept them there. Arthur suffered unspeakably. He imparted his awful anxiety to an old man in the same compartment. And the old man said:

" They always keep the express waiting for the Loop. Moreover, you've plenty o' time yet."

He knew that the Loop was supposed to catch the express, and that in actual practice it did catch it. He knew that there was yet enough time. Still, he continued to suffer. He continued to believe, at the bottom of his heart, that on this morning, of all mornings, the Loop would not catch the express.

However, he was wrong. The Loop caught the express, though it was a nearish thing. He dashed down into the subterranean passage at Knype Station, reappeared on the up-platform, ran to the fore-part of the express, which was in and waiting, and jumped; a porter banged the door, a guard inspired the driver by a tune on a whistle, and off went the express.   Arthur was now safe.   Nothing ever happened to a North-Western express.   He was safe.   He was shorn of his luggage (almost, but not quite, indispensable) and of Simeon; but he was safe.   He could not be disgraced in the world's eye.   He thought of poor, gallant, imperturbable, sprained Simeon freezing on the trunk in the middle of the cinder-waste.

III

THE train stopped momentarily at a station which he thought to be Lichfield.   Then (out of his waking dreams) it seemed to him that Lichfield Station had strangely grown in length, and just as the train was drawing out he saw the word " Stafford " in immense white enamelled letters on a blue ground.   There was nobody else in the compartment.   His heart and stomach in a state of frightful torture, he sprang out of it—not on to the line, but into the corridor (for it was a corridor train) and into the next compartment, where were seated two men.

" Is this the London train? " he demanded, not concealing his terror.

" No, it isn't.   It's the Birmingham train," said one of the men fiercely—a sort of a Levite.

" Great heavens! " ejaculated Arthur Cotterill.

" You ought to inquire before you get into a train," said the Levite.

" The fact is," said the other man, who was perhaps a cousin of a Good Samaritan, " the express from Manchester is split up at Knype—one part for London, and the other part for Birmingham."

" I know that," said Arthur Cotterill.

" Ever since I can remember the London part has gone off first."

" Of course," said Arthur; " I've travelled by it lots of times."

" But they altered it only last week."

" I only just caught the train," Arthur breathed.

" Seems to me you didn't catch it," said the Levite.

" *I must be in London before two o'clock,*" said Arthur, and he said it so solemnly, he said it with so much of his immortal soul, that even the Levite was startled out of his callous indifference.

" There are expresses from Birmingham to London that do the journey in two hours," said he.

" Let us see," said the cousin of a Good Samaritan, kindly, opening a bag and producing Bradshaw.

And he explained to Arthur that the train reached New Street, Birmingham, at 10.45, and that, by a singular good fortune, a very fast express left New Street at 11.40, and arrived at Euston at 1.45.

Arthur thanked him and retired with his pincers and anvil to his own compartment.

He was a ruined man, a disgraced man. The loss of his trunk was now nothing. At the best he would be over half an hour late, and it was quite probable that he would be too late altogether. He pictured the other people waiting, waiting for him anxiously, as minute after minute passed, until the fatal hour struck. The whole affair was unthinkable. Simeon's fault, of course. Simeon had convinced him that to go up to London on Christmas Day would be absurd, whereas it was now evident that to go up to London on Christmas Day was obviously the only prudent thing to do. Awful!

The train to Birmingham was in an ironical mood, for it ran into New Street to the very minute of the time-table. Thus Arthur had fifty-five futile minutes to pass. At another time New Street, as the largest single station in the British Empire, might have interested him. But now it was no more interesting than Purgatory when you know where you are ultimately going to. He sought

out the telegraph-office, and telegraphed to London—
a despairing, yet a manly telegram.   Then he sought out
the refreshment-room, and ordered a whisky.   He was
just putting the whisky to his lips when he remembered that if, after all, he did arrive in time, the whisky
would amount to a serious breach of manners.   So he
put the glass down untasted, and the barmaid justifiably
felt herself to have been insulted.

He watched the slow formation of the Birmingham-
London express.   He also watched the various clocks.
For whole hours the fingers of the clocks never budged,
and even then they would show an advance of only a
minute or two.

" Is this the train for London? " he asked an inspector at 11.35.

" Can't you see? " said the inspector, brightly.   As a
fact, " Euston " was written all over the train.   But
Arthur wanted to be sure this time.

The express departed from Birmingham with the
nicest exactitude, and covered itself with glory as far as
Watford, when it ran into a mist, and lost more than a
quarter of an hour, besides ruining Arthur's career.

Arthur arrived in London at one minute past two.
He got out of the train with no plan.   The one feasible
enterprise seemed to be that of suicide.

" Come on, now," said a voice—a voice that staggered Arthur.   It was a man with a crutch who spoke.
It was Simeon.   " Come on, quick, and don't talk too
much!   To the hotel first."   Simeon hobbled forward
rapidly, and somehow (he could not explain how) the
anvil and pincers had left Arthur.

" I got hold of a milk-cart with a sharpened horse,
and drove to Knype.   Horse fell once, but he picked
himself up again.   Cost me a sovereign.   Only just
caught the train.   Shouldn't have caught it if they hadn't
sent off the Birmingham part before the London part.
I was astonished, I can tell you, not to find you at

Euston. Went to the hotel. Found 'em all waiting, of course, and practically weeping over a telegram from you. However, I soon arranged things. Had to buy a crutch. . . . Here, boy, lift!" They were in the hotel.

On a bed all Arthur's finest clothes were laid out. The famous trunk was at the foot of the bed.

"Quick!"

"But 'ook here!" Arthur remonstrated. "It's after two l..w."

"Well, if it is? We've got till three. I've arranged with the mandarin chap for a quarter to three."

"I thought these things couldn't occur after two o'clock—by law."

"That's what's the matter with you," said Simeon; "you think too much. The two o'clock law was altered years ago. Had anything to eat?" He was helping Arthur with buttons.

"No."

"I expected not. Here! Swallow this whisky."

"Not I!" Arthur protested in a startled tone.

"Why not?"

"Because I shall have to kiss her after the ceremony."

"Bosh!" said Simeon. "Drink it. Besides, there's no kissing in a Registry Office. You're thinking of a church. I wish you wouldn't think so much. Here! Now the necktie, you cuckoo!"

In three minutes they were driving rapidly through the London mist towards the other sex, and in a quarter of an hour there was one bachelor the less in this vale of tears.

THE WIDOW OF THE
BALCONY

I

THEY stood at the window of her boudoir in the new
house which Stephen Cheswardine had recently
bought at Sneyd. The stars were pursuing their orbits
overhead in a clear dark velvet sky, except to the north,
where the industrial fires and smoke of the Five Towns
had completely put them out. But even these distant
signs of rude labour had a romantic aspect, and did not
impair the general romance of the scene. Charlie had
loved her; he loved her still; and she gave him odd
minutes of herself when she could, just to keep him
alive. Moreover, there was the log fire richly crackling
in the well-grate of the boudoir; there was the feminine-
ness of the boudoir (dimly lit), and the soft splendour of
her gown, and behind all that, pervading the house,
the gay rumour of the party. And in front of them the
window-panes, and beyond the window-panes the stars
in their orbits. Doubtless it was such influences which,
despite several degrees of frost outside, gave to Charlie
Woodruff's thoughts an Italian, or Spanish, turn. He
said:

"Stephen ought to have this window turned into a
French window, and build you a balcony. It could
easily be done. Just the view for a balcony. You can
see Sneyd Lake from here." (You could. People were
skating on it.)

He did not add that you could see the Sneyd Golf
Links from there, and *vice versa*. I doubt if the idea

occurred to him, but as he was an active member of the Sneyd Golf Club it would certainly have presented itself to him in due season.

" What a lovely scheme! " Vera exclaimed enthusiastically.

It appealed to her. It appealed to all that was romantic in her bird-like soul. She did not see the links; she did not see the lake; she just saw herself in exquisite frocks, lightly lounging on the balcony in high summer, and dreaming of her own beauty.

" And have a striped awning," she said.

" Yes," he said. " Make Stephen do it."

" I will," she said.

At that moment Stephen came in, with his bald head and his forty years.

" I say! " he demanded. " What are you up to? "

" We were just watching the skaters," said Vera.

" And the wonders of the night," said Charlie, chuckling characteristically. He always laughed at himself. He was a philosopher. He and Stephen had been fast friends from infancy.

" Well, you'd just better skate downstairs," said Stephen. (No romance in Stephen! He was netting a couple of thousand a year out of the manufacture of toilet-sets, in all that smoke to the north. How could you expect him to be romantic?)

" Charlie was saying how nice it would be for me to have a French window here, and a marble balcony," Vera remarked. It had not taken her long to think of marble. " You must do it for me, Steve."

" Bosh! " said Stephen. " That's just like you, Charlie. What an ass you are! "

" Oh, but you *must !* " said Vera, in that tone which meant business, and which also meant trouble for Stephen.

" *She's* come," Stephen announced curtly, determined to put trouble off.

" Oh, has she? " cried Vera.   " I thought you said she wouldn't."

" She hesitated, because she was afraid.   But she's come after all," Stephen answered.

" What fun! " Vera murmured.

And ran off downstairs back again into the midst of the black coats and the white toilettes and the holly-clad electricity of her Christmas gathering.

II

THE news that *she* had come was all over the noisy house in a minute, and it had the astonishing effect of producing what might roughly be described as a silence.   It stopped the reckless waltzing of the piano in the drawing-room; it stopped the cackle incident to cork-pool in the billiard-room; it even stopped a good deal of the whispering under the Chinese lanterns beneath the stairs and in the alcove at the top of the stairs.   What it did not stop was the consumption of mince-pies and claret-cup in the small breakfast-room; people mumbled about *her* between munches.

She, having been sustained with turkey and beer in the kitchen, was led by the backstairs up to Vera's very boudoir, that being the only suitable room.   And there she waited.   She was a woman of about forty-five; fat, unfair (in the physical sense), and untidy.   Of her hands the less said the better.   She had probably never visited a professional coiffeur in her life.   Her form was straitly confined in an atrocious dress of linsey-woolsey, and she wore an apron that was neither white nor black. Her boots were commodious.   After her meal she was putting a hat-pin to a purpose which hat-pins do not usually serve.   She gained an honest living by painting green leaves on yellow wash-basins in Stephen's re-nowned earthenware manufactory.   She spoke the dialect of the people. She had probably never heard of Christian Science, bridge, Paquin, Panhard, Father Vaughan, the fall of consols, osprey plumes, nor the new theology. Nobody in the house knew her name; even Stephen had forgotten it. And yet the whole house was agog concerning her.

The fact was that in the painting-shops of the various manufactories where she had painted green leaves on yellow wash-basins (for in all her life she had done little else) she possessed a reputation as a prophet, seer, oracle, fortune-teller—what you will. Polite persons would perhaps never have heard of her reputation, the toiling millions of the Five Towns being of a rather secretive nature in such matters, had not the subject of fortune-telling been made prominent in the district by the celebrated incident of the fashionable palmist. The fashionable palmist, having thriven enormously in Bond Street, had undertaken a tour through the provinces and had stopped several days at Hanbridge (our metropolis), where he had an immense vogue until the Hanbridge police hit on the singular idea of prosecuting him for an unlawful vagabond. Stripped of twenty pounds odd in the guise of a fine and costs, and having narrowly missed the rigours of our county jail, that fashionable palmist and soothsayer had returned to Bond Street full of hate and respect for Midland justice, which fears not and has a fist like a navvy's. The attention of the Five Towns had thus been naturally drawn to fortune-telling in general. And it was deemed that in securing a local celebrity (quite an amateur, and therefore, it was uncertainly hoped, on the windy side of the law) for the diversion of his Christmas party Stephen Cheswardine had done a stylish and original thing.

Of course no one in the house believed in fortune-telling. Oh no! But as an amusement it was amusing. As fun, it was fun. She did her business with tea-leaves: so the tale ran. This was not considered to be very dis-

tinguished.   A crystal, or even cards, or the anatomy of
a sacrificed fowl, would have been better than tea-leaves;
tea-leaves were decidedly lower class.   And yet, despite
these drawbacks, when the question arose who should
first visit the witch of Endor, there was a certain
hesitation.

" You go! "

" No, *you* go."

" Oh! *I'm* not going," (a superior laugh), etc.

At last it was decided that Jack Hall and Cissy
Woodruff (Charlie's much younger sister), the pair having been engaged to be married for exactly three days,
should make the first call.   They ascended, blushing
and brave.   In a moment Jack Hall descended alone,
nervously playing with the silk handkerchief that was
lodged in his beautiful white waistcoat.   The witch of
Endor had informed him that she never received the two
sexes together, and had expelled him.   This incident
greatly   enhanced   the   witch's   reputation.   Then
Stephen happened to mention that he had heard that
the woman's mother, and her grandmother before her,
had   been   fortune-tellers.   Somehow that statement
seemed to strike everybody full in the face; it set a seal
on the authority of the witch, made her genuine.   And
an uncanny feeling seemed to spread through the house
as the house waited for Cissy to reappear.

" She's very *good*," said Cissy, on emerging.   " She
told me all sorts of things."

A group formed at the foot of the stairs.

" What did she tell you? "

" Well, she said I must expect a very important
letter in a few days, and much would depend on it,
and next year there will be a big removal, and a large
lumbering piece of furniture, and I shall go a journey
over water.   It's quite right, you know.   I suppose the
letter's from grandma; I hope it is, anyway.   And if
we go to France—"

Thenceforward the witch without a name held continuous receptions in the boudoir, and the boudoir gradually grew into an abode of mystery and strangeness, hypnotizing the entire house. People went thither; people came back; and those who had not been pictured to themselves something very incantatory, and little by little they made up their minds to go. Some thought the woman excellent, others said it was all rot. But none denied that it was interesting. None could possibly deny that the fortune-telling had killed every other diversion provided by the hospitable Stephen and Vera (except the refreshments). The most scornful scoffers made a concession and kindly consented to go to the boudoir. Stephen went. Charlie went. Even the Mayor of Hanbridge went (not being on the borough Bench that night).

But Vera would not go. A genuine fear was upon her. Christmases had always been unlucky for her peace of mind. And she was highly superstitious. Yet she wanted to go; she was burning to go, all the while assuring her guests that nothing would induce her to go. The party drew to a close, and pair by pair the revellers drove off, or walked, into the romantic night. Then Stephen told Vera to give the woman half-a-sovereign and let her depart, for it was late. And in paying the half-sovereign to the woman Vera was suddenly overcome by temptation and asked for her fortune. The woman's grimy simplicity, her smiling face, the commonness of her teapot, her utter unlikeness to anything in the first act of *Macbeth*, encouraged Vera to believe in her magic powers. Vera's hand trembled as, under instructions, she tipped the tea-leaves into the saucer.

" Ay! " said the witch, in broadest Staffordshire, running her objectionable hand up and down the buttons of her linsey-wolsey bodice, and gently agitating the saucer. " Theer's a widder theer." [There's a

widow there.]   "Yo'll be havin' a letter, or it mit be a
talligram—"

Vera wouldn't hear any more. Her one fear in life was
the fear of Stephen's death (though she *did* console Charlie
with nice smiles and lots of *tête-à-tête*), and here was this
fiendish witch directly foreseeing the dreadful event.

III

EVERY day for many days Stephen expected to have to
take part in a pitched battle about the proposed balcony.
The sweet enemy, however, did not seem to be in fighting form.   It is true that she mentioned the balcony,
but she mentioned it in quite a reasonable spirit.   Astounding as the statement may appear to any personal
acquaintance of Vera's, Vera showed a capacity to perceive that there were two sides to the question.   When
Stephen pointed out that balconies were unsuited to the
English climate, she almost agreed.   When he said that
balconies were dangerous and that to have a safe one
would necessitate the strengthening of the wall, she
merely replied, with wonderful meekness, that she only
weighed seven stone twelve.   When he informed her
that the breakfast-room, already not too light, was
underneath the proposed balcony, which would further
darken it, she kept an angelic silence.   And when he
showed her that the view from the proposed balcony
would in any case be marred by the immense pall of
Five Towns smoke to the south, she still kept an angelic
silence.

Stephen could not understand it.

Nor was this all. She became extraordinarily
solicitous for his welfare, especially in the matter of
health.   She wrapped him up when he went out, and
unpacked him when he came in.   She cautioned him
against draughts, overwork, microbes, and dietary in-

discretions. Thanks to regular boxing exercise, his old dyspepsia had almost entirely disappeared, but this did not prevent her from watching every mouthful that vanished under the portals of his moustache. And she superintended his boxing too. She made a point of being present whenever he and Charlie boxed, and she would force Charlie to cease fighting at the oddest moments. She was flat against having a motor-car; she compelled Stephen to drive to the station in the four-wheeler instead of in the high dog-cart. Indeed, from the way she guarded him, he might have been the one frail life that stood between England and anarchy.

And she was always so kind, in a rather melancholy, resigned, wistful fashion.

No. Stephen could *not* understand it.

There came a time when Stephen could neither understand it nor stand it. And he tried to worm out of her her secret. But he could not. The fascinating little liar stoutly stuck to it that nothing was the matter with her, and that she had nothing on her mind. Stephen knew differently. He consulted Charlie Woodruff. She had not made a confidant of Charlie. Charlie was exactly as much in the dark as Stephen. Then Stephen (I regret to have to say it) took to swearing. For instance, he swore when she hid all his thin socks and so obliged him to continue with his thick ones. And one day he swore when, in answer to his query why she was pale, she said she didn't know.

He thus, without expecting to do so, achieved a definite climax.

For she broke out. She ceased in half a second to be pale. She gave him with cutting candour all that had been bottled up in her entrancing bosom. She told him that the witch had foreseen her a widow (which was the same thing as prophesying his death), and that she had done, and was doing, all that the ingenuity of a loving heart could suggest to keep him alive in spite of the prediction, but that, in face of his infamous brutality, she should do no more; that if he chose to die and leave her a widow he might die and leave her a widow for all she cared; in brief, that she had done with him.

When she had become relatively calm Stephen addressed her calmly, and even ingratiatingly.

" I'm sorry," he said, and added, " but you know you did say that you were hiding nothing from me."

" Of course," she retorted, " because I *was*." Her arguments were usually on this high plane of logic.

" And you ought not to be so superstitious," Stephen proceeded.

" Well," said she, with truth, " one never knows." And she wiped away a tear and showed the least hint of an inclination to kiss him. " And anyhow my only anxiety was for you."

" Do you really believe what that woman said? " Stephen asked.

" Well," she repeated, " one never knows."

" Because if you do, I'll tell you something."

" What? " Vera demanded.

At this juncture Stephen committed an error of tactics. He might have let her continue in the fear of his death, and thus remained on velvet (subject to occasional outbreaks) for the rest of his life. But he gave himself utterly away.

" She told *me* I should live till I was ninety," said he. " So you can't be a widow for quite half a century, and you'll be eighty yourself then."

IV

WITHIN twenty-four hours she was at him about the balcony.

" The summer will be lovely," she said, in reply to his argument about climate.

"Rubbish," she said, in reply to his argument about safety.

"Who cares for your old breakfast-room?" she said, in reply to his argument about darkness at breakfast.

"We will have trees planted on that side—big elms," she said, in reply to his argument about the smoke of the Five Towns spoiling the view.

Whereupon Stephen definitely and clearly enunciated that he should not build a balcony.

"Oh, but you must!" she protested.

"A balcony is quite impossible," said Stephen, with his firmest masculinity.

"You'll see if it's impossible," said she, "*when I'm that widow.*"

The curious may be interested to know that she has already begun to plant trees.

THE CAT AND CUPID

I

THE secret history of the Ebag marriage is now printed for the first time. The Ebag family, who prefer their name to be accented on the first syllable, once almost ruled Oldcastle, which is a clean and conceited borough, with long historical traditions, on the very edge of the industrial, democratic and unclean Five Towns. The Ebag family still lives in the grateful memory of Oldcastle, for no family ever did more to preserve the celebrated Oldcastilian superiority in social, moral and religious matters over the vulgar Five Towns. The episodes leading to the Ebag marriage could only have happened in Oldcastle. By which I mean merely that they could not have happened in any of the Five Towns. In the Five Towns that sort of thing does not occur. I don't know why, but it doesn't. The people are too deeply interested in football, starting prices, rates, public parks, sliding scales, excursions to Blackpool, and municipal shindies, to concern themselves with organists as such. In the Five Towns an organist may be a sanitary inspector or an auctioneer on Mondays. In Oldcastle an organist is an organist, recognized as such in the streets. No one ever heard of an organist in the Five Towns being taken up and petted by a couple of old ladies. But this may occur at Oldcastle. It, in fact, did.

The scandalous circumstances which led to the disappearance from the Oldcastle scene of Mr Skerritt, the original organist of St Placid, have no relation to the

present narrative, which opens when the ladies Ebag
began to seek for a new organist.   The new church of
St Placid owed its magnificent existence to the Ebag
family.   The apse had been given entirely by old
Caiaphas Ebag (ex-M.P., now a paralytic sufferer) at a
cost of twelve thousand pounds; and his was the
original idea of building the church.   When, owing to
the decline of the working man's interest in beer, and
one or two other things, Caiaphas lost nearly the whole
of his fortune, which had been gained by honest labour
in mighty speculations, he rather regretted the church;
he would have preferred twelve thousand in cash to a
view of the apse from his bedroom window; but he was
man enough never to complain.   He lived, after his
misfortunes, in a comparatively small house with his
two daughters, Mrs Ebag and Miss Ebag.   These two
ladies are the heroines of the tale.

Mrs Ebag had married her cousin, who had died.
She possessed about six hundred a year of her own.
She was two years older than her sister, Miss Ebag, a
spinster.   Miss Ebag was two years younger than Mrs
Ebag.   No further information as to their respective
ages ever leaked out.   Miss Ebag had a little money of
her own from her deceased mother, and Caiaphas had
the wreck of his riches.   The total income of the household was not far short of a thousand a year, but of this
quite two hundred a year was absorbed by young Edith
Ebag, Mrs Ebag's step-daughter (for Mrs Ebag had
been her husband's second choice).   Edith, who was
notorious as a silly chit and spent most of her time in
London and other absurd places, formed no part of the
household, though she visited it occasionally.   The
household consisted of old Caiaphas, bedridden, and his
two daughters and Goldie.   Goldie was the tomcat, so
termed by reason of his splendid tawniness.   Goldie
had more to do with the Ebag marriage than anyone or
anything, except the weathercock on the top of the

house. This may sound queer, but is as naught to the queerness about to be unfolded.

II

IT cannot be considered unnatural that Mrs and Miss Ebag, with the assistance of the vicar, should have managed the affairs of the church.   People nicknamed them " the churchwardens," which was not quite nice, having regard to the fact that their sole aim was the truest welfare of the church.   They and the vicar, in a friendly and effusive way, hated each other.   Sometimes they got the better of the vicar, and, less often, he got the better of them.   In the choice of a new organist they won.   Their candidate was Mr Carl Ullman, the artistic orphan.

Mr Carl Ullman is the hero of the tale.   The son of one of those German designers of earthenware who at intervals come and settle in the Five Towns for the purpose of explaining fully to the inhabitants how inferior England is to Germany, he had an English mother, and he himself was violently English.   He spoke English like an Englishman and German like an Englishman.   He could paint, model in clay, and play three musical instruments, including the organ.   His one failing was that he could never earn enough to live on. It seemed as if he was always being drawn by an invisible string towards the workhouse door.   Now and then he made half a sovereign extra by deputizing on the organ.   In such manner had he been introduced to the Ebag ladies.   His romantic and gloomy appearance had attracted them, with the result that they had asked him to lunch after the service, and he had remained with them till the evening service.   During the visit they had learnt that his grandfather had been Court Councillor in the Kingdom of Saxony.   Afterwards they often

said to each other how ideal it would be if only Mr
Skerritt might be removed and Carl Ullman take his
place. And when Mr Skerritt actually was removed,
by his own wickedness, they regarded it as almost an
answer to prayer, and successfully employed their
powerful interest on behalf of Carl. The salary was a
hundred a year. Not once in his life had Carl earned
a hundred pounds in a single year. For him the situation meant opulence. He accepted it, but calmly,
gloomily. Romantic gloom was his joy in life. He
said with deep melancholy that he was sure he could not
find a convenient lodging in Oldcastle. And the ladies
Ebag then said that he must really come and spend a
few days with them and Goldie and papa until he was
" suited." He said that he hated to plant himself on
people, and yielded to the request. The ladies Ebag
fussed around his dark-eyed and tranquil pessimism,
and both of them instantly grew younger—a curious but
authentic phenomenon. They adored his playing, and
they were enchanted to discover that his notions about
hymn tunes agreed with theirs, and by consequence dis-
agreed with the vicar's. In the first week or two they
scored off the vicar five times, and the advantage of
having your organist in your own house grew very
apparent. They were also greatly impressed by his
gentleness with Goldie and by his intelligent interest in
serious questions.

One day Miss Ebag said timidly to her sister: " It's
just six months to-day."

" What do you mean, sister? " asked Mrs Ebag, self-
consciously.

" Since Mr Ullman came."

" So it is! " said Mrs Ebag, who was just as well
aware of the date as the spinster was aware of it.

They said no more. The position was the least bit
delicate. Carl had found no lodging. He did not offer
to go. They did not want him to go. He did not offer

to pay. And really he cost them nothing except laundry, whisky and fussing. How could they suggest that he should pay? He lived amidst them like a beautiful mystery, and all were seemingly content. Carl was probably saving the whole of his salary, for he never bought clothes and he did not smoke. The ladies Ebag simply did what they liked about hymn-tunes.

III

You would have thought that no outsider would find a word to say, and you would have been mistaken. The fact that Mrs Ebag was two years older than Miss and Miss two years younger than Mrs Ebag; the fact that old Caiaphas was, for strong reasons, always in the house; the fact that the ladies were notorious cat-idolaters; the fact that the reputation of the Ebag family was and had ever been spotless; the fact that the Ebag family had given the apse and practically created the entire church; all these facts added together did not prevent the outsider from finding a word to say.

At first words were not said; but looks were looked, and coughs were coughed. Then someone, strolling into the church of a morning while Carl Ullman was practising, saw Miss Ebag sitting in silent ecstasy in a corner. And a few mornings later the same someone, whose curiosity had been excited, veritably saw Mrs Ebag in the organ-loft with Carl Ullman, but no sign of Miss Ebag. It was at this juncture that words began to be said.

Words! Not complete sentences! The sentences were never finished. " Of course, it's no affair of mine, but—" " I wonder that people like the Ebags should—" " Not that I should ever dream of hinting that—" " First one and then the other—well! " " I'm sure

that if either Mrs or Miss Ebag had the slightest idea
they'd at once—" And so on. Intangible gossamer
criticism, floating in the air!

IV

ONE evening—it was precisely the first of June—when
a thunderstorm was blowing up from the south-west,
and scattering the smoke of the Five Towns to the four
corners of the world, and making the weathercock of
the house of the Ebags creak, the ladies Ebag and Carl
Ullman sat together as usual in the drawing-room.
The French window was open, but banged to at intervals. Carl Ullman had played the piano and the ladies
Ebag—Mrs Ebag, somewhat comfortably stout and
Miss Ebag spare—were talking very well and sensibly
about the influence of music on character. They invariably chose such subjects for conversation. Carl
was chiefly silent, but now and then, after a sip of
whisky, he would say " Yes " with impressiveness and
stare gloomily out of the darkening window. The ladies
Ebag had a remarkable example of the influence of
music on character in the person of Edith Ebag. It
appeared that Edith would never play anything but
waltzes—Waldteufel's for choice—and that the foolish
frivolity of her flyaway character was a direct consequence of this habit. Carl felt sadly glad, after hearing the description of Edith's carryings-on, that Edith
had chosen to live far away.

And then the conversation languished and died with
the daylight, and a certain self-consciousness obscured
the social atmosphere. For a vague rumour of the
chatter of the town had penetrated the house, and the
ladies Ebag, though they scorned chatter, were affected
by it; Carl Ullman, too. It had the customary effect
of such chatter; it fixed the thoughts of those chatted

about on matters which perhaps would not otherwise have occupied their attention.

The ladies Ebag said to themselves: "We are no longer aged nineteen. We are moreover living with our father. If he is bedridden, what then? This gossip connecting our names with that of Mr Ullman is worse than baseless; it is preposterous. We assert positively that we have no designs of any kind on Mr Ullman."

Nevertheless, by dint of thinking about that gossip, the naked idea of a marriage with Mr Ullman soon ceased to shock them. They could gaze at it without going into hysterics.

As for Carl, he often meditated upon his own age, which might have been anything between thirty and forty-five, and upon the mysterious ages of the ladies, and upon their goodness, their charm, their seriousness, their intelligence and their sympathy with himself.

Hence the self-consciousness in the gloaming.

To create a diversion Miss Ebag walked primly to the window and cried:

"Goldie! Goldie!"

It was Goldie's bedtime. In summer he always strolled into the garden after dinner, and he nearly always sensibly responded to the call when his bed-hour sounded. No one would have dreamed of retiring until Goldie was safely ensconced in his large basket under the stairs.

"Naughty Goldie!" Miss Ebag said, comprehensively, to the garden.

She went into the garden to search, and Mrs Ebag followed her, and Carl Ullman followed Mrs Ebag. And they searched without result, until it was black night and the threatening storm at last fell. The vision of Goldie out in that storm desolated the ladies, and Carl Ullman displayed the nicest feeling. At length the rain drove them in and they stood in the drawing-room

with anxious faces, while two servants, under directions
from Carl, searched the house for Goldie.

" If you please'm," stammered the housemaid, rushing rather unconventionally into the drawing-room,
" cook says she thinks Goldie must be on the roof, in
the vane."

"On the roof in the vane? " exclaimed Mrs Ebag,
pale. " In the vane? "

" Yes'm."

" Whatever do you mean, Sarah? " asked Miss Ebag,
even paler.

The ladies Ebag were utterly convinced that Goldie
was not like other cats, that he never went on the roof,
that he never had any wish to do anything that was not
in the strictest sense gentlemanly and correct. And if by
chance he did go on the roof, it was merely to examine
the roof itself, or to enjoy the view therefrom out of
gentlemanly curiosity. So that this reference to the
roof shocked them. The night did not favour the
theory of view-gazing.

"Cook says she heard the weather-vane creaking
ever since she went upstairs after dinner, and now it's
stopped; and she can hear Goldie a-myowling like
anything."

" Is cook in her attic? " asked Mrs Ebag.

" Yes'm."

" Ask her to come out. Mr Ullman, will you be so
very good as to come upstairs and investigate? "

Cook, enveloped in a cloak, stood out on the second
landing, while Mr Ullman and the ladies invaded her
chamber. The noise of myowling was terrible. Mr
Ullman opened the dormer window, and the rain burst
in, together with a fury of myowling. But he did not
care. It lightened and thundered. But he did not
care. He procured a chair of cook's and put it under
the window and stood on it, with his back to the window,
and twisted forth his body so that he could spy up the

roof. The ladies protested that he would be wet through, but he paid no heed to them.

Then his head, dripping, returned into the room.

" I've just seen by a flash of lightning," he said in a voice of emotion. " The poor animal has got his tail fast in the socket of the weather-vane. He must have been whisking it about up there, and the vane turned and caught it. The vane is jammed."

" How dreadful! " said Mrs Ebag. " Whatever can be done? "

" He'll be dead before morning," sobbed Miss Ebag.

" I shall climb up the roof and release him," said Carl Ullman, gravely.

They forbade him to do so. Then they implored him to refrain. But he was adamant. And in their supplications there was a note of insincerity, for their hearts bled for Goldie, and, further, they were not altogether unwilling that Carl should prove himself a hero. And so, amid apprehensive feminine cries of the acuteness of his danger, Carl crawled out of the window and faced the thunder, the lightning, the rain, the slippery roof, and the maddened cat. A group of three servants were huddled outside the attic door.

In the attic the ladies could hear his movements on the roof, moving higher and higher. The suspense was extreme. Then there was silence; even the myowling had ceased. Then a clap of thunder; and then, after that, a terrific clatter on the roof, a bounding downwards as of a great stone, a curse, a horrid pause, and finally a terrific smashing of foliage and cracking of wood.

Mrs Ebag sprang to the window.

" It's all right," came a calm, gloomy voice from below. " I fell into the rhododendrons, and Goldie followed me. I'm not hurt, thank goodness! Just my luck! "

A bell rang imperiously. It was the paralytic's bell. He had been disturbed by these unaccustomed phenomena.

" Sister, do go to father at once," said Mrs Ebag, as they both hastened downstairs in a state of emotion, assuredly unique in their lives.

V

Mrs Ebag met Carl and the cat as they dripped into the gas-lit drawing-room. They presented a surprising spectacle, and they were doing damage to the Persian carpet at the rate of about five shillings a second; but that Carl, and the beloved creature for whom he had dared so much, were equally unhurt appeared to be indubitable. Of course, it was a miracle. It could not be regarded as other than a miracle. Mrs Ebag gave vent to an exclamation in which were mingled pity, pride, admiration and solicitude, and then remained, as it were, spellbound. The cat escaped from those protecting arms and fled away. Instead of following Goldie, Mrs Ebag continued to gaze at the hero.

" How can I thank you! " she whispered.

" What for? " asked Carl, with laconic gloom.

" For having saved my darling! " said Mrs Ebag. And there was passion in her voice.

" Oh! " said Carl. " It was nothing! "

" Nothing? " Mrs Ebag repeated after him, with melting eyes, as if to imply that, instead of being nothing, it was everything; as if to imply that his deed must rank hereafter with the most splendid deeds of antiquity; as if to imply that the whole affair was beyond words to utter or gratitude to repay.

And in fact Carl himself was moved. You cannot fall from the roof of a two-story house into a very high-class rhododendron bush, carrying a prize cat in your arms, without being a bit shaken. And Carl was a bit shaken, not merely physically, but morally and spiritually. He could not deny to himself that he had after all done something rather wondrous, which ought to be celebrated in sounding verse. He felt that he was in an atmosphere far removed from the commonplace.

He dripped steadily on to the carpet.

" You know how dear my cat was to me," proceeded Mrs Ebag. " And you risked your life to spare me the pain of his suffering, perhaps his death. How thankful I am that I insisted on having those rhododendrons planted just where they are—fifteen years ago! I never anticipated—"

She stopped. Tears came into her dowager eyes. It was obvious that she worshipped him. She was so absorbed in his heroism that she had no thought even for his dampness. As Carl's eyes met hers she seemed to him to grow younger. And there came into his mind all the rumour that had vaguely reached him coupling their names together; and also his early dreams of love and passion and a marriage that would be one long honeymoon. And he saw how absurd had been those early dreams. He saw that the best chance of a felici- tous marriage lay in a union of mature and serious per- sons, animated by grave interests and lofty ideals. Yes, she was older than he. But not much, not much! Not more than—how many years? And he remembered surprising her rapt glance that very evening as she watched him playing the piano. What had romance to do with age? Romance could occur at any age. It was occurring now. Her soft eyes, her portly form, exuded romance. And had not the renowned Beaconsfield espoused a lady appreciably older than himself, and did not those espousals achieve the ideal of bliss? In the act of saving the cat he had not been definitely aware that it was so particularly the cat of the household. But now, influenced by her attitude and her shining rever- ence, he actually did begin to persuade himself that an uncontrollable instinctive desire to please her and win her for his own had moved him to undertake the perilous passage of the sloping roof.

In short, the idle chatter of the town was about to be justified. In another moment he might have dripped into her generous arms . . . had not Miss Ebag swept into the drawing-room!

"Gracious!" gasped Miss Ebag. "The poor dear thing will have pneumonia. Sister, you know his chest is not strong. Dear Mr Ullman, please, please, do go and—er—change."

He did the discreet thing and went to bed, hot whisky following him on a tray carried by the house-maid.

VI

THE next morning the slightly unusual happened. It was the custom for Carl Ullman to breakfast alone, while reading *The Staffordshire Signal*. The ladies Ebag breakfasted mysteriously in bed. But on this morning Carl found Miss Ebag before him in the break-fast-room. She prosecuted minute inquiries as to his health and nerves. She went out with him to regard the rhododendron bushes, and shuddered at the sight of the ruin which had saved him. She said, following famous philosophers, that Chance was merely the name we give to the effect of laws which we cannot understand. And, upon this high level of conversation, she poured forth his coffee and passed his toast.

It was a lovely morning after the tempest.

Goldie, all newly combed, and looking as though he had never seen a roof, strolled pompously into the room with tail unfurled. Miss Ebag picked the animal up and kissed it passionately.

"Darling!" she murmured, not exactly to Mr Ullman, nor yet exactly to the cat. Then she glanced effulgently at Carl and said, "When I think that you risked your precious life, in that awful storm, to save my poor Goldie? . . . You must have guessed how

dear he was to me? . . . No, really, Mr Ullman, I
cannot thank you properly! I can't express my—"

Her eyes were moist.

Although not young, she was two years younger.
Her age was two years less. The touch of man had never
profaned her. No masculine kiss had ever rested on
that cheek, that mouth. And Carl felt that he might be
the first to cull the flower that had so long waited. He
did not see, just then, the hollow beneath her chin, the
two lines of sinew that, bounding a depression, disappeared beneath her collarette. He saw only her soul.
He guessed that she would be more malleable than the
widow, and he was sure that she was not in a position,
as the widow was, to make comparisons between husbands. Certainly there appeared to be some confusion
as to the proprietorship of this cat. Certainly he could
not have saved the cat's life for love of two different
persons. But that was beside the point. The essential
thing was that he began to be glad that he had decided
nothing definite about the widow on the previous
evening.

"Darling!" said she again, with a new access of
passion, kissing Goldie, but darting a glance at Carl.

He might have put to her the momentous question,
between two bites of buttered toast, had not Mrs Ebag,
at the precise instant, swum amply into the room.

"Sister! You up!" exclaimed Miss Ebag.

"And you, sister!" retorted Mrs Ebag.

VII

IT is impossible to divine what might have occurred for
the delectation of the very ancient borough of Oldcastle
if that frivolous piece of goods, Edith, had not taken it
into her head to run down from London for a few days,
on the plea that London was too ridiculously hot. She

was a pretty girl, with fluffy honey-coloured hair and
about thirty white frocks. And she seemed to be quite
as silly as her staid stepmother and her prim step-aunt
had said. She transformed the careful order of the
house into a wild disorder, and left a novel or so lying
on the drawing-room table between her stepmother's
Contemporary Review and her step-aunt's *History of
European Morals*. Her taste in music was candidly and
brazenly bad. It was a fact, as her elders had stated,
that she played nothing but waltzes. What was worse,
she compelled Carl Ullman to perform waltzes. And
one day she burst into the drawing-room when Carl was
alone there, with a roll under her luscious arm, and said:
" What do you think I've found at Barrowfoot's? "
" I don't know," said Carl, gloomily smiling, and
then smiling without gloom.
" Waldteufel's waltzes arranged for four hands.
You must play them with me at once."
And he did. It was a sad spectacle to see the
organist of St Placid's galloping through a series of
dances with the empty-headed Edith.
The worst was, he liked it. He knew that he ought
to prefer the high intellectual plane, the severe artistic
tastes, of the elderly sisters. But he did not. He was
amazed to discover that frivolity appealed more powerfully to his secret soul. He was also amazed to discover
that his gloom was leaving him. This vanishing of
gloom gave him strange sensations, akin to the sensations of a man who, after having worn gaiters into
middle-age, abandons them.
After the Waldteufel she began to tell him all about
herself; how she went slumming in the East End, and
how jolly it was. And how she helped in the Blooms-
bury Settlement, and how jolly that was. And, later,
she said:
" You must have thought it very odd of me, Mr
Ullman, not thanking you for so bravely rescuing my

poor cat; but the truth is I never heard of it till to-day.
I can't say how grateful I am.   I should have loved to
see you doing it."

"Is Goldie your cat?" he feebly inquired.

"Why, of course?" she said.   "Didn't you know?
Of course you did! Goldie always belonged to me.
Grandpa bought him for me.   But I couldn't do with
him in London, so I always leave him here for them to
take care of.   He adores me.   He never forgets me.
He'll come to me before anyone.   You must have
noticed that.   I can't say how grateful I am!   It was
perfectly marvellous of you!   I can't help laughing,
though, whenever I think what a state mother and
auntie must have been in that night!"

Strictly speaking, they hadn't a cent between them,
except his hundred a year.   But he married her hair and
she married his melancholy eyes; and she was content
to settle in Oldcastle, where there are almost no slums.
And her stepmother was forced by Edith to make the
hundred up to four hundred.   This was rather hard on
Mrs Ebag.   Thus it fell out that Mrs Ebag remained a
widow, and that Miss Ebag continues a flower unculled.
However, gossip was stifled.

In his appointed time, and in the fulness of years,
Goldie died, and was mourned.   And by none was he
more sincerely mourned than by the aged bedridden
Caiaphas.

"I miss my cat, I can tell ye!" said old Caiaphas
pettishly to Carl, who was sitting by his couch.   "He
knew his master, Goldie did!   Edith did her best to
steal him from me when you married and set up house.
A nice thing considering I bought him and he never belonged to anybody but me!   Ay!   I shall never have
another cat like that cat."

And this is the whole truth of the affair.

THE FORTUNE-TELLER

I

THE prologue to this somewhat dramatic history was of the simplest. The affair came to a climax, if one may speak metaphorically, in fire and sword and high passion, but it began like the month of March. Mr Bostock (a younger brother of the senior partner in the famous firm of Bostocks, drapers, at Hanbridge) was lounging about the tennis-court attached to his house at Hillport. Hillport has long been known as the fashionable suburb of Bursley, and indeed as the most aristocratic quarter strictly within the Five Towns; there certainly are richer neighbourhoods not far off, but such neighbourhoods cannot boast that they form part of the Five Towns—no more than Hatfield can boast that it is part of London. A man who lives in a detached house at Hillport, with a tennis-court, may be said to have succeeded in life. And Mr Bostock had succeeded. A consulting engineer of marked talent, he had always worked extremely hard and extremely long, and thus he had arrived at luxuries. The chief of his luxuries was his daughter Florence, aged twenty-three, height five feet exactly, as pretty and as neat as a new doll, of expensive and obstinate habits. It was Florence who was the cause of the episode, and I mention her father only to show where Florence stood in the world. She ruled her father during perhaps eleven months of the year. In the twelfth month (which was usually January—after the Christmas bills) there would be an insurrection, conducted by the father with much spirit for a

time, but ultimately yielding to the forces of the govern-
ment. Florence had many admirers; a pretty woman,
who habitually rules a rich father, is bound to have
many admirers. But she had two in particular; her
cousin, Ralph Martin, who had been apprenticed to
her father, and Adam Tellwright, a tile manufacturer
at Turnhill.

These four—the father and daughter and the rivals
—had been playing tennis that Saturday afternoon.
Mr Bostock, though touching on fifty, retained a youthful athleticism; he looked and talked younger than his
years, and he loved the society of young people. If he
wandered solitary and moody about the tennis-court
now, it was because he had a great deal on his mind
besides business. He had his daughter's future on his
mind.

A servant with apron-strings waving like flags in the
breeze came from the house with a large loaded tea-
tray, and deposited it on a wicker table on the small
lawn at the end of the ash court. The rivals were reclin-
ing in deck chairs close to the table; the Object of
Desire, all in starched white, stood over the table and
with quick delicious movements dropped sugar and
poured milk into tinkling porcelain.

" Now, father," she called briefly, without looking
up, as she seized the teapot.

He approached, gazing thoughtfully at the group.
Yes, he was worried. And everyone was secretly
worried. The situation was exceedingly delicate, fragile,
breakable. Mr Bostock looked uneasily first at Adam
Tellwright, tall, spick and span, self-confident, clever,
shining, with his indubitable virtues mainly on the outside. If ever any man of thirty-two in all this world was
eligible, Adam Tellwright was. Decidedly he had a
reputation for preternaturally keen smartness in trade,
but in trade that cannot be called a defect; on the contrary, if a man has virtues, you cannot precisely

quarrel with him because they happen to be on the outside; the principal thing is to have virtues. And then Mr Bostock looked uneasily at Ralph Martin, heavy, short, dark, lowering, untidy, often incomprehensible, and more often rude; with virtues concealed as if they were secret shames. Ralph was capricious. At moments he showed extraordinary talent as an engineer; at others he behaved like a nincompoop. He would be rich one day; but he had a formidable temper. The principal thing in favour of Ralph Martin was that he and Florence had always been " something to each other." Indeed of late years it had been begun to be understood that the match was " as good as arranged." It was taken for granted. Then Adam Tellwright had dropped like a bomb into the Bostock circle. He had fallen heavily and disastrously in love with the slight Florence (whom he could have crushed and eaten). At the start his case was regarded as hopeless, and Ralph Martin had scorned him. But Adam Tellwright soon caused gossip to sing a different tune, and Ralph Martin soon ceased to scorn him. Adam undoubtedly made a profound impression on Florence Bostock. He began by dazzling her, and then, as her eyes grew accustomed to the glare, he gradually showed her his good qualities. Everything that skill and tact could do Tellwright did. The same could not be said of Ralph Martin. Most people had a vague feeling that Ralph had not been treated fairly. Mr Bostock had this feeling. Yet why? Nothing had been settled. Florence's heart was evidently still open to competition, and Adam Tellwright had a perfect right to compete. Still, most people sympathized with Ralph. But Florence did not. Young girls are like that.

Now the rivals stood about equal. No one knew how the battle would go. Adam did not know. Ralph did not know. Florence assuredly did not know. Mr Bostock was quite certain, of a night, that Adam would win, but the next morning he was quite certain that his nephew would win.

No wonder that the tea-party, every member of it tremendously preoccupied by the great battle, was not distinguished by light and natural gaiety. Great battles cannot be talked about till they are over and the last shot fired. And it is not to be expected that people should be bright when each knows the others to be deeply preoccupied by a matter which must not even be mentioned. The tea-party was self-conscious, highly. Therefore, it ate too many cakes and chocolate, and forgot to count its cups of tea. The conversation nearly died of inanition several times, and at last it actually did die, and the quartette gazed in painful silence at its corpse. Anyone who has assisted at this kind of a tea-party will appreciate the situation. Why, Adam Tellwright himself was out of countenance. To his honour, it was he who first revived the corpse. A copy of the previous evening's *Signal* was lying on an empty deck-chair. It had been out all night, and was dampish. Tellwright picked it up, having finished his tea, and threw a careless eye over it. He was determined to talk about something.

" By Jove! " he said. " That Balsamo johnny is coming to Hanbridge! "

" Yes, didn't you know? " said Florence, agreeably bent on resuscitating the corpse.

" What! The palmistry man? " asked Mr Bostock, with a laugh.

" Yes." And Adam Tellwright read: " ' Balsamo, the famous palmist and reader of the future, begs to announce that he is making a tour through the principal towns, and will visit Hanbridge on the 22nd inst., remaining three days. Balsamo has thousands of testimonials to the accuracy of his predictions, and he absolutely guarantees not only to read the past correctly, but to foretell the future. Address: 22 Machin Street,

Hanbridge.   10 to 10.   Appointment advisable in order
to avoid delay.'   There!   He'll find himself in prison
one day, that gentleman will! "

"It's astounding what fools people are! " observed
Mr Bostock.

"Yes, isn't it! " said Adam Tellwright.

"If he'd been a gipsy," said Ralph Martin, savagely,
"the police would have had him long ago."   And he
spoke with such grimness that he might have been talking of Adam Tellwright.

"They say his uncle and his grandfather before him
were both thought-readers, or whatever you call it,"
said Florence.

"Do they? " exclaimed Mr Bostock, in a different
tone.

"Oh! " exclaimed Adam, also in a different tone.

"I wonder whether that's true! " said Ralph Martin.

The rumour that Balsamo's uncle and grandfather
had been readers of the past and of the future produced
of course quite an impression on the party.   But each
recognized how foolish it was to allow oneself to be so impressed in such an illogical manner.   And therefore all
the men burst into violent depreciation of Balsamo and
of the gulls who consulted him.   And by the time they
had done with Balsamo there was very little left of him.
Anyhow, Adam Tellwright's discovery in the *Signal*
had saved the tea-party from utter fiasco.

II

No. 22 Machin Street, Hanbridge, was next door to
Bostock's vast emporium, and exactly opposite the
more exclusive, but still mighty, establishment of
Ephraim Brunt, the greatest draper in the Five Towns.
It was, therefore, in the very heart and centre of
retail commerce.   No woman who respected herself

could buy even a sheet of pins without going past No. 22
Machin Street.   The ground-floor was a confectioner's
shop, with a back room where tea and Berlin pancakes
were served to the *élite* who had caught from London the
fashion of drinking tea in public places.   By the side of
the confectioner's was an open door and a staircase,
which led to the first floor and the other floors.   A card
hung by a cord to a nail indicated that Balsamo had
pitched his moving tent for a few days on the first floor,
in a suite of offices lately occupied by a solicitor.   Considering that the people who visit a palmist are just as
anxious to publish their doings as the people who visit a
pawnbroker—and no more—it might be thought that
Balsamo had ill-chosen his site.   But this was not so.
Balsamo, a deep student of certain sorts of human
nature, was perfectly aware that, just as necessity will
force a person to visit a pawnbroker, so will inherited
superstition force a person to visit a palmist, no matter
what the inconveniences.   If he had erected a wigwam
in the middle of Crown Square and people had had to
decide between not seeing him at all and running the
gauntlet of a crowd's jeering curiosity, he would still
have had many clients.

Of course when you are in love you are in love.
Anything may happen to you then.   Most things do happen.   For example, Adam Tellwright found himself
ascending the stairs of No. 22 Machin Street at an early
hour one morning.   He was, I need not say, mounting
to the third floor to give an order to the potter's modeller,
who had a studio up there.   Still he stopped at the first
floor, knocked at a door labelled " Balsamo," hesitated,
and went in.   I need not say that this was only fun on
his part.   I need not say that he had no belief whatever
in palmistry, and was not in the least superstitious.   A
young man was seated at a desk, a stylish young man.
Adam Tellwright smiled, as one who expected the stylish
young man to join in the joke.   But the young man did

not smile.   So Adam Tellwright suddenly ceased to smile.

" Are you Mr Balsamo? " Adam inquired.

" No.   I'm his secretary."

His secretary!   Strange how the fact that Balsamo was guarded by a secretary, and so stylish a secretary, affected the sagacious and hard-headed Adam!

" You wish to see him? " the secretary demanded coldly.

" I suppose I may as well," said Adam, sheepishly.

" He is disengaged, I think.   But I will make sure. Kindly sit down."

Down sat Adam, playing nervously with his hat, and intensely hoping that no other client would come in and trap him.

" Mr Balsamo will see you," said the secretary, emerging through a double black portière.   " The fee is a guinea."

He resumed his chair and drew towards him a book of receipt forms.

A guinea!

However, Adam paid it.   The receipt form said: " Received from Mr —— the sum of one guinea for professional assistance.—Per Balsamo, J. H. K.," and a long flourish.   The words " one guinea " were written.   Idle to deny that this receipt form was impressive.   As Adam meekly followed " J. H. K." in to the Presence, he felt exactly as if he was being ushered into a dentist's cabinet.   He felt as though he had been caught in the wheels of an unstoppable machine and was in vague but serious danger.

The Presence was a bold man, with a flowing light brown moustache, blue eyes, and a vast forehead.   He wore a black velvet coat, and sat at a small table on which was a small black velvet cushion.   There were two doors to the rooms, each screened by double black portières, and beyond a second chair and a large transparent ball, such as dentists use, there was no other furniture.

"Better give me your hat," said the secretary, and took it from Adam, who parted from it reluctantly, as if from his last reliable friend. Then the portières swished together, and Adam was alone with Balsamo.

Balsamo stared at him; did not even ask him to sit down.

"Why do you come to me? You don't believe in me," said Balsamo, curtly. "Why waste your money?"

"How can I tell whether I believe in you or not," protested Adam Tellwright, the shrewd man of business, very lamely. "I've come to see what you can do."

Balsamo snapped his fingers.

"Sit down then," said he, "and put your hands on this cushion. No!—palms up!"

Balsamo gaped at them a long time, rubbing his chin. Then he rose, adjusted the transparent glass ball so that the light came through it on to Adam's hands, sat down again and resumed his stare.

"Do you want to know everything?" he asked.

"Yes—of course."

"Everything?"

"Yes." A trace of weakness in this affirmative.

"Well, you mustn't expect to live much after fifty-two. Look at the line of life there." He spoke in such a casual, even antipathetic tone that Adam was startled.

"You've had success. You will have it continuously. But you won't live long."

"What have I to avoid?" Adam demanded.

"Can't avoid your fate. You asked me to tell you everything."

"Tell me about my past," said Adam, feebly, the final remnant of shrewdness in him urging him to get the true measure of Balsamo before matters grew worse.

"Your past?" Balsamo murmured. "Keep your left hand quite still, please. You aren't married. You're in business. You've never thought of marriage —till lately. It's not often I see a hand like yours. Your slate is clean. Till lately you never thought of marriage."

"How lately?"

"Who can say when the idea of marriage first came to you? You couldn't say yourself. Perhaps about three months ago. Yes—three months. I see water— you have crossed the sea. Is all this true?"

"Yes," admitted Adam.

"You're in love, of course. Did you know you have a rival?"

"Yes." Once more Adam was startled.

"Is he fair? No, he's not fair. He's dark. Isn't he?"

"Yes."

"Ah! The woman. Uncertain, uncertain. Mind you I never undertake to foretell anything; all I guarantee is that what I do foretell will happen. Now, you will be married in a year or eighteen months." Balsamo stuck his chin out with the gesture of one who imparts grave news; then paused reflectively.

"Whom to?"

"Ah! There are two women. One fair, one dark. Which one do you prefer?"

"The dark one," Adam replied in spite of himself.

"Perhaps the fair one has not yet come into your life? No. But she will do."

"But which shall I marry?"

"Look at that line. No, here! See how indistinct and confused it is. Your destiny is not yet settled. Frankly, I cannot tell you with certainty. No one can go in advance of destiny. Ah! Young man, I sympathize with you."

"Then, really you can't tell me."

" Listen! I might help you. Yes, I might help you."

" How? "

" The others will come to me."

" What others? "

" Your rival. And the woman you love."

" And then? "

" What is not marked on your hand may be very clearly marked on theirs. Come to me again."

" How do you know they will come? They both said they should not."

" You said you would not. But you are here. Rely on me. They will come. I might do a great deal for you. Of course it will cost you more. One lives in a world of money, and I sell my powers, like the rest of mankind. I am proud to do so."

" How much will it cost? "

" Five pounds. You are free to take it or leave it, naturally."

Adam Tellwright put his hand in his pocket.

" Have the goodness to pay my secretary," Balsamo stopped him icily.

" I beg pardon," said Adam, out of countenance.

" Of course if they do not come the money will be returned. Now, before you go, you might tell me all you know about him, and about her. All. Omit nothing. It is not essential, but it might help me. There is a chance that it might make things clearer than they otherwise could be. The true palmist never refuses any aid."

And Adam thereupon went into an elaborate account of Florence Bostock and Ralph Martin. He left out nothing, not even that Ralph had a wart on his chin, and had once broken a leg; nor that Florence had once been nearly drowned in a swimming-bath in London.

III

It was the same afternoon.

Balsamo stared calmly at a young dark-browed man who had entered his sanctuary with much the same air as a village bumpkin assumes when he is about to be shown the three-card trick on a race-course. Balsamo did not even ask him to sit down.

"Why do you come to me? You don't believe in me," said Balsamo, curtly. "Why waste your half-sovereign?"

Ralph Martin, not being talkative, said nothing.

"However!" Balsamo proceeded. "Sit down, please. Let me look at your hands. Ah! yes! Do you want to know anything?"

"Yes, of course."

"Everything?"

"Certainly."

"Let me advise you, then, to give up all thoughts of that woman."

"What woman?"

"You know what woman. She is a very little woman. Once she was nearly drowned—far from here. You've loved her for a long time. You thought it was a certainty. And upon my soul you were justified in thinking so—almost! Look at that line. But it isn't a certainty. Look at that line!"

Balsamo gazed at him coldly, and Ralph Martin knew not what to do or to say. He was astounded; he was frightened; he was desolated. He perceived at once that palmistry was after all a terrible reality.

"Tell me some more," he murmured.

And so Balsamo told him a great deal more, including full details of a woman far finer than Florence Bostock, whom he was destined to meet in the following year.

But Ralph Martin would have none of this new woman. Then Balsamo said suddenly:

"She is coming. I see her coming."

"Who?"

"The little woman. She is dressed in white, with a gold-and-white sunshade, and yellow gloves and boots, and she has a gold reticule in her hand. Is that she?"

Ralph Martin admitted that it was she. On the other hand, Balsamo did not admit that he had seen her an hour earlier and had made an appointment with her.

There was a quiet knock on the door. Ralph started.

"You hear," said Balsamo, quietly. "I fear you will never win her."

"You said just now positively that I shouldn't," Ralph exclaimed.

"I did not," said Balsamo. "I would like to help you. I am very sorry for you. It is not often I see a hand like yours. I might be able to help you; the destiny is not yet settled."

"I'll give you anything to help me," said Ralph.

"It will be a couple of guineas," said Balsamo.

"But what guarantee have I?" Ralph asked rudely, when he had paid the money—to Balsamo, not to the secretary. Such changes of humour were characteristic of him.

"None!" said Balsamo, with dignity, putting the sovereigns on the table. "But I am sorry for you. I will tell you what you can do. You can go behind those curtains there"—he pointed to the inner door—"and listen to all that I say."

A proposal open to moral objections! But when you are in the state that Ralph Martin was in, and have experienced what he had just experienced, your outlook upon morals is apt to be disturbed.

IV

"Young lady," Balsamo was saying. "Rest assured that I have not taken five shillings from you for nothing. Your lover has a wart on his chin."

Daintiness itself sat in front of him, with her little porcelain hands lying on the black cushion. And daintiness was astonished into withdrawing those hands.

"Please keep your hands still," said Balsamo, firmly, and proceeded: "But you have another lover, older, who has recently come into your life. Fair, tall. A successful man who will always be successful. Is it not so?"

"Yes," a little voice muttered.

"You can't make up your mind between them? Answer me."

"No."

"And you wish to learn the future. I will tell you —you will marry the fair man. That is your destiny. And you will be very happy. You will soon perceive the bad qualities of the one with the wart. He is a wicked man. I need not urge you to avoid him. You will do so."

"A bad man!"

"A bad man. You see there are two sovereigns lying here. That man has actually tried to bribe me to influence you in his favour?"

"Ralph?"

"Since you mention his Christian name, I will mention his surname. It is written here. Martin."

"He can't have—possibly—"

Balsamo strode with offended pride to the portière, and pulled it away, revealing Mr Ralph Martin, who for the second time that afternoon knew not what to say or to do.

"I tell you—" Ralph began, as red as fire.

" Silence, sir! Let this teach you not to try to corrupt an honest professional man! Surely I had amply convinced you of my powers! Take your miserable money! " He offered the miserable money to Ralph, who stuck his hands in his pockets, whereupon Balsamo flung the miserable money violently on to the floor.

A deplorable scene followed, in which the presence of Balsamo did not prevent Florence Bostock from conveying clearly to Ralph what she thought of him. They spoke before Balsamo quite freely, as two people will discuss maladies before a doctor. Ralph departed first; then Florence. Then Balsamo gathered up the sovereigns. He had honestly earned Adam's fiver, and since Ralph had refused the two pounds—

" I have seen their hands," said Balsamo the next day to Adam Tellwright. " All is clear. In a month you will be engaged to her."

" A month? "

" A month. I regret that I had a painful scene with your rival. But of course professional etiquette prevents me from speaking of that. Let me repeat, in a month you will be engaged to her."

This prophecy came true. Adam Tellwright, however, did not marry Florence Bostock. One evening, in a secluded corner at a dance, Ralph Martin, without warning, threw his arms angrily, brutally, instinctively round Florence's neck and kissed her. It was wrong of him. But he conquered her. Love is like that. It hides for years, and then pops out, and won't be denied. Florence's engagement to Adam was broken. She married Ralph. She knew she was marrying a strange, dark-minded man of uncertain temper, but she married him.

As for the unimpeachable Adam, he was left with nothing but the uneasy fear that he was doomed to die at fifty-two. His wife (for he got one, and a good one) soon cured him of that.

THE LONG-LOST UNCLE

ON a recent visit to the Five Towns I was sitting with my old schoolmaster, who, by the way, is much younger than I am after all, in the bow window of a house overlooking that great thoroughfare, Trafalgar Road, Bursley, when a pretty woman of twenty-eight or so passed down the street. Now the Five Towns contains more pretty women to the square mile than any other district in England (and this statement I am prepared to support by either sword or pistol). But do you suppose that the frequency of pretty women in Hanbridge, Bursley, Knype, Longshaw and Turnhill makes them any the less remarked? Not a bit of it. Human nature is such that even if a man should meet forty pretty women in a walk along Trafalgar Road from Bursley to Hanbridge, he will remark them all separately, and feel exactly forty thrills. Consequently my ever-youthful schoolmaster said to me:

"Good-looking woman that, eh, boy? Married three weeks ago," he added.

A piece of information which took the keen edge off my interest in her.

"Really!" I said. "Who is she?"

"Married to a Scotsman named Macintyre, I fancy."

"That tells me nothing," I said. "Who was she?"

"Daughter of a man named Roden."

"Not Herbert Roden?" I demanded.

"Yes. Art director at Jacksons, Limited."

"Well, well!" I exclaimed. "So Herbert Roden's got a daughter married. Well, well! And it seems like

a week ago that he and his uncle—you know all about
that affair, of course? "

" What affair? "

" Why, the Roden affair! "

" No," said my schoolmaster.

" You don't mean to say you've never—"

Nothing pleases a wandering native of the Five
Towns more than to come back and find that he knows
things concerning the Five Towns which another man
who has lived there all his life doesn't know. In ten
seconds I was digging out for my schoolmaster one of
those family histories which lie embedded in the general
grey soil of the past like lumps of quartz veined and
streaked with the precious metal of passion and glittering here and there with the crystallizations of scandal.

" You could make a story out of that," he said, when
I had done talking and he had done laughing.

" It is a story," I replied. " It doesn't want any
making."

And this is just what I told him. I have added on a
few explanations and moral reflections—and changed
the names.

I

SILAS RODEN, commonly called Si Roden—Herbert's
uncle—lived in one of those old houses at Paddock
Place, at the bottom of the hill where Hanbridge begins.
Their front steps are below the level of the street, and
their backyards look out on the Granville Third Pit and
the works of the Empire Porcelain Company. It was Si's
own house, a regular bachelor's house, as neat as a pin,
and Si was very proud of it and very particular about it.
Herbert, being an orphan, lived with his uncle. He
would be about twenty-five then, and Si fifty odd. Si
had retired from the insurance agency business, and
Herbert, after a spell in a lawyer's office, had taken to

art and was in the decorating department at Jackson's.
They had got on together pretty well, had Si and Herbert, in a grim, taciturn, Five Towns way.   The historical scandal began when Herbert wanted to marry Alice
Oulsnam, an orphan like himself, employed at a dressmaker's in Crown Square, Hanbridge.

" Thou'lt marry her if thou'st a mind," said Si to
Herbert, " but I s'll ne'er speak to thee again."

" But why, uncle? "

" That's why," said Si.

Now if you have been born in the Five Towns and
been blessed with the unique Five Towns mixture of
sentimentality and solid sense, you don't flare up and
stamp out of the house when a well-to-do and childless
uncle shatters your life's dream.   You dissemble.   You
piece the dream together again while your uncle is looking another way.   You feel that you are capable of out-
witting your uncle, and you take the earliest opportunity
of " talking it over " with Alice.   Alice is sagacity
itself.

Si's reasons for objecting so politely to the projected
marriage were various.   In the first place he had persuaded himself that he hated women.   In the second
place, though in many respects a most worthy man, he
was a selfish man, and he didn't want Herbert to leave
him, because he loathed solitude.   In the third place
—and here is the interesting part—he had once had an
affair with Alice's mother and had been cut out: his one
deviation into the realms of romance—and a disastrous
one.   He ought to have been Alice's father, and he
wasn't.   It angered him, with a cold anger, that Herbert should have chosen just Alice out of the wealth of
women in the Five Towns.   Herbert was unaware of
this reason at the moment.

The youth was being driven to the conclusion that he
would be compelled to offend his uncle after all, when
Alice came into two thousand two hundred pounds from

a deceased relative in Cheshire.   The thought of this
apt legacy does good to my soul.   I love people to come
into a bit of stuff unexpected.   Herbert instantly advised her to breathe not a word of the legacy to anyone.
They were independent now, and he determined that he
would teach his uncle a lesson.   He had an affection for
his uncle, but in the Five Towns you can have an affection for a person, and be extremely and justly savage
against that person, and plan cruel revenges on that
person, all at the same time.

Herbert felt that the legacy would modify Si's attitude towards the marriage, if Si knew of it.   Legacies,
for some obscure and illogical cause, do modify attitudes
towards marriages.   To keep a penniless dressmaker out
of one's family may be a righteous act.   But to keep a
level-headed girl with two thousand odd of her own out
of one's family would be the act of an insensate fool.
Therefore Herbert settled that Si should not know of the
legacy.   Si should be defeated without the legacy, or he
should be made to suffer the humiliation of yielding after
being confronted with the accomplished fact of a secret
marriage.   Herbert was fairly sure that he would yield,
and in any case, with a couple of thousand at his wife's
back, Herbert could afford to take the risks of war.

So Herbert, who had something of the devil in him,
approached his uncle once more, with a deceitful respect,
and he was once more politely rebuffed—as indeed he
had half hoped to be.   He then began his clandestine
measures—measures which culminated in him leaving
the house one autumn morning dressed in a rather
stylish travelling suit.

The tramcar came down presently from Hanbridge.
Not one of the swift thunderous electrical things that
now chase each other all over the Five Towns in every
direction at intervals of about thirty seconds; but the old
horse-car that ran between Hanbridge and Bursley twice
an hour and no oftener, announcing its departure by a

big bell, and stopping at toll-gates with broad eaves, and
climbing hills with the aid of a tip-horse and a boy
perched on the back thereof. That was a calm and
spacious age.

Herbert boarded the car, and raised his hat rather
stiffly to a nice girl sitting in a corner. He then sat
down in another corner, far away from her. Such is the
capacity of youth for chicane! For that nice girl was
exactly Alice, and her presence on the car was part of
the plot. When the car arrived at Bursley these
monsters of duplicity descended together, and went to a
small public building and entered therein, and were
directed to an official and inhospitable room which was
only saved from absolute nakedness by a desk, four
Windsor chairs, some blotting-paper, pens, ink and a
copy of Keats's Directory of the Five Towns. An
amiable old man received them with a perfunctory
gravity, and two acquaintances of Herbert's strolled in,
blushing. The old man told everybody to sit down,
asked them questions of no spiritual import, abruptly
told them to stand up, taught them to say a few phrases,
in the tone of a person buying a ha'-porth of tin-tacks,
told them to sit down, filled a form or two, took some
of Herbert's money, and told them that that was all,
and that they could go. So they went, secretly surprised. This was the august ritual, and this the imposing theatre, provided by the State in those far-off days
for the solemnizing of the most important act in a
citizen's life. It is different now; the copy of Keats's
Directory is a much later one.

Herbert thanked his acquaintances, who, begging
him not to mention it, departed.

"Well, that's over!" breathed Herbert with a sigh
of relief. "It's too soon to go back. Let us walk round
by Moorthorne."

"I should love to!" said Alice.

It was a most enjoyable walk. In the heights of

Moorthorne they gradually threw off the depressing influence of those four Windsor chairs, and realized their
bliss.   They reached Paddock Place again at a quarter
to one o'clock, which, as they were a very methodical
and trustworthy pair, was precisely the moment at
which they had meant to reach it.   The idea was that
they should call on Si and announce to him, respectfully:
" Uncle, we think it only right to tell you that we are
married.   We hope you will not take it ill, we should like
to be friends."   They would then leave the old man to
eat the news with his dinner.   A cab was to be at the
door at one o'clock to carry them to Knype Station,
where they would partake of the wedding breakfast in
the first-class refreshment room, and afterwards catch
the two-forty to Blackpool, there to spend a honeymoon
of six days.

This was the idea.

Herbert was already rehearsing in his mind the exact
tone in which he should say to Si: " Uncle, we think it
only right—" when, as they approached the house, they
both saw a white envelope suspended under the knocker
of the door.   It was addressed to " Mr Herbert Roden,"
in the handwriting of Silas.   The moment was dramatic.
As they had not yet discussed whether correspondence
should be absolutely common property, Alice looked
discreetly away while Herbert read: " Dear nephew,
I've gone on for a week or two on business, and sent
Jane Sarah home.   Her's in need of a holiday.   You
must lodge at Bratt's meantime.   I've had your things
put in there, and they've gotten the keys of the house.
—Yours affly, S. Roden."   Bratt's was next door but
one, and Jane Sarah was the Roden servant, aged fifty
or more.

" Well, I'm—! " exclaimed Herbert.

" Well, I never! " exclaimed Alice when she had
read the letter.   " What's the meaning—? "

" Don't ask me! " Herbert replied.

" Going off like this! " exclaimed Alice.

" Yes, my word! " exclaimed Herbert.

" But what are you to do? " Alice asked.

" Get the key from Bratt's, and get my box, if he hasn't had it carried in to Bratt's already, and then wait for the cab to come."

" Just fancy him shutting you out of the house like that, and no warning! " Alice said, shocked.

" Yes. You see he's very particular about his house. He's afraid I might ruin it, I suppose. He's just like an old maid, you know, only a hundred times worse." Herbert paused, as if suddenly gripped in a tremendous conception. " I have it! " he stated positively. " I have it! I have it! "

" What? " Alice demanded.

" Suppose we spend our honeymoon here? "

" In this house? "

" In this house. It would serve him right."

Alice smiled humorously. " Then the house wouldn't get damp," she said. " And there would be a great saving of expense. We could buy those two easy-chairs with what we saved."

" Exactly," said Herbert. " And after all, seaside lodgings, you know. . . . And this house isn't so bad either."

" But if he came back and caught us? " Alice suggested.

" Well, he couldn't eat us! " said Herbert.

The clear statement of this truth emboldened Alice. " And he'd no right to turn you out! " she said in wifely indignation.

Without another word Herbert went into Bratt's and got the keys. Then the cab came up with Alice's luggage lashed to the roof, and the driver, astounded, had to assist in carrying it into Si's house. He was then dismissed, and not with a bouncing tip either. We are in the Five Towns. He got a reasonable tip, no more.

The Bratts, vastly intrigued, looked inconspicuously on.

Herbert banged the door and faced Alice in the lobby across her chief trunk. The honeymoon had commenced.

"We'd better get this out of the way at once," said Alice the practical.

And between them they carried it upstairs, Alice, in the intervals of tugs, making favourable remarks about the cosiness of the abode.

"This is uncle's bedroom," said Herbert, showing the front bedroom, a really spacious and dignified chamber full of spacious and dignified furniture, and not a pin out of place in it.

"What a funny room!" Alice commented. "But it's very nice."

"And this is mine," said Herbert, showing the back bedroom, much inferior in every way.

When the trunk had been carried into the front bedroom, Herbert descended for the other things, including his own luggage; and Alice took off her hat and jacket and calmly laid them on Silas's ample bed, gazed into all Silas's cupboards and wardrobes that were not locked, patted her hair in front of Silas's looking-glass, and dropped a hairpin on Silas's floor.

She then kneeled down over her chief trunk, and the vision of her rummaging in the trunk in his uncle's bedroom was the most beautiful thing that Herbert had ever seen. Whether it was because the light caught her brown hair, or because she seemed so strange there and yet so deliciously at home, or because— Anyhow, she fished a plain white apron out of the trunk and put it on over her grey dress. And the quick, graceful, enchanting movements with which she put the apron on—well, they made Herbert feel that he had only that moment begun to live. He walked away wondering what was the matter with him. If you imagine that he ran up to her and kissed her you imagine a vain thing; you do not understand that complex and capricious organism, the masculine heart.

The wedding breakfast consisted of part of a leg of mutton that Jane Sarah had told the Bratts they might have, pikelets purchased from a street hawker, coffee, scrambled eggs, biscuits, butter, burgundy out of the cellar, potatoes out of the cellar, cheese, sardines, and a custard that Alice made with custard-powder. Herbert had to go out to buy the bread, the butter, the sardines and some milk; when he returned with these purchases, a portion of the milk being in his breast pocket, Alice checked them, and exhibited a mild surprise that he had not done something foolish, and told him to clear out of " her kitchen."

Her kitchen was really the back kitchen or scullery. The proper kitchen had always been used as a dining-room. But Alice had set the table in the parlour, at the front of the house, where food had never before been eaten. At the first blush this struck Herbert as sacri-lege; but Alice said she didn't like the middle room, be-cause it was dark and because there was a china pig on the high mantelpiece; and really Herbert could discover no reason for not eating in the parlour. So they ate in the parlour. Before the marvellous repast was over Alice had rearranged all the ornaments and chairs in that parlour, turned round the carpet, and patted the window curtains into something new and strange. Herbert frequently looked out of the window to see if his uncle was coming.

" Pity there's no dessert," said Herbert. It was three o'clock, and the refection was drawing to a re-luctant close.

" There is a dessert," said Alice. She ran upstairs, and came down with her little black hand-bag, out of which she produced three apples and four sponge-cakes, meant for the railway journey. Amazing woman! Yet in resuming her seat she mistook Herbert's knee for her chair. Amazing woman! Intoxicating mixture of sweet confidingness and unfailing resource.   And Si had wanted to prevent Herbert from marrying this pearl!

" Now I must wash up! " said she.

" I'll run out and telegraph to Jane Sarah to come back at once.   I expect she's gone to her sister's at Rat Edge.   It's absurd for you to be doing all the work like this."   Thus Herbert.

" I can manage by myself till to-morrow," Alice decided briefly.

Then there was a rousing knock at the door, and Alice sprang up, as it were, guiltily.   Recovering herself with characteristic swiftness, she went to the window and spied delicately out.

" It's Mrs Bratt," she whispered.   " I'll go."

" Shall I go? " Herbert asked.

" No—I'll go," said Alice.

And she went—apron and all.

Herbert overheard the conversation.

" Oh! "   Exclamation of feigned surprise from Mrs Bratt.

" Yes? "   In tones of a politeness almost excessive.

" Is Mr Herbert meaning to come to our house to-night?   That there bedroom's all ready."

" I don't think so," said Alice.   " I don't think so."

" Well, miss—"

" I'm Mrs Herbert Roden," said Alice, primly.

' Oh!   I beg pardon, miss—Mrs, that is—I'm sure. I didn't know—"

" No," said Alice.   " The wedding was this morning."

" I'm sure I wish you both much happiness, you and Mr Herbert," said Mrs Bratt, heartily.   " If I had but known—"

" Thank you," said Alice, " I'll tell my husband."

And she shut the door on the entire world.

II

ONE evening, after tea, by gaslight, Herbert was reading the newspaper in the parlour at Paddock Place, when he heard a fumbling with keys at the front door. The rain was pouring down heavily outside. He hesitated a moment. He was a brave man, but he hesitated a moment, for he had sins on his soul, and he knew in a flash who was the fumbler at the front door. Then he ran into the lobby, and at the same instant the door opened and his long-lost uncle stood before him, a living shower-bath, of which the tap could not be turned off.

"Well, uncle," he stammered, "how are—"

"Nay, my lad," Si stopped him, refusing his hand. "I'm too wet to touch. Get along into th' back kitchen. If I mun make a pool I'll make it there. So thou's taken possession o' my house!"

"Yes, uncle. You see—"

They were now in the back kitchen, or scullery, where a bright fire was burning in a small range and a great kettle of water singing over it.

"Run and get us a blanket, lad," said Si, stopping Herbert again, and turning up the gas.

"A blanket?"

"Ay, lad! A blanket. Art struck?"

When Herbert returned with the blanket Silas was spilling mustard out of the mustard tin into a large zinc receptacle which he had removed from the slop-stone to a convenient place on the floor in front of the fire. Silas then poured the boiling water from the kettle into the receptacle, and tested the temperature with his finger.

"Blazes!" he exclaimed, shaking his finger. "Fetch us the whisky, lad."

When Herbert returned a second time, Uncle Silas

was sitting on a chair wearing merely the immense blanket, which fell gracefully in rich folds around him to the floor. From sundry escaping jets of steam Herbert was able to judge that the zinc bath lay concealed somewhere within the blanket. Si's clothes were piled on the deal table.

"I hanna' gotten my feet in yet," said Si. "They're resting on th' edge. But I'll get 'em in in a minute. Oh! Blazes! Here! Mix us a glass o' that, hot. And then get out that clothes-horse and hang my duds on it nigh th' fire."

Herbert obeyed, as if in a dream.

"I canna do wi' another heavy cowd [cold] at my time o' life, and there's only one way for to stop it. There! That'll do, lad. Let's have a look at thee."

Herbert perched himself on a corner of the table. The vivacity of Silas astounded him.

"Thou looks older, nephew," said Silas, sipping at the whisky, and smacking his lips grimly.

"Do I? Well, you look younger, uncle, anyhow. You've shaved your beard off, for one thing."

"Yes, and a pretty cold it give me, too! I'd carried that beard for twenty year."

"Then why did you cut it off?"

"Because I had to, lad. But never mind that. So thou'st taken possession o' my house?"

"It isn't your house any longer, uncle," said Herbert, determined to get the worst over at once.

"Not my house any longer! Us'll see whether it inna' my house any longer."

"If you go and disappear for a twelvemonth and more, uncle, and leave no address, you must take the consequence. I never knew till after you'd gone that you'd mortgaged this house for four hundred pounds to Callear, the fish-dealer."

"Who towd thee that?"

"Callear told me."

THE LONG-LOST UNCLE   215

"Callear had no cause to be uneasy. I wrote him twice as his interest 'ud be all right when I come back."

"Yes, I know. But you didn't give any address. And he wanted his money back. So he came to me."

"Wanted his money back!" cried Silas, splashing about in the hidden tub and grimacing. "He had but just lent it me."

"Yes, but Tomkinson, his landlord, died, and he had the chance of buying his premises from the executors. And so he wanted his money back."

"And what didst tell him, lad?"

"I told him I would take a transfer of the mortgage."

"Thou! Hadst gotten four hundred pounds i' thy pocket, then?"

"Yes. And so I took a transfer."

"Bless us! This comes o' going away! But where didst find th' money?"

"And what's more," Herbert continued, evading the question, "as I couldn't get my interest I gave you notice to repay, uncle, and as you didn't repay—"

"Give me notice to repay! What the dev—? You hadna' got my address."

"I had your legal address—this house, and I left the notice for you in the parlour And as you didn't repay I—I took possession as mortgagee, and now I'm—I'm foreclosing."

"Thou'rt foreclosing!"

Silas stood up in the tub, staggered, furious, sweating. He would have stepped out of the tub and done something to Herbert had not common prudence and the fear of the blanket falling off restrained his passion. There was left to him only one thing to do, and he did it. He sat down again.

"Bless us!" he repeated feebly.

"So you see," said Herbert.

" And thou'st been living here ever since—alone, wi' Jane Sarah? "

" Not exactly," Herbert replied. " With my wife."

Fully emboldened now, he related to his uncle the whole circumstances of his marriage.

Whereupon, to his surprise, Silas laughed hilariously, hysterically, and gulped down the remainder of the whisky.

" Where is her? " Silas demanded.

" Upstairs."

" I' my bedroom, I lay," said Silas.

Herbert nodded. " May be."

" And everything upside down! " proceeded Uncle Silas.

" No! " said Herbert. " We've put all your things in my old room."

" Have ye! Ye're too obliging, lad! " growled Silas. " And if it isn't asking too much, where's that china pig as used to be on the chimney-piece in th' kitchen there? Her's smashed it, eh? "

" No," said Herbert, mildly. " She's put it away in a cupboard. She didn't like it."

" Ah! I was but wondering if ye'd foreclosed on th' pig too."

" Possibly a few things are changed," said Herbert. " But you know when a woman takes into her head—"

" Ay, lad! Ay, lad! I know! It was th' same wi' my beard. It had for go. Thou'st under the domination of a woman, and I can sympathize wi' thee."

Herbert gave a long, high whistle.

" So that's it? " he exclaimed. And he suddenly felt as if his uncle was no longer an uncle but a brother.

" Yes," said Silas. " That's it. I'll tell thee. Pour some more hot water in here. Dost remember when th' Carl Rosa Opera Company was at Theatre Royal last year? I met her then. Her was one o' Venus's maidens i' th' fust act o' *Tannhäuser*, and her was a

bridesmaid i' *Lohengrin*, and Siebel i' *Faust*, and a
cigarette girl i' summat else.   But it was in *Tannhäuser*
as I fust saw her on the stage, and her struck me like
that."   Silas clapped one damp hand violently on the
other.   "Miss Elsa Venda was her stage name, but her
was a widow, Mrs Parfitt, and had bin for ten years.
Seemingly her husband was of good family.   Finest
woman I ever seed, nephew.   And you'll say so.   Her'd
ha' bin a prima donna only for jealousy.   Fust time I
spoke to her I thought I should ha' fallen down.   Steady
with that water.   Dost want for skin me alive?   Yes, I
thought I should ha' fallen down.   They call'n it love.
You can call it what ye'n a mind for call it.   I nearly
fell down."

"How did you meet her, uncle?" Herbert inter-
posed, aware that his uncle had not been accustomed to
move in theatrical circles.

"How did I meet her?   I met her by setting about
to meet her.   I had for t' meet her.   I got Harry Buris-
ford, th' manager o' th' theatre thou knowst, for t'
introduce us.   Then I give a supper, nephew—I give
a supper at Turk's Head, but private like."

"Was that the time when you were supposed to be
at the Ratepayers' Association every night?" Herbert
asked blandly.

"It was, nephew," said Si, with equal blandness.

"Then no doubt those two visits to Manchester,
afterwards—"

"Exactly," said Si.   "Th' company went to Manchester and stopped there a fortnight.   I told her fair
and square what I meant and what I was worth.   There
was no beating about the bush wi' me.   All her friends
told her she'd be a fool if she wouldn't have me.   She
said her'd write me yes or no.   Her didn't.   Her telegraphed me from Sunderland for go and see her at once.
It was that morning as I left.   I thought to be back in a
couple o' days and to tell thee as all was settled.   But

women! Women! Her had me dangling after her from
town to town for a week.   I was determined to get her,
and get her I did, though it cost me my beard, and the
best part o' that four hundred.   I married her i' Halifax,
lad, and it were the best day's work I ever did.   You
never seed such a woman.   Big and plump—and sing!
By ——!   I never cared for singing afore.   And her
knows the world, let me tell ye."

" You might have sent us word," said Herbert.

Silas grew reflective.   " Ah! " he said.   " I might—
and I mightn't.   I didn't want Hanbridge chattering.
I was trapesing wi' her from town to town till her engagement was up—pretty near six months.   Then us
settled i' rooms at Scarborough, and there was other
things to think of.   I couldna' leave her.   Her wouldna'
let me.   To-day was the fust free day I've had, and so I
run down to fix matters.   And nice weather I've chosen!
Her aunt's spending the night wi' her."

" Then she's left the stage."

" Of course she's left th' stage.   What 'ud be th'
sense o' her painting her face and screeching her chest
out night after night for a crowd o' blockheads, when I
can keep her like a lady.   Dost think her's a fool?   Her's
the only woman wi' any sense as ever I met in all my
life."

" And you want to come here and live? "

" No, us dunna!   At least her dunna.   Her says her
hates th' Five Towns.   Her says Hanbridge is dirty and
too religious for her.   Says its nowt but chapels and
public-houses and pot-banks.   So her ladyship wunna'
come here.   No, nephew, thou shalt buy this house for
six hundred, and be d—d to thy foreclosure!   And th'
furniture for a hundred.   It's a dead bargain.   Us'll
settle at Scarborough, Liz and me.   Now this water's
getting chilly.   I'll nip up to thy room and find some
other clothes."

" You can't go up just now," said Herbert.

" But I mun go at once, nephew. Th' water's chilly, and I've had enough on it."

" The fact is we're using my old bedroom for a sort of a nursery, and Alice and Jane Sarah are just giving the baby its bath."

" Babby! " cried Silas. " Shake hands, nephew. Give us thy fist. I may as well out wi' it. I've gotten one mysen. Pour some more hot water in here, then."

THE TIGHT HAND

I

THE tight hand was Mrs Garlick's. A miser, she was not the ordinary miser, being exceptional in the fact that her temperament was joyous. She had reached the thirtieth year of her widowhood and the sixtieth of her age, with cheerfulness unimpaired. The people of Bursley, when they met her sometimes of a morning coming down into the town from her singular house up at Toft End, would be conscious of pleasure in her brisk gait, her slightly malicious but broad-minded smile, and her cheerful greeting. She was always in black. She always wore one of those nodding black bonnets which possess neither back nor front, nor any clue of any kind to their ancient mystery. She always wore a mantle which hid her waist and spread forth in curves over her hips; and as her skirts stuck stiffly out, she thus had the appearance of one who had been to sleep since 1870, and who had got up, thoroughly refreshed and bright, into the costume of her original period. She always carried a reticule. It was known that she suffered from dyspepsia, and this gave real value to her reputation for cheerfulness.

Her nearness, closeness, stinginess, close-fistedness—as the quality was variously called—was excused to her, partly because it had been at first caused by a genuine need of severe economy (she having been " left poorly off " by a husband who had lived " in a large way "), partly because it inconvenienced nobody save perhaps her servant Maria, and partly because it was so pictur-

esque and afforded much excellent material for gossip.
Mrs Garlick's latest feat of stinginess was invariably a
safe card to play in the conversational game. Each
successive feat was regarded as funnier than the one
before it.

Maria, who had a terrific respect for appearances,
never disclosed her mistress's peculiarities. It was Mrs
Garlick herself who humorously ventilated and discussed
them; Mrs Garlick, being a philosopher, got quite as
much amusement as anyone out of her most striking
quality.

"Is there anything interesting in the *Signal* to-
night? " she had innocently asked one of her sons.

"No," said Sam Garlick, unthinkingly.

"Well, then," said she, "suppose I turn out the gas
and we talk in the dark? "

Soon afterwards Sam Garlick married; his mother
remarked drily that she was not surprised.

It was supposed that this feat of turning out the gas
when the *Signal* happened to fail in interest would remain unparalleled in the annals of Five Towns skin-
flintry. But in the summer after her son's marriage,
Mrs Garlick was discovered in the evening habit of
pacing slowly up and down Toft Lane. She said that
she hated sitting in the dark alone, that Maria would not
have her in the kitchen, and that she saw no objection
to making harmless use of the Corporation gas by strolling to and fro under the Corporation gas-lamps on fine
nights. Compared to this feat the previous feat was as
naught. It made Mrs Garlick celebrated even as far as
Longshaw. It made the entire community proud of
such an inventive miser.

Once Mrs Garlick, before what she called her dinner,
asked Maria, "Will there be enough mutton for to-
morrow? " And Maria had gloomily and firmly said,
"No." "Will there be enough if I don't have any
to-day? " pursued Mrs Garlick. And Maria had said,

" Yes." " I won't have any then," said Mrs Garlick. Maria was offended; there are some things that a servant will not stand. She informed Mrs Garlick that if Mrs Garlick meant " to go on going on like that " she should leave; she wouldn't stay in such a house. In vain Mrs Garlick protested that the less she ate the better she felt; in vain she referred to her notorious indigestion. " Either you eats your dinner, mum, or out I clears! " Mrs Garlick offered her a rise of £1 a year to stay. She was already, because she would stop and most servants wouldn't, receiving £18, a high wage. She refused the increment. Pushed by her passion for economy in mutton, Mrs Garlick then offered her a rise of £2 a year. Maria accepted, and Mrs Garlick went without mutton. Persons unacquainted with the psychology of parsimoniousness may hesitate to credit this incident. But more advanced students of humanity will believe it without difficulty. In the Five Towns it is known to be true.

II

THE supreme crisis, to which the foregoing is a mere prelude, in the affairs of Mrs Garlick and Maria, was occasioned by the extraordinary performances of the Mayor of Bursley. This particular mayor was invested with the chain almost immediately upon the conclusion of a great series of revival services in which he had conspicuously figured. He had an earthenware manufactory half-way up the hill between Bursley and its loftiest suburb, Toft End, and the smoke of his chimneys and kilns was generally blown by a favourable wind against the windows of Mrs Garlick's house, which stood by itself. Mrs Garlick made nothing of this. In the Five Towns they think no more of smoke than the world at large used to think of small-pox. The smoke plague is exactly as curable as the small-pox plague. It continues to flourish, not because smokiness is cheaper than cleanliness—it is dearer—but because a greater nuisance than smoke is the nuisance of a change, and because human nature in general is rather like Mrs Garlick: its notion of economy is to pay heavily for the privilege of depriving itself of something—mutton or cleanliness.

However, this mayor was different. He had emerged from the revival services with a very tender conscience, and in assuming the chain of office he assumed the duty of setting an example. It was to be no excuse to him that in spite of bye-laws ten thousand other chimneys and kilns were breathing out black filth all over the Five Towns. So far as he could cure it the smoke nuisance had to be cured, or his conscience would know the reason why! So he sat on the borough bench and fined himself for his own smoke, and then he installed gas ovens. The town laughed, of course, and spoke of him alternately as a rash fool, a hypocrite, and a mere pompous ass. In a few months smoke had practically ceased to ascend from the mayoral manufactory. The financial result to the mayor was such as to encourage the tenderness of consciences. But that is not the point. The point is that Mrs Garlick, re-entering her house one autumn morning after a visit to the market, paused to look at the windows, and then said to Maria:

" Maria, what have you to do this afternoon? '

Now Mrs Garlick well knew what Maria had to do.

" I'm going to change the curtains, mum."

" Well, you needn't," said Mrs Garlick. " It's made such a difference up here, there being so much less smoke, that upon my word the curtains will do another three months quite well! "

" Well, mum, I never did! " observed Maria, meaning that so shocking a proposal was unprecedented in her experience. Yet she was thirty-five.

" Quite well! " said Mrs Garlick, gaily.

Maria said no more. But in the afternoon Mrs Garlick, hearing sounds in the drawing-room, went into the drawing-room and discovered Maria balanced on a pair of steps and unhooking lace curtains.

" Maria," said she, " what are you doing? "

Maria answered as busy workers usually do answer unnecessary questions from idlers.

" I should ha' thought you could see, mum," she said tartly, insolently, inexcusably.

One curtain was already down.

" Put that curtain back," Mrs Garlick commanded.

"I shall put no curtain back!" said Maria, grimly; her excited respiration shook the steps. " All to save the washing of four pair o' curtains! And you know you beat the washerwoman down to tenpence a pair last March! Three and fo'pence, that is! For the sake o' three and fo'pence you're willing for all Toft End to point their finger at these 'ere windows."

" Put that curtain back," Mrs Garlick repeated haughtily.

She saw that she had touched Maria in a delicate spot—her worship of appearances. The mutton was simply nothing to these curtains. Nevertheless, as there seemed to be some uncertainty in Maria's mind as to who was the mistress of the house, Mrs Garlick's business was to dispel that uncertainty. It may be said without exaggeration that she succeeded in dispelling it. But she did not succeed in compelling Maria to re-hang the curtain. Maria had as much force of character as Mrs Garlick herself. The end of the scene, whose details are not sufficiently edifying to be recounted, was that Maria went upstairs to pack her box, and Mrs Garlick personally re-hung the curtain. One's dignity is commonly an expensive trifle, and Mrs Garlick's dignity was expensive. To avoid prolonging the scene she paid Maria a month's wages in lieu of notice—£1, 13s. 4d. Then she showed her the door. Doubtless (Mrs Garlick

meditated) the girl thought she would get another rise
of wages. If so, she was finely mistaken. A nice thing
if the servant is to decide when curtains are to go to the
wash! She would soon learn, when she went into
another situation, what an easy, luxurious place she had
lost by her own stupid folly! Three and fourpences
might be picked up in the street, eh? And so on.

After Maria's stormy departure Mrs Garlick re-
gained her sense of humour and her cheerfulness; but
the inconveniences of being without Maria were important.

III

ON the second day following, Mrs Garlick received a
letter from " young Lawton," the solicitor. Young
Lawton, aged over forty, was not so-called because in
the Five Towns youthfulness is supposed to extend to
the confines of forty-five, but because he had succeeded
his father, known as " old Lawton "; it is true that the
latter had been dead many years. The Five Towns,
however, is not a country of change. This letter
pointed out that Maria's wages were not £1, 13s. 4d. a
month, but £1, 13s. 4d. a month plus her board and lodging, and that consequently, in lieu of a month's notice,
Maria demanded £1, 13s. 4d. plus the value of a month's
keep.

There was more in this letter than met the eye of Mrs
Garlick. Young Lawton's offices were cleaned by a
certain old woman; this old woman had a nephew; this
nephew was a warehouseman at the Mayor's works, and
lived up in Toft End, and at least twice every day he
passed by Mrs Garlick's house. He was a respectful
worshipper of Maria's, and it had been exclusively on his
account that Maria had insisted on changing the historic
curtains. Nobody else of the slightest importance ever
passed in front of the house, for important people have

long since ceased to live at Toft End. The subtle
flattering of an unspoken love had impelled Maria to
leave her situation rather than countenance soiled
curtains. She could not bear that the warehouseman
should suspect her of tolerating even the semblances of
dirt. She had permitted the warehouseman to hear the
facts of her departure from Mrs Garlick's. The warehouseman was nobly indignant, advising an action for
assault and battery. Through his aunt's legal relations
Maria had been brought into contact with the law, and,
while putting aside as inadvisable an action for assault
and battery, the lawyer had counselled a just demand
for more money. Hence the letter.

Mrs Garlick called at Lawton's office, and, Mr Lawton being out, she told an office-boy to tell him with her
compliments that she should not pay.

Then the County Court bailiff paid her a visit, and
left with her a blue summons for £2, 8s., being four
weeks of twelve shillings each.

Many house-mistresses in Bursley sympathized with
Mrs Garlick when she fought this monstrous claim. She
fought it gaily, with the aid of a solicitor. She might
have won it, if the County Court Judge had not happened to be in one of his peculiar moods—one of those
moods in which he felt himself bound to be original at
all costs. He delivered a judgment sympathizing with
domestic servants in general, and with Maria in particular. It was a lively trial. That night the *Signal* was
very interesting. When Mrs Garlick had finished with
the action she had two and threepence change out of a
five-pound note.

Moreover, she was forced to employ a charwoman—
a charwoman who had made a fine art of breaking china,
of losing silver teaspoons down sinks, and of going home
of a night with vast pockets full of things that belonged
to her by only nine-tenths of the law. The charwoman
ended by tumbling through a window, smashing panes

to the extent of seventeen and elevenpence, and irreparably ripping one of the historic curtains.

Mrs Garlick then dismissed the charwoman, and sat down to count the cost of small economics. The privilege of half-dirty curtains had involved her in an expense of £9, 19s. (call it £10). It was in the afternoon. The figure of Maria crossed the recently-repaired window. Without a second's thought Mrs Garlick rushed out of the house.

" Maria! " she cried abruptly—with grim humour. " Come here. Come right inside."

Maria stopped, then obeyed.

" Do you know how much you've let me in for, with your wicked, disobedient temper? "

" I'd have you know, mum—" Maria retorted, putting her hands on the hips and forwarding her face.

Their previous scene together was as nothing to this one in sound and fury. But the close was peace. The next day half Bursley knew that Maria had gone back to Mrs Garlick, and there was a facetious note about the episode in the " Day by Day " column of the *Signal*. The truth was that Maria and Mrs Garlick were " made for each other." Maria would not look at the ordinary "place." The curtains, as much as remained, were sent to the wash, but as three months had elapsed the mistress reckoned that she had won. Still, the cleansing of the curtains had run up to appreciably more than a sovereign per curtain.

The warehouseman did not ask for Maria's hand. The stridency of her behaviour in court had frightened him.

Mrs Garlick's chief hobby continues to be the small economy. Happily, owing to a rise in the value of a land and a fortunate investment, she is in fairly well-to-do circumstances.

As she said one day to an acquaintance, " It's a good thing I can afford to keep a tight hand on things."

WHY THE CLOCK STOPPED

I

MR MORFE and Mary Morfe, his sister, were sitting on either side of their drawing-room fire, on a Friday evening in November, when they heard a ring at the front door. They both started, and showed symptoms of nervous disturbance. They both said aloud that no doubt it was a parcel or something of the kind that had rung at the front door. And they both bent their eyes again on the respective books which they were reading. Then they heard voices in the lobby—the servant's voice and another voice—and a movement of steps over the encaustic tiles towards the door of the drawing-room. And Miss Morfe ejaculated:

" Really! "

As though she was unwilling to believe that somebody on the other side of that drawing-room door contemplated committing a social outrage, she nevertheless began to fear the possibility.

In the ordinary course it is not considered outrageous to enter a drawing-room—even at nine o'clock at night—with the permission and encouragement of the servant in charge of portals. But the case of the Morfes was peculiar. Mr Morfe was a bachelor aged forty-two, and looked older. Mary Morfe was a spinster aged thirty-eight, and looked thirty-seven. Brother and sister had kept house together for twenty years. They were passionately and profoundly attached to each other —and did not know it. They grumbled at each other freely, and practised no more conversation, when they

were alone, than the necessities of existence demanded
(even at meals they generally read), but still their
mutual affection was tremendous.   Moreover, they were
very firmly fixed in their habits.   Now one of these
habits was never to entertain company on Friday night.
Friday night was their night of solemn privacy.   The
explanation of this habit offers a proof of the sentimental
relations between them.

Mr Morfe was an accountant.   Indeed, he was *the*
accountant in Bursley, and perhaps he knew more
secrets of the ledgers of the principal earthenware manufacturers than some of the manufacturers did themselves.
But he did not live for accountancy.   At five o'clock
every evening he was capable of absolutely forgetting
it.   He lived for music.   He was organist of Saint
Luke's Church (with an industrious understudy—for he
did not always rise for breakfast on Sundays) and, more
important, he was conductor of the Bursley Orpheus Glee
and Madrigal Club.   And herein lay the origin of those
Friday nights.   A glee and madrigal club naturally com-
prises women as well as men; and the women are apt to
be youngish, prettyish, and somewhat fond of music.
Further, the conductorship of a choir involves many and
various social encounters.   Now Mary Morfe was jealous.   Though Richard Morfe ruled his choir with whips,
though his satiric tongue was a scorpion to the choir,
though he never looked twice at any woman, though she
was always saying that she wished he would marry,
Mary Morfe was jealous.   It was Mary Morfe who had
created the institution of the Friday night, and she had
created it in order to prove, symbolically and spectacu-
larly, to herself, to him, and to the world, that he and
she lived for each other alone.   All their friends, every
member of the choir, in fact the whole of the respectable
part of Bursley, knew quite well that in the Morfes'
house Friday was sacredly Friday.

And yet a caller!

" It's a woman," murmured Mary.   Until her ear
had assured her of this fact she had seemed to be more
disturbed than startled by the stir in the lobby.

And it was a woman.   It was Miss Eva Harracles,
one of the principal contraltos in the glee and madrigal
club.   She entered richly blushing, and excusably a
little nervous and awkward.   She was a tall, agreeable
creature of fewer than thirty years, dark, almost handsome, with fine lips and eyes, and an effective large hat
and a good muff.   In every physical way a marked contrast to the thin, prim, desiccated brother and sister.

Richard Morfe flushed faintly.   Mary Morfe grew
more pallid.

" I really must apologize for coming in like this,"
said Eva, as she shook hands cordially with Mary Morfe.
She knew Mary very well indeed.   For Mary was the
" librarian " of the glee and madrigal club; Mary never
missed a rehearsal, though she cared no more for music
than she cared for the National Debt.   She was a perfect librarian, and very good at unofficially prodding in-
dolent members into a more regular attendance too.

" Not at all! " said Mary.   " We were only reading;
you aren't disturbing us in the least."   Which, though
polite, was a lie.

And Eva Harracles sat down between them.   And
brother and sister abandoned their literature.

" I can't stop," said she, glancing at the clock immediately in front of her eyes.   " I must catch the last
car for Silverhays."

" You've got twenty minutes yet," said Mr Morfe.

" Because," said Eva, " I don't want that walk from
Turnhill to Silverhays on a dark night like this."

" No, I should think not, indeed! " said Mary Morfe.

" You've got a full twenty minutes," Mr Morfe repeated.   The clock showed three minutes past nine.

The electric cars to and from the town of Turnhill
were rumbling past the very door of the Morfes every

five minutes, and would continue to do so till midnight.
But Silverhays is a mining village a couple of miles be-
yond Turnhill, and the service between Turnhill and
Silverhays ceases before ten o'clock.   Eva's father
was a colliery manager who lived on the outskirts of
Silverhays.

" I've got a piece of news," said Eva.

" Yes? " said Mary Morfe.

Mr Morfe was taciturn.   He stooped to nourish the
fire.

" About Mr Loggerheads," said Eva, and stared
straight at Mary Morfe.

" About Mr Loggerheads! " Mary Morfe echoed,
and stared back at Eva.   And the atmosphere seemed
to have been thrown into a strange pulsation.

Here perhaps I ought to explain that it was not the
peculiarity of Mr Loggerheads' name that produced the
odd effect.   Loggerheads is a local term for a harmless
plant called the knapweed (*centaurea nigra*), and it is
also the appellation of a place and of quite excellent
people, and no one regards it as even the least bit
odd.

" I'm told," said Eva, " that he's going into the
Hanbridge Choir! "

Mr Loggerheads was the principal tenor of the
Bursley Glee and Madrigal Club.   And he was reckoned
one of the finest " after-dinner tenors " in the Five
Towns.   The Hanbridge Choir was a rival organization,
a vast and powerful affair that fascinated and swallowed
promising singers from all the choirs of the vicinity.
The Hanbridge Choir had sung at Windsor, and since
that event there had been no holding it.   All other
choirs hated it with a homicidal hatred.

" I'm told," Eva proceeded, " that the Birmingham
and Sheffield Bank will promote him to the cashiership
of the Hanbridge Branch on the understanding that he
joins the Hanbridge Choir.   Shows what influence they

have!   And it shows how badly the Hanbridge Choir
wants him."

(Mr Loggerheads was cashier of the Bursley branch
of the Birmingham and Sheffield Bank.)

" Who told you? " asked Mary Morfe, curtly.

Richard Morfe said nothing. The machinations of
the manager of the Hanbridge Choir always depressed
and disgusted him into silence.

" Oh! " said Eva Harracles. " It's all about."
(By which she meant that it was in the air.)   " Everyone's talking of it."

" And do they say Mr Loggerheads has accepted? "
Mary demanded.

" Yes," said Eva.

" Well," said Mary, " it's not true! . . . A mistake! " she added.

" How do you know it isn't true? " Mr Morfe inquired doubtfully.

" Since you're so curious," said Mary, defiantly,
" Mr Loggerheads told me himself."

" When? "

" The other day."

" You never said anything to me," protested Mr
Morfe.

" It didn't occur to me," Mary replied.

" Well, I'm very glad! " remarked Eva Harracles.
" But I thought I ought to let you know at once what
was being said."

Mary Morfe's expression conveyed the fact that in her
opinion Eva Harracles' evening call was a vain thing,
too lightly undertaken, and conceivably lacking in the
nicest discretion.   Whereupon Mr Morfe was evidently
struck by the advisability of completely changing the
subject.   And he did change it.   He began to talk
about certain difficulties in the choral parts of Havergal
Brian's *Vision of Cleopatra*, a work which he meant the
Bursley Glee and Madrigal Club to perform though it

should perish in the attempt. Growing excited, in his
dry way, concerning the merits of this composition, he
rose from his easy chair and went to search for it. Before doing so he looked at the clock, which indicated
twenty minutes past nine.

" Am I all right for time? " asked Eva.

" Yes, you're all right," said he. " If you go when
that clock strikes half-past, and take the next car down,
you'll make the connection easily at Turnhill. I'll put
you into the car."

" Oh, thanks! " said Eva.

Mr Morfe kept his modern choral music beneath a
broad seat under the bow window. The music was concealed by a low curtain that ran on a rod—the ingenious device of Mary. He stooped down to find the
Vision of Cleopatra, and at first he could not find it.
Mary walked towards that end of the drawing-room
with a vague notion of helping him, and then Eva did
the same, and then Mary walked back, and then Mr
Morfe happily put his hand on the *Vision of Cleopatra*.

He opened the score for Eva's inspection, and began
to hum passages and to point out others, and Eva also
began to hum, and they hummed in concert, at intervals exclaiming against the wantonness with which
Havergal Brian had invented difficulties. Eva glanced
at the clock.

" You're all right," Mr Morfe assured her somewhat
impatiently. And he, too, glanced at the clock:
" You've still nearly ten minutes."

And proceeded with his critical and explanatory
comments on the *Vision of Cleopatra*.

He was capable of becoming almost delirious about
music. Mary Morfe had seated herself in silence.

At last Eva and Mr Morfe approached the fire and
the mantelpiece again. Mr Morfe shut up the score,
dismissed his delirium, and looked at the clock, quite
prepared to see it pointing to twenty-nine and a half

minutes past nine. Instead, the clock pointed to only twenty-two minutes past nine.

" By Jove! " he exclaimed. He went nearer.

" By Jove! " he exclaimed again rather more loudly. " I do believe that clock's stopped! "

It had. The pendulum hung perpendicular, motionless, dead.

He was astounded. For the clock had never been known to stop. It was a presentation clock, of the highest guaranteed quality, offered to him as a small token of regard and esteem by the members of the Bursley Orpheus Glee and Madrigal Club to celebrate the twelfth anniversary of his felicitous connection with the said society. It had stood on his mantelpiece for four years and had earned an absolutely first-class reputation for itself. He wound it up on the last day of every month, for it was a thirty-odd day clock, specially made by a famous local expert; and he had not known it to vary more than ten minutes a month at the most. And lo! it had stopped in the very middle of the month.

" Did you wind it up last time? " asked Mary.

" Of course," he snapped. He had taken out his watch and was gazing at it. He turned to Eva. " It's twenty to ten," he said. " You've missed your connection at Turnhill—that's a certainty. I'm very sorry."

Obviously there was only one course open to a gallant man whose clock was to blame: namely, to accompany Eva Harracles to Turnhill by car, to accompany her on foot to Silverhays, then to walk back to Turnhill and come home again by car. A young woman could not be expected to perform that bleak and perhaps dangerous journey from Turnhill to Silverhays alone after ten o'clock at night in November. Such was the clear course. But he dared scarcely suggest it. He dared scarcely suggest it because of his sister. He was afraid of Mary. The names of Richard Morfe and Eva

Harracles had already been coupled in the mouth of gossip. And naturally Eva Harracles herself could not suggest that Richard should sally out and leave his sister alone on this night specially devoted to sisterliness and brotherliness. And of course, Eva thought, Mary will never, never suggest it.

But Eva was wrong there.

To the amazement of both Richard and Eva, Mary calmly said:

" Well, Dick, the least you can do now is to see Miss Harracles home. You'll easily be able to catch the last car back from Turnhill if you start at once. I daresay I shall go to bed."

And in three minutes Richard Morfe and Eva Harracles were being sped into the night by Mary Morfe.

The Morfes' house was at the corner of Trafalgar Road and Beech Street. The cars stopped at that corner in their wild course towards the town and towards Turnhill. A car was just coming. But instead of waiting for it Richard Morfe and Eva Harracles deliberately turned their backs on Trafalgar Road, and hurried side by side down Beech Street. Beech Street is a short street, and ends in a nondescript unlighted waste patch of ground. They arrived in the gloom of this patch, safe from all human inquisitiveness, and then Richard Morfe warmly kissed Eva Harracles in the mathematical centre of those lips of hers. And Eva Harracles showed no resentment of any kind, nor even shame. Yet she had been very carefully brought up. The sight would have interested Bursley immensely; it would have appealed strongly to Bursley's strong sense of the piquant. . . . That dry old stick Dick Morfe kissing one of his contraltos in the dark at the bottom end of Beech Street.

" Then you hadn't told her! " murmured Eva Harracles.

" No! " said Richard, with a slight hesitation. " I was just going to begin to tell her when you called."

Another woman might have pouted to learn that her lover had exhibited even a little cowardice in informing his family that he was engaged to be married. But Eva did not pout. She comprehended the situation, and the psychology of the relations between brothers and sisters. (She herself possessed both brothers and sisters.) All the courting had been singularly secret and odd.

" I shall tell her to-morrow morning at breakfast," said Richard, firmly. " Unless, after all, she isn't gone to bed when I get back."

By a common impulse they now returned towards Trafalgar Road.

" I say," said Richard, " what made you call? "

" I was passing," said the beloved. " And somehow I couldn't help it. Of course, I knew it wasn't true about Mr Loggerheads. But I had to think of something."

Richard was in ecstasy; had never been in such ecstasy.

" I say," he said again. " I suppose *you* didn't put your finger against the pendulum of that clock? "

" Oh, *no !* " she replied with emphasis.

" Well, I'm jolly glad it did stop, anyway," said Richard. " What a lark, eh? "

She agreed that the lark was ideal. They walked down the road till a car should overtake them.

" Do you think she suspects anything? " Eva asked.

" I'll swear she doesn't," said Richard, positively. " It'll be a bit of a startler for the old girl."

" No doubt you've heard," said Eva, haltingly, " that Mr Loggerheads has cast eyes on Mary."

" And do you think there's anything *in* that? " Richard questioned sharply.

" Well," she said, " I really don't know." Meaning that she decidedly thought that Mary *had* been encouraging advances from Mr Loggerheads.

" Well," said Richard, superiorly, " you may just

take it from me that there's nothing in it at all. . . .
Ha!" He laughed shortly. He knew Mary.

Then they got on a car, and tried to behave as though
their being together was a mere accident, as though
they had not become engaged to one another within the
previous twenty-four hours.

II

IMMEDIATELY after the departure of Richard Morfe and
Eva Harracles, his betrothed, from the front door of the
former, Mr Simon Loggerheads arrived at the same front
door, and rang thereat, and was a little surprised, and
also a little unnerved, when the door opened instantly,
as if by magic. Mr Simon Loggerheads said to himself,
as he saw the door move on its hinges, that Miss Morfe
must have discovered a treasure of a servant who, when
she had nothing else to do, spent her time on the inner
door-mat waiting to admit possible visitors—even on
Friday night. Nevertheless, Mr Simon Loggerheads regretted that prompt opening, as one regrets the prompt
opening of the door of a dentist.

And it was no servant who stood in front of him,
under the flickering beam of the lobby-lamp. It was
Mary Morfe herself. The simple explanation was that
she had just sped her brother and Eva Harracles, and had
remained in the lobby for the purpose of ascertaining by
means of her finger whether the servant had, as usual,
forgotten to dust the tops of the picture-frames.

"Oh!" said Mr Loggerheads, when he saw Mary
Morfe. For the cashier of the Bursley branch of the
Birmingham and Sheffield Bank it was not a very able
speech, but it was all he could accomplish.

And Miss Mary Morfe said:

"Oh!"

She was thirty-eight, and he was quite that (for the

Bank mentioned does not elevate its men to the august
situation of cashier under less than twenty years' service), and yet they neither of them had enough worldliness to behave in a reasonable manner.   Then Miss
Morfe, to whom it did at last occur that something must
be done, produced an invitation:

"Do come in!"   And she added, "Richard has just
gone out."

"Oh!" commented Mr Simon Loggerheads again.
(After all, it must be admitted that tenors as a class
have never been noted for their conversational powers.)
But he was obviously more at ease, and he went in, and
Mary Morfe shut the door.   At this very instant her
brother and Eva were in secret converse at the back end
of Beech Street.

"Do take your coat off!" Mary suggested to Simon.
Simultaneously the servant appeared at the kitchen extremity of the lobby, and Mary thrust her out of sight
again with the cold words: "It's all right, Susan."

Mr Loggerheads took his coat off, and Mary Morfe
watched him as he did so.

He made a pretty figure.   He was something of a
dandy.   The lapels of the overcoat would have showed
that, not to mention the correctly severe necktie.   All
his clothes, in fact, had "cut and style," even to his
boots.   In the Five Towns many a young man is a
dandy down to the edge of his trousers, but not down to
the ground.   Mr Loggerheads looked a young man.
The tranquillity of his career and the quietude of his
tastes had preserved his youthfulness.   And, further,
he had the air of a successful, solid, much-respected in-
dividual.   To be a cashier, though worthy, is not to be
a nabob, but a bachelor can save a lot out of over twenty
years of regular salary.   And Mr Loggerheads had saved
quite a lot.   And he had had opportunities of advan-
tageously investing his savings.   Then everybody knew
him, and he knew everybody.   He handed out gold at

least once a week to nearly half the town, and you cannot help venerating a man who makes a practice of
handing out gold to you. And he had thrilled thousands with the wistful beauty of his voice in "The
Sands of Dee." In a word, Simon Loggerheads was a
personage, if not talkative.

They went into the drawing-room. Mary Morfe
closed the door gently. Simon Loggerheads strolled
vaguely and self-consciously up to the fireplace, murmuring.

"So he's gone out?"

"Yes," said Mary Morfe, in confirmation of her first
statement.

"I'm sorry!" said Simon Loggerheads. A state-
ment which was absolutely contrary to the truth.
Simon Loggerheads was deeply relieved and glad that
Richard Morfe was out.

The pair, aged slightly under and slightly over forty,
seemed to hover for a fraction of a second uncertainly
near each other, and then, somehow, mysteriously,
Simon Loggerheads had kissed Mary Morfe. She
blushed. He blushed. The kiss was repeated. Mary
gazed up at him. Mary could scarcely believe that he
was hers. She could scarcely believe that on the previous evening he had proposed marriage to her—rather
suddenly, so it seemed to her, but delightfully. She
could comprehend his conduct no better than her own.
They two, staid, settled-down, both of them "old
maids," falling in love and behaving like lunatics!
Mary, a year ago, would have been ready to prophesy
that if ever Simon Loggerheads—at his age!—did
marry, he would assuredly marry something young,
something ingenuous, something cream-and-rose, and
probably something with rich parents. For twenty
years Simon Loggerheads had been marked down
for capture by the marriageable spinsters and
widows, and the mothers with daughters, of Bursley.

And he had evaded capture, despite the special temptations to which an after-dinner tenor is necessarily subject. And now Mary Morfe had caught him—caught him, moreover, without having had the slightest intention of catching him. She was one of the most spinsterish spinsters in the Five Towns; and she had often said things about men and marriage of which the recollection now, as an affianced woman, was very disturbing to her. However, she did not care. She did not understand how Simon Loggerheads had had the wit to perceive that she would be an ideal wife. And she did not care. She did not understand how, as a result of Simon Loggerheads falling in love with her, she had fallen in love with him. And she did not care. She did not care a fig for anything. She *was* in love with him, and he with her, and she was idiotically joyous, and so was he. And that was all.

On reflection, I have to admit that she did in fact care for one thing. That one thing was the look on her brother's face when he should learn that she, the faithful sardonic sister, having incomprehensibly become indispensable and all in all to a bank cashier, meant to desert him. She was afraid of that look. She trembled at the fore-vision of it.

Still, Richard had to be informed, and the world had to be informed, for the silken dalliance between Mary and Simon had been conducted with a discretion and a secrecy more than characteristic of their age and dispositions. It had been arranged between the lovers that Simon should call on that Friday evening, when he would be sure to catch Richard in his easy chair, and should, in presence of Mary, bluntly communicate to Richard the blunt fact.

"What's he gone out for? Anything special?" asked Simon.

Mary explained the circumstances.

"The truth is," she finished, "that girl is just throw

ing herself at Dick's head.   There's no doubt of it.   I
never saw such work! "

"Well," said Simon Loggerheads, " of course, you
know, there's been a certain amount of talk about them.
Some folks say that your brother—er—began—"

"And do you believe that? " demanded Mary.

" I don't know," said Simon.   By which he meant
diplomatically to convey that he had had a narrow
escape of believing it, at any rate.

"Well," said Mary, with conviction, "you may take
it from me that it isn't so.   I know Dick.   Eva Harracles may throw herself at his head till there's no
breath left in her body, and it'll make no difference to
Dick.   Do *you* see Dick a married man?   I don't.   I
only wish he *would* take it into his head to get married.   It
would make me much easier in my mind.   But all the same
I do think it's downright wicked that a girl should fling
herself *at* him, right *at* him.   Fancy her calling to-night!
It's the sort of thing that oughtn't to be encouraged."

" But I understood you to say that you yourself had
told him to see her home," Simon Loggerheads put in.
" Isn't that encouraging her, as it were? "

" Ah! " said Mary, with a smile.   " I only suggested
it to him because it came over me all of a sudden how
nice it would be to have you here all alone!   He can't
be back much before twelve."

To such a remark there is but one response.   A sofa
is, after all, made for two people, and the chance of the
servant calling on them was small.

" And so the clock stopped! " observed Simon
Loggerheads.

" Yes," said Mary.   " If it hadn't been for the sheer
accident of that clock stopping, we shouldn't be sitting
here on this sofa now, and Dick would be in that chair,
and you would just be beginning to tell him that we are
engaged."   She sighed.   " Poor Dick!   What on earth
will he do? "

"Strange how things happen!" Simon reflected in a low voice. "But I'm really surprised at that clock stopping like that. It's a clock that you ought to be able to depend on, that clock is."

He got up to inspect the timepiece. He knew all about the clock, because he had been chairman of the presentation committee which had gone to Manchester to buy it.

"Why!" he murmured, after he had toyed a little with the pendulum, "it goes all right. Its tick is as right as rain."

"How odd!" responded Mary.

Simon Loggerheads set the clock by his own impeccable watch, and then sat down again. And he drew something from his waistcoat pocket and slid it on to Mary's finger.

Mary regarded her finger in silent ecstasy, and then breathed "How lovely!"—not meaning her finger.

"Shall I stay till he comes back?" asked Simon.

"If I were you I shouldn't do that," said Mary. "But you can safely stay till eleven-thirty. Then I shall go to bed. He'll be tired and short [curt] when he gets back. I'll tell him myself to-morrow morning at breakfast. And you might come to-morrow afternoon early, for tea.'"

Simon did stay till half-past eleven. He left precisely when the clock, now convalescent, struck the half-hour. At the door Mary said to him:

"I won't have any secrets from you, Simon. It was I who stopped that clock. I stopped it while they were bending down looking for music. I wanted to be as sure as I could of a good excuse for me suggesting that he ought to take her home. I just wanted to get him out of the house."

"But why?" asked Simon.

"I must leave that to you to guess," said Mary, with a hint of tartness, but smiling.

Loggerheads and Richard Morfe met in Trafalgar Road.

" Good-night, Morfe."

" 'night, Loggerheads! "

And each passed on, without having stopped.

You can picture for yourself the breakfast of the brother and sister.

HOT POTATOES

I

IT was considered by certain people to be a dramatic
moment in the history of musical enterprise in the
Five Towns when Mrs Swann opened the front door of
her house at Bleakridge, in the early darkness of a
November evening, and let forth her son Gilbert. Gilbert's age was nineteen, and he was wearing evening
dress, a form of raiment that had not hitherto
happened to him. Over the elegant suit was his winter
overcoat, making him bulky, and round what may be
called the rim of the overcoat was a white woollen scarf,
and the sleeves of the overcoat were finished off with
white woollen gloves. Under one arm he carried a vast
inanimate form whose extremity just escaped the
ground. This form was his violoncello, fragile as a
pretty woman, ungainly as a navvy, and precious as
honour. Mrs Swann looked down the street, which
ended to the east in darkness and a marl pit, and up the
street, which ended to the west in Trafalgar Road and
electric cars; and she shivered, though she had a shawl
over her independent little shoulders. In the Five
Towns, and probably elsewhere, when a woman puts
her head out of her front door, she always looks first to
right and then to left, like a scouting Iroquois, and if the
air nips she shivers—not because she is cold, but merely
to express herself.

"For goodness sake, keep your hands warm," Mrs
Swann enjoined her son.

"Oh!" said Gilbert, with scornful lightness, as though his playing had never suffered from cold hands, "it's quite warm to-night!" Which it was not.

"And mind what you eat!" added his mother. "There! I can hear the car."

He hurried up the street. The electric tram slid in thunder down Trafalgar Road, and stopped for him with a jar, and he gingerly climbed into it, practising all precautions on behalf of his violoncello. The car slid away again towards Bursley, making blue sparks. Mrs Swann stared mechanically at the flickering gas in her lobby, and then closed her front door. He was gone! The boy was gone!

Now, the people who considered the boy's departure to be a dramatic moment in the history of musical enterprise in the Five Towns were Mrs Swann, chiefly, and the boy, secondarily.

II

AND more than the moment—the day, nay, the whole week—was dramatic in the history of local musical enterprise.

It had occurred to somebody in Hanbridge, about a year before, that since York, Norwich, Hereford, Gloucester, Birmingham, and even Blackpool had their musical festivals, the Five Towns, too, ought to have its musical festival. The Five Towns possessed a larger population than any of these centres save Birmingham, and it was notorious for its love of music. Choirs from the Five Towns had gone to all sorts of places—such as Brecknock, Aberystwyth, the Crystal Palace, and even a place called Hull—and had come back with first prizes—cups and banners—for the singing of choruses and part-songs. There were three (or

at least two and a half) rival choirs in Hanbridge alone.
Then also the brass band contests were famously attended. In the Five Towns the number of cornet
players is scarcely exceeded by the number of public-
houses. Hence the feeling, born and fanned into lusti-
ness at Hanbridge, that the Five Towns owed it to its
self-respect to have a Musical Festival like the rest of
the world! Men who had never heard of Wagner, men
who could not have told the difference between a sonata
and a sonnet to save their souls, men who spent all their
lives in manufacturing tea-cups or china door-knobs,
were invited to guarantee five pounds a-piece against
possible loss on the festival; and they bravely and
blindly did so. The conductor of the largest Hanbridge
choir, being appointed to conduct the preliminary rehearsals of the Festival Chorus, had an acute attack of
self-importance, which, by the way, almost ended fatally
a year later.

Double-crown posters appeared magically on all the
hoardings announcing that a Festival consisting of three
evening and two morning concerts would be held in the
Alexandra Hall, at Hanbridge, on the 6th, 7th and 8th
November, and that the box-plan could be consulted at
the principal stationers. The Alexandra Hall contained
no boxes whatever, but " box-plan " was the phrase
sacred to the occasion, and had to be used. And the
Festival more and more impregnated the air, and took
the lion's share of the columns of the *Staffordshire Signal*.
Every few days the *Signal* reported progress, even to intimate biographical details of the singers engaged, and of
the composers to be performed, together with analyses of
the latter's works. And at last the week itself had
dawned in exhilaration and excitement. And early on
the day before the opening day John Merazzi, the renowned conductor, and Herbert Millwain, the renowned
leader of the orchestra, and the renowned orchestra
itself, all arrived from London. And finally sundry

musical critics arrived from the offices of sundry London
dailies. The presence of these latter convinced an awed
population that its Festival was a real Festival, and not
a local make-believe. And it also tranquillized in some
degree the exasperating and disconcerting effect of a
telegram from the capricious Countess of Chell (who had
taken six balcony seats and was the official advertised
high patroness of the Festival) announcing at the last
moment that she could not attend.

III

Mrs Swann's justification for considering (as she in fact
did consider) that her son was either the base or the apex
of the splendid pyramid of the Festival lay in the following facts:—

From earliest infancy Gilbert had been a musical
prodigy, and the circle of his fame had constantly been
extending. He could play the piano with his hands
before his legs were long enough for him to play it with
his feet. That is to say, before he could use the pedals.
A spectacle formerly familiar to the delighted friends of
the Swanns was Gilbert, in a pinafore and curls, seated
on a high chair topped with a large Bible and a bound
volume of the *Graphic*, playing " Home Sweet Home "
with Thalberg's variations, while his mother, standing
by his side on her right foot, put the loud pedal on or off
with her left foot according to the infant's whispered
orders. He had been allowed to play from ear—playing
from ear being deemed especially marvellous—until
some expert told Mrs Swann that playing solely from
ear was a practice to be avoided if she wished her son to
fulfil the promise of his babyhood. Then he had lessons
at Knype, until he began to teach his teacher. Then he

said he would learn the fiddle, and he did learn the fiddle; also the viola. He did not pretend to play the flute, though he could. And at school the other boys would bring him their penny or even sixpenny whistles so that he might show them of what wonderful feats a common tin whistle is capable.

Mr Swann was secretary for the Toft End Brickworks and Colliery Company (Limited). Mr Swann had passed the whole of his career in the offices of the prosperous Toft End Company, and his imagination did not move freely beyond the company's premises. He had certainly intended that Gilbert should follow in his steps; perhaps he meant to establish a dynasty of Swanns, in which the secretaryship of the twenty per cent. paying company should descend for ever from father to son. But Gilbert's astounding facility in music had shaken even this resolve, and Gilbert had been allowed at the age of fifteen to enter, as assistant, the shop of Mr James Otkinson, the piano and musical instrument dealer and musicseller, in Crown Square, Hanbridge. Here, of course, he found himself in a musical atmosphere. Here he had at once established a reputation for showing off the merits of a piano, a song, or a waltz, to customers male and female. Here he had thirty pianos, seven harmoniums, and all the new and a lot of classical music to experiment with. He would play any " piece " at sight for the benefit of any lady in search of a nice easy waltz or reverie. Unfortunately ladies would complain that the pieces proved much more difficult at home than they had seemed under the fingers of Gilbert in the shop. Here, too, he began to give lessons on the piano. And here he satisfied his secret ambition to learn the violoncello, Mr Otkinson having in stock a violoncello that had never found a proper customer. His progress with the 'cello had been such that the theatre people offered him an engagement, which his father and his own sense of the

enormous respectability of the Swanns compelled him
to refuse. But he always played in the band of the
Five Towns Amateur Operatic Society, and was beloved by its conductor as being utterly reliable. His
connection with choirs started through his merits as a
rehearsal accompanist who could keep time and make
his bass chords heard against a hundred and fifty voices.
He had been appointed (*nem. con.*) rehearsal accompanist to the Festival Chorus. He knew the entire
Festival music backwards and upside down. And his
modestly-expressed desire to add his 'cello as one of the
local reinforcements of the London orchestra had been
almost eagerly complied with by the Advisory Committee.

Nor was this all. He had been invited to dinner by
Mrs Clayton Vernon, the social leader of Bursley. In
the affair of the Festival Mrs Clayton Vernon loomed
larger than even she really was. And this was due to an
accident, to a sheer bit of luck on her part. She happened to be a cousin of Mr Herbert Millwain, the leader
of the orchestra down from London. Mrs Clayton
Vernon knew no more about music than she knew about
the North Pole, and cared no more. But she was Mr
Millwain's cousin, and Mr Millwain had naturally to
stay at her house. And she came in her carriage to
fetch him from the band rehearsals; and, in short, anyone might have thought from her self-satisfied demeanour (though she was a decent sort of woman at heart)
that she had at least composed " Judas Maccabeus."
It was at a band rehearsal that she had graciously commanded Gilbert Swann to come and dine with her and
Mr Millwain between the final rehearsal and the opening concert. This invitation was, as it were, the over-
flowing drop in Mrs Swann's cup. It was proof, to her,
that Mr Millwain had instantly pronounced Gilbert to
be the equal of London 'cellists, and perhaps their
superior. It was proof, to her, that Mr Millwain relied

on him particularly to maintain the honour of the band in the Festival.

Gilbert had dashed home from the final rehearsal, and his mother had helped him with the unfamiliarities of evening dress, while he gave her a list of all the places in the music where, as he said, the band was " rocky," and especially the 'cellos, and a further list of all the smart musical things that the players from London had said to him and he had said to them.   He simply knew everything from the inside.   And not even the great Merazzi, the conductor, was more familiar with the music than he.   And the ineffable Mrs Clayton Vernon had asked him to dinner with Mr Millwain!   It was indubitable to Mrs Swann that all the Festival rested on her son's shoulders.

IV

" It's freezing, I think," said Mr Swann, when he came home at six o'clock from his day's majestic work at Toft End.   This was in the bedroom.   Mrs Swann, a comely little thing of thirty-nine, was making herself resplendent for the inaugural solemnity of the Festival, which began at eight.   The news of the frost disturbed her.

" How annoying! " she said.

" Annoying? " he questioned blandly.   " Why? "

" Now you needn't put on any of your airs, John! " she snapped.   She had a curt way with her at critical times.   " You know as well as I do that I'm thinking of Gilbert's hands. . . .   No! you must wear your frock-coat, of course! . . . All that drive from the other end of the town right to Hanbridge in a carriage!   Perhaps outside the carriage, because of the 'cello!   There'll never be room for two of them and the 'cello and Mrs Clayton Vernon in her carriage!   And he can't keep his hands in his pockets because of holding the 'cello.   And

he's bound to pretend he isn't cold. He's so silly. And
yet he knows perfectly well he won't do himself justice
if his hands are cold. Don't you remember last year at
the Town Hall? "

" Well," said Mr Swann, " we can't do anything;
anyway, we must hope for the best."

" That's all very well," said Mrs Swann. And it was.

Shortly afterwards, perfect in most details of her
black silk, she left the bedroom, requesting her husband to be quick, as tea was ready. And she came into
the little dining-room where the youthful servant was
poking up the fire.

" Jane," she said, " put two medium-sized potatoes
in the oven to bake."

" Potatoes, mum? "

" Yes, potatoes," said Mrs Swann, tartly.

It was an idea of pure genius that had suddenly
struck her; the genius of common sense.

She somewhat hurried the tea; then rang.

" Jane," she inquired, " are those potatoes ready? "

" Potatoes? " exclaimed Mr Swann.

" Yes, hot potatoes," said Mrs Swann, tartly. " I'm
going to run up with them by car to Mrs Vernon's. I
can slip them quietly over to Gil. They keep your
hands warm better than anything. Don't I remember
when I was a child! I shall leave Mrs Vernon's immediately, of course, but perhaps you'd better give me my
ticket and I will meet you at the hall. Don't you think
it's the best plan, John? "

"As you like," said Mr Swann, with the force of habit.

He was supreme in most things, but in the practical
details of their son's life and comfort she was supreme.
Her decision in such matters had never been questioned.
Mr Swann had a profound belief in his wife as a uniquely
capable and energetic woman. He was tremendously
loyal to her, and he sternly inculcated the same loyalty
to her in Gilbert.

V

Just as the car had stopped at the end of the street for Gilbert and his violoncello, so—more than an hour later —it stopped for Mrs Swann and her hot potatoes.

They were hot potatoes—nay, very hot potatoes—·of a medium size, because Mrs Swann's recollections of youth had informed her that if a potato is too large one cannot get one's fingers well around it, and if it is too small it cools somewhat rapidly. She had taken two, not in the hope that Gilbert would be able to use two at once, for one cannot properly nurse either a baby or a 'cello with two hands full of potatoes, but rather to provide against accident. Besides, the inventive boy might after all find a way of using both simultaneously, which would be all the better for his playing at the concert, and hence all the better for the success of the Musical Festival.

It never occurred to Mrs Swann that she was doing anything in the least unusual. There she was, in her best boots, and her best dress, and her best hat, and her sealskin mantle (not easily to be surpassed in the town), and her muff to match (nearly), and concealed in the muff were the two very hot potatoes. And it did not strike her that women of fashion like herself, wives of secretaries of flourishing companies, do not commonly go about with hot potatoes concealed on their persons. For she was a self-confident woman, and after a decision she did not reflect, nor did she heed minor consequences. She was always sure that what she was doing was the right and the only thing to do. And, to give her justice, it was; for her direct, abrupt common sense was indeed remarkable. The act of climbing up into the car warned her that she must be skilful in the control of these potatoes; one of them nearly fell out of the right end of her muff as she grasped the car rail with her right hand. She had to let go and save the potato, and begin again,

while the car waited.   The conductor took her for one of
those hesitating, hysterical women who are the bane of
car conductors.   " Now, missis! " he said.   " Up with
ye! "   But she did not care what manner of woman the
conductor took her for.

The car was nearly full of people going home from
their work, of people actually going in a direction contrary to the direction of the Musical Festival.   She sat
down among them, shocked by this indifference to the
Musical Festival.   At the back of her head had been an
idea that all the cars for Hanbridge would be crammed
to the step, and all the cars from Hanbridge forlorn and
empty.   She had vaguely imagined that the thoughts of
a quarter of a million of people would that evening be
centred on the unique Musical Festival.   And she was
shocked also by the conversation—not that it was in the
slightest degree improper—but because it displayed no
interest whatever in the Musical Festival.   And yet
there were several Festival advertisements adhering to
the roof of the car.   Travellers were discussing football,
soap, the weather, rates, trade; travellers were dozing;
travellers were reading about starting prices; but not
one seemed to be occupied with the Musical Festival.
" Nevertheless," she reflected with consoling pride, " if
they knew that our Gilbert was playing 'cello in the
orchestra and dining at this very moment with Mr Millwain, some of them would be fine and surprised, that
they would! "   No one would ever have suspected, from
her calm, careless, proud face, that such vain and two-
penny thoughts were passing through her head.   But
the thoughts that do pass through the heads of even the
most common-sensed philosophers, men and women,
are truly astonishing.

In four minutes she was at Bursley Town Hall,
where she changed into another car—full of people
equally indifferent to the Musical Festival—for the
suburb of Hillport, where Mrs Clayton Vernon lived.

" Put me out opposite Mrs Clayton Vernon's, will you? " she said to the conductor, and added, " you know the house? "

He nodded as if to say disdainfully in response to such a needless question: " Do I know the house? Do I know my pocket? "

As she left the car she did catch two men discussing the Festival, but they appeared to have no intention of attending it. They were earthenware manufacturers. One of them raised his hat to her. And she said to herself: " He at any rate knows how important my Gilbert is in the Festival! "

It was at the instant she pushed open Mrs Clayton Vernon's long and heavy garden gate, and crunched in the frosty darkness up the short winding drive, that the notion of the peculiarity of her errand first presented itself to her. Mrs Clayton Vernon was a relatively great lady, living in a relatively great house; one of the few exalted or peculiar ones who did not dine in the middle of the day like other folk. Mrs Clayton Vernon had the grand manner. Mrs Clayton Vernon instinctively and successfully patronized everybody. Mrs Clayton Vernon was a personage with whom people did not joke. And lo! Mrs Swann was about to invade her courtly and luxurious house, uninvited, unauthorized, with a couple of hot potatoes in her muff. What would Mrs Clayton Vernon think of hot potatoes in a muff? Of course, the Swanns were " as good as anybody." The Swanns knelt before nobody. The Swanns were of the cream of the town, combining commerce with art, and why should not Mrs Swann take practical measures to keep her son's hands warm in Mrs Clayton Vernon's cold carriage? Still, there was only one Mrs Clayton Vernon in Bursley, and it was impossible to deny that she inspired awe, even in the independent soul of Mrs Swann.

Mrs Swann rang the bell, reassuring herself. The next instant an electric light miraculously came into

existence outside the door, illuminating her from head
to foot.   This startled her.   But she said to herself that
it must be the latest dodge, and that, at any rate, it was
a very good dodge, and she began again the process of
reassuring herself.   The door opened, and a prim
creature stiffly starched stood before Mrs Swann.
" My word! " reflected Mrs Swann, " she must cost her
mistress a pretty penny for getting up aprons! "   And
she said aloud curtly:

" Will you please tell Mr Gilbert Swann that someone wants to speak to him a minute at the door? "

" Yes," said the servant, with pert civility.   " Will
you please step in? "

She had not meant to step in.   She had decidedly
meant not to step in, for she had no wish to encounter
Mrs Clayton Vernon; indeed, the reverse.   But she immediately perceived that in asking to speak to a guest
at the door she had socially erred.   At Mrs Clayton
Vernon's refined people did not speak to refined people
at the door.   So she stepped in, and the door was closed,
prisoning her and her potatoes in the imposing hall.

" I only want to see Mr Gilbert Swann," she insisted.

"Yes," said the servant.   " Will you please step into
the breakfast-room?   There's no one there.   I will tell
Mr Swann."

VI

As Mrs Swann was being led like a sheep out of the hall
into an apartment on the right, which the servant styled
the breakfast-room, another door opened, further up the
hall, and Mrs Clayton Vernon appeared.   Magnificent
though Mrs Swann was, the ample Mrs Clayton Vernon,
discreetly *décolletée*, was even more magnificent.   Dressed
as she meant to show herself at the concert, Mrs Clayton
Vernon made a resplendent figure worthy to be the
cousin of the leader of the orchestra—and worthy even

to take the place of the missing Countess of Chell. Mrs Clayton Vernon had a lorgnon at the end of a shaft of tortoise-shell; otherwise, a pair of eye-glasses on a stick. She had the habit of the lorgnon; the lorgnon seldom left her, and whenever she was in any doubt or difficulty she would raise the lorgnon to her eyes and stare patronizingly. It was a gesture tremendously effective. She employed it now on Mrs Swann, as who should say, " Who is this insignificant and scarcely visible creature that has got into my noble hall? " Mrs Swann stopped, struck into immobility by the basilisk glance. A courageous and even a defiant woman, Mrs Swann was taken aback. She could not possibly tell Mrs Clayton Vernon that she was the bearer of hot potatoes to her son. She scarcely knew Mrs Clayton Vernon, had only met her once at a bazaar! With a convulsive unconscious movement her right hand clenched nervously within her muff and crushed the rich mealy potato it held until the flesh of the potato was forced between the fingers of her glove. A horrible sticky mess! That is the worst of a high-class potato, cooked, as the Five Towns phrase it, " in its jacket." It will burst on the least provocation. There stood Mrs Swann, her right hand glued up with escaped potato, in the sober grandeur of Mrs Clayton Vernon's hall, and Mrs Clayton Vernon bearing down upon her like a Dreadnought.

Steam actually began to emerge from her muff.

" Ah! " said Mrs Clayton Vernon, inspecting Mrs Swann. " It's Mrs Swann! How do you do, Mrs Swann? "

She seemed politely astonished, as well she might be. By a happy chance she did not perceive the wisp of steam. She was not looking for steam. People do not expect steam from the interior of a visitor's muff.

" Oh! " said Mrs Swann, who was really in a pitiable state. " I'm sorry to trouble you, Mrs Clayton Vernon. But I want to speak to Gilbert for one moment."

She then saw that Mrs Clayton Verron's hand was graciously extended. She could not take it with her right hand, which was fully engaged with the extremely heated sultriness of the ruined potato. She could not refuse it, or ignore it. She therefore offered her left hand, which Mrs Clayton Vernon pressed with a well-bred pretence that people always offered her their left hands.

"Nothing wrong, I do hope!" said she, gravely.

"Oh no," said Mrs Swann. "Only just a little matter which had been forgotten. Only half a minute. I must hurry off at once as I have to meet my husband. If I could just see Gilbert—"

"Certainly," said Mrs Clayton Vernon. "Do come into the breakfast-room, will you? We've just finished dinner. We had it very early, of course, for the concert. Mr Millwain—my cousin—hates to be hurried. Maria, be good enough to ask Mr Swann to come here. Tell him that his mother wishes to speak to him."

In the breakfast-room Mrs Swann was invited, nay commanded by Mrs Clayton Vernon, to loosen her mantle. But she could not loosen her mantle. She could do nothing. In clutching the potato to prevent bits of it from falling out of the muff, she of course effected the precise opposite of her purpose, and bits of the luscious and perfect potato began to descend the front of her mantle. The clock struck seven, and ages elapsed, during which Mrs Swann could not think of anything whatever to say, but the finger of the clock somehow stuck motionless at seven, though the pendulum plainly wagged.

"I'm not too warm," she said at length, feebly but obstinately resisting Mrs Clayton Vernon's command. This, to speak bluntly, was an untruth. She was too warm.

"Are you sure that nothing is the matter˺" urged Mrs Clayton Vernon, justifiably alarmed by the expression of her visitor's features. "I beg you to confide in me if—"

"Not at all," said Mrs Swann, trying to laugh. "I'm only sorry to disturb you. I didn't mean to disturb you."

"What on earth is that?" cried Mrs Clayton Vernon.

The other potato, escaping Mrs Swann's vigilance, had run out of the muff and come to the carpet with a dull thud. It rolled half under Mrs Swann's dress. Almost hysterically she put her foot on it, thus making pulp of the second potato.

"What?" she inquired innocently.

"Didn't you hear anything? I trust it isn't a mouse! We have had them once."

Mrs Clayton Vernon thought how brave Mrs Swann was, not to be frightened by the word "mouse."

"I didn't hear anything," said Mrs Swann. Another untruth.

"If you aren't too warm, won't you come a little nearer the fire?"

But not for a thousand pounds would Mrs Swann have exposed the mush of potato on the carpet under her feet. She could not conceive in what ignominy the dreadful affair would end, but she was the kind of woman that nails her colours to the mast.

"Dear me!" Mrs Clayton Vernon murmured. "How delicious those potatoes do smell! I can smell them all over the house."

This was the most staggering remark that Mrs Swann had ever heard.

"Potatoes?" very weakly.

"Yes," said Mrs Clayton Vernon, smiling. "I must tell you that Mr Millwain is very nervous about getting his hands cold in driving to Hanbridge. And he has asked me to have hot potatoes prepared. Isn't it amusing? It seems hot potatoes are constantly used

for this purpose in winter by the pupils of the Royal
College of Music, and even by the professors. My
cousin says that even a slight chilliness of the hands
interferes with his playing. So I am having potatoes
done for your son too. A delightful boy he is! "

" Really! " said Mrs Swann. " How queer! But
what a good idea! "

She might have confessed then. But you do not
know her if you think she did. Gilbert came in, anxious
and alarmed. Mrs Clayton Vernon left them together.
The mother explained matters to the son, and in an
instant of time the ruin of two magnificent potatoes was
at the back of the fire. Then, without saluting Mrs
Clayton Vernon, Mrs Swann fled.

HALF-A-SOVEREIGN

THE scene was the up-platform of Knype railway
station on a summer afternoon, and, more particularly, that part of the platform round about the
bookstall. There were three persons in the neighbourhood of the bookstall. The first was the principal book
stall clerk, who was folding with extraordinary rapidity
copies of the special edition of the *Staffordshire Signal ;*
the second was Mr Sandbach, an earthenware manufacturer, famous throughout the Five Towns for his ingenious invention of teapots that will pour the tea into
the cup instead of all over the table; and a very shabby
man, whom Mr Sandbach did not know. This very
shabby man was quite close to the bookstall, while Mr
Sandbach stood quite ten yards away. Mr Sandbach
gazed steadily at the man, but the man, ignoring Mr
Sandbach, allowed dreamy and abstracted eyes to rest
on the far distance, where a locomotive or so was impatiently pushing and pulling waggons as an excitable
mother will drag and shove an inoffensive child. The
platform as a whole was sparsely peopled; the London
train had recently departed, and the station was suffering from the usual reaction; only a local train was signalled.

Mr Gale, a friend of Mr Sandbach's, came briskly on
to the platform from the booking-office, caught sight of
Mr Sandbach, and accosted him.

" Hello, Sandbach! "

" How do, Gale? "

To a slight extent they were rivals in the field of invention. But both had succeeded in life, and both had

the alert and prosperous air of success. Born about the same time, they stood nearly equal after forty years of earthly endeavour.

" What are you doing here? " asked Gale, casually.

" I've come to meet someone off the Crewe train."

" And I'm going by it—to Derby," said Mr Gale. " They say it's thirteen minutes late."

" Look here," said Mr Sandbach, taking no notice of this remark, " you see that man there? "

" Which one—by the bookstall? "

" Yes."

" Well, what about him? "

" I bet you you can't make him move from where he is—no physical force, of course."

Mr Gale hesitated an instant, and then his eye glistened with response to the challenge, and he replied:

" I bet you I can."

" Well, try," said Mr Sandbach.

Mr Sandbach and Mr Gale frequently threw down the glove to each other in this agreeable way. Either they asked conundrums, or they set test questions, or they suggested feats. When Mr Sandbach discovered at a Christmas party that you cannot stand with your left side close against a wall and then lift your right leg, his first impulse was to confront Mr Gale with the trick. When Mr Gale read in a facetious paper an article on the lack of accurate observation in the average man, entitled, "Do 'bus horses wear blinkers? " his opening remark to Mr Sandbach at their next meeting was: " I say, Sandbach, do 'bus horses wear blinkers? Answer quick! " And a phrase constantly in their mouths was, " I'll try that on Gale; " or, " I wonder whether Sandbach knows that? " All that was required to make their relations artistically complete was an official referee for counting the scores. Such a basis of friendship may seem bizarre, but it is by no means uncommon in the Five Towns, and perhaps elsewhere.

So that when Mr Sandbach defied Mr Gale to induce the shabby man to move from where he stood, the nostrils of the combatants twitched with the scent of battle.

Mr Gale conceived his tactics instantly and put them into execution. He walked along the platform some little distance, then turned, and taking a handful of silver from his pocket, began to count it. He passed slowly by the shabby man, almost brushing his shoulder; and, just as he passed, he left fall half-a-crown. The half-crown rolled round in a circle and lay down within a yard and a half of the shabby man. The shabby man calmly glanced at the half-crown and then at Mr Gale, who, strolling on, magnificently pretended to be unaware of his loss; and then the shabby man resumed his dreamy stare into the distance.

" Hi! " cried Mr Sandbach after Mr Gale. " You've dropped something."

It was a great triumph for Mr Sandbach.

" I told you you wouldn't get him to move! " said Mr Sandbach, proudly, having rejoined his friend at another part of the platform.

" What's the game? " demanded Mr Gale, frankly acknowledging by tone and gesture that he was defeated.

" Perfectly simple," answered Mr Sandbach, condescendingly, " when you know. I'll tell you—it's really very funny. Just as everyone was rushing to get into the London express I heard a coin drop on the platform, and I saw it rolling. It was half-a-sovereign. I couldn't be sure who dropped it, but I think it was a lady. Anyhow, no one claimed it. I was just going to pick it up when that chap came by. He saw it, and he put his foot on it as quick as lightning, and stood still. He didn't notice that I was after it too. So I drew back. I thought I'd wait and see what happens."

" He looks as if he could do with half-a-sovereign,"
said Mr Gale.

" Yes; he's only a station loafer."

" Then why doesn't he pick up his half-sovereign
and hook it? "

" Can't you see why? " said Mr Sandbach, patronizingly. " He's afraid of the bookstall clerk catching him at it. He's afraid it's the bookstall clerk that
has dropped that half-sovereign. You wait till the
bookstall clerk finishes those papers and goes inside,
and you'll see."

At this point Mr Gale made the happy involuntary
movement of a man who has suddenly thought of something really brilliant.

" Look here," said he. " You said you'd bet. But
you didn't bet. I'll bet you a level half-crown I get him
to shift this time."

" But you mustn't say anything to him."

" No—of course not."

" Very well, I'll bet you."

Mr Gale walked straight up to the shabby man, drew
half-a-sovereign from his waistcoat pocket, and held it
out. At the same time he pointed to the shabby man's
boots, and then in the most unmistakable way he
pointed to the exit of the platform. He said nothing,
but his gestures were expressive, and what they clearly
expressed was: " I know you've got a half-sovereign
under your foot; here's another half-sovereign for you
to clear off and ask no questions."

Meanwhile the ingenious offerer of the half-sovereign
was meditating thus: " I give half-a-sovereign, but I
shall gather up the other half-sovereign, and I shall also
win my bet. Net result: Half-a-crown to the good."

The shabby man, who could not have been a fool,
comprehended at once, accepted the half-sovereign, and
moved leisurely away—not, however, without glancing
at the ground which his feet had covered. The result

of the scrutiny evidently much surprised him, as it surprised, in a degree equally violent, both Mr Gale and Mr Sandbach. For there was no sign of half-a-sovereign under the feet of the shabby man. There was not even nine and elevenpence there.

Mr Gale looked up very angry and Mr Sandbach looked very foolish.

"This is all very well," Mr Gale exploded in tones low and fierce. "But I call it a swindle." And he walked, with an undecided, longing, shrinking air, in the wake of the shabby man who had pocketed his half-sovereign.

"I'm sure I saw him put his foot on it," said Mr Sandbach in defence of himself (meaning, of course, the other half-sovereign), "and I've never taken my eyes off him."

"Well, then, how do you explain it?"

"I don't explain it," said Mr Sandbach.

"I think some explanation is due to me," said Mr Gale, with a peculiar and dangerous intonation. "If this is your notion of a practical joke."

"There was no practical joke about it at all," Mr Sandbach protested. "If the half-sovereign has disappeared it's not my fault. I made a bet with you, and I've lost it. Here's your half-crown."

He produced two-and-six, which Mr Gale accepted, though he had a strange impulse to decline it with an air of offended pride.

"I'm still seven-and-six out," said Mr Gale.

"And if you are!" snapped Mr Sandbach, "you thought you'd do me down by a trick. Offering the man ten shillings to go wasn't at all a fair way of winning the bet, and you knew it, my boy. However, I've paid up; so that's all right."

"All I say is," Mr Gale obstinately repeated, "if this is your notion of a practical joke—"

"Didn't I tell you—" Mr Sandbach became icily furious.

The friendship hitherto existing between these two excellent individuals might have been ruined and annihilated for a comparative trifle, had not a surprising and indeed almost miraculous thing happened, by some kind of freak of destiny, in the nick of time.   Mr Sandbach was sticking close to Mr Gale, and Mr Gale was following in the leisurely footsteps of the very shabby man, possibly debating within himself whether he should boldly demand the return of his half-sovereign, when lo! a golden coin seemed to slip from the boot of the very shabby man.   It took the stone-flags of the platform with scarcely a sound, and Mr Sandbach and Mr Gale made a simultaneous, superb and undignified rush for it.   Mr Sandbach got it.   The very shabby man passed on, passed eternally out of the lives of the other two.   It may be said that he was of too oblivious and dreamy a nature for this world.   But one must not forget that he had made a solid gain of ten shillings.

" The soles of the fellow's boots must have been all cracks, and it must have got lodged in one of them," cheerfully explained Mr Sandbach as he gazed with pleasure at the coin.   " I hope you believe me now. You thought it was a plant.   I hope you believe me now."

Mr Gale made no response to this remark.   What Mr Gale said was:

" Don't you think that in fairness that half-sovereign belongs to me? "

" Why? " asked Mr Sandbach, bluntly.

" Well," Mr Gale began, searching about for a reason.

" You didn't find it," Mr Sandbach proceeded firmly.   " You didn't see it first.   You didn't pick it up.   Where do you come in? "

" I'm seven and sixpence out," said Mr Gale.

" And if I give you the coin, which I certainly shall not do, I should be half-a-crown out."

Friendship was again jeopardized, when a second interference of fate occurred, in the shape of a young and pretty woman who was coming from the opposite direction and who astonished both men considerably by stepping in front of them and barring their progress.

" Excuse me," said she, in a charming voice, but with a severe air. " But may I ask if you have just picked up that coin? "

Mr Sandbach, after looking vaguely, as if for inspiration, at Mr Gale, was obliged to admit that he had.

" Well," said the young lady, " if it's dated 1898, and if there's an ' A ' scratched on it, it's mine. I've lost it off my watch-chain." Mr Sandbach examined the coin, and then handed it to her, raising his hat. Mr Gale also raised his hat. The young lady's grateful smile was enchanting. Both men were bachelors and invariably ready to be interested.

" It was the first money my husband ever earned," the young lady explained, with her thanks.

The interest of the bachelors evaporated.

" Not a profitable afternoon," said Mr Sandbach, as the train came in and they parted.

" I think we ought to share the loss equally," said Mr Gale.

" Do you? " said Mr Sandbach. " That's like you."

THE BLUE SUIT

I WAS just going into my tailor's in Sackville Street, when who should be coming out of the same establishment but Mrs Ellis! I was startled, as any man might well have been, to see a lady emerging from my tailor's. Of course a lady might have been to a tailor's to order a tailor-made costume. Such an excursion would be perfectly legal and not at all shocking. But then my tailor did not " make " for ladies. And moreover, Mrs Ellis was not what I should call a tailor-made woman. She belonged to the other variety—the fluffy, lacy, flowing variety. I had made her acquaintance on one of my visits to the Five Towns. She was indubitably elegant, but in rather a Midland manner. She was a fine specimen of the provincial woman, and that was one of the reasons why I liked her. Her husband was a successful earthenware manufacturer. Occasionally he had to make long journeys—to Canada, to Australia and New Zealand—in the interests of his business; so that she was sometimes a grass-widow, with plenty of money to spend. Her age was about thirty-five; bright, agreeable, shrewd, downright, energetic; a little short and a little plump. Wherever she was, she was a centre of interest! In default of children of her own she amused herself with the children of her husband's sister, Mrs Carter. Mr Carter was another successful earthenware manufacturer. Her favourite among nephews and nieces was young Ellis Carter, a considerable local dandy and " dog." Such was Mrs Ellis.

" Are you a widow just now? " I asked her, after we had shaken hands.

267

" Yes," she said. " But my husband touched at Port Said yesterday, thank Heaven."

" Are you ordering clothes for him to wear on his arrival? " I adopted a teasing tone.

" Can you picture Henry in a Sackville Street suit? " she laughed.

I could not. Henry's clothes usually had the appearance of having been picked up at a Jew's.

" Then what *are* you doing here? " I insisted.

" I came here because I remembered you saying once that this was your tailor's," she said, " so I thought it would be a pretty good place."

Now I would not class my tailor with the half-dozen great tailors of the world, but all the same he is indeed a pretty good tailor.

" That's immensely flattering," I said. " But what have you been doing with h m? "

" Business," said she. " And if you want to satisfy your extraordinary inquisitiveness any further, don't you think you'd better come right away now and offer me some tea somewhere? "

" Splendid," I said. " Where? "

" Oh! The Hanover, of course! " she answered.

" Where's that? " I inquired.

" Don't you know the Hanover Tea-rooms in Regent Street? " she exclaimed, staggered.

I have often noticed that metropolitan resorts which are regarded by provincials as the very latest word of London style, are perfectly unknown to Londoners themselves. She led me along Vigo Street to the Hanover. It was a huge white place, with a number of little alcoves and a large band. We installed ourselves in one of the alcoves, with supplies of China tea and multitudinous cakes, and grew piquantly intimate, and then she explained her visit to my tailor's. I propose to give it here as nearly in her own words as I can.

I

I WOULDN'T tell you anything about it (she said) if I didn't know from the way you talk sometimes that you are interested in *people*. I mean any people, anywhere. Human nature! Everybody that I come across is frightfully interesting to me. Perhaps that's why I've got so many friends—and enemies. I *have*, you know. I just like watching people to see what they do, and then what they'll do next. I don't seem to mind so much whether they're good or naughty—with me it's their interestingness that comes first. Now I suppose you don't know very much about my nephew, Ellis Carter. Just met him once, I think, and that's all. Don't you think he's handsome? Oh! *I* do. I think he's very handsome. But then a man and a woman never do agree about what being handsome is in a man. Ellis is only twenty, too. He has such nice curly hair, and his eyes—haven't you noticed his eyes? His father says he's idle. But all fathers say that of their sons. I suppose you'll admit anyhow that he's one of the best-dressed youths in the Five Towns. Anyone might think he got his clothes in London, but he doesn't. It seems there's a simply marvellous tailor in Bursley, and Ellis and all his friends go to him. His father is always grumbling at the bills, so his mother told me. Well, when I was at their house in July, there happened to come for Ellis one of those flat boxes that men's tailors always pack suits in, and so I thought I might as well show a great deal of curiosity about it, and I did. And Ellis undid it in the breakfast-room (his father wasn't there) and showed me a lovely blue suit. I asked him to go upstairs and put it on. He wouldn't at first, but his sisters and I worried him till he gave way.

He came downstairs again like Solomon in all his glory. It really was a lovely suit. No—seriously, I'm not joking. It was a dream. He was very shy in it. I must say men are funny. Even when they really *like* having new clothes and cutting a figure, they simply hate putting them on for the first time. Ellis is that way. I don't know how many suits that boy hasn't got —sheer dandyism!—and yet he'll keep a new suit in the house a couple of months before wearing it! Now that's the sort of thing that I call "interesting." So curious, isn't it? Ellis wouldn't keep that suit on. No; as soon as we'd done admiring it he disappeared and changed it.

Now I'd gone that day to ask Ellis to escort me to Llandudno the week after. He likes going about with his auntie, and his auntie likes to have him. And of course she sees that it doesn't cost *him* anything. But his father has to be placated first. There's another funny thing! His father is always grumbling that Ellis is absolutely no good at all at the works, but the moment there's any question of Ellis going away for a holiday —even if it's only a week-end—then his father turns right round and wants to make out that Ellis is absolutely indispensable. Well, I got over his father. I always do, naturally. And it was settled that Ellis and I should go on the next Saturday.

I said to Ellis:

" You must be sure to bring that suit with you."

And then—will you believe me?—he stuck to it he wouldn't! Truly I was under the impression that I could argue either Ellis or his father into any mortal thing. But no! I couldn't argue Ellis into agreeing to bring that suit with him to Llandudno. He said he should wear whites. He said it was a September suit. He said that everybody wore blue at Llandudno, and he didn't want to be mistaken for a schoolmaster! Imagine him being mistaken for a schoolmaster! He even said there were some things I didn't understand! I told him there was a very particular reason why I wanted him to take that suit. And there *was*. He said:

" What is the reason? "

But I wouldn't tell him that. I wasn't going to knuckle down to him altogether. So it ended that we didn't either of us budge. However, I didn't mean to be beaten by a mere curly-headed boy. I can do what I please with his mother, though she *is* my eldest sister-in-law. And before he started in the dogcart to meet me at the station on our way to Llandudno she gave Ellis a bonnet-box to hand to me, and told him to take great care of it. He handed it over to me, and I also told him to take great care of it. Of course he became very curious to know what was in it. I said to him:

" You may see it on the pier on Monday. In fact, I believe you will."

He said: " It's heavy for a hat."

So I informed him that hats were both heavy and large this summer.

He said, " Well, I pity you, auntie! "

Naturally it was his blue suit that was in the box. His mother had burgled it after he'd done his packing, while he was having lunch.

I was determined he *should* wear that suit. And I felt pretty sure that when he saw my *reason* for asking him to bring it he'd be glad at the bottom of his heart that I'd brought it in spite of him. There is one good thing about Ellis—he can see a joke against himself. . . . Have another cake. Well, I will, then. . . . Yes, I'm coming to the reason.

II

A GIRL, you say? Well, of course. But you mustn't look so proud of yourself. A body needn't be anything like so clever as you are to be able to guess that there's a girl in it. Do you suppose I should have imagined for a moment that it would interest you if there hadn't been a girl in it? Not exactly! Well, it's a girl from Winnipeg. Came to England in June with her parents. Or rather, perhaps, her parents came with *her*. I'd never seen any of the three before—didn't know them from Adam and Eve. But my husband had made friends with them out there last year—great friends. And they wanted to make the acquaintance of my husband's wife. I'd gathered from Harry that they were quite my sort. . . . What *is* my sort? You know perfectly well what my sort is. There are only two sorts of people—the decent sort and the other sort. Well, they were doing England—you know, like Colonial people do—seriously, leaving nothing out. By the way, their name was only " Smith," without even a " y " in it or an " e " at the end. They wished to try a good seaside place, so I wrote to them and suggested Llandudno as a fair specimen, and it was arranged that we should meet there and spend at least a week together, and afterwards they were to come to the Five Towns. I suggested we should all stay at Hawthornden's . . . Hawthornden's? Don't you know —it's easily the best private hotel in Llandudno. Lift and a French chef and all kinds of things; but surely you must have seen all about it in the papers!

Now that was why I took Ellis with me. I hate travelling about alone, especially when my husband's away. And it was particularly on account of the girl that I stole the blue suit. But I didn't tell Ellis a word about the girl, and I only just mentioned the father and mother—and not even that until we were safely in the train. These young dandies are really very nervous and timid at bottom, you know, in spite of their airs. Ellis would walk ten miles sooner than have to meet a stranger of the older generation. And he's just as shy about girls too. I believe most men are, if you ask *me*.

The great encounter occurred in the hall, just before dinner. They were late, and so were we. I tell you, we were completely outshone. I tell you, we were not *in* it, not anywhere near being in it! For one thing, they were in evening-dress. Now at Hawthornden's you never dress for dinner. There isn't a place in Llandudno where it's the exception not to dress for dinner. They seemed rather surprised; not put out, not ashamed of themselves for being too swagger, but just mildly disappointed with Hawthornden's. The fact is, they didn't think much of Hawthornden's. I learnt all manner of things during dinner. They'd been in Scotland when I corresponded with them, but before that they'd stayed at the Ritz in London, and at the Hotel St Regis in New York, and the something else—I forget the name—at Chicago. I was expecting to meet " Colonials," but it was Ellis and I who were " colonial." I could have borne it better if they hadn't been so polite, and so anxious to hide their opinion of Hawthornden's. The girl—oh! the girl. . . . Her name is Nellie. Really very pretty. Only about eighteen, but as self-possessed as twenty-eight. Evidently she had always been used to treating her parents as equals; she talked quite half the time, and contradicted her mother as flatly as Ellis contradicts me. Mr Smith didn't talk much. And Ellis didn't at first—he was too timid and awkward— really not at all like himself. However, Miss Nellie soon made him talk, and they got quite friendly and curt with each other. Curious thing—Ellis never notices women's clothes; very interested in his own, and in other men's, but not in women's! So I expect Nellie's didn't make much impression on him. But truly they were stylish. Much too gorgeous for a young girl— oh! you've no idea!—but not vulgar. They'd been bought in London, in Dover Street. Better than mine, and better than her mother's. I will say this for her— she wore them without any self-consciousness, though she came in for a good deal of staring. Heaven knows what they cost! I'd be afraid to guess. But then you see the Smiths had come to England to spend money, and—well—they were spending it. All their ideas were larger than ours.

When dinner was over Nellie wanted to know what we could do to amuse ourselves. Well, it was a showery night, and of course there was nothing. Then Ellis said, in his patronizing way:

"Suppose we go and knock the balls about a bit?"

And Nellie said, "Knock the balls about a bit?"

"Yes," said Master Ellis, "billiards—you know."

All four of us went to the billiard-room. And Ellis began to knock the balls about a bit. His father installed a billiard-table in his own house a few years ago. The idea was to "keep the boy at home." It didn't, of course, not a bit. Ellis is a pretty good player, but he did nearly all his practising at his club. I've often heard his mother regret the eighty pounds odd that that billiard-table cost. . . . *I* play a bit, you know. Nellie Smith would not try at first, and Papa Smith was smoking a cigar and he said he couldn't do justice to a cigar and a cue at the same time. So Ellis and I had a twenty-five up. He gave me ten and I beat him—probably because he would keep on smoking cigarettes, just to show Papa Smith how well he could keep the smoke out of his eyes. Then he asked Nellie if she'd "try." She said she would if her pa would. And she and her pa put themselves against Ellis and me.

Well, I'll cut it short. That girl, with her pink-and-white complexion—she began right off with a break of twenty-eight. You should have seen Ellis's face. It was the funniest thing I ever saw in my life. I can't remember anything that ever struck me as half so funny. It seems that they have plenty of time for billiards out in Winnipeg, and a very high-class table. After a while Ellis saw the funniness of it too. He made a miss and then he said:

"Will someone kindly take me out and bury me?"

That kind of speech is supposed to be very smart at his club. And the Smiths thought it was very smart too. Nellie and her pa beat us hollow, and then Nellie began to take her pa to task for showing off with too much screw instead of using the natural angle!

Ellis went to bed. He was very struck by Nellie's talents. But he went to bed. Probably he wanted to think things over, and consider how he could be impressive with her. I should like to have broken it to him about his blue suit, because it was Sunday the next day, and Nellie was bound to be gorgeous for chapel and the pier, and I felt sure he'd be really glad to have that suit —whatever he might *say* to me. And I wanted him to wear it too. But there was no chance for me to tell him. He went off to bed like a streak of lightning. And usually, you know, he simply will not go to bed. Nothing will induce him to go to bed, just as nothing will induce him to get up. I said to myself I would send the suit into his room early in the morning with a note. I did want him to look his best.

And then of course there was the fire. The fire was that very night. What? . . .

III

Do you actually mean to sit there and tell me you never heard about the fire at Hawthornden's Hotel last July? Why, it was the sensation of the season. There was over a column about it in the *Manchester Guardian*. Everybody talked of it for weeks. . . . And no one ever told you that we were in it? Half the annexe was burnt down. We were in the annexe, all four of us. I fancy the Smiths had chosen it because the rooms in the annexe are larger. Have you ever been in a fire? . . . Well, thank your stars! We were wakened up at three o'clock. It was getting light, even. Somehow that made it worse. The confusion—you can't imagine it. We got out all right. Oh! there was no special danger to life and limb. But after all we only *did* get out just in time. And with practically nothing but our

dressing-gowns—some not even that! It's queer, in a
fire, how at first you try to save things, and keep calm,
and pretend you *are* calm, until the thing gets hold of
you. I actually began to shovel clothes into my trunks.
Somebody said we should have time for that. Well—
we hadn't. And it was a very good thing there wasn't
a lift in the annexe. It seems a lift well acts like a
chimney, and half of us might have been burnt alive.

I must say the fire-brigade was pretty good. They
got the fire out very well—very quickly in fact. We
women, or most of us, had been bundled into private
parlours and things in'the main part of the hotel, which
wasn't threatened, and when we knew that the fire was
out we naturally wanted to go back and see whether any
of our things could be saved out of the wreck.

Oh! what a sight it was! What a sight it was!
You'd never believe that so much damage could be done
in an hour or so. Chiefly by water, of course. All the
ground floor was swimming in water. In fact there was
a river of it running across the promenade into the sea.
About five-sixths of Llandudno, dressed nohow, was on
the promenade. However, policemen kept the people
outside the gates.

The firemen began bringing trunks down the stairs;
they wouldn't let us go up at first. It really was a
wonderful scene, at the foot of the stairs, lots of us pad-
dling about in that lake, and perfectly lost to all sense of
—what shall I say?—well, correctness. I do believe
most of us had forgotten all about civilization. We
wanted our things. We wanted our things so badly
that we even lost our interest in the origin of the fire
and in the question whether we should get anything out
of the insurance company. By the way, I mustn't omit
to tell you that we never saw the proprietors after the
fire was out; the proprietors could only be seen by appointment. The German and Swiss waiters had to bear
the brunt of us.

I was very lucky. I received both my trunks nearly
at once. They came sliding on a plank down those
stairs. And most of my things were in them too. I
was determined to be energetic then, and to get out of
all that crowd. Do you know what I did? I simply
called two men in out of the street, and told them to
shoulder my trunks into the main building of the hotel.
I defied policemen and the superintendent of the fire-
brigade. And in the main building I demanded a bedroom, and I was told that everything would be done to
accommodate me as quickly as possible. So I went
straight upstairs and told the men to follow me, and I
began knocking at every door till I found a room that
wasn't occupied, and I took possession of it, and gave
the men a shilling a piece. They seemed to expect half-
a-crown, because I'd been in a fire, I suppose! Curious
ideas odd job men have! Then I dressed myself out of
what was left of my belongings and went down again.

All the people said how lucky I was, and what presence of mind I had, and how calm and practical I was,
and so on and so on. But they didn't know that I'd
been stupid enough not to give a thought to Ellis's blue
suit. One can't think of everything, and I didn't think
of that. I believe if I had thought of it, at the start, I
should have taken the bonnet-box with me at any cost.

I came across Ellis; smoking a cigarette, of course,
just to show, I suppose, that a fire was a most ordinary
event to him. He was completely dressed, like me. He
had saved the whole of his belongings. He said the
Smiths were fixing themselves up in private rooms somewhere, and would be down soon. So we moved along
into the dining-room and had breakfast. The place was
full and noisy. Ellis was exceedingly facetious. He
said:

" Well, auntie, did you have a pretty good night? "
Also:

" A fire is a very clumsy way of waking you up in the

morning.   A bell would be much simpler, and cost less,"
etcetera, etcetera.   And then he said:

" A nice thing, auntie, if I'd followed your advice and
brought my beauteous new suit!   It would have been
bound to be burnt to a cinder.   One's best suit always is
in a fire."

I ought to have told him then the trick I'd played
on him, but I didn't.   I merely agreed with him in a
lame sort of way that it *would* have been a nice thing if
he'd brought his beauteous suit.   I hoped that I might
be able later on to invent some good excuse, something
really plausible, for having brought along with me his
newest suit unknown to him.   But the more I reflected
the more I couldn't think of anything clever enough.

Then the three Smiths came in.   There was some
queer attire in that dining-room, but I think that Mrs
Smith won the gold medal for queerness.   All her
" colonialness " had come suddenly out.   They evidently hadn't been very fortunate.   But they didn't seem
to mind much.   They hadn't thought very highly of the
hotel before, and they accepted the fire good-humouredly as one of the necessary drawbacks of a hotel that
wasn't quite up to their Winnipeg form.   Nellie Smith
was delightful.   I must say she was delightful, and she
looked delightful.   She was wearing a blue-and-red
striped petticoat, rather short, and a white jersey, and
over that a man's blue jacket, which fitted her pretty
well.   She looked indescribably pert and charming,
though the jacket was dirty and stained.

I noticed Ellis staring and staring at that jacket. . . .

I needn't tell you.   You can see a mile off what had
happened.

Ellis said in his casual way:

" Hello!   Where did you pick up that affair, Miss
Smith? "   Meaning the jacket.

She said she had picked it up on one of the landings,
and that there was a pair of continuations lying in a

broken bonnet-box just close to it, and that the continuations were ruined by too much water.

I could feel myself blushing redder and redder.

" In a bonnet-box, eh? " said Master Ellis.

Then he said: " Would you mind letting me look at the right-hand breast-pocket of that jacket? "

She didn't mind in the least. He looked at the strip of white linen that your men's tailors always stitch into that pocket with your name and address and date, and age and weight, and I don't know what.

He said, " Thank you."

And she asked him if the jacket was his.

" Yes," he said, " but I hope you'll keep it."

Everybody said what a very curious coincidence! Ellis avoided my eyes, and I avoided his. . . . Will you believe me that when we "had it out" afterwards, he and I, that boy was seriously angry. He suspected me of a plan " to make the best of him " during the stay with the Smiths, and he very strongly objected to being " made the best of." His notion apparently was that even his worst was easily good enough for my Colonial friends, although, as he'd have said, they *had* " simply wiped the floor with him " in the billiard-room. Anyhow, he was furious. He actually used the word " unwarrantable," and it was rather a long word for a mere stripling of a nephew to use to an auntie who was paying all his expenses. However, he's a nice enough boy at the bottom, and soon got down off his high horse. I must tell you that Nellie Smith wore that jacket all day, quite without any concern. These Colonials don't really seem to mind what they wear. At any rate she didn't. She was just as much at ease in that jacket as she had been in her gorgeousness the evening before. And she and Ellis were walking about together all day. The next day of course we all left. We couldn't stay, seeing the state we were in. . . . Now, don't you think it's a very curious story?

.   .   .   .   .   .

Thus spake Mrs Ellis across the tea-table in an alcove at the Hanover.

" But you've not finished the story! " I explained.

" Yes, I have," she said.

" You haven't explained what you were doing at my tailor's in Sackville Street."

" Oh! " she cried, " I was forgetting that. Well, I promised Ellis a new suit. And as I wanted to show him that after all I had larger ideas about tailoring than he had, I told him I knew a very good tailor's in Sackville Street—a real West End tailor—and that if he liked he could have his presentation suit made there. He pooh-poohed the offer at first, and pretended that his Bursley tailor was just as good as any of your West End tailors. But at last he accepted. You see—it meant an authorized visit to London. . . . I'd been into the tailor's just now to pay the bill. That's all."

" But even now," I said, " you haven't finished the story."

" Yes, I have," she replied again.

" What about Nellie Smith? " I demanded. " A story about a handsome girl named Nellie, who could make a break of twenty-eight at billiards, and a hand-some dog like Ellis Carter, and a fire, and the girl wear-ing the youth's jacket—it can't break off like that."

" Look here," she said, leaning a little across the table. " Did you expect them to fall in love with each other on the spot and be engaged? What a senti-mental old thing you are, after all! "

" But haven't they seen each other since? "

" Oh yes! In London, and in Bursley too."

" And haven't they—"

" Not yet. . . . They may or they mayn't. You must remember this isn't the reign of Queen Victoria. . . . If they *do*, I'll let you know."

THE TIGER AND THE BABY

I

GEORGE PEEL and Mary, his wife, sat down to breakfast. Their only son, Georgie, was already seated. George the younger showed an astounding disregard for the decencies of life, and a frankly gluttonous absorption in food which amounted to cynicism. Evidently he cared for nothing but the satisfaction of bodily desires. Yet he was twenty-two months old, and occupied a commanding situation in a high chair! His father and mother were aged thirty-two and twenty-eight respectively. They both had pale, intellectual faces; they were dressed with elegance, and their gestures were the gestures of people accustomed to be waited upon and to consider luxuries as necessaries. There was silver upon the table, and the room, though small and somewhat disordered, had in it beautiful things which had cost money. Through a doorway half-screened by a portière could be seen a large studio peopled with heroic statuary, plaster casts, and lumps of clay veiled in wet cloths. And on the other side of the great window of the studio green trees waved their foliage. The trees were in Regent's Park. Another detail to show that the Peels had not precisely failed in life: the time was then ten-thirty o'clock! Millions of persons in London had already been at hard work for hours.

And indeed George Peel was not merely a young sculptor of marked talent; he was also a rising young sculptor. For instance, when you mentioned his name

in artistic circles the company signified that it knew
whom you meant, and those members of the company
who had never seen his work had to feel ashamed of
themselves. Further, he had lately been awarded the
Triennial Gold Medal of the International Society, an
honour that no Englishman had previously achieved.
His friends and himself had, by the way, celebrated this
dazzling event by a noble and joyous gathering in the
studio, at which famous personages had been present.

Everybody knew that George Peel, in addition to
what he earned, had important "private resources."
For even rising young sculptors cannot live luxuriously
on what they gain, and you cannot eat gold medals.
Nor will gold medals pay a heavy rent or the cost of
manual help in marble cutting. All other rising young
sculptors envied George Peel, and he rather condescended
to them (in his own mind) because they had to keep up
appearances by means of subterfuges, whereas there
was no deception about his large and ample existence.

On the table by Mary's plate was a letter, the sole
letter. It had come by the second post. The contents
of the first post had been perused in bed. While Mary
was scraping porridge off the younger George's bib with
a spoon, and wiping porridge out of his eyes with a
serviette, George the elder gave just a glance at the
letter.

"So he has written after all!" said George, in a
voice that tried to be nonchalant.

"Who?" asked Mary, although she had already
seen the envelope, and knew exactly what George
meant. And her voice also was unnatural in its
attempted casualness.

"The old cock," said George, beginning to serve
bacon.

"Oh!" said Mary, coming to her chair, and beginning to dispense tea.

She was dying to open the letter, yet she poured

out the tea with superhuman leisureliness, and then indicated to Georgie exactly where to search for bits of porridge on his big plate, while George with a great appearance of calm unfolded a newspaper. Then at length she did open the letter. Having read it, she put her lips tighter together, nodded, and passed the letter to George. And George read:

"DEAR MARY,—I cannot accede to your request. —Your affectionate uncle, SAMUEL PEEL.

"P.S.—The expenses connected with my County Council election will be terrible. S. P."

George lifted his eyebrows, as if to indicate that in his opinion there was no accounting for the wild stupidity of human nature, and that he as a philosopher refused to be startled by anything whatever.

"Curt!" he muttered coldly.

Mary uneasily laughed.

"What shall you do?" she inquired.

"Without!" replied George, with a curtness that equalled Mary's uncle's.

"And what about the rent?"

"The rent will have to wait."

A brave young man! Nevertheless he saw in that moment chasms at his feet—chasms in which he and his wife and child and his brilliant prospects might be swallowed up. He changed the subject.

"You didn't see this cutting," he said, and passed a slip from a newspaper gummed to a piece of green paper.

George, in his quality of rising young sculptor, received Press cuttings from an agency. This one was from a somewhat vulgar Society journal, and it gave, in two paragraphs, an account of the recent festivity at George's studio. It finished with the words: "Heidsieck flowed freely." He could not guess who had written it. No! It was not in the nicest taste, but it furnished indubitable proof that George was still rising, that he was a figure in the world.

"What a rag!" he observed, with an expression of repugnance. "Read by suburban shop-girls, I suppose."

II

GEORGE had arranged his career in a quite exceptional way. It is true that chance had served him; but then he had known how to make use of chance to the highest advantage. The chance that had served him lay in the facts that Mary Peel had fallen gravely in love with him, that her sole surviving relative was a rich uncle, and that George's surname was the same as hers and her uncle's. He had met niece and uncle in Bursley in the Five Towns, where old Samuel Peel was a personage, and, timidly, a patron of the arts. Having regard to his golden hair and affection-compelling appearance, it was not surprising that Mary, accustomed to the monotony of her uncle's house, had surrendered her heart to him. And it was not surprising that old Peel had at once consented to the match, and made a will in favour of Mary and her offspring. What was surprising was that old Peel should have begun to part with his money at once, and in large quantities, for he was not of a very open-handed disposition.

The explanation of old Samuel Peel's generosity was due to his being a cousin of the Peels of Bursley, the great eighteenth-century family of earthenware manufacturers. The main branch had died out, the notorious Carlotta Peel having expired shockingly in Paris, and another young descendant, Matthew, having been forced under a will to alter his name to Peel-Swynnerton. So that only the distant cousin, Samuel Peel, was left, and he was a bachelor with no prospect

of ever being anything else.   Now Samuel had made a
fortune of his own, and he considered that all the honour
and all the historical splendours of the Peel family were
concentrated in himself.   And he tried to be worthy
of them.   He tried to restore the family traditions.
For this he became a benefactor to his native town, a
patron of the arts, and a candidate for the Staffordshire
County Council.   And when Mary set her young mind
on a young man of parts and of ambition, and bearing by
hazard the very same name of Peel, old Samuel Peel
said to himself: " The old family name will not die out.
It ought to be more magnificent than ever."   He said
this also to George Peel.

Whereupon George Peel talked to him persuasively
and sensibly about the risks and the prizes of the
sculptor's career.   He explained just how extremely
ambitious he was, and all that he had already done,
and all that he intended to do.   And he convinced his
uncle-in-law that young sculptors were tremendously
handicapped in an expensive and difficult profession
by poverty or at least narrowness of means.   He convinced his uncle-in-law that the best manner of succeed-
ing was to begin at the top, to try for only the highest
things, to sell nothing cheaply, to be haughty with
dealers and connoisseurs, and to cut a figure in the very
centre of the art-world of London.   George was a good
talker, and all that he said was perfectly true.   And
his uncle was dazzled by the immediate prospect of
new fame for the ancient family of Peel.   And in the
end old Samuel promised to give George and Mary five
hundred a year, so that George, as a sculptor, might
begin at the top and " succeed like success."   And
George went off with his bride to London, whence he
·had come.   And the old man thought he had done a
very noble and a very wonderful thing, which, indeed,
he had.

This had occurred when George was twenty-five.

Matters fell out rather as George had predicted. The youth almost at once obtained a commission for three hundred pounds' worth of symbolic statues for the front of the central offices of the Order of Rechabites, which particularly pleased his uncle, because Samuel Peel was a strong temperance man. And George got one or two other commissions.

Being extravagant was to George Peel the same thing as " putting all the profits into the business " is to a manufacturer. He was extravagant and ostentatious on principle, and by far-sighted policy—or, at least, he thought that he was.

And thus the world's rumours multiplied his success, and many persons said and believed that he was making quite two thousand a year, and would be an A.R.A. before he was grey-haired. But George always related the true facts to his uncle-in-law; he even made them out to be much less satisfactory than they really were. His favourite phrase in letters to his uncle was that he was "building," "building "—not houses, but his future reputation and success.

Then commissions fell off or grew intermittent, or were refused as being unworthy of George's dignity. And then young Georgie arrived, with his insatiable appetites and his vociferous need of doctors, nurses, perambulators, nurseries, and lacy garments. And all the time young George's father kept his head high and continued to be extravagant by far-sighted policy. And the five hundred a year kept coming in regularly by quarterly instalments. Many a tight morning George nearly decided that Mary must write to her uncle and ask for a little supplementary estimate. But he never did decide, partly because he was afraid, and partly from sheer pride. (According to his original statements to his uncle-in-law, seven years earlier, he ought at this epoch to have been in an assured position with a genuine income of thousands.)

But the state of trade worsened, and he had a cheque dishonoured. And then he won the Triennial Gold Medal. And then at length he did arrange with Mary that she should write to old Samuel and roundly ask him for an extra couple of hundred. They composed the letter together; and they stated the reasons so well, and convinced themselves so completely of the righteousness of their cause, that for a few moments they looked on the two hundred as already in hand. Hence the Heidsieck night. But on the morrow of the Heidsieck night they thought differently. And George was gloomy. He felt humiliated by the necessity of the application to his uncle—the first he had ever made. And he feared the result.

His fears were justified.

III

THEY were far more than justified. Three mornings after the first letter, to which she had made no reply, Mary received a second. It ran:

" DEAR MARY,—And what is more, I shall henceforth pay you three hundred instead of five hundred a year. If George has not made a position for himself it is quite time he had. The Gold Medal must make a lot of difference to him. And if necessary you must economize. I am sure there is room for economy in your household. Champagne, for instance.—Your affectionate uncle,   SAMUEL PEEL.

" P.S.—I am, of course, acting in your best interests.
                                             " S. P."

This letter infuriated George, so much so that George the younger, observing strange symptoms on his father's face, and strange sounds issuing from his father's mouth,

stopped eating in order to give the whole of his attention
to them.

"Champagne!   What's he driving at?" exclaimed
George, glaring at Mary as though it was Mary who had
written the letter.

"I expect he's been reading that paper," said Mary.

"Do you mean to say," George asked scornfully,
"that your uncle reads a rag like that?   I thought all
his lot looked down on worldliness."

"So they do," said Mary.   "But somehow they
ike reading about it.   I believe uncle has read it every
week for twenty years."

"Well, why didn't you tell me?"

"The other morning?"

"Yes."

"Oh, I didn't want to worry you.   What good
would it have done?"

"What good would it have done!" George repeated in accents of terrible disdain, as though the
good that it would have done was obvious to the lowest
intelligence.   (Yet he knew quite well that it would
have done no good at all.)   "Georgie, take that spoon
out of your sleeve."

And Georgie, usually disobedient, took the porridge-
laden spoon out of his sleeve and glanced at his mother
for moral protection.   His mother merely wiped him
rather roughly.   Georgie thought, once more, that he
never in this world should understand grown-up people.
And the recurring thought made him cry gently.

George lapsed into savage meditation.   During all
the seven years of his married life he had somehow supposed himself to be superior, as a man, to his struggling
rivals.   He had regarded them with easy toleration,
as from a height.   And now he saw himself tumbling
down among them, humiliated.   Everything seemed
unreal to him then.   The studio and the breakfast-room
were solid; the waving trees in Regent's Park were

solid; the rich knick-knacks and beautiful furniture and excellent food and fine clothes were all solid enough; but they seemed most disconcertingly unreal. One letter from old Samuel had made them tremble, and the second had reduced them to illusions, or delusions. Even George's reputation as a rising sculptor appeared utterly fallacious. What rendered him savage was the awful injustice of Samuel. Samuel had no right whatever to play him such a trick. It was, in a way, worse than if Samuel had cut off the allowance altogether, for in that case he could at any rate have gone majestically to Samuel and said: " Your niece and her child are starving." But with a minimum of three hundred a year for their support three people cannot possibly starve.

" Ring the bell and have this kid taken out," said he.

Whereupon Georgie yelled.

Kate came, a starched white-and-blue young thing of sixteen.

" Kate," said George, autocratically, " take baby."

" Yes, sir," said Kate, with respectful obedience. The girl had no notion that she was not real to her master, or that her master was saying to himself: " I ought not to be ordering human beings about like this. I can't pay their wages. I ought to be starving in a garret."

When George and Mary were alone, George said: " Look here! Does he mean it? "

" You may depend he means it. It's so like him. Me asking for that £200 must have upset him. And then seeing that about Heidsieck in the paper—he'd make up his mind all of a sudden—I know him so well."

" H'm! " snorted George. " I shall make my mind up all of a sudden, too! "

" What shall you do? "

" There's one thing I shan't do," said George.

" And that is, stop here. Do you realize, my girl,
that we shall be absolutely up a gum-tree? "

" I should have thought you would be able—"

" Absolute gum-tree! " George interrupted her.
" Simply can't keep the shop open! To-morrow, my
child, we go down to Bursley."

" Who? "

" You, me, and the infant."

" And what about the servants? "

" Send 'em home."

" But we can't descend on uncle like that without
notice, and him full of his election! Besides, he's cross."

" We shan't descend on him."

" Then where shall you go? "

" We shall put up at the Tiger," said George, im-
pressively.

" The Tiger? " gasped Mary.

George had meant to stagger, and he had staggered.

" The Tiger," he iterated.

" With Georgie? "

" With Georgie."

" But what will uncle say? I shouldn't be surprised
if uncle has never been in the Tiger in his life. You
know his views—"

" I don't care twopence for your uncle," said George,
again implicitly blaming Mary for the peculiarities of
her uncle's character. " Something's got to be done,
and I'm going to do it."

IV

Two days later, at about ten o'clock in the morning,
Samuel Peel, J.P., entered the market-place, Bursley,
from the top of Oldcastle Street. He had walked down,
as usual, from his dignified residence at Hillport. It
was his day for the Bench, and he had, moreover, a lot of
complicated election business. On a dozen hoardings

between Hillport and Bursley market-place blazed the red letters of his posters inviting the faithful to vote for Peel, whose family had been identified with the district for a century and a half. He was pleased with these posters, and with the progress of canvassing. A slight and not a tall man, with a feeble grey beard and a bald head, he was yet a highly-respected figure in the town. He had imposed himself upon the town by regular habits, strict morals, a reasonable philanthropy, and a successful career. He had, despite natural disadvantages, upheld on high the great name of Peel. So that he entered the town on that fine morning with a certain conquering jauntiness. And citizens saluted him with respect and he responded with benignity.

And as, nearly opposite that celebrated hotel, the Tiger, he was about to cross over to the eastern porch of the Town Hall, he saw a golden-haired man approaching him with a perambulator. And the sight made him pause involuntarily. It was a strange sight. Then he recognized his nephew-in-law. And he blanched, partly from excessive astonishment, but partly from fear.

" How do, uncle? " said George, nonchalantly, as though he had parted from him on the previous evening. " Just hang on to this pram a sec., will you? " And, pushing the perambulator towards Samuel Peel, J.P., George swiftly fled, and, for the perfection of his uncle-in-law's amazement, disappeared into the Tiger.

Then the occupant of the perambulator began to weep.

The figure of Samuel Peel, dressed as a Justice of the Peace should be dressed for the Bench, in a frock-coat and a ceremonious neck-tie, and (of course) spats over his spotless boots; the figure of Samuel Peel, the wrinkled and dry bachelor (who never in his life had held a saucepan of infant's food over a gas-jet in the middle of the night), this figure staring horror-struck

through spectacles at the loud contents of the perambulator, soon excited attention in the market-place of
Bursley.   And Mr Peel perceived the attention.

He guessed that the babe was Mary's babe, though
he was quite incapable of recognizing it.   And he could
not imagine what George was doing with it (and the
perambulator) in Bursley, nor why he had vanished so
swiftly into the Tiger, nor why he had not come out
again.   The whole situation was in the acutest degree
mysterious.   It was also in the acutest degree amazing.
Samuel Peel had no facility in baby-talk, so, to tran-
quillize Georgie, he attempted soothing strokes or pats
on such portions of Georgie's skin as were exposed.
Whereupon Georgie shrieked, and even dogs stood still
and lifted noses inquiringly.

Then Jos Curtenty, very ancient but still a wag,
passed by, and said:

" Hello, Mr Peel.   Truth will out.   And yet who'd
ha' suspected you o' being secretly married! "

Samuel Peel could not take offence, because Jos
Curtenty, besides being old and an alderman, and an
ex-Mayor, was an important member of his election
committee.   Of course such a friendly joke from an
incurable joker like Jos Curtenty was all right; but
supposing enemies began to joke on similar lines—how
he might be prejudiced at the polls!   It was absurd,
totally absurd, to conceive Samuel Peel in any other
relation than that of an uncle to a baby; yet the more
absurd a slander the more eagerly it was believed, and
a slander once started could never be overtaken.

What on earth was George Peel doing in Bursley
with that baby?   Why had he not announced his
arrival?   Where was the baby's mother?   Where
was their luggage?   Why, in the name of reason, had
George vanished so swiftly into the Tiger, and what
in the name of decency and sobriety was he doing in
the Tiger such a prodigious time?

It occurred to him that possibly George had written to him and the letter had miscarried.

But in that case, where had they slept the previous night? They could not have come down from London that morning; it was too early.

Little Georgie persevered in the production of yells that might have been heard as far as the Wesleyan Chapel, and certainly as far as the Conservative Club.

Then Mr Duncalf, the Town Clerk, went by, from his private office, towards the Town Hall, and saw the singular spectacle of the public man and the perambulator. Mr Duncalf, too, was a bachelor.

" So you've come down to see 'em," said Mr Duncalf, gruffly, pretending that the baby was not there.

" See whom? "

" Well, your niece and her husband, of course."

" Where are they? " asked Mr Peel, without having sufficiently considered the consequences of his question.

" Aren't they in the Tiger? " said Mr Duncalf. " They put up there yesterday afternoon, anyhow. But naturally you know that."

He departed, nodding. The baby's extraordinary noise incommoded him and seemed somehow to make him blush if he stood near it.

Mr Peel did not gasp. It is at least two centuries since men gasped from astonishment. Nevertheless, Mr Duncalf with those careless words had simply knocked the breath out of him. Never, never would he have guessed, even in the wildest surmise, that Mary and her husband and child would sleep at the Tiger ! The thought unmanned him. What! A baby at the Tiger!

Let it not be imagined for a moment that the Tiger is not an utterly respectable hotel. It is, always was, always will be. Not the faintest slur had ever been cast upon its licence. Still, it had a bar and a barmaid, and indubitably people drank at the bar. When a prominent man took to drink (as prominent men sometimes

did), people would say, " He's always nipping into the
Tiger! " Or, " You'll see him at the Tiger before eleven
o'clock in the morning! " Hence to Samuel Peel, total
abstainer and temperance reformer, the Tiger, despite
its vast respectability and the reputation of its eighteen-
penny ordinary, was a place of sin, a place of contamina-
tion; briefly, a " gin palace," if not a " gaming saloon."
On principle, Samuel Peel (as his niece suspected) had
never set foot in the Tiger. The thought that his great-
nephew and his niece had actually slept there horrified
him.

And further and worse; what would people say
about Samuel Peel's relatives having to stop at the
Tiger, while Samuel Peel's large house up at Hillport
was practically empty? Would they not deduce
family quarrels, feuds, scandals? The situation was
appalling.

He glanced about, but he did not look high enough
to see that George was watching him from a second-
floor window of the Tiger, and he could not hear Mary
imploring George: " Do for goodness sake go back to
him." Ladies passed along the pavement, stifling their
curiosity. At the back of the Town Hall there began
to collect the usual crowd of idlers who interest themselves in the sittings of the police-court.

Then Georgie, bored with weeping, dropped off into
slumber. Samuel Peel saw that he could not, with
dignity, lift the perambulator up the steps into the
porch of the Tiger, and so he began to wheel it cautiously
down the side-entrance into the Tiger yard. And in the
yard he met George, just emerging from the side-door
on whose lamp is written the word " Billiards."

" So sorry to have troubled you, uncle. But the
wife's unwell, and I'd forgotten something. Asleep,
is he? "

George spoke in a matter-of-fact tone, with no hint
whatever that he bore ill-will against Samuel Peel for

having robbed him of two hundred a year. And Samuel felt as though he had robbed George of two hundred a year.

" But—but," asked Samuel, " what are you doing here? "

" We're stopping here," said George. " I've come down to look out for some work—modelling, or anything I can get hold of. I shall begin a round of the manufacturers this afternoon. We shall stay here till I can find furnished rooms, or a cheap house. It's all up with sculpture now, you know."

" Why! I thought you were doing excellently. That medal—"

" Yes. In reputation. But it was just now that I wanted money for a big job, and—and—well, I couldn't have it. So there you are. Seven years wasted. But, of course, it was better to cut the loss. I never pretend that things aren't what they are. Mind you, I'm not blaming you, uncle. You're no doubt hard up like other people."

" But—but," Samuel began stammering again. " Why didn't you come straight to me—instead of here? "

George put on a confidential look.

" The fact is," said he, " Mary wouldn't. She's vexed. You know how women are. They never understand things—especially money."

" Vexed with me? "

" Yes."

" But why? " Again Samuel felt like a culprit.

" I fancy it must be something you said in your letter concerning champagne."

" It was only what I read about you in a paper."

" I suppose so. But she thinks you meant it to insult her. She thinks you must have known perfectly well that we simply asked the reporter to put champagne in because it looks well—seems very flourishing, you know."

"I must see Mary," said Samuel. "Of course the idea of you staying on here is perfectly ridiculous, perfectly ridiculous. What do you suppose people will say?"

"I'd like you to see her," said George. "I wish you would. You may be able to do what I can't. You'll find her in Room 14. She's all dressed. But I warn you she's in a fine state."

"You'd better come too," said Samuel.

George lifted Georgie out of the perambulator.

"Here," said George. "Suppose you carry him to her."

Samuel hesitated, and yielded. And the strange procession started upstairs.

In two hours a cab was taking all the Peels to Hillport.

In two days George and his family were returning to London, sure of the continuance of five hundred a year, and with a gift of two hundred supplementary cash.

But it was long before Bursley ceased to talk of George Peel and his family putting up at the Tiger. And it was still longer before the barmaid ceased to describe to her favourite customers the incredible spectacle of Samuel Peel, J.P., stumbling up the stairs of the Tiger with an infant in his arms.

THE REVOLVER

W HEN friends observed his occasional limp, Alderman Keats would say, with an air of false casualness, " Oh, a touch of the gout."

And after a year or two, the limp having increased in frequency and become almost lameness, he would say, " My gout! "

He also acquired the use of the word " twinge." A scowl of torture would pass across his face, and then he would murmur, " Twinge."

He was proud of having the gout, " the rich man's disease." Alderman Keats had begun life in Hanbridge as a grocer's assistant, a very simple person indeed. At forty-eight he was wealthy, and an alderman. It is something to be alderman of a town of sixty thousand inhabitants. It was at the age of forty-five that he had first consulted his doctor as to certain capricious pains, which the doctor had diagnosed as gout. The diagnosis had enchanted him, though he tried to hide his pleasure, pretending to be angry and depressed. It seemed to Alderman Keats a mark of distinction to be afflicted with the gout. Quite against the doctor's orders he purchased a stock of port, and began to drink it steadily. He was determined that there should be no mistake about his gout; he was determined to have the gout properly and fully. Indulgence in port made him somewhat rubicund and " portly,"—he who had once been a pale little counter-jumper; and by means of shooting-coats, tight gaiters, and the right shape of hat he turned himself into a passable imitation of the fine old English gentleman. His tone altered, too, and instead of being uniformly diplomatic, it varied abruptly between a sort of Cheeryble philanthropy and a sort of Wellingtonian ferocity. During an attack of gout he was terrible in the house, and the oaths that he " rapped out " in the drawing-room could be heard in the kitchen and further. Nobody minded, however, for everyone shared in the glory of his gout, and cheerfully understood that a furious temper was inseparable from gout. Alderman Keats succeeded once in being genuinely laid up with gout. He then invited acquaintances to come and solace him in misfortune, and his acquaintances discovered him with one swathed leg horizontal on a chair in front of his arm-chair, and twinging and swearing like anything, in the very manner of an eighteenth-century squire. And even in that plight he would insist on a glass of port, " to cheat the doctor."

He had two boys, aged sixteen and twelve, and he would allow both of them to drink wine in the evening, saying they must learn to " carry their liquor like gentlemen." When the lad of twelve calmly ordered the new parlour-maid to bring him the maraschino, Alderman Keats thought that that was a great joke.

Quickly he developed into the acknowledged champion of all ancient English characteristics, customs, prejudices and ideals.

It was this habit of mind that led to the revolver.

He saw the revolver prominent in the window of Stetton's, the pawnbroker in Crown Square, and the notion suddenly occurred to him that a fine old English gentleman could not be considered complete without a revolver. He bought the weapon, which Stetton guaranteed to be first-rate and fatal, and which was, in fact, pretty good. It seemed to the alderman bright, complex and heavy. He had imagined a revolver to be smaller and lighter; but then he had never handled an instrument more dangerous than a razor. He hesitated

about going to his cousin's, Joe Keats, the ironmonger;
Joe Keats always laughed at him as if he were a farce;
Joe would not be ceremonious, and could not be corrected because he was a relative and of equal age with
the alderman. But he was obliged to go to Joe Keats,
as Joe made a speciality of cartridges. In Hanbridge,
people who wanted cartridges went as a matter of course
to Joe's. So Alderman Keats strolled with grand
casualness into Joe's, and said:

" I say, Joe, I want some cartridges."

" What for? " the thin Joe asked.

" A barker," the alderman replied, pleased with this
word, and producing the revolver.

" Well," said Joe, " you don't mean to say you're
going about with that thing in your pocket, you? "

" Why not? "

" Oh! No reason why not! But you ought to be
preceded by a chap with a red flag, you know, same as a
steam-roller."

And the alderman, ignoring this, remarked with curt
haughtiness:

" Every man ought to have a revolver."

Then he went to his tailor and had a right-hand hippocket put into all his breeches.

Soon afterwards, walking down Slippery Lane, near
the Big Pits, notoriously a haunt of mischief, he had an
encounter with a collier who was drunk enough to be
insulting and sober enough to be dangerous. In relating
the affair afterwards Alderman Keats said:

" Fortunately I had my revolver. And I soon
whipped it out, I can tell you."

" And are you really never without your revolver? "
he was asked.

" Never! "

" And it's always loaded? "

" Always! What's the good of a revolver if it isn't
loaded? "

Thus he became known as the man who never went out without a loaded revolver in his pocket. The revolver indubitably impressed people; it seemed to match the gout. People grew to understand that evil-doers had better look out for themselves if they meant to disturb Alderman Keats, with his gout, and his revolver all ready to be whipped out.

One day Brindley, the architect from Bursley, who knew more about music than revolvers, called to advise the alderman concerning some projected alterations to his stabling—alterations not necessitated by the purchase of a motor-car, for motor-cars were not old English. And somehow, while they were in the stable-yard, the revolver got into the conversation, and Brindley said: "I should like to see you hit something. You'll scarcely believe me, but I've never seen a revolver fired —not with shot in it, I mean."

Alderman Keats smiled bluffly.

"I've been told it's difficult enough to hit even a door with a revolver," said Brindley.

"You see that keyhole," said the alderman, startlingly, pointing to a worn rusty keyhole in the middle of the vast double-doors of the carriage-house.

Brindley admitted that he did see it.

The next moment there was an explosion, and the alderman glanced at the smoking revolver, blew on it suspiciously, and put it back into his celebrated hippocket.

Brindley, whom the explosion had intimidated, examined the double-doors, and found no mark.

"Where did you hit?" he inquired.

"Through the keyhole," said the alderman, after a pause. He opened the doors, and showed half a load of straw in the dusk behind them.

"The bullet's imbedded in there," said he.

"Well," said Brindley, "that's not so bad, that isn't."

" There aren't five men in the Five Towns who could do that," the alderman said.

And as he said it he looked, with his legs spread apart, and his short-tailed coat, and his general bluff sturdiness, almost as old English as he could have desired to look. Except that his face had paled somewhat. Mr Brindley thought that that transient pallor had been caused by legitimate pride in high-class revolver-shooting. But he was wrong. It had been caused by simple fear. The facts of the matter were that Alderman Keats had never before dared to fire the revolver, and that the infernal noise and the jar on his hand (which had held the weapon too loosely) had given him what is known in the Five Towns as a fearful start. He had offered to shoot on the spur of the moment, without due reflection, and he had fired as a woman might have fired. It was a piece of the most heavenly good fortune that he had put the bullet through the keyhole. Indeed, at first he was inclined to believe that marksmanship must be less difficult than it was reported to be, for his aim had been entirely casual. In saying to Brindley, " You see that keyhole," he had merely been boasting in a jocular style. However, when Brindley left, Brindley carried with him the alderman's reputation as a perfect Wild West shot.

The alderman had it in mind to practise revolver-shooting seriously, until the Keats coachman made a discovery later in the day. The coachman slept over the carriage-house, and on going up the ladder to put on his celluloid collar he perceived a hole in his ceiling and some plaster on his bit of carpet. The window had been open all day. The alderman had not only failed to get the keyhole, he had not only failed to get the double-doors, he had failed to hit any part whatever of the ground floor!

And this unsettled the alderman. This proved to the alderman that the active use of a revolver incurred

serious perils. It proved to him that nearly anything
might happen with a revolver. He might aim at a lamp-
post and hit the town hall clock; he might mark down
a burglar and destroy the wife of his affections. There
were no limits to what could occur. And so he resolved
never to shoot any more. He would still carry the
revolver; but for his old English gentlemanliness he
would rely less on that than on the gout.

But the whole town (by which I mean the councillors
and the leading manufacturers and tradesmen and their
sons) had now an interest in the revolver, for Brindley,
the architect, had spoken of that which he had seen with
his own eyes. Some people accepted the alderman
without demur as a great and terrible shot; but others
talked about a fluke; and a very small minority mentioned that there was such a thing as blank cartridge.
It was the monstrous slander of this minority that induced the alderman to stand up morally for his revolver
and to continue talking about it. He suppressed the
truth about the damaged ceiling; he deliberately
allowed the public to go on believing, with Brindley,
that he had aimed at the keyhole and really gone
through it, and his conscience was not at all disturbed.
But that wicked traducers should hint that he had been
using blank cartridge made him furiously indignant, and
also exacerbated his gout. And he called on his cousin
Joe to prove that he had never spent a penny on blank
cartridge.

It was a pity that he dragged the sardonic Joe back
into the affair. Joe observed to him that for a man in
regular revolver practice he was buying precious few
cartridges; and so he had to lay in a stock. Now he
dared not employ these cartridges; and yet he wished
to make a noise with his revolver in order to convince
the neighbourhood that he was in steady practice. Nor
dare he buy blank cartridges from Joe. It was not safe
to buy blank cartridges anywhere in the Five Towns, so

easily does news travel there, and so easily are reputa-
tions blown. Hence it happened that Alderman Keats
went as far as Crewe specially to buy blank cartridge,
and he drowned the ball cartridge secretly in the Birches
Pond. To such lengths may a timid man be driven in
order to preserve and foster the renown of being a dog of
the old sort. All kinds of persons used to hear the bark-
ing of the alderman's revolver in his stable-yard, and the
cumulative effect of these noises wore down calumny
and incredulity. And, of course, having once begun to
practise, the alderman could not decently cease. The
absurd situation endured. And a coral reef of ball
cartridges might have appeared on the surface of Birches
Pond had it not been for the visit (at enormous expense)
of Hagentodt's ten tigers to the Hanbridge Empire.

This visit, epoch-making in the history of music-
hall enterprise in the Five Towns, coincided with the
annual venison feast of a society known as Ye Ancient
Corporation of Hanbridge, which society had no connection whatever with the real rate-levying corporation,
but was a piece of elaborate machinery for dinner-
eating. Alderman Keats, naturally, was prominent in
the affair of the venison feast. Nobody was better fitted
than he to be in the chair at such a solemnity, and in the
chair he was, and therein did wonderful things. In
putting the loyal toasts he spoke for half an hour concerning the King's diplomacy, with a reference to royal
gout; which was at least unusual. And then, when the
feast was far advanced, he uprose, ignoring the toast list,
and called upon the assembled company to drink to Old
England and Old Port for ever, and a fig for gout! And
after this, amid a genial informality, the conversation
of a knot of cronies at the Chair end of the table de-
viated to the noble art of self-defence, and so to revolvers. And the alderman, jolly but still aldermanic,
produced his revolver, proving that it went even with
his dress-suit.

" Look here," said one.   " Is it loaded? "

" Of course," said the alderman.

" Ball cartridge? "

" Of course," said the alderman.

" Well, would you mind putting it back in your pocket—with all this wine and whisky about—"

The alderman complied, proud.

He was limping goutily home with the Vice, at something after midnight, when, as they passed the stage-door of the Empire, both men were aware of fearsome sounds within the building. And the stage-door was ajar. Being personages of great importance, they entered into the interior gloom and collided with the watchman, who was rushing out.

" Is that you, Alderman Keats? " exclaimed the watchman. " Thank Heaven! "

The alderman then learnt that two of Hagentodt's Bengal tigers were having an altercation about a lady, and that it looked like a duel to the death. (Yet one would have supposed that after two performances, at eight-thirty and ten-thirty respectively, those tigers would have been too tired and bored to quarrel about anything whatever.) The watchman had already fetched Hagentodt from his hotel, but Hagentodt's revolver was missing—could not be found anywhere, and the rivals were in such a state of fury that even the unique Hagentodt would not enter their cage without a revolver. Meanwhile invaluable tigers were being mutually destructive, and the watchman was just off to the police-station to borrow a revolver.

The roaring grew terrific.

" Have you got your revolver, Alderman Keats? " asked the watchman.

" No," said the alderman, " I haven't."

" Oh! " said the Vice.   " I thought I saw you showing it to your cousin and some others."

At the same moment Joe and some others, equally attracted by the roaring, strolled in.

The alderman hesitated.

" Yes, of course; I was forgetting."

" If you'll lend it to the professor a minute or so? " said the watchman.

The alderman pulled it out of his pocket, and hesitatingly handed it to the watchman, and the watchman was turning hurriedly away with it when the alderman said nervously:

" I'm not sure if it's loaded."

" Well, you're a nice chap! " Joe Keats put in.

" I forget," muttered the alderman.

" We'll soon see," said the watchman, who was accustomed to revolvers. And he opened it. " Yes," glancing into it, " it's loaded right enough."

And turned away again towards the sound of the awful roaring.

" I say," the alderman cried, " I'm afraid it's only blank cartridge."

He might have saved his reputation by allowing the unique Hagentodt to risk his life with a useless revolver. But he had a conscience. A clear conscience was his sole compensation as he faced the sardonic laughter which Joe led and which finished off his reputation as a dog of the old sort. The annoying thing was that his noble self-sacrifice was useless, for immediately afterwards the roaring ceased, Hagentodt having separated the combatants by means of a burning newspaper at the end of a stick. And the curious thing was that Alderman Keats never again mentioned his gout.

AN UNFAIR ADVANTAGE

JAMES PEAKE and his wife, and Enoch Lovatt, his
wife's half-sister's husband, and Randolph Sneyd,
the architect, were just finishing the usual Saturday
night game of solo whist in the drawing-room of Peake's
large new residence at Hillport, that unique suburb of
Bursley. Ella Peake, twenty-year-old daughter of the
house, sat reading in an arm-chair by the fire which
blazed in the patent radiating grate. Peake himself
was banker, and he paid out silver and coppers at the
rate of sixpence a dozen for the brass counters handed
to him by his wife and Randolph Sneyd.

" I've made summat on you to-night, Lovatt," said
Peake, with his broad easy laugh, as he reckoned up
Lovatt's counters. Enoch Lovatt's principles and the
prominence of his position at the Bursley Wesleyan
Chapel, though they did not prevent him from playing
cards at his sister-in-law's house, absolutely forbade
that he should play for money, and so it was always
understood that the banker of the party should be his
financier, supplying him with counters and taking the
chances of gain or loss. By this kindly and ingenious
arrangement Enoch Lovatt was enabled to live at peace
with his conscience while gratifying that instinct for
worldliness which the weekly visit to Peake's always
aroused from its seven-day slumber into a brief activity.

" Six shillings on my own; five and fourpence on
you," said Peake. " Lovatt, we've had a good night;

no mistake." He laughed again, took out his knife, and cut a fresh cigar.

"You don't think of your poor wife," said Mrs Peake, "who's lost over three shillings," and she nudged Randolph Sneyd.

"Here, Nan," Peake answered quickly. "You shall have the lot." He dropped the eleven and fourpence into the kitty-shell, and pushed it across the table to her.

"Thank you, James," said Mrs Peake. "Ella, your father's given me eleven and fourpence."

"Oh, father!" The long girl by the fire jumped up, suddenly alert. "Do give me half-a-crown. You've no conception how hard up I am."

"You're a grasping little vixen, that's what you are. Come and give me a light." He gazed affectionately at her smiling flushed face and tangled hair.

When she had lighted his cigar, Ella furtively introduced her thin fingers into his waistcoat-pocket, where he usually kept a reserve of money against a possible failure of his trouser-pockets.

"May I?" she questioned, drawing out a coin. It was a four-shilling piece.

"No. Get away."

"I'll give you change."

"Oh! take it," he yielded, "and begone with ye, and ring for something to drink."

"You are a duck, pa!" she said, kissing him. The other two men smiled.

"Let's have a tune now, Ella," said Peake, after she had rung the bell. The girl dutifully sat down to the piano and sang "The Children's Home." It was a song which always touched her father's heart.

Peake was in one of those moods at once gay and serene which are possible only to successful middle-aged men who have consistently worked hard without permitting the faculty for pleasure to deteriorate through disuse. He was devoted to his colliery, and his com-

mercial acuteness was scarcely surpassed in the Five
Towns, but he had always found time to amuse himself;
and at fifty-two, with a clear eye and a perfect digestion,
his appreciation of good food, good wine, a good cigar,
a fine horse, and a pretty woman was unimpaired. On
this night his happiness was special; he had returned in
the afternoon from a week's visit to London, and he was
glad to get back again. He loved his wife and adored
his daughter, in his own way, and he enjoyed the
feminized domestic atmosphere of his fine new house with
exactly the same zest as, on another evening, he might
have enjoyed the blue haze of the billiard-room at the
Conservative Club. The interior of the drawing-room
realized very well Peake's ideals. It was large, with
two magnificent windows, practicably comfortable, and
unpretentious. Peake despised, or rather he ignored, the
æsthetic crazes which had run through fashionable
Hillport like an infectious fever, ruthlessly decimating
its turned and twisted mahogany and its floriferous
carpets and wall-papers. That the soft thick pile under
his feet would wear for twenty years, and that the
Welsbach incandescent mantles on the chandelier saved
thirty per cent. in gas-bills while increasing the light by
fifty per cent.: it was these and similar facts which
were uppermost in his mind as he gazed round that
room, in which every object spoke of solid, unassuming
luxury and represented the best value to be obtained
for money spent. He desired, of a Saturday night,
nothing better than such a room, a couple of packs of
cards, and the presence of wife and child and his two
life-long friends, Sneyd and Lovatt—safe men both.
After cards were over—and on Lovatt's account play
ceased at ten o'clock—they would discuss Bursley and
Bursley folk with a shrewd sagacity and an intimate and
complete knowledge of circumstance not to be found in
combination anywhere outside a small industrial town.
To listen to Sneyd and Mrs Peake, when each sought to

distance the other in tracing a genealogy, was to learn
the history of a whole community and the secret
springs of the actions which constituted its evolution.

"Haven't you any news for me?" asked Peake,
during a pause in the talk. At the same moment the
door opened and Mrs Lovatt entered. "Eh, Auntie
Lovatt," he went on, greeting her, "we'd given
ye up." Mrs Lovatt usually visited the Peakes
on Saturday evenings, but she came later than her
husband.

"Eh, but I was bound to come and see you to-night,
Uncle Peake, after your visit to the great city. Well,
you're looking bonny." She shook hands with him
warmly, her face beaming goodwill, and then she kissed
her half-sister and Ella, and told Sneyd that she had
seen him that morning in the market-place.

Mrs Peake and Mrs Lovatt differed remarkably in
character and appearance, though this did not prevent
them from being passionately attached to one another.
Mrs Lovatt was small, and rather plain; content to be
her husband's wife, she had no activities beyond her
own home. Mrs Peake was tall, and strikingly handsome in spite of her fifty years, with a brilliant complexion and hair still raven black; her energy was ex-
haustless, and her spirit indomitable; she was the
moving force of the Wesleyan Sunday School, and
there was not a man in England who could have driven
her against her will. She had a fortune of her own.
Enoch Lovatt treated her with the respect due to an
equal who had more than once proved herself capable
of insisting on independence and equal rights in the
most pugnacious manner.

"Well, auntie," said Peake, "I've won eleven and
fourpence to-night, and my wife's collared it all from
me." He laughed with glee.

"Eh, you should be ashamed!" said Mrs Lovatt,
embracing the company in a glance of reproof which

rested last on Enoch Lovatt. She was a Methodist of the strictest, and her husband happened to be chapel steward. " If I had my way with those cards I'd soon play with them; I'd play with them at the back of the fire. Now you were asking for news when I came in, Uncle Peake. Have they told you about the new organ? We're quite full of it at our house."

" No," said Peake, " they haven't."

" What! " she cried reproachfully. " You haven't told him, Enoch—nor you, Nan? "

" Upon my word it never entered my head," said Mrs Peake.

" Well, Uncle Peake," Mrs Lovatt began, " we're going to have a new organ for the Conference."

" Not before it's wanted," said Peake. " I do like a bit of good music at service, and Best himself couldn't make anything of that old wheezer we've got now."

" Is that the reason we see you so seldom at chapel? " Mrs Lovatt asked tartly.

" I was there last Sunday morning."

" And before that, Uncle Peake? " She smiled sweetly on him.

Peake was one of the worldlings who, in a religious sense, existed precariously on the fringe of the Methodist Society. He rented a pew, and he was never remiss in despatching his wife and daughter to occupy it. He imagined that his belief in the faith of his fathers was unshaken, but any reference to souls and salvation made him exceedingly restless and uncomfortable. He could not conceive himself crowned and harping in Paradise, and yet he vaguely surmised that in the last result he would arrive at that place and state, wafted thither by the prayers of his womenkind. Logical in all else, he was utterly illogical in his attitude towards the spiritual—an attitude which amounted to this: " Let a sleeping dog lie, but the animal isn't asleep and means mischief."

He smiled meditatively at Mrs Lovatt's question, and turned it aside with another.

" What about this organ? "

" It's going to cost nine hundred pounds," continued Mrs Lovatt, " and Titus Blackhurst has arranged it all. It was built for a hall in Birmingham, but the manufacturers have somehow got it on their hands. Young Titus the organist has been over to see it, and he says it's a bargain. The affair was all arranged as quick as you please at the Trustees' meeting last Monday. Titus Blackhurst said he would give a hundred pounds if eight others would do the same within a fortnight—it must be settled at once. As Enoch said to me afterwards, it seemed, as soon as Mr Blackhurst had made his speech, that we *must* have that organ. We really couldn't forshame to show up with the old one again at *this* Conference—don't you remember the funny speech the President made about it at the last Conference, eleven years ago? Of course he was very polite and nice with his sarcasm, but I'm sure he meant us to take the hint. Now, would you believe, seven out of those eight subscriptions were promised by Wednesday morning! I think that was just splendid! "

" Well, well! " exclaimed Peake, genuinely amazed at this proof of religious vitality. " Who are the subscribers? "

" I'm one," said Enoch Lovatt, quietly, but with unconcealed pride.

" And I'm another," said Mrs Lovatt. " Bless you, I should have been ashamed of myself if I hadn't responded to such an appeal. You may say what you like about Titus Blackhurst—I know there's a good many that don't like him—but he's a real good sort. I'm sure he's the best Sunday School superintendent we ever had. Then there's Mr Clayton-Vernon, and Alderman Sutton, and young Henry Mynors and—"

" And Eardley Brothers—they're giving a hundred apiece," put in Lovatt, glancing at Randolph Sneyd.

" I wish they'd pay their debts first," said Peake, with sudden savageness.

" They're all right, I suppose? " said Sneyd, interested, and leaning over towards Peake.

" Oh, they're all *right*," Peake said testily. " At least, I hope so," and he gave a short, grim laugh. " But they're uncommon slow payers. I sent 'em in an account for coal only last week—three hundred and fifty pound. Well, auntie, who's the ninth subscriber? "

" Ah, that's the point," said Enoch Lovatt. " The ninth isn't forthcoming."

Mrs Lovatt looked straight at her sister's husband. " We want you to be the ninth," she said.

" Me! " He laughed heartily, perceiving a broad humour in the suggestion.

" Oh, but I mean it," Mrs Lovatt insisted earnestly. " Your name was mentioned at the trustees' meeting, wasn't it, Enoch? "

" Yes," said Lovatt, " it was."

" And dost mean to say as they thought as I 'ud give 'em a hundred pound towards th' new organ? " said Peake, dropping into dialect.

" Why not? " returned Mrs Lovatt, her spirit roused. " I shall. Enoch will. Why not you? "

" Oh, you're different. You're *in* it."

" You can't deny that you're one of the richest pew-holders in the chapel. What's a hundred pound to you? Nothing, is it, Mr Sneyd? When Mr Copinger, our superintendent minister, mentioned it to me yesterday, I told him I was sure you would consent."

" You did? "

" I did," she said boldly.

" Well, I shanna'."

Like many warm-hearted, impulsive and generous

men, James Peake did not care that his generosity should be too positively assumed. To take it for granted was the surest way of extinguishing it. The pity was that Mrs Lovatt, in the haste of her zeal for the amelioration of divine worship at Bursley Chapel, had overlooked this fact. Peake's manner was final. His wife threw a swift glance at Ella, who stood behind her father's chair, and received a message back that she too had discerned finality in the tone.

Sneyd got up, and walking slowly to the fireplace emitted the casual remark: " Yes, you will, Peake."

He was a man of considerable education, and though in neither force nor astuteness was he the equal of J mes Peake, it often pleased him to adopt towards his friend a philosophic pose—the pose of a seer, of one far removed from the trivial disputes in which the colliery-owner was frequently concerned.

" Yes, you will, Peake," he repeated.

" I shanna', Sneyd."

" I can read you like a book, Peake." This was a favourite phrase of Sneyd's, which Peake never heard without a faint secret annoyance. " At the bottom of your mind you mean to give that hundred. It's your duty to do so, and you will. You'll let them persuade you."

" I'll bet thee a shilling I don't."

" Done! "

" Ssh! " murmured Mrs Lovatt, " I'm ashamed of both of you, betting on such a subject—or on any subject," she added. " And Ella here too! "

" It's a bet, Sneyd," said Peake, doggedly, and then turned to Lovatt. " What do you say about this, Enoch? "

But Enoch Lovatt, self-trained to find safety in the middle, kept that neutral and diplomatic silence which invariably marked his demeanour in the presence of an argument.

"Now, Nan, you'll talk to James," said Mrs Lovatt, when they all stood at the front-door bidding good-night.

"Nay, I've nothing to do with it," Mrs Peake replied, as quickly as at dinner she might have set down a very hot plate. In some women profound affection exists side by side with a nervous dread lest that affection should seem to possess the least influence over its object.

II

PEAKE dismissed from his mind as grotesque the suggestion that he should contribute a hundred pounds to the organ fund; it revolted his sense of the fitness of things; the next morning he had entirely forgotten it. But two days afterwards, when he was finishing his midday dinner with a piece of Cheshire cheese, his wife said:

"James, have you thought anything more about that organ affair?" She gave a timid little laugh.

He looked at her thoughtfully for a moment, holding a morsel of cheese on the end of his knife; then he ate the cheese in silence.

"Nan," he said at length, rather deliberately, "have they been trying to come round you? Because it won't work. Upon my soul I don't know what some people are dreaming of. I tell you I never was more surprised i' my life than when your sister made that suggestion. I'll give 'em a guinea towards their blooming organ if that's any use to 'em. Ella, go and see if the horse is ready."

"Yes, father."

He felt genuinely aggrieved.

"If they'd get a new organist," he remarked, with ferocious satire, five minutes later, as he lit a cigar, "and a new choir—I could see summat in that."

In another minute he was driving at a fine pace towards his colliery at Toft End. The horse, with swift instinct, had understood that to-day its master was not in the mood for badinage.

Half-way down the hill into Shawport he overtook a lady walking very slowly.

"Mrs Sutton!" he shouted in astonishment, and when he had finished with the tense frown which involuntarily accompanied the effort of stopping the horse dead within its own length, his face softened into a beautiful smile. "How's this?" he questioned.

"Our mare's gone lame," Mrs Sutton answered, "and as I'm bound to get about I'm bound to walk."

He descended instantly from the dogcart.

"Climb up," he said, "and tell me where you want to go to."

"Nay, nay."

"Climb up," he repeated, and he helped her into the dogcart.

"Well," she said, laughing, "what must be, must. I was trudging home, and I hope it isn't out of your way."

"It isn't," he said; "I'm for Toft End, and I should have driven up Trafalgar Road anyhow."

Mrs Sutton was one of James Peake's ideals. He worshipped this small frail woman of fifty-five, whose soft eyes were the mirror of as candid a soul as was ever prisoned in Staffordshire clay. More than forty years ago he had gone to school with her, and the remembrance of having kissed the pale girl when she was crying over a broken slate was still vivid in his mind. For nearly half a century she had remained to him exactly that same ethereal girl. The sole thing about her that puzzled him was that she should have found anything attractive in the man whom she allowed to marry her— Alderman Sutton. In all else he regarded her as an

angel. And to many another, besides James Peake,
it seemed that Sarah Sutton wore robes of light. She
was a creature born to be the succour of misery, the
balm of distress. She would have soothed the two
thieves on Calvary. Led on by the bounteous instinct
of a divine, all-embracing sympathy, the intrepid
spirit within her continually forced its fragile physical
mechanism into an activity which appeared almost
supernatural. According to every rule of medicine
she should have been dead long since; but she lived—
by volition. It was to the credit of Bursley that the
whole town recognized in Sarah Sutton the treasure it
held.

"I wanted to see you," Mrs Sutton said, after they
had exchanged various inquiries.

"What about?"

"Mrs Lovatt was telling me yesterday you hadn't
made up your mind about that organ subscription."
They were ascending the steepest part of Oldcastle
Street, and Peake lowered the reins and let the horse
into a walk.

"Now look here, Mrs Sutton," he began, with passionate frankness, "I can talk to you. You know me;
you know I'm not one of their set, as it were. Of
course I've got a pew and all that; but you know as
well as I do that I don't belong to the chapel lot. Why
should they ask me? Why should they come to me?
Why should I give all that sum?"

"Why?" she repeated the word, smiling. "You're
a generous man; you've felt the pleasure of giving. I
always think of you as one of the most generous men
in the town. I'm sure you've often realized what a
really splendid thing it is to be able to give. D'you
know, it comes over me sometimes like a perfect shock
that if I couldn't give—something, do—something, I
shouldn't be able to live; I would be obliged to go to
bed and die right off."

" Ah! " he murmured, and then paused. " We
aren't all like you, Mrs Sutton. I wish to God we were.
But seriously, I'm not for giving that hundred; it's
against my grain, and that's flat—you'll excuse me
speaking plain."

" I like it," she said quickly. " Then I know where
I am."

" No," he reiterated firmly, " I'm not for giving
that hundred."

" Then I'm bound to say I'm sorry," she returned
kindly. " The whole scheme will be ruined, for it's
one of those schemes that can only be carried out in
a particular way—if they aren't done on the inspiration
of the moment they're not done at all. Not that I
care so much for the organ itself. It's the idea that
was so grand. Fancy—nine hundred pounds all in
a minute; such a thing was never known in Bursley
Chapel before! "

" Well," said Peake, " I guess when it comes to
the pinch they'll find someone else instead of me."

" They won't; there isn't another man who could
afford it and trade so bad."

Peake was silent; but he was inflexible. Not even
Mrs Sutton could make the suggestion of this subscription seem other than grossly unfair to him, an
imposition on his good-nature.

" Think it over," she said abruptly, after he had
assisted her to alight at the top of Trafalgar Road.
" Think it over, to oblige me."

" I'd do anything to oblige you," he replied. " But
I'll tell you this "—he put his mouth to her ear and
whispered, half-smiling at the confession. " You call me
a generous man, but whenever that organ's mentioned
I feel just like a miser—yes, as hard as a miser. Good-
bye! I'm very glad to have had the pleasure of
driving you up." He beamed on her as the horse
shot forward.

III

THIS was on Tuesday. During the next few days Peake went through a novel and very disturbing experience. He gradually became conscious of the power of that mysterious and all-but-irresistible moral force which is called public opinion. His own public of friends and acquaintances connected with the chapel seemed to be, for some inexplicable reason, against him on the question of the organ subscription. They visited him, even to the Rev. Mr Copinger (whom he heartily admired as having "nothing of the parson" about him), and argued quietly, rather severely, and then left him with the assurance that they relied on his sense of what was proper. He was amazed and secretly indignant at this combined attack. He thought it cowardly, unscrupulous; it resembled brigandage. He felt most acutely that no one had any right to demand from him that hundred pounds, and that they who did so transgressed one of those unwritten laws which govern social intercourse. Yet these transgressors were his friends, people who had earned his respect in years long past and kept it through all the intricate situations arising out of daily contact. They could defy him to withdraw his respect now; and, without knowing it, they did. He was left brooding, pained, bewildered. The explanation was simply this: he had failed to perceive that the grandiose idea of the ninefold organ fund had seized, fired, and obsessed the imaginations of the Wesleyan community, and that under the unwonted poetic stimulus they were capable of acting quite differently from their ordinary selves.

Peake was perplexed, he felt that he was weakening; but, being a man of resourceful obstinacy, he was by no means defeated. On Friday morning he told his

wife that he should go to see a customer at Blackpool
about a contract, and probably remain at the seaside
for the week-end.   Accustomed to these sudden movements, she packed his bag without questioning, and he
set off for Knype station in the dogcart.   Once behind
the horse he felt safe, he could breathe again.   The
customer at Blackpool was merely an excuse to enable
him to escape from the circle of undue influence.
Ardently desiring to be in the train and on the other
side of Crewe, he pulled up at his little order-office in
the market-place to give some instructions.   As he
did so his clerk, Vodrey, came rushing out and saw
him.

"I have just telephoned to your house, sir," the
clerk said excitedly.   "They told me you were driving
to Knype and so I was coming after you in a cab."

"Why, what's up now?"

"Eardley Brothers have called their creditors
together."

"*What?*"

"I've just had a circular-letter from them, sir."

Peake stared at Vodrey, and then took two steps
forward, stamping his feet.

"The devil!" he exclaimed, with passionate
ferocity.   "The devil!"

Other men of business, besides James Peake, made
similar exclamations that morning; for the collapse of
Eardley Brothers, the great earthenware manufacturers,
who were chiefly responsible for the ruinous cutting of
prices in the American and Colonial markets, was no
ordinary trade fiasco.   Bursley was staggered, especially when it learnt that the Bank, the inaccessible and
autocratic Bank, was an unsecured creditor for twelve
thousand pounds.

Peake abandoned the Blackpool customer and
drove off to consult his lawyer at Hanbridge; he stood
to lose three hundred and fifty pounds, a matter suffi-

ciently disconcerting. Yet, in another part of his mind, he felt strangely serene and happy, for he was sure now of winning his bet of one shilling with Randolph Sneyd. In the first place, the failure of Eardleys would annihilate the organ scheme, and in the second place no one would have the audacity to ask him for a subscription of a hundred pounds when it was known that he would be a heavy sufferer in the Eardley bankruptcy.

Later in the day he happened to meet one of the Eardleys, and at once launched into a stream of that hot invective of which he was a master. And all the while he was conscious of a certain hypocrisy in his attitude of violence; he could not dismiss the notion that the Eardleys had put him under an obligation by failing precisely at this juncture.

IV

On the Saturday evening only Sneyd and Mrs Lovatt came up to Hillport, Enoch Lovatt being away from home. Therefore there were no cards; they talked of the Eardley affair.

" You'll have to manage with the old organ now," was one of the first things that Peake said to Mrs Lovatt, after he had recited his own woe. He smiled grimly as he said it.

" I don't see why," Sneyd remarked. It was not true; he saw perfectly; but he enjoyed the rousing of Jim Peake into a warm altercation.

" Not at all," said Mrs Lovatt, proudly. " We shall have the organ, I'm sure. There was an urgency committee meeting last night. Titus Blackhurst has most generously given another hundred; he said it would be a shame if the bankruptcy of professed Methodists was allowed to prejudice the interests of the chapel. And the organ-makers have taken fifty pounds off their price. Now, who do you think has given another fifty? Mr Copinger! He stood up last night, Mr Blackhurst told me this morning, and he said, 'Friends, I've only seventy pounds in the world, but I'll give fifty pounds towards this organ.' There! What do you think of that? Isn't he a grand fellow?"

"He is a grand fellow," said Peake, with emphasis, reflecting that the total income of the minister could not exceed three hundred a year.

"So you see you'll *have* to give your hundred," Mrs Lovatt continued. "You can't do otherwise after that."

There was a pause.

"I won't give it," said Peake. "I've said I won't, and I won't."

He could think of no argument. To repeat that Eardley's bankruptcy would cost him dear seemed trivial. Nevertheless, the absence of any plausible argument served only to steel his resolution.

At that moment the servant opened the door.

"Mr Titus Blackhurst, senior, to see you, sir."

Peake and his wife looked at one another in amazement, and Sneyd laughed quietly.

"He told me he should come up," Mrs Lovatt explained.

"Show him into the breakfast-room, Clara," said Mrs Peake to the servant.

Peake frowned angrily as he crossed the hall, but as he opened the breakfast-room door he contrived to straighten out his face into a semblance of urbanity. Though he could have enjoyed accelerating the passage of his visitor into the street, there were excellent commercial reasons why he should adopt a less strenuous means towards the end which he had determined to gain.

"Glad to see you, Mr Blackhurst," he began, a little awkwardly.

" You know, I suppose, what I've come for, Mr
Peake," said the old man, in that rich, deep, oily voice
of which Mrs Lovatt, in one of those graphic phrases
that came to her sometimes, had once remarked that
it must have been " well basted in the cooking."

" I suppose I do," Peake answered diffidently.

Mr Blackhurst took off a wrinkled black glove,
stroked his grey beard, and started on a long account
of the inception and progress of the organ scheme.
Peake listened and was drawn into an admission that
it was a good scheme and deserved to succeed.   Mr
Blackhurst then went on to make plain that it was in
danger of utterly collapsing, that only one man of " our
Methodist friends " could save it, and that both Mrs
Sutton and Mrs Lovatt had advised him to come and
make a personal appeal to that man.

Peake knew of old, and in other affairs, the wily
diplomatic skill of this Sunday School superintendent,
and when Mr Blackhurst paused he collected himself
for an effort which should conclude the episode at a
stroke.

" The fact is," he said, " I've decided that I can't
help you.   It's no good beating about the bush, and
so I tell you this at once.   Mind you, Mr Blackhurst,
if there's anyone in Bursley that I should have liked
to oblige, it's you.   We've had business dealings, you
and me, for many years now, and I fancy we know one
another.   I've the highest respect for you, and if you'll
excuse me saying so, I think you've some respect for
me.   My rule is always to be candid.   I say what I
mean and I mean what I say; and so, as I've quite
made up my mind, I let you know straight off.   I
can't do it.   I simply *can't* do it."

" Of course if you put it that way, if you *can't*—"

" I do put it that way, Mr Blackhurst," Peake continued quickly, warming himself into eloquence as he
perceived the most effective line to pursue.   " I admire

your open-handedness. It's an example to us all. I
wish I could imitate it. But I mustn't. I'm not one
o' them as rushes out and promises a hundred pound
before they've looked at their profit and loss account.
Eardleys, for example. By the way, I'm pleased to
hear from Sneyd that you aren't let in there. I'm one
of the flats. Three hundred and fifty pound—that's
my bit; I'm told they won't pay six shillings in the
pound. Isn't that a warning? What right had they
to go offering their hundred pound apiece to your
organ fund?"

"It was very wrong," said Mr Blackhurst, severely,
"and what's more, it brings discredit on the Methodist
society."

"True!" agreed Peake, and then, leaning over
confidentially, he spoke in a different voice: "If you
ask me, I don't mind saying that I think that magnificent subscription o' theirs was a deliberate and fraudu-
lent attempt to inspire pressing creditors with fresh
confidence. That's what I think. I call it monstrous."

Mr Blackhurst nodded slowly, as though meditating
upon profound truths ably expressed.

"Well," Peake resumed, "I'm not one of that sort.
If I can afford to give, I give; but not otherwise. How
do I know how I stand? I needn't tell you, Mr Blackhurst, that trade in this district is in a very queer
state—a very queer state indeed. Outside yourself,
and Lovatt, and one or two more, is there a single manufacturer in Bursley that knows how he stands? Is
there one of them that knows whether he's making
money or losing it? Look at prices; can they go lower?
And secret discounts; can they go higher? And all
this affects the colliery-owners. I shouldn't like to
tell you the total of my book-debts; I don't even care
to think of it. And suppose there's a colliers' strike—
as there's bound to be sooner or later—where shall we
be then?"

Mr Blackhurst nodded once more, while Peake, intoxicated by his own rhetoric, began actually to imagine that his commercial condition was indeed perilous.

" I've had several very severe losses lately," he went on. " You know I was in that newspaper company; that was a heavy drain; I've done with newspapers for ever more. I was a fool, but calling myself a fool won't bring back what I've lost. It's got to be faced. Then there's that new shaft I sunk last year. What with floodings, and flaws in the seam, that shaft alone is running me into a loss of six pound a week at this very moment, and has been for weeks."

" Dear me! " exclaimed Mr Blackhurst, sympathetically.

" Yes! Six pound a week! And that isn't all " —he had entirely forgotten the immediate object of Mr Blackhurst's visit—" that isn't all. I've got a big lawsuit coming on with the railway company. Goodness knows how that will end! If I lose it . . . well! "

" Mr Peake," said the old man, with quiet firmness, " if things are as bad as you say we will have a word of prayer."

He knelt down and forthwith commenced to intercede with God on behalf of this luckless colliery-owner, his business, his family, his soul.

Peake jumped like a shot rabbit, reddening to the neck with stupefaction, excruciating sheepishness and annoyance. Never in the whole course of his life had he been caught in such an ineffable predicament. He strode to and fro in futile speechless rage and shame. The situation was intolerable. He felt that at no matter what cost he must get Titus Blackhurst up from his knees. He approached him, meaning to put a hand on his shoulder, but dared not do so. Inarticulate sounds escaped from his throat, and then at last he burst out:

" Stop that, stop that! I canna stand it. Here, I'll give ye a cheque for a hundred. I'll write it now."

When Mr Blackhurst had departed he rang for a brandy-and-soda, and then, after an interval, returned to the drawing-room.

" Sneyd," he said, trying to laugh, " here's your shilling. I've lost."

" There! " exclaimed Mrs Lovatt. " Didn't I say that Mr Copinger's example would do it? Eh, James! Bless you! "